SOMEONE WICKED

A Written Remains Anthology

SOMEONE WICKED

A Written Remains Anthology

Edited by JM Reinbold
& Weldon Burge

Smart Rhino Publications
www.smartrhino.com

First Edition

ISBN-13: 978-0-9847876-8-5

DEDICATION

For the Written Remains Writers Guild
—its members and friends!

CONTENTS

ACKNOWLEDGMENTS

Thanks go to Jamie Mahon for his amazing cover illustration, to Amy York for designing the cover, and to Terri Gillespie for her excellent proofreading skills.

We must also point out that, although most of the stories are original to this volume, a number are reprints. Mike Dunne's story, "The Fire of Iblis," was originally published in *Twilight Times: A Digital Journal of Speculative Fiction* (2003). Billie Sue Mosiman's story, "The Flenser," was self-published under the title "White Skulls" in July 2013. "Sometimes the Good Witch Sings to Me," by L.L. Soares, first appeared in the anthology *Cover of Darkness*, published by Sam's Dot Publishing in 2007.

FOREWARD:
THE WRITTEN REMAINS WRITERS GUILD

BY JM REINBOLD

The Written Remains Writers Guild was founded in 2009 by a small group of Delaware writers. We believed that writers can achieve greater literary excellence and more success in developing careers as authors by working together and sharing knowledge, skills, and resources.

Over the past five years, the Guild has doubled its membership. And, along with our increase in membership, we have also increased the number of opportunities for Guild members to present their work to the public, as well as providing free, quality programs and events to the Delaware writing community.

For example, Guild members and other writers from the Delaware area get together on the first Saturday of every month for Writers Breakfast Club, where we have an opportunity to meet, talk about the writing life, and network. Guild members are the featured speakers at our quarterly Get Out & Write! events, which are held at local libraries and are open to the public, as are our writing workshops. Guild members hone their writing skills in our Mixed Genre and Literary Critique groups, as well as through our two annual writing challenges, the Summer Writing Challenge in July and MiniWriMo (an alternative to NaNoWriMo) in November. We offer two online groups for writers—the 250 Words Plus Facebook Group for Writers, which offers daily support and inspiration for working writers, and the Delaware Writers Network, where writers from all around the state can share information about classes, events, readings, workshops, and other information of interest. Our members also participate together in public book signings, readings, and other author events. And, there are opportunities for publication in our anthologies, on our blog, and our Write Around Here! podcast.

The Guild's success is rooted in our "all for one and one for all" credo. I am grateful to all our members for their willingness to share their energy, enthusiasm, expertise, ideas, inspiration, resources, skills, and talent in service of their fellow Guild members. This willingness to share and support one another as authors is nowhere more apparent than in our combined effort to produce the *Someone Wicked* anthology.

Many of you may not realize that *Someone Wicked* is the second Written Remains anthology. Our first, *Stories From the Inkslingers*, was published in 2008 by Gryphonwood Press. It is a small volume—only 116 pages—of excellent stories (two nominated for awards) by eight accomplished writers, some of whom have stories in *Someone Wicked*.

My hope for the future of the Written Remains Writers Guild is that we continue to grow, enrich one another's lives, help our members achieve success as authors, and produce many more excellent anthologies!

JM Reinbold, Director
The Written Remains Writers Guild

INTRODUCTION: ACQUIRING A TASTE FOR ANTHOLOGIES

BY WELDON BURGE

I blame Scholastic Books.

In 1969, when I was thirteen, I purchased that fine little anthology, *11 Great Horror Stories*, published by Scholastic Book Services. The book contains classics like "The Dunwich Horror" by H.P. Lovecraft, "The Oblong Box" by Edgar Allan Poe, "The Judge's House" by Bram Stoker, and "Thus I Refute Beelzy" by John Collier. My favorite story in the collection was the gruesome, stomach-churning tale "Flies" by Anthony Vercoe. What thirteen-year-old boy, who already loved horror comic books, wouldn't be impressed? I've loved anthologies ever since.

Looking at my bookshelves now, I see *Dark Forces*, edited by Kirby McCauley; *Prime Evil*, Doug Winter; *The Dark Descent*, David Hartwell; *The New Dead*, Christopher Golden; *Stalkers* and *Predators*, Ed Gorman and Martin Greenberg; and so many more that I could go on listing them for another page or so. I love anthologies of every genre (although horror and suspense dominate my shelves).

To me, a successful anthology is like an excellent all-you-can-eat seafood restaurant. The spread of food should have something for everyone. Some people hate clams and go straight for the shrimp.

Others prefer scallops or crab cakes. Yet others head straight for the Alaskan crab legs. But, to be successful, the restaurant ensures every patron leaves satisfied. A successful anthology should leave each reader satisfied as well, even if some of the stories included don't match his/her "tastes." I always look for anthologies with a wide selection of writing styles and ideas from a variety of writers—the more diverse, the better. Taking the analogy another step, patrons at the seafood smorgasbord are free to experiment with foods they might not otherwise purchase a la carte. A successful anthology provides not only work from familiar writers, but introduces readers to new talent that they perhaps wouldn't otherwise read.

Which brings me to the collection of stories you now hold in your hands, *Someone Wicked: A Written Remains Anthology*.

Whenever I assemble an anthology for Smart Rhino Publications, I strive for a diversity of voices and styles around a common theme (e.g., the *Zippered Flesh* anthos on the theme of body enhancements; *Uncommon Assassins* based on ... well ... killers and assassins). When my co-editor, JM Reinbold, and I first discussed pulling together this anthology, we decided early on to (1) invite members of the Written Remains Writers Guild to contribute stories, and (2) invite writers outside the membership who would provide an excellent mix of stories that would balance those of the WR writers. (We started the anthology with Written Remains member Gail Husch, and then alternated between members and guest writers before ending with member Shannon Connor Winward—twenty-one stories in all.)

We're thrilled with the results! You may recognize a few names; many you may not. But we hope, like visiting a good seafood smorgasbord, you'll come away satisfied—and perhaps acquire a "taste" for several new authors!

And a diverse collection of stories it is!

Here you will find serial killers in the "The Flenser" by Billie Sue Mosiman, "The Chances" by Ramona DeFelice Long, "Abracadabra" by Russell Reece, and "Sometimes the Good Witch Sings to Me" by Bram Stoker Award Winner L.L. Soares.

Some stories have elements of fairy tales, including "Mirror Mirror" by Chantal Noordeloos, "Sisters: A Fairy Tale" by Liz DeJesus, and "The Flowering Princess of Dreams" by Doug Blakeslee.

There are stories of suburban horror, including Shannon Connor Winward's "The Devil Inside," Maria Masington's "Impresario," and Barbara Ross's "Home Improvements," as well as a tale of psychological horror, "Despair" by Shaun Meeks.

Enjoy humorous fiction? Then you'll likely enjoy the dark comedic turn of Carson Buckingham's "The Plotnik Curse" and the experimental/absurdist tale "The Semi-Aquatic Blue Baker of Borneo" by Justynn Tyme.

Revenge stories your thing? Check out Gail Husch's "Reckonings," Joe Badal's "Ultimate Betrayal," and my own hit man story, "Right-Hand Man." There are wicked characters carrying out evil schemes in "The Next King" by Patrick Derrickson and "The Tail of Fate" by Ernestus Jiminy Chald, and an Arabian fantasy with demonic entities, "The Fire of Iblis" by Mike Dunne.

If you enjoy Brit whodunits, you'll love "Missing" by JM Reinbold. And there's even the tale of a bloodthirsty Viking, "Sven Bloodhair," by Christine Morgan.

If you love anthologies as much as I do, I'm sure you'll find stories to savor in this collection. There's something "tasty" for everyone!

Bon appétit!

Weldon Burge, Executive Editor
Smart Rhino Publications

RECKONINGS

BY GAIL HUSCH

The first thing you need to know: I don't own a single cat. Not one. I don't even like them, selfish, arrogant creatures. But seeing me perched small and tight on the seat across from you, glancing at me with that sly, hooded curiosity strangers sometimes display when trapped together in subway cars, I'm sure you think I support a whole pride of them, cats, purring on every cushion in my tiny studio apartment, lapping up milk in my kitchen nook, prowling my pink-tiled bathroom.

If you cared to look closely, though, if you lifted your eyes from that shiny rectangular toy that has you so mesmerized, you'd realize that I have not a single strand of cat hair on my sensible tweed coat. The tiles in my bathroom are tastefully beige. They are spotless. And I have a living room, separated from my bedroom by a hallway. A short hallway, I admit, but a hallway nonetheless. More of a hallway, I suspect, than you have in whatever overstuffed, overpriced closet you call home.

It's my hair that's fooled you—the pulled back bun, the slight halo of frizz. And the glasses, steel-rimmed and severe. The thin lips, too, without a hint of color. No man ever thought to kiss *those*, you're certain, and you feel sorry for me. Poor lonely spinster, you think, she's filled that hole with cats.

Don't waste your pity. I have no hole to fill, not anymore. I am stronger than you imagine, stronger than I ever thought possible.

So, on second thought, it's better if you don't know.

It's better if you notice me clutching my purse in my lap and think, what a weak, fragile, pathetic little woman, hanging on to the pittance in her handbag. It's better if you see me slip off my seat and stand back when the door slides open, letting the crowd push past me while I wait, timidly polite, until it's my turn to leave. It's too bad you won't be there to see me smile a shy good morning to all my office colleagues, each one lazier and stupider than the next.

Still, I want to tell someone. You, there, staring at me from one table over, pretending you're just gazing off into space, nursing your coffee, dawdling after lunch, I wish I could tell you. Not a confession, certainly. A boast, if you will. A brag. I would so love to see the look on your face.

The first act of retribution wasn't much to speak of, just a momentary flash, but it changed everything. Last Friday evening, not quite a week ago, the grocery store was hideously crowded, gangs of young people clogging the aisles, shouting, shoving, pushing carts packed with bags of nasty orange chips and bottles of electric blue and green liquid—you know the disgusting things I'm talking about. I won't even call it food. I never would have been there, but that morning I noticed a brown spot on my last banana. I cannot stand overripe bananas, so cloyingly sweet and slimy.

I carried nothing but two unblemished bananas toward the checkout lane; the young thug held a hand basket piled high. I was closer, I know that for a fact, just about to place my items on the conveyor belt when he pushed ahead of me as if I weren't there, as if he had a God-given right to barrel his way in front of me because he was a man, because he was bigger, because he was younger, because he wore a ridiculous turned around baseball cap on his thick head, because I was no more than a mouse or a flea to him, because I was an insignificant nothing.

So I did it; I still don't know why then, why there. A straw, perhaps, the last one. Breaking the camel's back.

I didn't think, I didn't plan, I just lifted my shoe—my boot, to be precise—and pressed hard on the back of his foot. As luck would have it, he was stepping forward; I felt his shoe—one of those monstrous puffy things—slip down and my sole scrape his heel.

You must understand: I am not a cruel woman. I've never deliberately caused another's pain, never wanted to until that moment. It surprises me still, how good it felt, the brutal contact of my foot against his.

"Hey!" he whined, and turned around to glare at me. You would have laughed to see the look of horrified contrition on my face. Such an acting job—I deserve an Oscar. "Oh, I'm so sorry!" I said. "Please forgive me!" But, of course, I wanted no forgiveness. The righteous need no forgiveness.

And then he mumbled "s'okay" or something like that, but I could tell by the way he limped that his heel still hurt. As it should.

Not much of a story, I realize. Not terribly exciting. But wait: the next one is better, the one from the day before yesterday, the one from Monday, the one in my office.

Damn. I've barely had time to hang up my coat and settle at my desk before I catch a whiff of your cheap aftershave. Old Spice, perhaps, or something meant for younger men, Axe or Meat Cleaver or whatever it is they call such a stench these days.

In all these years, you've never noticed that I flinch every time you sidle up to my desk. A slight hunching of my shoulders, a momentary pucker of my forehead—movements that would be visible to anyone who deigned a glance in my direction while bringing me yet another job to be completed, ASAP.

I'm flinching now, inside at least, although the only expression on my face is a small and expectant smile.

"Yes?" I ask, as if all I cared about in this world was to help you and do your bidding.

3

You shove a handful of paper in my direction, your eyes fixed somewhere above my head.

"Look this over, will you."

You never say my name. I wonder if you know it.

"I need it done pronto, soon as you can. Sooner." That guffaw, more snort than laugh. No please, of course. No thank you.

I breathe through my mouth, trying to avoid the smell wafting toward me.

And look at that—a dark spot on your yellow tie. No surprise. Oil of some sort, greasy evidence of your gobbled-down lunch, just like the crumb stuck to your beard.

"How's your thumb?" I ask.

Now I have your attention. You lower the hand clutching the paper, raise the other one, thumb upward. We both stare at it, mournfully.

I care a great deal about that thumb. I wish you'd let me examine it so I could find the tiny puncture wound, look for a reddened swelling, some sign of infection.

You asked for it, of course, the day before yesterday, lumbering up to my desk as you always do, thrusting a sheaf of misaligned, dog-eared pages at me, a sheaf with no staple, nothing, not even a paper clip to hold it together, as if for all the world it were *my* job to neaten the pile and keep it straight.

I straightened the pages, of course, and I stapled them. I read through them, made the proper notations and corrections—you're as slovenly in your spelling and punctuation as you are in your grooming—and rose to make my obedient way to your office. But I wasn't feeling obedient.

It was a stroke of genius, an inspiration quick as the one that made me tread on the thug's heel. A pry at the staple with my thumbnail, and the trap was set. I gave the pages back to you, stapled corner first, stapled corner up. You, of course, paid no attention when you grabbed them.

"Ouch!" you bellowed, and stuck your thumb in your mouth like the big, overgrown baby that you are.

I made no apology this time, but I cooed my sympathy. "Oh, dear," I said, "Little jabs like that can be very painful. Please be sure to wash it out. "

"Still hurts," you say now, and I do believe I hear a quiver in your voice.

I click concern with my tongue; you shrug like a brave little boy and give me the papers in your hand, another disheveled sheaf. Lesson unlearned, I see.

Well. We'll have to do something about that. More unfortunate pricks, I think, until you get the message.

On your way then; good riddance. Oh, and when you pass her cubicle, you might tell your larcenous friend that I saw what she did yesterday morning. It was mine, the half-eaten yogurt she stole from the back of the break room refrigerator.

I'll tend to that as well. How, precisely, I have not yet determined.

This is a public street corner, Miss Blond Hair Black Leather Jacket. You could have the decency to dangle that cigarette somewhere else, away from the sleeve of my coat, at least for the few moments we're forced to stand side by side. Clearly, my strangled coughs mean nothing to you. Stick it in your mouth if you must and turn your head, blow your smoke somewhere else. Blow it in the stubbly face of the boy you're kissing. I can't decide which is more disgusting, the smoking or the shameless display.

Rules don't apply to you, do they, princess, young and pretty as you think you are. Foul the city with your filth, drop that lit cigarette at my feet, no matter. I'll just shrug indulgently, let it slide, let it go, a proud parent.

But I am not your mother. Ignorant girl, you have no idea who I am, what I am becoming.

A quick bend; I pick up the smoldering butt, drop it in the gap at the top of your boot. No one notices—why would they? I'm just a drab and dowdy thing, scavenging a fallen penny or a dime.

"Shit!" you shriek, and stomp your foot like a spoiled child.

Your stubbly boyfriend is no help. All he can manage is a stream of unrepeatable words.

Still yowling, you unzip the boot and slip it off. I give you my arm and my sympathy; together we find the blistering spot, a hole burned through black stocking into flesh, just above the anklebone. It is beautiful.

"O dear," I say, my voice soft and soothing, "Burns are so painful."

You whimper and nod; I relinquish my position to Stubble Face and walk away through a small, staring crowd.

I stride through the darkened streets, savoring the memory of those shrieks. My mind is sharp and clear; I feel a sense of purpose more potent than any I have ever experienced. Now I'm sure of what I'd begun to suspect: I am an agent of something larger than myself. I am a tool in the hand of justice, human or divine, I don't care which. In the clarity of this moment, I think of you, my yogurt thief, and I devise a plan.

I have no peanuts. No matter—a quick stop at the grocery store on the corner. Then just one, dry roasted and unsalted, ground into fine powder, mixed with the container of yogurt I have at home, the same flavor as the one you stole.

Finally! I thought you'd never lift your ample rump from the chair; I have nothing but sympathy for that poor, abused piece of furniture. You're later than usual this morning; I'm surprised you held out so long—a full hour at your desk without a break, without a trip to forage something sweet, a donut, a candy bar, a half-eaten container of somebody else's blueberry yogurt. I'd almost given up hope.

You've made me wait, unable to concentrate, anticipating the whisper of wheels as you push back, the soft grunt you make before standing. I hear those sounds and my heart beats faster, my chest tightens. My first three acts were spontaneous; this one, plotted and premeditated, marks a turning point in my career and I feel its gravity.

I can tell that your face has risen like a pale moon above the partition separating us, your eyes vacant and befuddled as a sheep's. Don't expect me to look up, although I feel the pressure of your gaze. You clear your throat, take a breath, preparing to speak. I hold my own, keep my eyes fixed on my work. Certainly you see that I'm too busy to pause, even for a moment. No offense intended.

One glance from me, and you'd never shut up; I have better things to do than listen to your blather. I've heard too much of it already, your whining voice, that nasal New York bray. I know all about your husband's surgery, your father's dementia, your dog's antics. And I know more than I should about *your* health, your weight problem, and your allergies.

A little sigh as you turn away, defeated by my diligence. I'll count a few seconds—one, two, three one thousand—and then I'll lift my head.

Strange, how hard the thumping in my chest.

You must be there by now. I can see you, hesitating with one fist curled around the refrigerator handle and the other around a plastic spoon, just the way you paused the morning that I caught you, hidden as I was outside the break room door. The coast is clear, you'll determine. Gently, you open the refrigerator, bend over until your haunches press like hams against your polyester trousers, and, with one furtive gesture, grab the container.

I can almost hear your moist and greedy slurps.

I have to stand, do something to distract myself. But carefully, with no indication of excitement, no sign I sense disaster, no trace of nerves. I busy myself at the file cabinet near the entrance to my cubicle, but my hands shake.

A gasp and fumbling footfalls; I'm sure I hear them. An invisible current of surprise breaks toward me, heads popping up like mushrooms above each cubicle. What can I do but rush to see what's happening, a lemming among lemmings.

Such a satisfying shade of crimson, those plump cheeks of yours. And your lower lip, fat as a blood-filled leech. You can't see me, not through those eyelids swollen nearly shut. If you could, you'd be gratified by the way I clasp my hands against my open mouth, a look of horrified pity in my widened eyes.

"Epi ..." you manage to choke out. At least, I think that's what you're attempting to say. "Epi ..."

Ah, the Good Samaritans, running this way and that, one on her way to your desk to rummage for the sharp little antidote, one that has you by your arm, saving you from the indignity of sprawling like a beached whale on the floor, another yelling "911." What can I do, weak and ineffective as I am? My job: watch in helpless admiration of those better fit to act.

You look so peaceful as they wheel you away, an inert lump on a gurney, oxygen mask covering your face. You'll return a better person, I promise you, chastised and humble. No more taking what isn't yours, grabbing what you haven't earned.

I'd wave goodbye, but that would call attention. The last thing I want is attention. To go forward with my mission, I must remain invisible.

A cool glass of water; I've earned it after such commotion. Besides, I need to check the trashcan in the break room, make sure the yogurt container is well hidden in its depths.

It's not too much to ask, is it, just a quiet moment with a pot of tea, snug in one's robe and slippers at the kitchen table, enjoying the early morning silence, feeling like the only person awake and alive in the world.

I had years of such moments, until you ruined them.

I hear you directly above my head, clomping around your kitchen like an elephant, no doubt gulping coffee, fueling up for your descent.

Before they moved and you replaced them, I barely heard a peep from my upstairs neighbors, a doddering old couple who kept to themselves. Oh, once in a while a soft tapping, a shuffling, a hint of television noise through my ceiling, but always perfect silence before I went to bed, always absolute quiet in the morning.

There it is: the slam of your apartment door. Let me count: one, two, three, four, five—always five stomps in your hard-soled boots on the bare wooden landing. Then, the deafening clatter as you race downstairs.

Even now with my hands over my ears, I hear you. I hear you rush past my apartment, barrel down the next flight of stairs and the next and the last. I hear you reach the outside door and I hear you slam that, too.

Every single morning since you moved in. Two solid weeks now, every single morning, even weekends, even Sundays.

I could ask you to please be more careful, walk more softly, think about someone other than yourself, but I shouldn't have to. Besides, I've seen you—we passed that time going up, me carrying two heavy bags of groceries, you elbowing by with no offer of help—and I know your kind. So cool, so self-important in your tight black pants. I saw the tattoo on your neck and the earring. You probably consider yourself an artist. I know the type. You'd never listen. You'd sneer in my face. You'd say you have the right to walk any way you want. People like you think the world belongs to them. People like you are beyond redemption.

So. A spot of oil at the top of the stairs, just a few feet from my door? A puddle of water? An invisible fishing line strung low to the ground?

No. Something smaller, barely perceptible.

A sip of chamomile tea helps me think. It tastes grassy in my mouth, feels warm as sunshine in my throat.

I have it.

Late tonight, with my pink-handled hammer. A few tugs upward on the rubber tread laid across the top step outside my door, meant to keep the clumsy from slipping. An eighth of an inch should do it, even less, just enough to catch the toe of a thick and heavy boot.

THE FLENSER

BY BILLIE SUE MOSIMAN

The scalpel, a spear of flickering silver, sliced up beneath the skin of the jaw all the way to the cheekbone. Sawing right, then left, it slipped, releasing flesh from bone.

The head, technically not yet a skull, was that of a man in his fifties. Muscles from his neck hung down out of the head's cavity, red and dark blue as exotic snakes. The cadaver's head possessed ears, elephant large; nostrils, wide and hairy; and flat planes of beige cheeks bleached down to almost alabaster. His matted eyelashes were black as streaks of soot against his face.

Boris thought of Sheila, her lashes black too, long and stiff with mascara, her eyes brown, and her lips pomegranate even without lipstick. She wouldn't like it when she discovered what he did for a living. She'd hate him for it. They all did. He had lost five girlfriends already.

"Keirnan, how's your wife taking to you wiping skulls?" Their job was really "flensing" skulls, but none of them called it that among themselves.

Keirnan worked next to him at the long white table with the ridged funnels for catching the bits and pieces. At an identical table behind them worked three others—George, Barry, and Thomas—but they usually didn't talk. Only Keirnan would talk while working.

"She cries herself to sleep most nights," Keirnan said.

Boris nodded his head, knowing that was no doubt the truth. What woman wouldn't? If they stayed with a flenser long enough to sleep with him, it didn't surprise him at all they cried. Women, it seemed to him, were so sentimental about death.

"You had this job when you met her?" Boris asked.

"Yeah, I've been doing this for fifteen years."

Keirnan was the oldest guy in the facility at thirty-nine. Boris couldn't imagine being thirty-nine. He'd want to kill himself before he reached thirty-nine. He was twenty-five and that was already feeling too old to do much of anything in the world that would ever matter. He'd been working at Sci-Clean six months. He didn't mind the work and it paid well. But he wouldn't be doing it when he was past thirty, that was for shit.

Good thing the job didn't call for any real skills. Boris applied and was tested, given a head and told to clean off the flesh. He had thirty minutes. He was always good with knives. Growing up in the South skinning the carcasses of animals he hunted gave him the only background he needed. And he didn't change expression when he defleshed the head during his test. He was watched over by a skinny man with thinning hair and a mole on his chin. He looked like an extra from *The Walking Dead*. The test didn't make Boris nervous. If this didn't work out, he would find some other odd job. Besides, what was a human head but just a dead thing that needed the rotten matter taken off it? Once cleaned, it was a sterile piece of artwork.

Sci-Clean sold skulls all over the world. Their international sales made an astounding amount of money for the company. The owner was a multimillionaire. Skulls were used in universities, schools of anatomy, and they were bought by individuals who, Boris assumed, wanted a trophy for the bookshelf. People were strange. Boris knew that for damn sure.

His hands made quick work flensing the skull and before the thirty minutes were up he had a bloody skull with the brains removed ready for the beetle box. The beetles finished cleaning the meat remnants still attached to the bone. Then the skull was dropped in a bleaching solution, coming out the purest white. Human skulls were pretty cool when they were all cleaned up that way. Boris wouldn't pay $2900 for one, though—no way. He had stolen one to take home during his first month on the job, just to have it, but he wasn't about to waste hard-earned money buying one.

The workday wound down. As Boris left the building, he lit a cigarette. He was taking Sheila out for drinks tonight and maybe she'd come back to his place. He hadn't been laid in months and if Sheila didn't put out soon, he was going to have to move on. There was any number of unattached females in the clubs he could pick up. Just as long as he didn't tell them he cleaned skulls, he might get one of them into bed.

After a shower and a shave, Boris looked around his small apartment and decided it was tidy enough to pass cursory inspection. He contemplated hiding the human skull sitting on top of the end table next to the convertible sofa, but then decided to leave it. If he had to hide *everything* about himself, he didn't want a girl to hang around anyway.

Sheila agreed to come back to his place after three cocktails and some light, meaningless banter. There was a little twinkle in her eyes and he thought he might get lucky. "I can't stay long," she added. He thought that a little queer, stating she couldn't stay long. He felt as if she was hedging her bets. She needed an excuse to leave quickly. She was his timid little squirrel, ready to bolt.

She was hardly inside the door when she turned to him and said, "Why do you have a skull?"

It sounded like an accusation and he frowned slightly. "Why, don't you think it's beautiful?"

She wrinkled her nose as if smelling something soured, but his apartment was odorless. He never even smoked inside, stepping onto the concrete apron in front of his door outside to smoke.

"It's ... it's creepy." She stepped away from him and found the end of the sofa farthest from the end table to sit.

"I might as well tell you the truth. I work at a company that cleans human skulls and sells them. Well, they clean all human bones, but they sell more skulls than anything else on the skeletons. I work in the skull division." He laughed at what he'd just said. The skull division. That was funny.

"You're kidding," she said.

He sat next to her and put a hand on her left breast, moving in close to her. "Let's not talk about our jobs." He knew she worked as a

13

law secretary. How boring it was going to be if they spent their time talking about their mundane lives.

She took his hand as if it were a wet fish and removed it from her breast. She turned a little away from him. "I have to go home. My roommate gets nervous if I'm out too late."

He sank back onto the sofa and looked at the bare wall across the room. A single lamp threw their shadows there, two tall stick figures humped on a sofa like praying mantises. Outside, he could hear a couple giggling as they passed by his door. Inside, he heard Sheila's soft breathing.

"I want to have sex," he said bluntly.

Sheila stood up clutching her purse. "I must go home."

He made up his mind solely on the tone of her voice. "You're not going home," he said, rising from the sofa to face her. "I told you what I wanted."

The skull Boris worked on was female. They got so few female cadavers in the company. Nearly all of their bodies belonged to the indigent, released to them from the coroner's office. Lately, many of their heads were shipped without the bodies from India and the Philippines. Boris didn't know how much was paid for them, but he imagined it was a pauper's dowry. It appeared females often had family members claim the bodies, but not many claimed the men.

Keirnan glanced over at Boris' lady skull. "Lucky you. We hardly ever get a woman."

Boris almost laughed aloud. Keirnan could say that again. Getting women was a real problem for skull flensers, something he was finding out.

He lifted the head by the stringy gray-blonde hair and looked into the woman's face. "Rode hard, died badly," he said. There were deep lines on each side of her mouth, wrinkles in her forehead and between her eyes. Her lips were pale, straight ropes opening on gums showing missing teeth in the front, top and bottom. Only a few gray molars remained in the back.

Keirnan shrugged and went back to his own skull task. He was having trouble getting one of the ears off. He sawed at it like a chunk of stringy steak.

Boris lowered the woman's head and, handling it with more care than he did for male heads, he hummed as he worked, taking the skin, tendons, and muscles off the soon-to-be-beautiful white skull.

That evening after work, he stopped off at the Paper Tiger and sat on a high stool, hooking his feet in the rungs. The bar was a neighborhood joint, too dark, not very clean, but the beer was cold. People sitting at the tables and booths were older and spoke in whispers. At the bar front sat a woman several years older than Boris.

"Buy you the next round?" he asked, gesturing with his beer glass toward her. She looked all right for her age, whatever it was. Her hair was still shiny brown, even if it was colored, and her eyes looked sleepy and as calm as a small, windless pond.

"Sure, thanks." She took her whiskey sour glass and a little black purse off the bar and moved down to sit next to him on a stool. Their shoulders touched.

He held out his hand to shake. "I'm Boris."

She shook with him, her hand delicate and bare of jewelry. "Beatrice. You can call me Bea."

"Bzzzz." He made the sound of a bee and grinned.

She picked up her new drink the barkeep set before her and didn't remark on his little joke.

"Live around here?" he asked. He wanted to win over her attention. So what if she was ten or fifteen years older than him? She ought to kill herself, of course, being that old, but no one her age thought that way.

"I live across the street and down two blocks," she said. She sipped the whiskey sour, having first taken out the little red sword with the cherry stuck on it and placing it precisely centered on a napkin.

"You work?"

She gave him a direct stare to search his face. He knew then she was trying to determine if he was asking her if she worked on her back and she was about to get offended. "I'm the assistant manager in Broadmoor, the antique shop downtown."

"I know that place. They carry the coolest shit."

15

He bought her two more drinks and around ten o'clock consulted his wristwatch. "I need to beat it. You want to come by for a last call?"

She already had her little clutch purse in hand. "I don't mind if I do."

He smiled, took her hand, and led her from the bar. He felt light as a fairy inside, and more than a little tipsy. When he had his door unlocked and they were inside his apartment, he felt himself stagger a little and caught her arm to steady himself. The first thing she said to him was, "Where'd you get the skulls? We could sell those in our store."

After having a beer, his vision wavered, making the world look under water. Her face appeared demonic to him and he asked himself what the hell he was doing with this old broad. He wasn't really that hard up. He had to be drunk. She sat next to him with one of the two skulls in her lap. She turned it in the lamplight, admiring it.

"This one looks pretty fresh," she said.

He wasn't drunk enough to talk about Sheila. He just shrugged his shoulders and took the skull from her fingers to put it back on the table. It wobbled on the mandible and the silver fillings in the teeth sparkled at him. "It's old," he lied. "Old as the grave." This made him laugh until he caught himself sounding hysterical and swallowed the rest of his laughter.

"Well, I better scoot on outta here." She stood, took her empty beer bottle to the kitchen counter, and suddenly stood back in front of his knees. "I'd like to see you again," she said.

He knew she was waiting for him to get up and plant a big sloppy kiss on her lips, but they looked like rubber to him and it would be like kissing a big, fake dolly. He waved his hand weakly and mumbled, "I'll see you at the bar."

She swooped down and kissed his cheek, and then let herself out of the apartment.

Alone in the shadow-filled living room, the beer swirling in his stomach and the skulls grinning at him from the table, he realized he was going to be sick.

"I met a woman at the bar last night who didn't cringe when I talked about skulls," Boris told Keirnan. He wasn't about to mention how she'd admired the two skulls he owned.

"You don't say. That's a rare woman. You better snatch her up." Keirnan stood over the vacuum machine that sucked out the brains from the cadaver heads. It took sometimes twenty minutes to get all the goop out of the skull.

Boris slipped the waxy face off a male head that had the smallest nose he'd ever seen. His nasal passages must have been infinitesimal. "She's too old for me."

Keirnan laughed. "Mature women can give you a mature experience, Boris. I wouldn't discount them."

Boris thought about the woman and realized he couldn't remember her name. Or had she ever told him? Had he ever asked? He knew she worked at the antique emporium downtown, but that's about all he really knew about her.

After work, curious, he went back to the Paper Tiger where the neon light over the door advertised Bud Light. He made sure this time to eat a burger before he went drinking. He didn't like feeling out of control around women, and he certainly didn't like hugging the toilet to throw up his guts.

She was sitting at the same place at the bar. She glanced his way and smiled sweetly. She wasn't all that old, was she? Ten years older than him, maybe thirty-five. Shouldn't she be married and raising a pack of kids at her age? He'd have to get to know more about her.

She wore black slacks that were shiny as sharkskin and fit the curves of her buttocks. She had on a flimsy, see-through, black-and-white printed blouse over a black tank top. Her hair was loose around her shoulders. She didn't look like a dream or a super model, but she roused the randy part of his brain until he pictured her naked in bed with him.

He slid onto the stool next to her. "Hey. I don't think we introduced ourselves properly. I'm Boris Trazenski."

"Beatrice. Bea, remember?" She made a buzzing sound and he remembered now. Bee. The buzzing little bee. "Bea Calloway."

He bought her a whiskey sour and ordered a draft. He'd nurse it tonight. Just the smell of beer made him slightly nauseous.

17

He learned she'd been married once and divorced, no children. She was originally from Toronto, a transplanted Canadian. "You're pretty far South," he said. To him, Memphis was the heart of the South, no matter what anybody said.

"I like the climate," she said. "The snow got boring."

That night, he didn't take her home with him, unsure he really wanted her in his apartment. On Friday night, he returned to the bar and, thinking about her curvy body, he did want her. He had a real need and it had stopped mattering to him about her age. How many women was he going to find who were fascinated by skulls?

Friday night he turned to her at the bar and in a low, private voice he said, "I flense skulls for a living. I work at Sci-Clean and we ship skulls all over the world."

Her brown eyes opened only slightly wider. "That sounds bloody ... clever," she said.

He laughed. "I guess it is. I don't usually talk about it with women. Most of them are turned off, wondering how I can handle parts of a cadaver all day."

"I think it's fascinating. How do you get all the ..." She made a circle around her face with her hand. "... all the, you know, face off a skull?"

"With a super-sharp scalpel. It's tedious work, exacting, you don't want to leave nicks on the bone, but when it's done, the skull is like a pristine ..."

"Work of art," she finished for him. "Like the ones in your apartment."

"About those ..." He couldn't look her in the eyes now. He nursed the beer. "I didn't buy those the way I should have. I ..."

"You took them."

He dared not look at her. He didn't know why he was telling her so much. Her age made him confess like a child to a mother.

"I'd be tempted to do that, too," she said when he remained silent. "They're so lovely, so white and clean. Like owning a ball of untouched snow that doesn't melt."

He looked at her then and saw the look in her eyes. She was really into it. She wasn't faking a lie to make him feel better about himself. "You want to spend the night with me?"

She reached for her clutch purse. "Don't mind if I do." Her voice was jaunty and she was off the stool waiting for him to pay the tab.

They grew inseparable. Skipping the bar, she came directly to his apartment almost every night. First Bea brought him an antique cloche to hold one of his skulls under glass. She apologized the shop didn't have another so he could have matching covers for his prizes.

Next she told him she'd been caught stealing the cloche and had to pay for it—"$400," she said—and was fired.

Finally, weeks into their relationship, she told him her daydream fantasy of flensing the skull of her boss, the owner of the antique store.

He sat in the gloom of his apartment feeling two warring emotions. He was ecstatic she wanted to wipe a skull. He was terrified she thought he might agree to it.

Best to be cautious, he thought. "I don't know, Bea. That's murder, you know. And if you were just fired, you'll be the first suspect."

"You're right." She sat gnawing a nail and looking into the gloom. She had one of the skulls in her lap, petting the rounded head with her free hand the way she might caress a cat.

"On the other hand ..."

She looked at him in eagerness. "Yes?"

"There are several homeless guys down near the overpass and the river. Waste of life, you'd say."

"I would say that," she agreed. "The homeless and crack addicts and winos are like city litter. It makes the whole town look dirty. One thing I could say about Toronto—it was clean."

"So you want to go for a ride? To the river?"

It was Saturday and they had all night and all of Sunday before he had to be back to work.

"Keirnan, you notice after so many years doing this you have a whole new perspective on death?"

"How do you mean?"

"Like you aren't afraid to be around it. Like it holds no mystery. It's just not scary anymore, is it?"

Keirnan steadily and carefully removed tiny clots of flesh stuck to the skull in his hands and said without raising his gaze from the work, "It's a protective coping mechanism. It's known about in medical schools. Interns start out idealistic and empathetic and end up cynical, almost the whole lot of them. It happens." He shrugged and scraped at the skull as gently as any surgeon.

Boris thought he'd never had empathy in the first place. He'd never had to lose it to work at Sci-Clean. It's what made them all good at their jobs. They felt no taboo about handling the dead, no recognition of the thoughts that used to be in the brains they sucked down the drain, no idea about the parents, children, siblings, or friends of the owners of the lone heads brought to them in antiseptic plastic containers.

Then Boris began to wonder about Bea and if she had always been like him—someone without an ounce of kind feeling for his fellow men and no remorse for that lack.

"We're just cold," he said, thinking aloud.

Keirnan was ready to take his wiped skull to the brain sucking vacuum. "Cold as ice," he said and walked away.

Bea moved into his apartment, unable to afford her own any longer. They were awake late into the night, sitting cross-legged on the bed together, talking about what they wanted and the direction they hoped their lives would go. Slowly, Boris began to buy and bring home equipment. Each new piece thrilled Bea. In the living room, he situated a big glass fish tank housing thousands of dermestid beetles for eating the last of the flesh off bones. There was a fifty-gallon drum in the kitchen where they used a vacuum tube for extracting the brains. Buckets sat everywhere holding cleaning and whitening solutions. He set up a sturdy table in the living room, a plastic drop cloth below it, where the real flensing work was done.

Boris and Bea loved their nights and weekends together working on their own cadavers. The whole place was covered with various deodorizers, both electronic and organic. It was difficult to keep the bad smells from reaching outside the door, but so far they'd managed it. With all the flesh taken off a skeleton, they had to bag and haul the stinking mess the same night to the river bridge to throw it over during dark midnight hours. They trusted the river to carry the swill downriver and away where fish could eat it like chum.

On one of those nights, a homeless man braced them. Crossing the bridge on foot, he saw them pull over to the break-down lane and lob a heavy trash bag over the railing to the river below.

"Yo!" he called, trotting toward them. "We got people living down there, you know. You can't throw your garbage out like that in the river, it's against the law. You're a couple of filthy hooligans."

Bea and Boris looked at him, looked at each other as they decided whether to kill him, and both shook their heads in the negative. The bridge was much too public for abducting victims.

"Sorry, man," Boris called. As they drove away, they could see the bum behind them shaking a fist above his head.

A week later, they saw the same bum beneath the bridge overpass. It was night and the overpass was downstream from the main bridge. As a couple they were trolling, having just finished the skull of a hitchhiker Boris had picked up on a freeway off-ramp. They were ready for another victim with another perfect skull. Plenty of room for more specimens waited on the shelves of the bookcase against the bedroom wall.

"Isn't that ...?" Boris thought he recognized the man.

"The bum who yelled at us last week on the bridge, yeah," Bea said.

"There they are!" the bum rushed toward them weaving like a man having a seizure. From behind a concrete column three more bums appeared, following their mate down the incline toward the river and the couple standing there. Two more bums shakily rose from their little camp fire and tottered behind the rest. From out of a large cardboard box partially covered with corrugated tin, three more homeless men crawled forth into the night. They drew together like shadowy ectoplasm.

"Hold on, boys." Boris raised his hand in a halt position. "My girl and I, we're just walking along the river."

"At midnight?" the first bum asked, closing in on them. They could see now that he carried a baseball bat.

"We have to get the hell out of here." Bea backed up two steps, then three, then four.

"I ... I ..." Boris felt a trembling starting in his lower legs moving up to his thighs. He hadn't felt this afraid in years. In some way it was exhilarating, which was a surprise. He had trouble getting his breath.

"These are the guys threw over Joey's bloody parts and pieces," the old bum with the baseball bat said to his companions gathering at his back. They all carried something in their hands. Broken bottles, thick lengths of driftwood, even knives glinting in the moonlight.

"You left Joey's clothes in the bag, you monsters. You left his shirt with his pack of Winstons in it and the faded picture of his mother."

Boris looked at Bea. It was true they threw all the garbage away together in the trash bags. Clothes, entrails, eyeballs, genitals. All the useless stuff.

"Run," he said.

Bea was moving before the word left his mouth. Her eyes were round as shooter marbles and the lines in her face deepened to harsh trenches. Fear brought out the worst in people, Boris thought. He wondered what his own face reflected. Did he look like a clown whose greasepaint had smeared and made him look grotesque? Did he look as bad as he felt? He had seen fear on the faces of his victims and it was never pretty. He was so scared now he shook all over and had a hard time holding onto his urine, clenching his muscles for control.

But now he was running behind Bea, making tracks up the hillside overgrown with kudzu and blackberry vines. The verdant green smell filled his nostrils as he tore at the vines for purchase. He could hear the gang of homeless men at their backs cursing them. He could hear his labored breathing. The night was full of sound, full of fury, and ripe with the specter of death.

Why had he thought he'd never be afraid of dying, having dispensed it himself and handled the results of it in both the lab and his apartment? Why had he ever thought he was immune to fear and the idea of his own painful end?

Because he was ... he was ... he was so afraid, piss ran down his trousers hot and sharply pungent, and he was crying like a baby imagining the bludgeoning he was going to suffer if he couldn't get up the hillside in time to escape the wrath of almost a dozen men.

Then Bea fell. She was in front of him and her flats slipped on the dew-laden vines, sending her plummeting into his knees and knocking him backward off his feet. He landed on his back staring up at the half-moon in the dark starless sky. The wind had been knocked out of him. He tried to roll onto his side and get to his knees when the first blow came.

It was a crack of sound and of pain that landed on his shoulder and slammed through his arm all the way to his wrist. He screamed and knew instantly his shoulder and collar bone were broken.

The man standing over him, backed by fearsome shadows, said, "We know what you've been doing. We know about people like you. We watch out for people like you."

Bea clambered up his legs and into a sitting position. She was moaning and trying to get her feet beneath her. A man stepped forward and buried a long knife in her belly. She bent over, covering the knife with her hands, and let out a loud despairing groan.

"Wait," Boris said. His mind scrambled for something to say, anything to stop this from going forward. "Wait, listen, you've got us mixed up with somebody else. We're just on our honeymoon and were walking ..."

The bum reached down and felt under Boris' jacket. He removed a blackjack and held it up for the others to see. They searched Bea and found a sharp kitchen knife in the clutch purse she carried.

"You're the ones," the bum said. His gums were empty on the bottom, but Boris noticed his head was beautifully shaped. It was so symmetrically round beneath a scalp covered with short crew cut hair that Boris couldn't stop staring. The man's skull would have yielded such a *prize*.

"They're the ones," the man with the beautiful skull repeated, gesturing to the other men to join him as he commenced beating the couple to bloody death.

Keirnan stood in the Sci-Clean manager's office shifting from one foot to the other. "Did you know he'd stolen one of our skulls?" the manager asked.

"No, I didn't know."

"You're the one who talked to him all the time, you should have had some clue. You know what they found in his apartment? Skulls! Only one of them came from here. The rest were from murders Boris committed, him and his crazy bitch woman. I'm going to have to insist all of you take psychological tests before continuing the work in the lab. You're not opposed to that are you, Keirnan? I know you've been here a long time, but if one has to be tested, all of you do."

"No sir, I don't mind."

"Okay, go tell the others. I'll call in a psychologist tomorrow. This scandal is a publicity nightmare for the company. We hired a maniac, for Christ's sake!"

"Yes, sir."

Keirnan left the office with a hangdog look. This was sad news, very sad news indeed. Boris was such a putz. He was sloppy. He worked at Sci-Clean less than a year and thought he was an expert flenser. Keirnan could have told him he was no such thing. He was an amateur. It took a man many years to become a real artist.

That night, at home, Keirnan went into his bedroom and said to his wife, "Honey, there's trouble at work. There's going to be psychological testing. I don't think I can pass it. What do you think?"

When he received no answer, he moved closer in the shadows, and stared down with hollow, sad eyes. "Well, what do you think I should do?"

His wife's clean white skull lying on the pillow in the center of the bed stared at him from her big empty eye sockets and didn't say a word.

Keirnan sat down on the bed and took her skull into his hands. His tears fell onto the cheek bones and made it look as if the skull wept from open, shadowed sockets.

He glanced up at the wall of shelves next to the bed and the skulls arranged there with such care. He kept them dusted. He adored them with all his heart and soul. They each had a name and a past. They harbored dead dreams that beckoned to him in his sleep.

"You're right," he said as if answering someone in the room with him. "We need to pack everything up and move to another city. I could work in a hospital. We'll get along all right."

The skull in his hands slipped and the mandible fell open. Keirnan closed it with a clacking that sounded to him like soft distant laughter.

THE FIRE OF IBLIS

BY MIKE DUNNE

The sun rose in the east, sneaking underneath the gathering clouds and glistening off the ebony backs of the slaves as they loaded the camels. Abdullah Al Hamadi squinted as the morning light reflected into his dark eyes from the brass armbands the slaves wore. An uncommon rumble of thunder caused him to look up at the sky from under his red and white kufiyya. After sipping from his tiny cup of spiced coffee, he looked at Mustafa and asked, "Do you think the storm brings water?"

Mustafa, a lean and sharp-nosed man, stepped out from under the tent's overhanging flap and scanned the sky, his black jalabiyya flapping around his legs in the unusually strong dawn breeze. "It will be as Allah wishes. Peace be upon Him."

Al Hamadi grunted and started tapping his foot, his leather sandal creating a miniature sandstorm around their ankles.

Mustafa looked toward the tent nearby that served as a mosque. "I would think a man such as you would pay heavy favor to Allah. Surely, it is He that watches over your trade routes and has made you wealthy."

"It is *I* who has made me wealthy, Mustafa," said Al Hamadi sourly. "Allah does not pay your exorbitant fees. He does not bring you rare sweetmeats for your table, nor does he bring you fine silks for your wives."

Mustafa bowed his head and said, "You are indeed a generous man, Abdullah. But I fear the Imam believes differently."

"That addled old man is no better than a whore!" Abdullah exclaimed as he spat. "He takes my golden baksheesh easily enough."

Moving well for such a heavy man, Al Hamadi hurried over to the nearest slave and struck him on the back with his camel whip. "Careful with our provisions, you eater of dung! For that is *all* you will be eating if you drop them in the sand again!"

The slave bowed in apology and quickly bent to pick up the sack of aged cheese that had slipped to the ground. Securing it next to the dried meat, he looked over the camel's neck and into the desert outside of their camp. Nearby, at the top of a low dune, stood a woman; her black asaba was blowing loosely about her shoulders. The slave, an Ethiopian whose name was Faraji, finished tightening the leather straps on the camel and looked again. She was gone. Faraji searched in every direction but could see no other women walking back toward the caravanserai. Shrugging, he bent to the next task so as not to get another beating from his master.

Securing the whip on his wide leather belt, Al Hamadi threw his empty cup into Mustafa's tent as he strode by, moving behind the beige canvas enclosure to relieve himself. Rearranging his robes, he settled his old, curved dagger in place and looked again at the sky. Swollen black clouds were moving slowly toward Jeddah, far to the west. This journey would take him to that coastal city, where his camels would bring a high price at the Red Sea markets. It would take him roughly thirty days to make the trip from Riyadh and he did not want some unseasonable storm slowing him down and working additional fat from his herd. Heading back to camp, he was surprised to see a woman at the top of the closest dune.

What is she doing up there? he wondered.

Her right hand raised and beckoned to him. He was taking no harem for this trip but could always use good women—and the Nubians loved to trade in female slaves. Thinking he could turn a tidy profit from her if she was pretty enough, Al Hamadi strode away from the caravan and worked his way up the dune. Puffing loudly as he reached the top, he leaned on his knees while catching his breath.

That is odd, he thought. *Where did she go?*

The wind was not blowing hard enough to wipe out her tracks, but all he saw were faint traces of cloven hoof prints in the sand. Straightening to his full height, he looked all around. To the south and west was bare desert and rolling red dunes. To the north and east, the Bedouin camp bustled about its morning routine as the city gates opened in the distance, signaling the start of the business day.

Frowning, he sidestepped back down through the thick sand and noticed his caravan was finally packed and ready to go. The camels rested on their knees and the slaves were checking the hobbles to make sure no animals got loose. Al Hamadi had one more purchase to make before they left. His last strong box had broken and he needed a new one to carry his valuables. He walked quickly through the maze of tents until he reached the souk area and found the shop of the woodworker. Just inside the entrance, he stopped to let his eyes adjust to the dim light.

"Ah, Sheikh Al Hamadi," a man said obsequiously from the shadowy interior. "As-salaam alaykum."

"Wa alaykum as-salaam," Al Hamadi spoke the expected response.

"What can a humble merchant provide your greatness this morning?" the woodworker asked as he continued to bow.

"I need a chest," Al Hamadi said.

"A chest, a chest," murmured the shopkeeper. "Of course, I have only one that will suit a man of your eminence."

Moving swiftly to the back of the tent, the man knelt behind some finished work—camel saddles, decorative door panels, and such—and brought forward a small wooden chest. In its lid were set many fine jewels and heavy gold filigree.

"Here is the best chest my humble shop can offer you, effendi," said the man, bowing low once more.

"Is it strong?" Al Hamadi eyed the fancy box suspiciously. "Strong enough to make many journeys to Jeddah?"

"Yes, effendi, very strong is this box! This is my finest work and fit for a king."

"No doubt you shall charge me a king's ransom for it as well."

"My sheikh, I will give you the very best price!" offered the merchant. "But first, let me show you how truly special this box is."

The woodworker cleared off a space on his workbench and gestured Al Hamadi closer. "See how the lock is unusual?"

Pulling a chain from within the neck of his grimy jalabiyya, he brandished a key. The key was shaped like a miniature angel. It had ornate silver wings spread regally from its back amidst luminous robes delicately molded from mother of pearl. On its tiny feet were sandals of intricately woven gold. The merchant showed Al Hamadi how the golden sandals were removed and the ankles shifted on the smallest of hinges to position the feet and toes so as to be the teeth of the key. Once the puzzle of the key was revealed, it was inserted gently into the lock and the box was opened. Outside, thunder boomed causing Al Hamadi to look up with a start.

"Are you sure you want to be traveling today, effendi?" the woodworker asked with concern. "It sounds as if Allah is looking for children to punish."

"Let's be about our business, merchant, so that I can be away and leave Allah to his search!"

"As you wish, effendi," the woodworker answered softly.

The merchant quickly showed Al Hamadi the remaining features of his most precious wooden chest. Over sweet mint tea, the two men concluded their deal and Al Hamadi slipped the key chain around his neck, securing it within the folds of his white robes. Hoisting the small but surprisingly heavy box under his arm, he hurried through the camp and back to his caravan. There, Mustafa was waiting, apparently taking it upon himself to keep an eye on the slaves and camels while Al Hamadi was in the souk.

"Sheikh Al Hamadi!" Mustafa cried over a crack of thunder. "Surely you will stay in the caravanserai one more night until the storm has passed?"

"The Red Sea merchants will not wait on my camels and I must be in Jeddah to make sure it is *my* camels that are bought!" exclaimed Al Hamadi. "I will be away and we will run before the storm. It will die, out there in the desert, as all storms do."

Mustafa nodded. "So it has always been, my sheikh. Then may Allah go with you and speed you on your journey, and may you return in three months wealthy and wise." He clasped Al Hamadi's shoulders and kissed the sheikh three times, alternating cheeks.

With Mustafa's assistance, Al Hamadi mounted his camel and secured the new box in front of the saddle. With a lash of his whip and a shout, he bid his camel to rise, causing Mustafa to jump back. Slaves moved quickly down the line of animals pulling the hobbles as Mustafa, his kufiyya whipping about his head in the strengthening wind, bid farewell to the caravan.

As the last of the camels moved into the desert, Mustafa turned to go inside his tent. A flash of black caught his eye. He could have sworn he saw a woman following the last of the camels, but her image vanished as swiftly as a mirage into the desert. Shaking his head, as if to clear it of nonsense, Mustafa gathered his billowing robes and ducked inside, calling for tea and breakfast.

Al Hamadi scowled again. He watched as the slave Faraji continued his efforts to lead the caravan toward the west. Usually it was quite easy to follow the caravan route. It had been carved deeply into the desert by thousands of plodding hooves and shuffling feet—despite the ever-shifting sands—over hundreds of years. This accursed storm, however, was making it increasingly difficult to be sure of one's direction. He had been so certain that the storm would fade away quickly once the caravan entered the deep desert. But it had stayed with them. It almost seemed as though the storm was following him, circling like a pack of vicious black dogs, waiting to hamstring a straggler.

31

They had been in the desert two weeks and still the dark clouds glowered all around them. Great spears of lightning crackled earthward, flashing in their eyes and raising the hair on their arms. Rolling crashes of thunder assaulted their ears and threatened to spook the camels. Without the sun to guide him, and with the fierce wind blowing sand over the trail, doubt was slowly creeping into the corners of Al Hamadi's mind.

"Allow me to guide you, effendi," spoke a soft voice between claps of thunder.

Al Hamadi, jolted from his somber thoughts, looked for the speaker. Puzzled, he lifted up from his camel saddle to scratch his rear end. He was riding a few lengths off to one side and no one was nearby.

"Wise effendi, my wish is but to serve you. I humbly submit that we are moving too far north to reach our destination safely."

"Who said that?" Al Hamadi spoke in a low voice, glancing around nervously.

"It is I, my sheikh."

Startled, Al Hamadi looked down at the strong box. Shaking his head, he looked around again to see if anyone else had noticed the voice.

"How is it that a strong box can talk?" he whispered.

"I am called Hiraz, effendi. I am a jinni."

"If you are a jinni, why can I not see you?"

"I am not that type of jinni, effendi. Some of my kind can only inhabit inanimate objects."

Thunder boomed again as Al Hamadi looked over at the main body of the caravan. Rubbing the heavy stubble on his ample jowls, he said, "I must be going crazy. The storm has addled my mind."

"On the contrary, my sheikh. You are as sane as the next man. Simply luckier!"

"Lucky?" Al Hamadi laughed without humor. "How can this be true? My business, my very reputation, hinges on people believing in my shrewdness. If I am caught talking to a box, I will be ruined!"

"Effendi, I am here to help you. Even now, your untrustworthy slaves are taking you far to the north of your intended course."

Al Hamadi looked up at the caravan. His slaves were guiding the camels along the ridge of a low dune. Strong winds were blowing the sand into a stinging mist; the slaves had wrapped cloths around their heads to try and protect their eyes from the coarse grains. Al Hamadi looked down at the strong box once more. It sat there, silent.

"How can you tell we are off course, jinni?" Al Hamadi asked, still not sure whether he was imagining things.

"I am a jinni, effendi." Hiraz sounded amused. "We know many things."

Feeling apprehensive but overcome with desire to escape the storm and reach his destination quickly, Al Hamadi relented and asked, "In which direction should we go then, jinni?"

Hiraz answered, "Do you see that tall dune off to your left, effendi?"

Al Hamadi looked and saw a towering dune in the distance. It stood taller than any around it. In fact, it was unusually tall. Shivering in the breeze, he said, "I see it."

"Steer your caravan toward that dune, effendi, and you will be back on course to your destination."

With the wind howling about his ears, it had almost sounded like Hiraz had said, '*On course to your destiny.*' Al Hamadi considered his caravan. The camels were plodding along, seemingly oblivious to the storm, while the slaves struggled through the deep sand and fierce winds. Pulling hard on the reins and tapping his whip, Al Hamadi guided his camel over to where Faraji worked to keep the camels on course.

"Faraji!" Al Hamadi yelled.

The slave looked up, his black eyes peering through a slit in his head cloth.

"Turn the caravan!" Al Hamadi shouted over the wind, pointing at the large dune to their left.

Faraji nodded and, taking a firm grip on the lead camel's reins, began turning the caravan. The other slaves followed suit and soon the caravan was heading in the new direction. Almost at once, Al Hamadi felt the wind slacken. He looked down at the silent box, wondering. Directly ahead, he could see the huge dune, and even stranger, he also saw that on either side of the caravan were two large ridges of red sand, stretching ahead as far as he could see. With the dark clouds above and the walls of sand on either side, it was as if they were in a tunnel that led toward the giant dune in the distance.

Many hours later, Al Hamadi noticed no difference in their surroundings other than it was getting dark. Urging his camel over to Faraji, he said, "Let us make camp for the night. It looks like the storm is passing and we should be able to get new bearings in the morning."

At that moment, the caravan moved into a wide area between the towering dune walls. Date palms arose from the desert and a glistening pond, unruffled by the softening wind, appeared in the middle of an unexpected oasis. Al Hamadi and Faraji looked at each other then looked back at the oasis that had appeared seemingly out of nowhere.

"Effendi, shall we make camp here?"

Al Hamadi thought for a moment and then said, "Of course we shall make camp here. Look around you, Faraji. We have everything we need here for the night. Hobble the camels and set up my tent quickly. The storm has tired me!"

"As you command, my sheikh," Faraji said, bowing his head.

Faraji quickly began organizing the other slaves to do Al Hamadi's bidding. All of them looked worried, Faraji noticed. He didn't blame them. There was something wrong here. He felt it in his bones. Faraji had traveled the deserts of Arabia with his master for many years. They had camped in many oases and he had never felt this feeling of doom and despair before. Busying himself with setting up camp, he glanced over at Al Hamadi. The sheikh sat on his camel, staring at his new strong box and talking to himself. More worried than ever, Faraji spoke sharply to the other slaves, urging them to hurry.

Flickering light from copper braziers carved deep shadows in Al Hamadi's heavy face. He sat inside his tent with the flap closed. The braziers dimly illuminated a large room richly appointed with lustrous carpets and silken cushions. The strong box sat before him and he twisted the unusual key slowly at the end of its chain.

"Effendi, you should sleep after such a hard day's journey," Hiraz said.

As if in a trance, Abdullah Al Hamadi nodded and settled more comfortably on his cushions. His eyes closed, and soon his snores filled the tent.

Outside, Faraji stood sentinel at the entrance. He had heard voices emanating from within all evening. When he had entered to offer food and drink to his sheikh, he had been rudely dismissed. Now, he looked around the strange oasis and shivered in the desert night. No moon could be seen, shielded as it was by a low ceiling of clouds. The other slaves had completed their labors and eaten a meager supper. Settled down for the night, they appeared as shadows along the ground, dimly seen specters glimpsed from the corner of Faraji's weary eyes.

Some time later, his eyes flew open, the sound of horrible screams echoing in Faraji's ears. He looked around frantically, hoping the screams had been in his dreams. The other slaves were in a group at the edge of camp, staring into the desert night.

Glancing back at the sheikh's tent, Faraji hurried over to the other slaves. "What is this?" he asked sharply.

In a fearful voice, one of the men whispered, "They are gone."

"Of whom do you speak?" asked Faraji, eyes searching the darkness.

The same man, still whispering, said, "Six of our number have disappeared into the night. We were all asleep. I was having a dream of paradise. A beautiful woman was beckoning me. Just over the dune from here was a wonderful place. My heart's desires fulfilled!"

"That was the same dream I was having!" exclaimed another.

Faraji looked at the remaining slaves. All of them were nodding and whispering in agreement. "We must go and find our brothers," he said.

"We cannot search for them in the darkness," the first slave responded. "Whatever is out there will surely attack us as well." Others nodded, their eyes wide with dread.

"You would have us leave them to whatever roams the desert?" Faraji questioned.

Looking ashamed, the slaves hung their heads and made no argument. Faraji was a brave man. Before becoming a slave, he had been a warrior in the country of his birth. But the memory of the screams, and the certain knowledge that none of the men would venture out of camp this night to help, dampened his desire to discover the fate of his fellows.

With a last glance toward the blackness of the surrounding dunes, he said, "Move your pallets in close tonight. Let us stay near the fires and then we will investigate at first light." As the men hesitated, he spoke again, "We still have a long journey ahead of us. Quickly now, so that we may get what rest Allah will grant us."

Crowding close together, the slaves picked up their bedding and moved into the center of camp. Faraji went to the tent of Abdullah Al Hamadi and looked inside. By the light of the dying braziers, he could see the sheikh sleeping, soft snores coming from his open mouth.

How could he not have heard? Faraji wondered.

Entering quietly to tend the braziers, he looked down and saw a key resting against the chest of his master. In the dim light, it looked dark red, almost black. Tiny horns sprouted from a small, angular head. Dark, spiny wings jutted menacingly from the back of the figure. Tiny black eyes, like polished onyx, glistened in the dim, amber light of the braziers. The eyes seemed to follow Faraji as he finished feeding the coals and straightening the pillows under his master. With a last worried glance at his sheikh, Faraji left the tent and resumed his post outside.

Dawn was still far off as Al Hamadi yawned and sat up. The inside of his tent was uncomfortably warm.

That idiot Faraji must have stoked the braziers too much, he thought. Yet, as he looked around, both braziers were so low, they gave off hardly any light or heat.

Al Hamadi was tired, despite having slept many hours. Vaguely, he began to remember the events of the previous day.

It must've been a dream.

He felt a sharp pain in his chest. He reached with his left hand to rub the soreness and was shocked as his hand came away covered in a warm, dark liquid. Looking down, he cried out as he saw the front of his white jalabiyya also soaked with blood. What was happening to him?

Al Hamadi staggered to his feet and tried to move toward the entrance of his tent. He tripped over something hard and fell heavily. Frightened, he looked back and saw his new strong box. Remembering the madness he felt when speaking to Hiraz, he became frantic and started crawling toward the tent flap. Another sharp pain in his chest caused him to look down. When he saw what had become of his beautiful, angelic key, he screamed.

Outside, Faraji heard his master's scream and bolted upright. Al Hamadi sounded as if he was under attack from the knife-wielding assassins of Alumut. But as he rose and turned toward his sheikh's tent, he froze. Standing at the entrance were two women. Faraji stared incredulously. How did they get here, so many miles from the caravanserai? Then, he remembered the woman he had seen on the dunes the day the caravan had departed. He also recalled with a chill the screams he had heard earlier in the night, screams of men dying horribly.

"Demons," he said. Then more loudly, "What is it you want from us?"

The two women smiled, revealing glistening white teeth, tapered to razor sharp points. Their canines extended further down, like the fangs of a tiger. Faraji looked more closely at them in the dim light of the campfire and could make out dark stains, darker than the fabric of their black asabas—or perhaps wetter, as he now noticed that the stains reflected the firelight.

"What have you done with my master?" Faraji shouted at them.

The one on the left stepped forward, her tongue peeking out from between her fangs. "We have done nothing with your sheikh, poor slave," she said in a low and sultry voice. "He is being attended by Hiraz."

Faraji trembled. She was close enough now that he felt her breath upon his cheek like a fetid breeze. Her scent was sweet and sickly at the same time. As he looked at her, he began to notice other things. Her eyes were nearly luminous, angling upward from the corners. At her breast, where her asaba had parted, the swell of her bosom was covered in a fine, black down. Bowing his head in fear, he saw that her feet were not feet at all, but cloven hooves, leaving small goat-like tracks in the sand.

Straining against his fright, Faraji raised his eyes and was captured by the creature's gaze. His whole world became her eyes. He felt as if his soul was being sucked into her. She took a final step toward him and he mercifully lost consciousness.

Inside the tent, Sheikh Abdullah was gibbering. His jalabiyya was soaking wet with blood. He lay on the carpeted floor, panting. The key that had been around his neck lay by one of the braziers. It glistened darkly and began to shimmer. Slowly, the hideous key began to pulse and grow. Before his eyes, Al Hamadi watched it become a man. Well, not exactly a man. It looked like a man crossed with some vile animal. The monster had skin the color of dark red blood and its black spiny wings were stretched wide and peaked high above its thickly horned skull, as if in anticipation of a kill. Al Hamadi's fear caused him to soil himself and tremble uncontrollably. With chattering teeth, he met the creature's dark-eyed gaze and managed to ask, "Who ... *what* are you?"

The voice that answered was awful. Images of loathing filled the sheikh's mind. Cries of the wretched, long dead, moaned and wailed, intertwined with the sound of the creature's voice. Al Hamadi screamed in terror, and then fell to whimpering, his hands clapped to his ears. Try as he might he could not block out the answers he did not want to hear.

"Know me not?" it asked, smiling, fangs twinkling wetly as the brazier's light grew stronger of its own volition. "I am Iblis, Lord of all Darkness and Eater of Souls"

Barely able to speak and unable to look at Iblis directly, Al Hamadi asked, "Why? Why do you do this to me? What have I done to deserve this horror?"

Iblis glared down at the broken figure of Al Hamadi. "Know you not the sins of your own miserable life?"

"I am but a humble businessman," sobbed Al Hamadi.

Through a force of will far greater than his own, he was commanded to look up into the glowing red eyes of Iblis. "You are a cheater of men," it began. "You are a seller of flesh and an abuser of women. You, who thinks so highly of himself and so lowly of others, are but a blight on the face of the earth. It is given to me to rid the world of such as you and I will make you quake before me as I eat your heart and consume your everlasting soul!"

Al Hamadi soiled himself again as the sound of Iblis thundered in the tent.

His being stripped bare by the power of the Dark Lord, Al Hamadi was forced to remember every unkind word, every underhanded deed, and each treacherous thought throughout the length of his existence. He begged for Allah to save him, but Iblis filled the tent, excluding all else. His awesome might and terrible presence permeated the air with evil darkness, driving all from Al Hamadi's mind but abject terror.

Finally, after reliving his every fault and failing, the sheikh looked up once more into the dreadful gaze of Iblis. His last mortal sight was of the Lord of Darkness descending upon him. As the powerful wings closed about him, their jagged spines piercing his flesh, Al Hamadi knew with awful despair that his soul was to be eaten, consumed each day in the fiery belly of Iblis for all eternity.

The Emir was a corpulent man. He did not stoop to go abroad in his Emirate. All his wants and needs were fulfilled without requiring him to move his great bulk. Slaves and hugely muscled guards filled his audience chamber as belly dancers moved seductively in the background. Today, a finely dressed merchant displayed wares of the finest metals, jewels of the highest quality and unsurpassed beauty.

"I would humbly offer you this rich chest of jewels, effendi," the sharp-nosed merchant began. "See how the lock is unusual?"

Pulling a chain from within the neck of his ornately embroidered jalabiyya, he showed the Emir a key. The key was shaped like a miniature angel. It had tiny silver wings spreading regally from its back amidst the luminous folds of its mother-of-pearl robes. On its tiny feet were sandals of intricately woven gold. The merchant showed the enchanted Emir how the golden sandals were removed and the ankles shifted on the smallest of hinges to position the feet and toes so as to be the teeth of the key.

Outside, thunder boomed.

SVEN BLOODHAIR

BY CHRISTINE MORGAN

"They say he was a great and fearsome warlord, in his time."

The words stung like wasps, burned like fire.

Was a great and fearsome warlord. Was.

In his time.

They say he was. They *say*.

Had he known who said it, had he seen the speaker as well as overheard the speech, he would have replied with his fists. King's peace or no king's peace, by Thor and by thunder he would have replied!

But he had not seen, and when he began to rise from his seat in the crowded and smoky feast-hall to demand that whoever said such a thing should stand forth and show himself, Gunnar, his brother, gripped his arm.

There would be, Gunnar told him, time enough to prove otherwise on the morrow.

"They insulted me," Sven said.

"By calling you a great and fearsome warlord?"

"That I *was* ... in my time ... they *say*." He ground his teeth until his jaw ached and the sound of millstones scraping filled his head.

"And so you were," said Gunnar.

"Were?"

"Were and are. What of it? They're brash young cocks. Look at them. Barely weaned, beardless as yearling goats. Half of them will piss themselves in the shield-wall for all their talk."

"They think me a used-up old man," said Sven.

"Nothing of the sort—" Gunnar began, but that was when their drunken excuse for a brother-in-law just had to stick his oar in.

"Well," Fjal Frodisson said, pausing to belch, "to be fair, you have seen, what, forty winters?"

"Thirty-seven!" Sven snarled.

Fjal gave an idle wave, rings glittering on his greasy, pudgy hand. "Thirty-seven, forty, close enough in their eyes. The eldest of those pups must be twenty, at most. They see someone of their fathers' age."

Gunnar gripped Sven's arm all the tighter, when Sven would have replied to *that* with his fists. Whatever had led their sister to marry such a fat fool as Fjal, Sven never had been able to comprehend.

"He makes me laugh," she said whenever the question was asked.

Made her laugh. A fine quality for the husband of Gunhild Sveingunsdottir. Even now, when they had come in the company of their jarl to the aid of the king, when Sven and Gunnar would fight, when they would win honor and plunder and fame, Fjal would stay behind here in the hall's safety. Stay behind, resting upon his well-padded ass, for he was a merchant and no kind of warrior at all.

Ever the good-natured one quick to placate, Gunnar urged Sven to enjoy more of the king's feast. "Save your temper for our foes, brother," he said, and beckoned to a serving girl to refill their drinking-horns. "Let them have reason aplenty to fear, when the Sveingunssons take the field!"

Sven, with one final glower at the insolent youths, let himself be grudgingly persuaded. All a man had forever was his reputation, and any who doubted his would find themselves well-educated on the morrow.

The king had laid a good table to welcome his allies. There was boiled meat and stewed fish ... barley beer, honey mead, and wine ... cheese and bread and spiced sweet-cakes. Dogs nosed eagerly among the floor rushes for scraps. Voices rang in song; talk and laughter rose to the high ceiling timbers. Now and then a woman squealed, and once there was a mighty slap followed by a boisterous roar.

All was great and hearty good cheer.

But Sven, Sven Sveingunsson, called Sven Bloodhair in battle, brother of Gunnar and Gunhild, did not much share it.

The insult rankled at him, a prickle-burr to his pride.

In his time.

In his *time?*

It was *still* his time! What did they take him for, some ancient white-beard suited only for whittling by the hearth?

Among his kindred had been Jarl Harald Bloodhair himself, by whose reputation and from tales of whom Sven had earned his own battle name!

He had been a mere lad when he'd slain his first man, an outlaw who'd sought to help himself to the contents of larder and hall while his father was away! He remembered that moment as if it had happened yesterday, his mother too weak with fever to rise from her bed, while little Gunnar and Gunhild looked on wide-eyed with fright.

The outlaw, unwashed and filthy, stinking of dung, sweat, and soured milk, had been armed with a long knife and a fierce-looking club. He'd expected no trouble from a house where there was only a sick woman and her children. He most certainly had not expected a boy of eight winters to come at him with a wood-axe, let alone cleave his thigh to the bone.

Sven had, of course, seen his fair share of blood before that fateful day, but never in such gushing and copious quantity as this. It leaped from the outlaw's gaped flesh in a spurting, crimson gout, dousing Sven, splashing him head to toe, hot and thick.

How the man had screamed! Like a pig being slaughtered! Dropping his weapons as he dropped to the floor, he'd clamped both hands over the terrible wound. The blood pumped and streamed between his dirty fingers.

He'd looked up at young Sven, sobbing with supplication, pleading for help and for mercy. And Sven, lifting the red-stained axe high over his head, had with all the strength in his boy-body buried the blade between his eyes.

Sven remembered vividly as well how the mess had been settled. He'd caused quite the commotion when he appeared at the neighbors' threshold, blood-drenched with flecks of the dead man's skull and brains spattered on his face. They'd come at once, beheld the carnage, and cleared it away. The men had clapped Sven on the back like an equal. One of them gave him an arm ring, a shoddy thing of hammered bronze, all but worthless, but he prized it as if it had been made from dwarf gold.

Later that night, Gunnar and Gunhild finally sleeping, his mother bade him sit beside her. He'd scrubbed the blood from his skin and his hair by then, and put on his spare tunic of nut-brown wool; a neighbor woman had taken his other clothes, promising to wash them.

As he sat with his mother, holding one of her fevered hands—it was warm as a coal!—in his, she'd told him of Jarl Harald Bloodhair, and what a great warlord and shipmaster he'd been, how famed and feared.

"So, too, shall you be," she'd told him, weakly squeezing his hand.

And so too had he become.

Never once had he forgotten the sensation of the outlaw's blood sluicing over him, the meaty smell and salty taste of it, the wet stickiness soaking through his clothes, dripping from his chin, running down his neck. Never once had he forgotten the wailing shrieks of his little brother and sister when he turned to them, or the startled uproar among the neighbors, their shock and horror, their reactions to the grisly sight.

Jarl Harald Bloodhair had, according to Sven's mother's stories, made faithful sacrifice to the gods before going into battle. Most often, it would be a dog, pig, or goat; sometimes an ox or even a horse. The throat would be put to the knife, slit so that the red life poured to fill a soapstone basin, and then into this basin Harald would dunk his head, until his hair and beard were sodden with it.

"To his foes," Sven's mother had said, "he was more monster than man, a blood beast of nightmares, a troll, a dread creature. Many a man who might otherwise have won his way to Valhalla by dying bravely threw down his sword instead and tried to flee, and was sent as a coward to Hel."

This became Sven's own practice as soon as he was of age to wage war. The sacrifice, the basin, the dunking of his head, the splatter when he threw back his long hair in wet, ropey strands. He sought not only to intimidate his enemies but honor his ancestor, and found it glorious on both counts.

Oddly, however, as well and clearly as he remembered the rest, he could not recall just when it was he'd decided to do Harald's legacy one better. When it was that he'd decided even a horse wouldn't be sufficient offering ... but a man *would*.

A man, or a woman. Bought slaves if need be. Captives were preferable, hostages even more so. High-born hostages were best of all.

Those Sven did remember with both clarity and satisfaction. He smiled over his mead to think of it. He'd bring them before the battle line, in full view of the other side. Sometimes he would not just dunk his head but upend the basin over it, pouring the thick blood down his face. He'd let it course into his mouth, even drink it, relishing the taste, that life broth, that blood stew. He'd guzzle it, gargle it, spit a triumphant laughing spray, and grin across at his foes with red, dripping teeth.

An enemy chieftain had once turned over a much-loved friend— his "sword companion" by rumor—as a pledge of truce. The friend had even volunteered for it, so confident were they that the truce would be upheld. When the chieftain's allies then broke it and attacked nonetheless, he sent messengers pleading, offering rich ransom.

Which, of course, Sven refused. The chieftain wailed and beat his breast like a woman when he saw the knife cut, the deed done—and the hot blood brought Sven much luck and favor in the ensuing battle.

He sadly had no such prize for tomorrow, when the horns sounded to call them to their places upon the field where reputation would be won. Only a slave, this time, a squat and sullen peasant purchased from a trader who claimed to have acquired him from a land across the sea. The slave was defiant, already often-beaten, and spoke no sensible tongue. It made him of little use.

For Sven, however, the slave's stubborn strength would make a fine sacrifice, pleasing to the gods.

More bursts of raucous laughter erupted into the smoke-filled air. Though he did not overhear his name spoken this time as the butt of some joke, Sven again glowered.

Yes, Fjal was right; they were young and insolent pups, barely weaned from the teats of their mothers. They knew nothing. And yet the very fact of *Fjal* being right, Gunhild's fat fool of a husband, only stung Sven's pride all the further. He drained off his drinking horn, the mead potent and sweet, and was glad when the king bade them all a good night.

45

"Rest well, my friends, my war brothers," the king said. "When next we gather here, in celebration of our sure victory, my gifts of gratitude will seem but small tokens compared to the honor your brave deeds will earn."

A hearty cheer greeted this. The king was well-known as generous, a ring giver, a bestower of riches and silver and gold. To speak with such obvious humility and self-deprecation showed his humor, and raised his approval in the eyes of all there assembled.

The hall began to empty as men left the benches. Sven watched for any smirks glancing his way, but there was too much jostle of backs, shoulders, cloaks, and heads to notice anything to take overt offense at.

He, Gunnar, and Fjal walked out together, making their way to the encampment outside of the log palisade. They passed through a village of houses, huts, and hovels, and then reached the place where their jarl's banner flew.

Fjal, who was wealthy, traveled with fine tents and servants and ox-carts of furnishings and goods. If Sven and Gunnar benefitted in comfort from their brother-in-law's hospitality, Fjal in turn benefitted in other ways from their kinship bonds. Bonds that, to be sure, Sven sometimes found burdensome, strained and constricting ... and rarely more so than when he returned that night.

The slave he'd purchased, the sullen and stubborn man who spoke no sensible tongue, had been tied with burdensome bonds of his own, fettered at wrist and ankle, tethered to a post by a short leash of leather. Tied, he still was, but he'd managed to strangle himself, the leather leash wrapped and twisted so tight around the post that it dug furrows in the choke-swollen flesh of his neck.

His face had gone the color of an overripe fruit. His clouded eyes bulged. He'd befouled himself in his death throes. The body was still warm, not yet fly-touched. An uneaten chunk of brown bread and an unfinished wooden cup of barley beer sat nearby.

Sven stood for a long moment with fists clenched at his sides, teeth grinding like millstones, feeling as if a vein pulsed and throbbed, boiling, in his brain. Then he turned and stalked from his tent.

Gunnar saw him and must have read the storm on his brow at a glimpse; he came running. "Sven?"

"Where is that fat clot of goat shit and that piss-dribble boy of his?" demanded Sven in a voice of Thor's thunder.

"Ah, now, think what you will of Fjal," Gunnar said lightly, as if hoping to deflect Sven's anger, "but that piss-dribble boy of his is still our nephew, our dear Gunhild's son."

Fjal, meanwhile, had heard Sven's bellow—all whose tents were within a spear's throw must have—and and stepped out of his own, looking puffed and indignant. He opened his mouth to bluster a protest or question, but before a word passed his lips, Sven shook off Gunnar's placating hand to jab a finger at Fjal's soft, flabby chest.

"That boy! That piss-dribble *boy* of yours! Where is he?"

"Frodi? He ... he's here, he's—" Fjal glanced over his shoulder, to where his son sat on a wooden stool draped with sheepskins.

"You left him to look after the camp, to mind the animals and our belongings!"

"Yes, that's why I brought him, he's thirteen, he's old enough to take on the responsibility, to learn the merchant trade."

"Quit your goat's-bleating! My slave is dead!"

"What? But ... Frodi, you did feed him, didn't you?"

"I did!" cried the boy, who was round-cheeked and pug-nosed, not fat yet but already plump as a suckling pig.

Just the sight of him, the sight of them both, the *being* of them ... a torrent of thoughts and images rushed in his mind like white water ... that his sister would allow this, this spoiled indulgence ... what manner of man would Frodi become with an example such as this for a father?

If his *own* wife, Sven knew, had not divorced him and gone home to her family's farmstead because she objected to his efforts to toughen up *their* frail and sickly son ...

He cast that aside as fiercely as he cast off yet again Gunnar's intervening hand. Fine and well for Gunnar, whose wife and girls were amiable and pretty, whose little boy was bold, healthy, and strong.

He cast that aside too. All he, Sven Sveingunsson, Sven Bloodhair, had was his war glory, his battle name, his reputation! And how would he go forth tomorrow with no slave to sacrifice? With no blood for the basin, no blood to drench his hair and beard?

"They say he was a great and fearsome warlord, in his time," uttered a mocking echo no one else heard.

How would he prove to them that his *time* had not passed?

Frodi whined on that he had fed the slave, had taken him a piece of bread and cup of beer, and made sure he was well-tied and well-tethered. "I even had Islunn offer him a bath!" he said, referring to one of Fjal's servant women. "She speaks his tongue, and explained to him that he was to be sacrificed—"

"And then he strangled himself to death!"

"But ..." Frodi's chin trembled. "But the gods ... the honor ..."

"Leave him be," said Fjal. "How could he have known?" He patted for his belt purse. "I'll pay for the slave, of course, and we'll buy you another—"

"By morning? When the horn calls sound?"

Gunnar sighed, grimacing, and pinched the bridge of his nose. "Sven ... Fjal ... both of you, please, for Gunhild's sake ..."

But not even invoking their sister's name could quell Sven's fury at Fjal's condescending tone. He would not be spoken to as if he were a child who'd lost a favorite toy, not by this fat clot of goat shit who could make Gunhild laugh.

"And if there's no slaves to be had? Will you give me one of your servants? Islunn, perhaps, since this was her doing?"

"Islunn has been a faithful family retainer since I was Frodi's age! You could do without your gory ritual just once, couldn't you? Or use an animal; you've done that before!"

"You'd have me use an animal rather than a woman?"

Frodi unwisely chose that moment to mutter something about how Sven *had* been planning to use a *man* instead.

"Shall I use a *boy*, then?" He turned toward his nephew and Gunnar interposed himself between them as Fjal sputtered.

"Let's go, Sven," Gunnar said, having now forsaken any note of amiability. His gaze held Sven's, so that Sven could almost feel the push of his brother's will, urging him, reminding him of oaths and obligations.

Sven slowly released a shuddering breath that whistled through his teeth. "I'll have a walk," he said, each word cut curt. "The night air will do me good."

He went without awaiting a reply, went without giving Gunnar the chance to offer to accompany him. As he left Fjal's tent, he heard their hurried conversation behind him, making hasty arrangements to dispose of the dead slave before he returned.

As he walked, drawing more deep and steadying breaths, Sven did his best to ignore the looks cast his way—their loud argument had not gone unnoticed. Around him was the general bustle of the camp's settling activity. Men took to their tents, or to their bedrolls and sleeping furs. Some, the poorest among them, wrapped themselves in cloaks or blankets against the chill. Those who'd brought, found, or hired women made vigorous use of them.

Tattered clouds scudded across the sky, wind-blown ships on a black sea. A haze smeared the half moon. Day would dawn, Sven knew, gray and damp, but not so rainy as to forestall the call to battle.

Watch fires burned. Guards kept wakeful sentry over the horses. There were no slaves to be found for sale, not at this hour, not even when Sven inquired of the most disreputable trader.

Fjal would have him forego his ritual altogether? Or use an animal instead? Sven noted sourly that his brother-in-law had not offered up one of his own oxen to the blade and the basin. Fjal had no understanding of these matters.

And that boy of his, that pug-nosed piglet ...

The dark notion lingered in Sven's mind, dark but strangely gleaming with tempting appeal. Was it so unthinkable, at that? Had not the mighty king Aun the Old gained long life with the sacrifice of each of his own sons?

He walked on, brooding, heavy with these thoughts. He had to do something. He could not go unprepared to war, and prove right those who'd given him such insult. They needed reminding that Sven Bloodhair was, had been, and would be a great warlord.

His path had taken him some distance from the main encampment by then, near to the clustered hovels and huts of the village. Some men had sought lodgings there, and whores' company. Others stumbled about or sprawled snoring in the brewer's yard, drunk from fishing for courage in bowls of barley beer.

Sven saw one such of these being led toward a wretched-looking shed by an even more wretched-looking woman. The man, swaying on his feet like a wave-tossed ship, had the look of a thick-bodied laborer, a peasant, a bondsman more suited to farming than fighting. He reeked of beer and of piss.

The woman was stick-thin and flat-chested, straggle-haired, far from pretty. She wore a shabby cloak, its hem flapping around dirty bare feet and knobby ankles. Skin paler than the bone-moon stretched tight over the half-starved angles of her face. A crone, a young one perhaps but a crone nonetheless.

And a whore, but one more by recent opportunity than profession, Sven suspected. Only with so many strangers in town, men far from home, desperate, drunk, and frightened of facing death in battle, might a creature such as this hope to earn a paltry sum for her dubious favors.

What a life that must be, a miserable life of drudgery and humiliation, of begging for every scrap. Ugly, unloved, unmarried, without family ... no one to miss her, no one to care about her disappearance or lament her loss ... slavery would be preferable ... and being sacrificed to the gods would be a greater privilege and honor than the likes of her could ever dream to attain.

He crept near the shed and lurked in the shadows pooled around it. The torches mounted atop the log palisade did not shed much firelight this far. He listened to a drunken chuckle and slurred mumble from within, then a grunt, and then wet, slurping sounds.

The whore emerged first, wiping her mouth as she ducked through the doorway. Her other hand held a belt purse and the dull glint of metal. He watched her open the purse to dump in some cheap trinkets of copper and bronze.

A whore *and* a thief, then.

But ...

His nostrils flared as another smell reached him, the smell not of sex but of fresh-spilled blood, and a lot of it. He realized he heard no other movement from the shed, not the rustling of the man adjusting his clothes, not even his breathing.

A whore, a thief, and a murderess as well?

Sven sprang from the shadows and seized the woman before she could react to the sudden surprise. He hit her in the belly, driving the breath from her lungs so as to stop a scream. Then he forced her back into the shed.

The blood-smell was thicker. His boots squelched. An errant crack in the planks let a line of torchlight through, enough to show him the man's head lolling from a mortal wound to the throat. A puddle had spread around him, soaking into the shed's hard-packed dirt floor.

The woman thrashed in his grasp. Scrawny though she was, she was ferociously strong. He pinned her arms at her sides so she could not get at whatever weapon she'd used. She still did not try to scream, but writhed and struggled and twisted.

Then she *bit* him, the she-dog, bit him where his neck met his shoulder, just above the braid-trimmed collar of his tunic. A mouthful of teeth tore into his flesh. The pain was enormous, the shock such that Sven recoiled and dropped her.

Or would have, but she hung on, hung on by her *teeth*, teeth sharp as *knives*, jaws clamped, digging in, chewing and gouging. Freed, her arms whipped around him and so did her legs, her limbs thin bands of iron. Blood ran down his chest and back, such a familiar sensation, but this blood was his *own*!

A murderess *and* a madwoman!

Battened onto him like a *leech*!

Sven snagged a fistful of her straggly hair and yanked. There was a ripping, a loathsome tearing of skin and sinew, a grotesque stretch-and-*give*, as he tugged her away with shreds of meat—shreds of *him*!—trailing from a mouthful of snarling, crooked teeth coursing with blood and drool.

Afire with agony, reeling with revulsion, he struck her as hard as he could. Her head snapped sideways. The iron bands of her limbs released him. Her body shuddered and went slack.

He swore at himself, furious that he'd killed her with the force of the blow and all this had been for nothing.

But then she stirred, uttering a low groan. Her fingers groped feebly for his arm, the fist of which still held her aloft by the hair. He struck her again, a more careful blow, and then wrapped her limp form in her shabby cloak.

His neck burned. He felt dizzy, light-headed. But he refused to succumb to weakness; he was Sven Sveingunsson, Sven Bloodhair ... so he fashioned a pad to cover the gouged hole in his neck and tied a strip of cloth to hold it in place.

Slinging the cloak-wrapped bundle over his other shoulder, Sven staggered from the shed. He stepped over the man's corpse—the scatter of coins and trinkets spilled from his belt-purse—and began making his way back.

Somehow, though his head spun and swam, though his stomach churned and a clammy sweat sheened his brow, he did so without being seen. It had grown late, which helped; the encampment for the most part slept.

Gunnar, however, did not. Gunnar had waited up for his brother at their tents. He came out with a small stone whale-oil lamp cupped flickering in his palm. His look of relief changed to one of concern the moment his gaze found Sven's face.

"By the gods, Sven, what happened? You're gray as death!"

"Later," Sven said. "Help me with her. I need a moment to rest."

"Who is she?" asked Gunnar, eyeing the bare legs and dirty feet poking out from the cloak bundle.

"No one. A whore. No one who'll be missed. I'm doing her a kindness."

"You're bleeding."

"She bit me."

"She what?"

"Teeth like a lynx. She bit me. I caught her just after she'd murdered a man, robbed him as well." He undid the strip of cloth holding the pad to his neck. The blood flow had slowed to a trickle when he lifted it away. "Tie her at the post. Tie her well, hand and foot. She's stronger than she looks."

"How badly are you hurt? Should I send for someone?"

"No. I'll be fine. Fine and ready for battle."

"For battle? Sven, son of my father, you're in no fit sta—"

His expression alone must have been stony, for it silenced Gunnar mid-word. "Bring me water," he said, "and my spare tunic. I want to wash. Then I'll sleep a bit, then be much better. You'll see."

Gunnar obliged. "It must not be as bad as it seemed," he said, upon inspecting the side of Sven's neck. "The way you bled, I expected your head half torn off."

"Felt like it," Sven said with a snort. "I'm lucky she didn't go for *my* throat with whatever she used to kill that other poor fool."

"I saw no weapons on her."

"She must have dropped it as well, when she dropped his purse."

Together, they got Sven cleaned up and into his spare tunic. He settled onto his sleeping platform, piled with thick fleeces and furs, and exhaled as a great heavy weariness sank into his bones.

52

"What shall I tell Fjal?" Gunnar asked.

"Tell him to lick a pig's ass."

This, more than anything else Sven had said, seemed to convince Gunnar that he was indeed himself. Snorting a laugh, he went out.

Sven glanced over once to see that the crone-whore who'd bitten him was well-secured at the post. Without her cloak, she wore nothing but a grubby linen under-tunic, no wool apron dress, no belt, no brooches.

Before, he'd thought her bone-moon pale, but by the whale-oil lamp's faint glow she looked almost ruddy. Nor did she seem as scrawny as he remembered, but he supposed that was because he now knew first-hand of her strength.

Whoever she was, he decided, she would make a fitting sacrifice, and much please the gods. Ugly, yes, but fierce and tenacious.

When he woke some time later, he was thirsty enough to drink dry the Hvergelmir, wellspring of all rivers. But beer, mead, wine, and water all tasted sour; only when Gunnar had the servant woman Islunn bring a pail of warm milk could he keep it down. As for hunger, he had it, a faint growl in his belly, but the mere thought of food made him gag.

His head still ached and his sweat still clammy. His eyes watered with protest at the wan light. Gunnar, bringing their mail coats that had been sand-scoured so they shone, did not find his countenance reassuring of health, but Sven waved away his brother's hen-fussing.

Dawn had not yet fully come, but the sky brightened. Fires were rekindled and more torches lit. By the silvery sheen of that misty morning, men armed and armored themselves and readied for war. Their foes, encamped along a hill ridge to the west, would be doing likewise.

Sven washed and dressed, trimmed his nails, combed his hair, and brushed his full beard. His mirror, antler-handled, had been a gift from his mother. Either the polished metal had gotten smudged and tarnished, or his watering eyes were more sensitive than he'd thought, because in his reflection he saw only a distorted, misshapen dark blotch.

No matter. Those who faced him in battle would not be impressed by handsomeness or grooming. He had other, better ways to intimidate and strike fear into them.

He touched the side of his neck, wincing in expectation of a pain that proved not to be there. Upon removing the bandage, his probing fingertips found the spot sore and tender but otherwise nicely healed.

The crone-whore's bite had not been so bad after all. He glanced at her, where she lay bound and tethered to the post. She slept deeply. So deeply, in fact, that he had a bad moment of worry she'd died in the night. Not even when he nudged her ribs with his boot-toe did she stir in her slumber.

She would wake soon enough, if only briefly.

After donning his mail coat and leathers, he opened a wooden chest carved all about with intricate knot work and designs of wolf heads and ravens, and, on the lid, a magnificent eight-legged horse. Inside, folded in cloth of soft wool dyed rich red, were a smooth soapstone basin and a short-bladed knife.

The whore's eyelids fluttered weakly when he lifted her head by the hair. He set the sharp edge to her slender throat.

"Now I give you to Odin," Sven said. "And to Thor and to Tyr, to the battle gods for whose honor and pleasure my arm strikes!"

He slashed hard and sure, with the skill of much practice.

Now the whore's eyes flew open, black and glittering like jet. She uttered a glottal cry that drowned in a gurgle. Her body lurched with a convulsion that snapped the bonds at her wrists and her ankles.

The blood flowed, but not in a hot red flood to which Sven was accustomed. It flowed slow and thick, dark and strange, oozing into the basin. It flowed like tree sap and tar, like winter honey.

A hand clawed at Sven's chest, fingernails scraping for purchase on the links of his mail coat. Then it fell away, and she twitched once more, and then she was still.

Sven raised the basin. Its contents had the color of mire-mud streaked with crimson. The smell was raw meat and turned soil, sea salt, and death.

Never had he seen blood such as this. It must, he knew, have some meaning, be some sign or omen.

Just then from outside sounded the first horns, summoning men to their places. Sven heard his jarl calling out jovial encouragement. They would, he told them, butcher their foes and strip them of plunder where they fell, do great deeds and make great names for themselves, win victory and honor!

Lusty shouts of approval met these words. Eagerness swelled in each man's breast, and no less so in Sven's. He tipped the basin over his head and laughed as the dark, strange, thick blood coated his hair and coursed down his face.

As it had smelled, so too did it taste as it ran in his mouth—raw meat, turned soil, sea salt, and death. Earlier, the mere thought of food made his gorge heave; this should have sent him to all fours vomiting like a dog, but it only wakened from nowhere a wild and ravenous hunger.

He laughed again. He pushed his head into the basin, sopping up the dregs until his beard stuck to his chin in a wet plaster, lapping the smears with his tongue.

Then he set the basin back into the chest, strapped his sword belt across his back, hung an axe at one hip and a stabbing blade on the other, picked up his round shield painted red and yellow, grasped an ash-shafted spear with a barbed iron point, and strode forth from his tent.

Sven Bloodhair would bring terror and slaughter to his enemies.

And on that day, he did.

Never before, in all his many battles, had the war-passion held him so strongly, the killing purpose burned so clean and decisive a force. Each thrust of his spear, each stroke of his sword, each block of a blow with his shield, seemed god-guided. The steel blade sang, the iron rim and boss rang.

It was exhilaration, exultation, a violent and savage and beautiful joy. He felt invincible, unstoppable. Nothing could harm him beyond slight nicks and scratches; he'd suffered worse wounds as a boy, picking thorn berries!

The dead and the dying dropped before him in droves. Sven offered no mercy, nor granted it when men groveled, begging, on their knees. He did pause to gather a few scraps of wealth here and there—a gold neck chain, a brooch set with amber, a ring of twisted silver wire—but, for the most part, it was the blood ... the blood and the killing, the blood and the death.

Only once, when the sun's rays shot through gaps in the clouds to stab at his eyes like needles of fire, did he falter. Such a pain split his head that he thought his skull had been shattered.

Gunnar called out and began hacking his way toward his brother, but two men in green cloaks and boar-bristle helms were already there. With a long-hafted axe, the taller of the two hooked the edge of Sven's shield and yanked it down. The other drove a spear at him. The tip pierced Sven's mail coat and sank into his side.

Then the cloud gaps closed up, the sun obscured again by cool shadow. Sven roared. He cast off his shield from his arm and swung his sword two-handed in a fast, sweeping arc. The blade, all but whistling in the air, caught the taller of the men just under the ear and took off his entire head with one stroke.

The boar-bristled helm spun high, the severed head still inside it. Blood leaped from the neck-stump in a fountain.

Sven wrenched the spear point from his side, barely feeling it, as Gunnar's sword cleaved the second man's mail coat to tatters. The spouting blood held all his attention. The body had only begun to topple when Sven sprang upon it and buried his face in the red, pulsing life-gush. He fastened his mouth to it as if sucking from a punctured goatskin wine-sack, gulping and guzzling, glutting himself on it, the blood overflowing his lips.

The hunger, oh, the ravenous hunger roared in him now! There was nothing to be done but indulge it, to drink and drink and drink until he was sated!

When he at length let go of the corpse, he sat back on his heels, gasping, exhausted, more spent and more fulfilled than he'd ever been with a woman.

Elsewhere on the field, battles yet raged. Nearby ...

He looked up at a ring of men. Enemies and allies alike stared aghast at him, their quarrel forgotten in that moment.

Even Gunnar, his brother, had recoiled, eyes wide with horror. The spearman's blood glistened on his blade, which dangled all but forgotten at the end of his strengthless arm.

No one spoke.

The war clangor seemed very far away.

Then a horse shrieked, its galloping hooves a shaking thunder on the earth. Wounded, wild, foaming with panic, it crashed into their midst with its dying rider clinging to the saddle.

The spell was broken. Men remembered where they were and why they had come.

"Attack!" someone cried.

"Kill them!" yelled another.

"Fight!" Sven's jarl brandished his sword, and his standard bearer blew a loud horn blast, and once again the weapons met in the clashing steel storm.

They fought on. They fought until the battle was done, the battle was won. Their foes fled in retreat. The slain and the injured littered the vale. Already, the ravens gathered, black-winged harbingers eager for their share.

Word spread of Sven's deeds—his strength and skill, his fearlessness, how no weapon seemed to hurt him. He had been, they said, more like legend than man. But word spread as well of the beheading, and his actions that followed. As he left the field, many uneasy looks were cast his way.

Only Gunnar, his brother, dared broach the subject. "What happened out there?" he asked. "You drank that man's blood, gorged on it like wine."

Sven shook his head. He had never felt so weary, and the westering sun through the clouds pained his eyes more than ever. "Later," he said to Gunnar. "I want to rest."

"There will be a feast tonight," Gunnar said. "I've heard the king and our jarl both wish to give you rich gifts."

At some other time, this news would have pleased him most greatly. But treasures of gold and silver did not much interest him now. Sven made a noise of acknowledgment, squinting against the sun's glare that felt summer-hot against his skin. He groaned.

"How bad is it?" Gunnar asked. "The spear wound?"

"Hm?" That, he had all but forgotten, craning his neck now to look. The point had gone through his mail coat, through the quilting and clothing beneath. Dried blood had crusted. But when he wiped it away, he revealed just a small scab, and bruises already fading. "It's nothing. A pinprick."

"It looked far worse than a pinprick."

"You are my brother, not my mother or nurse."

They returned to their tents. Gunnar continued to look troubled, but held his silence.

"Let me sleep for a while," Sven told him. "Then, if you still must fuss and fret, have someone bring me another jug of milk, and perhaps some bread, before the feast."

He went into his tent, into the welcome shade.

The crone-whore's corpse lay where he'd left it. Sven supposed he should dispose of her, but was too tired. She did not yet smell of rot—or, if she did, he was so covered himself in blood and viscera that he could discern nothing else. Besides, there'd be no shortage of graves dug and pyres built the next day for the fallen.

In the meanwhile, he simply flung a wool blanket over the body, then stripped off his arms and armor, splashed his face with water, and collapsed into his bed. Dark sleep dragged him down like an iron ship's anchor.

A thump and a muffled outcry awoke him some length of time later. He sat up to cool dusk and the single flame of a whale-oil lantern set on a stool by the foot of his bed. A milk pail had been set beside it, its top draped with a cloth.

His head felt clear, his body rested. But for a soreness in his jaw, as of many teeth aching, not the slightest pain remained from his wounds. Had he been hit in the face and could not remember? He worked his tongue around, seeking missing teeth or looseness ... finding them all firmly rooted and accounted for ... and if they seemed overlarge, oversharp to his probing, he attributed that to the fog of just-waking.

Fresh blood-scent slid into his nostrils. Eager saliva filled his mouth and hollow pangs rumbled his belly. He looked around for the source of the smell and gasped when he saw it.

An old woman, Islunn, Fjal's servant, lay flat on her back with one outstretched hand fitfully twitching. A figure crouched over her. It was the crone-whore, bone-moon pale and scrawny in her grubby linen under-tunic, her head buried in the hollow of Islunn's shoulder the way an ardent lover might affectionately nuzzle ... but the blood scent and the sucking, slurping sounds said otherwise.

She lifted her head, jet-black eyes glittering, hair falling in knots and straggles. Crimson-painted from nose to chin and ear to ear, she bared her red teeth in a malicious snarl. Of the cut he'd made when he slashed open her throat, only the faintest white trace of a scar line could be seen.

The side of Islunn's neck, however, was a savaged, ragged hole from which more blood sluggishly bubbled. Sven had to swallow before he began drooling into his own beard.

He forced himself to meet the crone-whore's cruel gaze. "I killed you," he said. "I sacrificed you to the gods."

"The gods don't want *me*," she replied in a voice like the scraping of flint. "They don't want the accursed, Sven Sveingunsson."

"You know my name?"

"I know enough," she said. "And you, you know nothing. Nothing of what you do, nothing at all."

Sven's mind spun with stories he'd heard ... stories of ghosts, yes, and barrow wights to protect burial mounds ... stories of unburied corpses that rose to walk again ... stories of shape-changers who donned the pelts of bears or of wolves ... but ...

"What are you?" he asked.

"What you'll become."

"What have you done to me?" He stood up from his bed, swiping the back of his hand across his mouth, feeling the oversized jut of his newly sharp teeth. "What have you done to me, you blood-drinking bitch?"

"What have you done to yourself? You brought this fate down upon your own head. Asgard and Valhalla will have no place for you."

To be dead but deathless, ancient but ageless, eternal. Would that, he wondered, be such a bad thing? No one would ever say again what a great and fearsome warlord he'd been in his time ... not when he would be greater and more fearsome than ever, not when his time did not end!

With his full attention fixed upon her and these thoughts, he had not been aware of the heavy footsteps approaching until the tent flap opened and his brother-in-law stepped inside.

"Sven? Is Islunn here? I heard shouting—"

Fjal's jaw dropped into the rolls of his chins. He struggled for breath. His right hand clutched at his lard-layered chest. His shocked eyes met Sven's, brimming with dread and accusation.

"And," said the crone-whore, slicking the tip of her gray tongue over her fangs, "you must be hungry."

A rage and madness took him.

Somehow, his arms shot out to seize Fjal by the shoulders. Somehow, as Fjal gibbered and screamed, Sven dragged him forward.

Fjal's terror-sweat stink sharpened as his bladder let go. He was an immense and disgusting creature, globs of fat encased in greasy sausage skin, but when Sven's teeth dug through the blubber to find the hot, savory blood pumping fast through Fjal's veins ...

The blood, oh the blood, a rushing scarlet river, well-flavored with melted butter and bacon drippings! Sven grunted and snuffled like a feeding beast, unable to help himself, the greedy feasting sounds, the ravenous ravaging! He felt his hunger inflame all the hotter even as it was quenched.

Then Fjal's considerable weight went to dead weight, seeming to double, and despite Sven's newfound strength he could not hold on. Fjal dropped like a felled ox. Loose limbs wobbled. Fatty flesh jiggled and bounced.

Sven went to his knees. Sensation surged and seethed through him, a lightning-struck power. He looked at the crone-whore, and began to wolfishly grin.

She had by then moved to the back of the tent, and torn a hole there large enough to go through. As she readied to do so, she smirked at him. "Across every land of Midgard, you'll be hunted and hated and feared, an outcast among men. No jarl, king, or lord will want you. You'll have no hall and no home."

His grin faded.

"Your wealth will be worthless," she said. "You'll never again marry ... no more children ... no family at all, Sven Bloodhair."

A deep shiver touched him. He stifled a sound of despair.

"They'll call you monster!" She barked a laugh as inhuman as a gore-crow's caw. "And they'll be right. Look at you already! Murderer! Oath breaker and kin slayer!"

He glanced at the quivering body beside him. His brother-in-law, his sister's husband ... he had not liked Fjal, true, but there were laws, there was honor, there were oaths and obligations ...

"Will his son avenge him?" the crone-whore asked. "Only a lad, but that is his duty, is it not? Or will you slaughter the boy as well? Your own nephew, your dear sister's son? Who, then, must be called upon to avenge young Frodi?"

He tried to retch but managed only a juicy and meaty, red-misted belch.

"And what of Gunnar?" she pressed on, relentless. "Your own brother, think what a place you've put him in—"

"Enough!" he wailed, sinking his hands into his hair, clotted and congealed with dark, sticky blood.

Outside, out front, coming closer, were many more footsteps and querying voices drawn by the disturbance. Gunnar would, Sven knew, be among them.

"But, what of it?" She spoke in a light and mocking lilt, and gave a revoltingly girlish giggle. "You got what you've always most dearly wanted."

Sven looked up again, disbelieving.

Her smile was grave-cold as she slipped through the gap at the back of the tent, leaving him with only her final words as the front flap was pulled open.

"All a man has forever is his reputation."

THE CHANCES

BY RAMONA DEFELICE LONG

Margot never goes into Bangor anymore, not since Steve left, but she has to today. She could get the test done locally, but this clinic is the best in the state and, with her family history, she should get the best. That's what Steve said, when he was still around. When he still cared.

But he's not and he doesn't, and so she must take care of herself. Just because he left doesn't mean she no longer deserves the best.

"No deodorant or powder," the office reminded her. Despite that, Margot dresses nicely—wide-legged, cream wool pants; a black cashmere turtleneck; black boots with heels. At the last minute, she adds a long necklace of bleached bone carved into geometric shapes. Her sister sent it from Morocco two years ago. It's not her usual style—too jangly and showy—but in the mirror, the shapes stand out against her dark sweater. It looks interesting. Artsy. The heels make her feel tall. She likes that.

At the clinic, she is called right away, but every year they seem to take more views. Later, she will be sore. Probably bruised by nightfall. Getting dressed, she wonders if she has any Tylenol in her purse.

"Miss Leigh, you're good to go," the technician tells her. "Oh my, what a pretty necklace."

It's past noon. She's hungry and feels virtuous after her morning of responsible self-care. She'll stay for lunch, she decides. She told her office she might be gone all day, not mentioning that it's only an annual mammogram. Now she calls and says she won't be back in today. Getting your boobs flattened like pancakes rates a nice sandwich at least; maybe she should indulge herself with a new pair of earrings, too.

She drives down State Street, where Steve works. She grips the steering wheel and watches the traffic, and not the people out in the brisk, late April sunshine. She doesn't look at the dark-haired man tapping a newspaper against his leg while waiting at the crosswalk. Or the dark-haired man walking with a blond woman, both of them laughing. Or the dark-haired man scowling at his iPhone. She is not looking for dark-haired men at all.

She drives past the Starbucks where Steve gets coffee. She turns onto the street with his bank, and goes by the Italian deli with the anisette biscotti he likes; the Greek place where he dribbled olive oil onto his favorite tie; the burger joint where he got the call that his brother was in a car accident; the soul food place with the coleslaw he'd buy in pints to bring home. Every Wednesday, she drove into Bangor to meet him for lunch, even though it was out of her way and, sometimes, she had to lie at work and say she had a doctor's appointment.

It's not a lie today. But it's also not Wednesday and even if it were, she hasn't seen Steve in months. She finds a restaurant where they never went together. An hour goes by while she eats a sandwich and lingers over coffee and a slice of lemon pound cake. Finally she leaves, shops until three o'clock, and then until four. By the time she gets in her car and heads to the bridge, traffic is heavy. Her right breast aches when she turns the steering wheel. She forgot to buy Tylenol. Darn. She should have planned better. Who knew the appointment would take the whole day?

"I deserved it," she says, to no one, as she crosses the bridge into Brewer. Dusk has fallen, and both of her breasts feel heavy and tender. She could kick herself for hanging around for so long, blowing off work for no good reason other than to prove ... what? That she could be in the same city as Steve without flipping out?

Ten miles from home, Margot takes a shortcut. It's a two-lane road with no lights, barely any shoulder, and iffy cell phone service. Trees grow a few feet from the roadside. People avoid it on spring nights because of the deer, but it would cut several minutes off her trip. Her chest aches. She just wants to be home.

She's about three miles in when she sees the woman.

She is huddled on the roadside, knees to chest, hands near her ankles. The second the headlights hit the figure, Margot's foot instinctively hits the brake. She leans forward, staring through the windshield, slowing with every yard. Head down, forehead on her knees, the woman's dark hair spills down her thighs. Her naked thighs. Which, Margot sees and gasps in shock, are bound by two strands of rope wrapped around her back and over her calves.

"Oh my god!" She slows to a stop in the road. The woman does not move. Margot stares, holding her breath, and then her foot moves again and the car lurches forward, speeds up, and jerks to the side of the road.

Cell phone. She grabs her purse, checking the rearview mirror at the same time. The woman's skin is red now, reflecting the brake lights.

"Oh my god," Margot says again. She finds the phone.

No service.

"No," she says. "No, no, no."

She shifts into park and lets off the brake. She hits the emergency flashers, and looks again in the rear view. The flashing red lights bounce off the woman's skin. Behind her, to the sides, everything is black.

Margot opens the car door. Closes it. Turns off the engine, pulls out the key, and opens the door again. It is so quiet, she can hear her own quick, shallow breaths as she steps onto the road and runs on tiptoe toward the woman.

She slows down a few feet away. The temperature has dropped considerably but she hardly feels it.

"Hello?" Margot says, her voice shaking. She can see the rope clearly now, two thick rough strands, and her stomach feels like it drops to her feet.

No movement. Margot tiptoes closer. Her breaths have turned into sharp, quick pants. She looks up and down the road but sees nothing—no cars, no deer, just the woman illuminated off and on, on and off, in the red from her flashers and the light from her open door.

Is she dead? Is she ...

Margot swallows. She reaches out to touch the woman's hair. She

65

barely makes contact before she pulls sharply away. Her breath is so jagged she feels light-headed. She reaches out again, this time laying her hand on the woman's head, and then Margot screams, and stumbles backward, as the head rolls off the knees, down the shins and stops, rocking, at the woman's feet.

It takes a moment for Margot's brain to processes what she sees. Screws sticking out from the knee joints. A knob at the base of the neck. The plaster white skin and red painted lipstick on the face. Eyes that are wide, unblinking. Unseeing.

A mannequin.

Margot stops shaking. Her breaths stop completely and then she is running, back to the car, wanting to scream but not having time, just time to grab the door, close it, lock it, fumble to get the key in the ignition and shift into drive, and then the tires squeal and the car shoots down the road, straddling the white line because—the deer be damned—she has to get away from it, from her, from that *thing*, on the roadside.

"Nine-one-one, what's your emergency?"

Margot is home, in her kitchen, still shaking from the crazy drive home. She had to run from her driveway to her front door because Steve, the bastard, left his skis and kayak in her garage. He's had months to come and pick up his crap, but she had to run through the dark because they don't want the same things anymore and his assistant won't put through any of her calls.

"I saw a woman—I thought it was a woman—by the side of the road," Margot begins, still panting to catch her breath. She reports what just happened, realizing she probably sounds nuts. But the dispatcher must be used to hearing bizarre stories because she asks questions (Are you sure she wasn't real? Do you recall the exact location? Did you see anyone in the area?) in a calm, matter-of-fact tone.

"Will somebody check it out?" Margot asks, after giving her name and address.

"An officer is already on the way, ma'am," the dispatcher says.

"Good," Margot says. "Because some other woman might ..." She has to stop and swallow. "You think somebody's trying to, like, lure a person out of their car and ..." She doesn't finish. The frozen moment of terror returns. My god. Was someone watching, back in the trees where she couldn't see, watching her, waiting for—

"I don't know, ma'am," the dispatcher says. "It could just be a prank."

Margot grips the phone. "A prank?" She had not for one second considered it might be a joke. Her stomach starts to burn now—not in fear, but in anger. Somebody thought scaring the life out of her would be *funny?*

The dispatcher says, "The trooper will need to speak with you. Will you be at this address tonight?"

The police will come to her house. That has never happened before.

"Yes," she says. "I'll be here."

She goes upstairs to freshen up. Her feet ache from the boots, but she doesn't want to wear fuzzy slippers for her first police interview. She takes a double dose of Tylenol. She'd love to have a drink with it, but that's probably not a good idea. She wants to be sharp, a good witness. She hopes the cops find the bastard who did this and string him up by his balls. The anger calms her. By the time she touches up her lipstick, her hands are steady.

She turns on all the outside lights—porch, garage, driveway. She peeks at her car. She can't remember if she locked it, but no way is she going out there to find out.

Her irritation returns. She had to park in the driveway all winter. She looks at the time. He's not at the office anymore. She doesn't even try to reach him but calls his assistant, at home. When Bridget answers, Margot says, "I need to leave a message for Steve. I want his stuff out of my garage. This weekend."

Bridget says she'll tell him. Margot glances outside again. No police car. She makes tea. Just as the kettle whistles, the phone rings. Steve.

"You can't call Bridget at home," he says. "She's not part of this."

"If you took my calls, I wouldn't have to," Margot says, and before he can respond, adds, "Fine, tell her I'm sorry. Come and get your stuff and I'll never call either of you again."

Silence. Then, "Margot, this is not going to work. You have to stop calling. You have to accept—"

"I *do*," she says, allowing her irritation to fly, something she never did when they were together. His ego is unbearable. How did she ever put up with him?

"I want your stuff out of my garage," she says. "My home is not a free storage facility." She considers telling him what happened, but decides not. If he cared about her, she wouldn't have been driving down that road in the first place. This is all his damn fault.

"Come Saturday. I'll put it down by the road. If you don't show up, I'm sure some college kid would love a free kayak. Come at ..." She pauses, thinks. "Ten. I won't be here. I'll stay out until noon." She hangs up without waiting for him to respond.

She is hungry. She fixes a sandwich. She's rinsing dishes when the doorbell rings. She does a quick look in the mirror in the hallway as she goes to answer it.

"Ms. Leigh?" The officer glances down at a notepad in his hand. "Margot Leigh?"

He's wearing one of those hats with the wide brims. It shadows his face under the porch light. She can't see what he looks like, but he's tall and slim, his voice polite.

"I'm Margot Leigh," she says, and opens the screen door. "Come in, Officer."

"Trooper," he says, as if it's a correction. He steps inside. "I have some questions about your call."

"Fine." He didn't say his name, so she reads it on his nametag. "Why don't we talk in the kitchen, Trooper Pedersen?"

She closes the door behind him and says, "This way." He follows her. The clicking of her heels on the wooden floors sounds purposeful. Businesslike. Like she is the kind of person on whom you would not want to play some cheap trick.

At the kitchen island where her teacup is sitting, she turns. He has removed his hat. His hair is very blond. She glances at the nametag again. Pedersen. Is that Scandinavian? She looks at the Maine State

Police patch on his blue shirt. It's obvious he's wearing a bulletproof vest. As she glances up again, she catches him scanning her kitchen, his eyes sweeping the room.

He sets his hat next to her teacup. When he moves his arm, she notices muscles. His posture is straight, his movements precise. Controlled. She wonders what he'd be like in bed.

"Did you find her?" she says. "I mean, it?"

"No, ma'am. Drove up and down that road and didn't see a thing."

She starts in disbelief. "I can't believe it! It was right there on the side of the road. Someone must have moved it."

He nods, but it is more noncommittal than agreement. He clicks the pen in his hand and says, "Why don't you tell me what you saw?"

She does. Like the dispatcher, he questions her: How was the mannequin tied? How long was the hair? What position were the hands in? Did she see anything off to the side? Hear any noises? Did any other cars go by?

Margot answers, a little confused. What do all of these details matter, if it wasn't a real woman?

He clicks the pen again and taps the pad with it. Twice. Three times. Looks up at her. His eyes are small and cornflower blue. "Do you remember anything else, ma'am?"

She wants to tell him to call her Margot. Instead she says, "I ... no." She shakes her head. He really has the most lovely eyes. "I'm sorry. I keep thinking, how stupid was I to get out of my car? You must think I'm an idiot. But, if it was a real woman, how could I not stop to help?"

His lips compress slightly. They are a little on the thin side, but she doesn't mind.

"It wasn't the wisest thing to do, ma'am. You should have driven to a safe place and called 911 as soon as you had service. Your intentions may have been good, but your personal safety comes first." The words sound like a statement.

"I will, next time," she says, and then laughs. "Listen to me, *next time*. Like something this bizarre could happen to somebody twice."

"True," he says, and his thin lips move into a small smile. "Just be glad that nothing bad went down tonight and be more cautious in the future."

"I will," she promises. How nice of him not to make her feel bad.

He closes the pad and puts the pen in his pocket.

"Now, do me a favor," he says. His voice is calm, quiet. "Close your eyes and picture the scene. Is there anything you forgot to tell me about?"

She obeys. She gets goose bumps as the woman fills the blank spot in front of her eyelids.

"Take your time," he says, sounding closer, as if he has taken a step toward her. She can hear him breathing. Her breasts start to ache again, but in an entirely different way than before.

She squeezes her eyes harder, tries to see beyond the woman—the mannequin—into the woods, up and down the roadside. She sees the throbbing red light, the bottoms of the trees ...

He moves again, closer now. He's so close, she can feel him, though he's not touching her. Her sister would call it his aura, but Margot doesn't believe in that stuff.

She doesn't want to disappoint him. She squeezes her eyes harder still. What can she say that would help?

"Shoes! She was wearing shoes!"

She opens her eyes as she says it. He moves back a step, and his eyebrows raise, like he's impressed. Or maybe surprised. She crosses her arms over her waist. Her necklace jangles with the movement.

"Shoes?" he says. "She was completely naked but wearing shoes?"

Does his voice hold the tiniest bit of disbelief? She wants to kick herself, but too late now. "Yes. I guess that is weird. But the whole thing is weird, right?"

"Right," he says. He opens his pad again, pulls the pen from his pocket. Clicks it. "What kind of shoes? Can you describe them?"

Oh, Jesus. Now she has to compound the lie.

"Um," she says, closing her eyes again, stalling for time. Even with the step back, he's so close, she can smell him. She couldn't describe the smell, give it a name. It's just a "him" smell.

She opens her eyes and matches his direct gaze.

"She was wearing Mary Janes," she says. "I have a pair upstairs."

In her closet, she rifles through boxes for the shoes she's had since forever. What possessed her to say the mannequin wore shoes—and Mary Janes in particular—she has no idea, but what can it hurt?

She finds the box and carries it downstairs. He's waiting, standing there, in the same spot.

"I'm so sorry," she says. "You must think I have awful manners. Would you like tea? Or I could make coffee."

"No, ma'am, I'm good. But thank you, that's nice of you," he says. He points at the box. "These are the shoes?"

She opens the box and pulls out the black shoes, dangling them by the straps. "Every girl has a pair of Mary Janes. I've had these since college." As soon as she says it, she's sorry. Will he think she's too cheap to get rid of old shoes?

"I didn't know that," he says.

"You must not have sisters."

He doesn't confirm or deny, but takes one of the shoes, grabbing it at the instep. His hand doesn't make contact with hers. "Why are they called Mary Janes?"

"I have no idea," she says, truthfully. "Could that be important?"

"Possibly," he says in the noncommittal tone again. He puts the shoe back into the box. She is tempted to offer them to him, as evidence, but she stops herself. What if they give her a lie detector test?

He closes his notebook. Picks up his hat. "Now I have another favor to ask."

"Of course," she says, completely sincere. Right now, she'd do any single thing he asked. "I just want to help."

"I appreciate that. Would you mind going for a ride, to show me where you saw this thing?"

In his patrol car, there's a laptop mounted on a stand and a console with notepads and pens and other items she can't make out in the few seconds the overhead light stays on. The car is impeccably clean. She sits with her hands clasped in her lap like a child. After he slides into the driver's seat, he presses the walkie-talkie thing on his shoulder and says he's taking a witness to a scene. He names the road.

"Do you work in this area?" he asks as they pull out of her

driveway. For the next few miles, she tells him about herself, where she works, how she moved here four years ago from down the coast when she inherited her grandparents' home. She doesn't mention Steve. Why would she? He's no longer part of her life.

She's nervous, so she babbles until she realizes he probably asked this question because he expected her—someone with no experience with the police—to be nervous, instead of being actually interested. While he drives, his gaze remains focused straight ahead, never once turning to face her. She thought he was paying attention to his driving, but maybe he's just bored. She stops talking, disappointed. Why does she always fall for stuff like this?

He glances her way, as if the silence surprises him. In the dark, his profile is handsome but he's got that polite look of the not very interested. She knows this one—and what to do about it.

"Enough about me," she says. Makes herself say, "Are you from this area?"

"Yes, ma'am. Born and raised here."

"Did you know my grandparents? They lived here, I don't know, maybe sixty years." She gives him their names and, for good measure, tells him her grandmother's maiden name. But he says no, the names are not familiar. After that, the car is quiet. In the movies, it seems there is always a police radio crackling, but his is not. All she hears is the heater going.

The quiet makes her antsy. She's an excellent conversationalist. Gifted, even. That's one of the things Steve admired about her, how she could draw people out, get them to talk to her, and how she remembered every word they shared. She puts people at ease. It's her thing.

But Trooper Pedersen, he's not reacting like most people do. It's not natural for people to sit a couple of feet apart and not interact. It feels wrong. After a minute, she can't stand it.

"Growing up here, that has to be helpful," she says. "You must know all the back roads."

His head flicks her way so quickly, it's like it didn't happen. "Most of them," he says. "After a while, you get to know the layout."

"How long have you been a state trooper?" she asks, glad she caught herself before she said "cop." The way he corrected her after saying "officer," she has a feeling he wouldn't like "cop."

"A few years," he says. And that is all.

They near the shortcut, and before she can tell him to, he hits the turn signal. On the road, he flips his high beams. There are no other cars in sight. He drives slowly.

"Now, Ms. Leigh, I want you to try to remember the spot where you stopped."

She clenches her hands in her lap, more nervous now. She was at the spot for a minute, two minutes tops. It was dark, and the road has no markings. What if she can't remember?

"It's darker than before," she says. "I don't know if—"

He raises a hand from the steering wheel. He remains facing forward, but says, "Just do your best, Ms. Leigh, that's all I ask," in a tone that is soft, comforting. In the darkness, it sounds almost intimate, but she curses the darkness at the same time. She'd love to see his face right now.

She leans forward and peers through the windshield. "I was coming from the other way," she says.

"That's right," he says, and speeds up. "Tell you what. We'll swing around and come at it from that way. Can you spare the time to do that?"

"Of course," she says. She has all the time in the world to spare for him, even in this car, which makes her a little afraid to move around. Before she can change her mind, she says, "Please, call me Margot. When someone says Ms. Leigh, I think they mean my mother."

He doesn't turn his head again, but she can see him smile. "Okay, Margot."

She wishes he'd ask her to call him by his first name, but that might be unprofessional. After all, they hardly know each other. She's just a really friendly person. He can probably tell that. He's probably trained to read people's personalities. She hopes he can tell she doesn't mean it as a come-on.

They don't meet any other cars on the road. She leans as forward as she can until the seat belt bites into her neck.

"Take your time," Trooper Pedersen says, not rushing her or the car. He drives more and more slowly, until they are crawling along the dark road.

To her surprise, she sees a spot and instantly knows it's the right place.

"Here!" she cries, pointing. He stops in the middle of the road. She is leaning forward, excited. "Yes. Right here."

"You're sure?" he says.

"Positive," she says, and his "Great. Good job," makes her nearly squeal in response. She can't stop a small wiggle—of excitement, or desire, or both, she can't tell.

He shifts into park and opens his door. "I need you to stay in the car, ma'am."

"Margot," she says, correcting him just the way he said "Trooper" to her before.

He nods. "Margot. Just wait for me here, all right?"

She folds her hands in her lap and watches him. The headlights illuminate the road, but he also holds a heavy-duty flashlight that he shines up and down the narrow shoulder. She glances at the woods, and her excitement fades away. What if someone had been waiting? What if—

What if they're waiting now? She gasps as the thought hits her like a blow. He's standing in the glow of the headlights and, though his uniform is dark, he might as well be under a spotlight. He is aiming the flashlight into the trees, and she wants to tell him to stop doing that! She puts her hand on the door, frightened enough to be disobedient, amazed that he can act so unconcerned when he is actually a sitting duck.

Not to mention, if there is someone hiding in the woods and something terrible happened to him ... what would become of her? She leans toward the steering wheel. Could she even operate this car? She's not sure she could climb over to his seat with all this stuff in the way. She checks for a radio, and then she remembers how he spoke into his shoulder.

She puts her hand on the door handle again, and he suddenly crouches down. She watches him pick up something from the ground. He holds it up, aiming the flashlight at it, and straightens up to return to the car.

"Did you find something?" she asks, hoping yes, but hoping no, depending what he finds.

He extends his hand and shines the flashlight at it. In his palm is a small clump of long dark hair. Margot gasps at it, horrified—and impressed. She was right about the spot, she knew it, but with all the stuff on the roadside, he must have really good eyes to have spotted a thing this small.

"Is it real hair, or is it from her?" Margot asks.

He squints at it. His hand is perfectly steady. "It doesn't look real. I think it's hers."

Back at the house, he walks her back to her kitchen. He opens the flap of his right pocket and pulls out a business card. *Karl Pedersen*, it says, *Trooper First Class, Maine State Police*. There's a little blue policeman embossed on the corner.

He pulls out the pen and clicks it again. "Here's the barracks number and my extension." He circles the number on the card, turns it over. "And here's my cell number. If you think of anything new, give me a call."

He hands her the card. Their fingers touch. She looks at the policeman on the card, or pretends to, but she's really waiting for the blush on her cheeks to fire down.

"I will," she says.

He picks up his hat and thanks her for her cooperation. At the door, he turns. His glance runs up and down her face and stops at her eyes. He looks stern. Her stomach clutches.

"Remember now, no more getting out of your car like that," he says. "You ever see anything odd, you get yourself to a safe location and call 911. Understand?"

"Absolutely," she says. She's so relieved, her knees actually feel weak. "I promise."

He wishes her a good night. She watches him back out and drive off, and then she's up the stairs, in her office, pulling off the boots because her arches are positively screaming now, but as soon as she kicks them off, she turns on her laptop and starts searching online.

Half an hour later, she's rubbing lotion on her feet with one hand and reading the cache of information she's found about him—old articles when he ran track at the local college; one from last year when he led the torch ceremony for the kickoff of the Special Olympics; a few police beat stories from the newspaper archives; his testimony in a couple of lawsuits that, from what she can tell, he totally did nothing wrong.

No marriage or engagement announcements. She leans back in her chair, squeezing her foot. She didn't notice if he was wearing a ring. Darn it. How could she have missed a detail like that?

It's late when she finishes searching. In the shower, she lets the warm water run over her sore breasts, but she hardly notices the bruising or the ache radiating toward her arms. All she thinks about is being squeezed in her shower with Trooper Pedersen, with his uniform in a crumpled heap on her bathroom floor.

On Saturday morning, a neighbor boy helps her drag Steve's belongings to the curb. She waits until ten-fifteen. No Steve. She backs out of the driveway and leaves her car running while she places a poster board with *FREE* written across it. She goes into Brewer and has a manicure and a pedicure. When she comes home, everything is gone but the sign. She can't tell if Steve picked it up or some kids had a lucky morning. It doesn't matter. She's just glad his junk is gone.

In the afternoon, she sees a little blurb in the newspaper: Local woman reported seeing a mannequin bound and left on the side of the road. It was removed by the time officers investigated. Police are warning local residents, especially women, about the dangers of exiting their cars in unfamiliar or deserted areas. Anyone with information should call this number. Neither her name nor Trooper Pedersen's name is mentioned.

The next day, she drives by the state trooper barracks. It's a few miles from her house, and she's driven past it countless times, but she's never stopped there. Two evenings later, she does, at exactly six o'clock. She guesses that's when his shift begins. She shows the receptionist his card and says she has some information to leave for him.

"Or, if he's here, I could give it to him," she says. "Whatever's easier."

The woman says she'll check. Margot sits on the waiting area bench. She's in her work clothes, a maroon dress that's professional looking and complements her coloring. She's careful to cross her legs at the ankles while she waits. She's wearing heels today, classic black slingbacks she bought on her lunch hour.

The door opens. He walks in. She blinks. She'd forgotten how tall he is.

"Hello, Margot," he says, and a shiver of excitement runs all through her. "What do you have for me?"

She stands. She hands him the sheet of paper she's brought along.

"You asked why Mary Janes were called Mary Janes," she said. "I looked it up. I saw the story in the paper and I wondered if ... well, it's probably not useful, but I printed it for you."

"You did that for me?" He takes the page, but doesn't look at it. He looks at her, so intently, her stomach flip-flops. "So why are they called Mary Janes?"

"She was a character in a cartoon called Buster Brown," Margot says. "When the shoe company was formed, in 1902, they named the girl's shoe Mary Janes. In the cartoon, she was Buster Brown's little sister."

"Hmm," he says. Hmm?

"Do you think that means something?" she asks, wondering what it might mean. Then remembers that it can't mean anything, since she made it up. For the first time, the enormity of what she's done descends on her. What if that messes up the investigation? What if Trooper First Class Karl Pedersen of the Maine State Police can't solve the case because of her misinformation?

"I don't know," he says. But his smile makes her sway a tiny bit in her heels. He folds the paper in half, in fourths, in eighths, and puts it in his pocket. "Thank you for this. I appreciate you being so cooperative."

That's all she meant, to be cooperative. That's all she wants. Well, that, and maybe to run her fingers through his blond hair while they are naked in the dark.

He escorts her down the hall. As they walk, she thinks of a question she should have asked before. It's so obvious, she's embarrassed to ask it belatedly, but she does anyway.

"I feel a little foolish asking this," she begins, "but should I avoid the road? The shortcut, I mean. It's so deserted. What if it happens again?"

He narrows his eyes at her. "Why do you think it would happen again?" he says. "Margot?"

The way he says her name gives her shivers of a different, oddly unpleasant kind. God, what is wrong with her? Why did she ask such a stupid question?

"I don't know," she says. Her purse is in her hand. She can feel her hands start to twist the strap and thinks, a guilty person would do that. So she stops. And remembers what she said before, at her house, about next time, about the chances of this happening to someone twice. She feels like a flaming idiot.

"I'm sorry, I'm being foolish, aren't I?"

He gives her a polite smile and says, "The road's on my regular patrol route now," which doesn't deny her comment about being foolish. Tears prickle her eyes. Everything was going so well, and then she had to go and make an idiot out of herself.

Steve used to say she always embellished things. It hurts to admit it, but maybe he was right. She'd give anything to take back the question, and more than that, the moment at her house when she mentioned the stupid, stupid Mary Janes.

She follows Trooper Pedersen to the door. When he says, "Thanks for coming by. Drive safely," she responds with a nod. She's learned her lesson. She's not going to open her mouth and say something foolish again.

She is too upset to make eye contact. He opens the door for her and she walks through; as she does, he touches the small of her back, as if guiding her. The touch is so light, someone else might think they imagined it. But not Margot. She's sure she didn't imagine it.

She walks to her car, feeling relieved and energized and a hundred different emotions. Trooper Pedersen—Karl—wouldn't have touched her, even a feathery touch on her back as she walked by, if he thought she was a fool.

Nothing happens over the next few days. He doesn't have a Facebook page, and though she scans every page on the Maine State Police web site and signs up for Google alerts, she doesn't find anything new on him.

That doesn't mean she gives up. All she can think about is that night. She doesn't tell anyone at work and doesn't mention it to her mom and dad during her weekly call home, but the minute she gets home at night, she rushes to her laptop. She researches the history of the road. She researches mannequins. She looks at true crime web sites, searching for serial killers who bound women with rope and decapitated them. She reads about copycats, about psychopaths who escalate from hurting animals to hurting people, wackos who leave bodies in certain positions like calling cards. She reads about killers triggered by innocuous events, those who kill on impulse or by opportunity, and others who plan and plot and wait for the exact, perfect moment to commit the perfect crime.

Reading that, she shivers, wondering if her stop was a close call.

She recalls her fear that night with Karl, when he stood in the middle of the road as if he didn't have a worry in the world, while she was cowering in his police car. A tiny voice, a microscopic whisper, suggests maybe that was not wise of him, but she won't listen to that voice. Instead, she listens to the one that says he must be brave and self-assured to stand there in the open, in possible danger, for her.

One night, she forgets her lie and looks up killers with shoe fetishes. What she sees disturbs her more than the dismemberment ones. After that, she searches online about Mary Janes. She scrolls through a slew of hits about marijuana to shoe sites. She's shocked by all the styles and colors. She had no idea Mary Janes had progressed beyond black, patent-leather flats. Because she can't think of anything else to search, she orders a pair of updated Mary Janes, black patent leather with the ubiquitous strap, but these have a three-inch heel. She pays more than the sticker cost of the shoes for overnight shipping. The box is waiting when she gets home from work the next day. She tries them on in her foyer. They pinch her toes, but they make her feel sexy. She walks up and down her hardwood floors like it's a runway.

She wears them to work the next day, but only when she drives. She removes them in the parking lot of her office and hides the box in her trunk. As she does, the little worry voice pops up, reminding her the shoes could be a problem. Relationships are built on trust. How can theirs be honest with this between them? Then she tells herself to stop worrying. Couples have overcome bigger obstacles than a little white lie.

Every day she checks the newspaper for stories from the state police, but there is no mention of mannequins or women on the roadside or Karl. At night, she stays dressed in her good work clothes until bedtime. She parks in her now-cleared garage, but leaves lights on in the house so it's obvious she is home. If he has a question. Should he decide to drop by.

After the week turns into a second week, and he hasn't called or come by, she fears she was wrong and she did mess up by asking if she should avoid the road. Everything was going so well, and she blew it. Whenever she gets discouraged, she remembers his hand on her back. He touched her. That's important. The first clue when things went wrong with Steve was that he stopped touching her. When she asked why, he said her behavior was becoming repellant.

What an ugly word. Why oh why had she wasted so much time on such an ugly guy?

Karl's silence is worrisome, but she had to help Steve along a little, too. Make him feel special, show him he was worthy of her attention, stroke his ego. She is not sure how she will do that with Karl—short of finding another mannequin, of course.

She is driving home from work, wearing the Mary Janes, a few hundred yards before the turn to the shortcut, when she has the epiphany.

It's been warm all week, and spring is starting to show. The days are getting longer; the underbrush of the woods are sprouting new leaves. She's driving along, glancing out her side window, thinking how the woods look different now and would be even easier for someone to hide in, when it hits her. What did he say, when she asked if she should avoid the shortcut?

The road's on my regular patrol route now.

She slams on her brakes and curses. How stupid is she? The road's on his regular route now. That means, drive down the shortcut and I will be there. How could she have missed his message all this time?

She flips the signal and barely makes the turn. If there had been even a hint of ice on the road, she'd have fishtailed for sure. But the road is clear, so her turn is ugly and wide but she makes it. It's not quite dusk. She meets one other car, a van that's going way too fast and hugs the center line, but she is not discouraged. She's peeved at herself for taking so long to catch his meaning, but now that she has, all she needs is patience. She barely looks at the roadside. She's too busy watching for, hoping for, waiting for, an oncoming police car.

She drives the road every night. The days get longer and the traffic increases, but she never sees Karl. Maybe his schedule has changed. Maybe the state police rotate. She decides to take the shortcut in the morning, too. Soon she knows every curve, every rise, every dip, though the trees fill in and the road hardly resembles the barren one she recalls from that night.

One morning, a month after she first saw the mannequin, she turns down the shortcut on the way to work. It's foggy and she thinks, this could be an entirely different road. She's not sure if she is relieved or disappointed. Her fear from that night is all gone. Surely it was a prank, after all, but she's not angry about that. If whoever had never planted the mannequin, she'd have never met Karl.

A couple of miles in, she sees it.

"Holy mama," she says. She slams on the brakes and stares, her mouth hanging open in shock. Then she remembers Karl's warning about being safe and smashes her foot on the gas.

She grabs her phone, which she now keeps on the console, but she doesn't call 911. She's programmed his number in her cell phone and, thank goodness, there is service in this spot. While it rings, she sees a dirt road, the sides a tangle of brush. She turns onto it. He answers just when she kills the engine.

"You're not going to believe this!" she says, and he must think something of that, because when she tells him where she is and what she just saw, there is silence on the other end. A long silence.

"Are you there?" she says.

"Yes," he says. "I'm here." Another pause. "Where are you?"

"I'm up the road. I pulled over to call."

"Stay there," he says. "Lock your doors. Don't get out of your car." No ma'am. No Margot. He sounds terse. Cold. She starts to be

81

upset at his tone, but of course he's doing his job, telling her how to stay safe, and the upset flips over. This just proves he cares, after all.

"All right," she says. "I'll stay right here."

He hangs up.

She obeys his instructions and locks the doors. She sits in the car. It's cold. She looks back at the road. She can't see the woman—the mannequin—from here. She wonders how far she drove. A quarter mile? The road is straight so she can see up and down, but the fog lingers low in the woods.

She waits, excited. She will see him. Karl. But the little voice returns and reminds her of that first night, and the fearful thought she has forgotten these past weeks returns with it. Was there a car sitting on a dirt road then, in the dark, waiting, watching her? Is there one here now?

She twists all around but the interior of the woods is masked by clumps of white. She shivers and wishes she could turn on the heater, but the woods are still, and she's afraid someone might hear her car running. She wonders if Karl will use his siren.

The minutes click and her anxiety rises. No other cars drive down the road, and it occurs to her she didn't tell him where she was, exactly. It's a different spot, a different side of the road. She starts to call him again, but changes her mind when she remembers his abrupt tone. It seems like he's taking a long time. Her car is hidden. What if he can't find her? What if there really is someone in the woods, and it's not a prank but a lure, and whoever put it there has been waiting for the exact, right, perfect time for the real thing? And the mannequin was just practice?

She puts her hand on the ignition. She's shaking so badly her fingers slip off the keys, and then she sees a glint through the fog, and the glint turns blue and his patrol car is coming, speeding, from the other direction. She rests her forehead on the steering wheel and lets out a slow, long, sigh of relief.

"Calm down," she tells herself. "Just be calm."

She starts her car, backs out, drives slowly toward him. He's standing in the road, in front of the mannequin, just the way he did that night in the headlights. Something about it strikes her as odd. Maybe because he's not in uniform, but in jeans and a dark blue jacket with STATE TROOPER on the back. And oddest of all, he's not wearing his hat.

His head whips around when she stops her car. His hand goes to his hip, under his jacket, as she opens the door. She freezes.

"It's me," she calls. "Margot."

The fog has burned off. From across the road, she can see his frown. It makes her almost stumble, or maybe it's the high heels that are really not meant for walking on a country road. It's a good thing he is here with her; if she had to run away, she wouldn't get ten feet.

"I told you to stay in your car," he says.

"I know, but ..." she begins, but stops. He's close enough now she can see he looks haggard. He needs a shave. She feels a punch of guilt. He must have been on duty all night.

She is openly staring at him, but the expression on his face doesn't alter, and he's still got his hand under his jacket.

"It's so weird," she says, giddy with nervousness. And upset. He's mad at her for getting out of her car. She was cold, and she was only trying to help, and now he's mad at her. It reminds her of Steve, who used to get mad at her for all the wrong reasons too. "I mean, it's crazy, isn't it? Me finding this twice. What are the chances?"

She holds her hands out, palms open.

"Yes," he says, his voice flat. "What are the chances?"

Her open hands frame the mannequin, and she looks at it now. It appears just like before, every detail just as she told him, but not quite. Something is off. She bends a little to peer closer. The hair is brown, not black, and wavy, and the skin looks softer. Quite real, as a matter of fact. As do the hands, curled this time into fists, positioned down near the feet.

Her heart clutches. The feet are wearing shoes.

She straightens up and looks up at him. His face has no expression at all.

"Mary Janes," she says, confused. "She's wearing Mary Janes."

His free hand points at her feet. "So are you," he says.

"But she wasn't—" She stops, still confused, not sure what to say. Will he get angry if she admits it was a lie?

"Did you tell anyone, about the shoes?" he asks.

"No," she says truthfully. "I only told you."

He smiles. It lights up his face, and her heart, and she thinks yes, now, everything is all right.

He pulls his hand out from under his jacket. He's holding his key. He aims it at his car and presses down. The trunk clicks open.

He takes a step toward her. "I need you to come with me. You'll do that for me, won't you, Margot?"

ABRACADABRA

BY RUSSELL REECE

The last twenty-four hours had been a tumbling blur of headlights, road signs and tollbooths. Wallace had been swept up in it all, not caring where he went, just rolling with the flow of traffic as his mind raced over images of Rhonda in the foyer, holding her open lipstick and looking at him standing next to her in the reflection of the mirror. *"Just what is it that you do, Wallace? How do you contribute to this household?"* she asked.

He smelled her perfume; saw her white, silk blouse, her tailored, navy blue business suit, and the familiar stern gaze. He looked at himself—a rumpled, balding man, an inch shorter than Rhonda in her heels—with his usual hangdog expression, but also with the hammer this time. Rhonda glared. *"You and your Bible and your ridiculous church. You're pathetic."* She leaned forward and applied the lipstick. He was used to her criticism. It was something that came with living with a strong woman. He had learned that from his mother. But then he saw himself whack Rhonda in the side of her forehead, heard her whine as she crumpled onto the floor. He heard the floorboards creak as he, catlike, went down on his knees and delivered a final blow. All this repeated again and again in the moving frenzy of the interstate, of truck wheels turning, of red taillights glowing in the night. He glanced at the heavy silver necklace dangling from his rearview mirror and felt a chill. He couldn't let himself think about that now. He couldn't.

He crossed into Michigan and drove for another hour. The sign ahead said Jackson. He was tired. He pulled into the first motel he came to.

From his window-booth in the diner, Wallace closed his Bible and watched two thirty-something waitresses in pink uniforms take a smoke break. The mousy brunette leaned on the counter and twisted a strand of hair as she listened to the blonde with the Marilyn Monroe hairdo complain about her boyfriend. The blonde held her cigarette at ear level and puffed between dramatic gestures and rapid-fire speech. She finally pointed toward the parking lot. "Any day now, he's going to pull into the lot and that'll be it. I gotta get out of here." The brunette nodded.

The blonde caught Wallace's gaze and put her cigarette in the shared ashtray. She picked up a pot of coffee and headed to his table. "Everything okay here, hon?" She topped off the thick ceramic cup. "So, what brings you out at three in the morning?"

He motioned through the window at the ramshackle motel across the road. "I don't sleep well in strange beds."

"There's never much sleeping going on over there." She picked up his dirty plate. "It's just an in-and-out place, if you know what I mean." She glanced at the Bible. "You ready for the check?"

"Yeah, I'll take it."

She pulled her order pad and a pencil from the pocket of her apron. Wallace shifted his gaze out the window. A car with two occupants backed out of the motel parking lot and disappeared down the deserted highway. His truck and an old sedan a few spaces away were the only vehicles left in the lot. He slowly moved his fingers in a small circle on the tabletop and recalled the car that had almost stopped yesterday morning as he pulled out of the potato field outside St. Louis, the man and woman inside the car straining to see him. They could have gotten his number, identified his truck. The police might already be involved.

The waitress slid the check onto the table. "Take your time, honey." She smiled and turned away.

He pulled out his wallet, sorted through bills, and took out a ten. He grabbed the check and started to slide out of the booth, then stopped. At the edge of the counter the blonde looked into a mirrored compact and touched up her lipstick. He drew a deep breath. He saw Rhonda lying on the floor, eyes wide open, fresh lipstick smeared across her cheek, and for a moment he was overcome again with the same tingling rush he had felt that afternoon as he hovered over Rhonda's body.

The blonde slipped the makeup back into a patent leather purse and shoved it under the counter.

He shook it off, slid from the booth, and walked to the register.

The brunette slouched behind the glass-topped counter and took his check. "That's $5.85." She speared the receipt on a wire post.

"Give me a pack of those Life Savers," he said.

She reached under the counter, pointed with her nail-bitten finger. "Which do you want?"

"The Cryst-O-Mints."

"Ugh. Too strong for me," she said as she slid the roll toward him. She tapped on the register keys with both hands. "Total is $6.25."

He handed her the ten and she counted out his change. He returned to the booth, dropped a single, then picked up the cup and drained the remaining coffee.

The blonde walked up alongside him. "Be glad to get you more."

Without looking at her, he shook his head, picked up his Bible, and headed toward the entrance.

"Thanks," she said. She slipped the bill into her apron pocket. "Come see me again, honey."

As he crossed the deserted highway, he opened the roll of mints and popped one of the clear candies in his mouth. It was a crisp, summer night and the fresh air was a complement to the sweet menthol flavor erupting over his taste buds. He fingered the motel key with the large plastic fob.

At the diner with other people around, he had been able to control himself, to push the thoughts away and read his Bible. But he knew when he was alone in his room he would relive every second, from the moment Rhonda collapsed to the floor until he piled on the last shovelful of dirt in the potato field. And he would recall the first time when he killed the soldier, the amazing adrenaline rush that came after he pulled the man into the alley, the sense of power, and the surprising feelings of arousal that he experienced for weeks after. How he had succumbed to those feelings, again and again, just as he had begun to do now after killing Rhonda. He shook his head, wondered what made him do that.

He looked across the road at the diner. Through the window he could see the two waitresses standing by the counter, smoking. He pulled out his truck keys, opened the door, and got inside. Maybe a ride would calm him. He started the engine and sat there tapping his fingers on the wheel, listening to the muffler burble. He poked at the necklace, watched it swing back and forth. He could see it slipping off Rhonda's headless torso and he fought to contain a smile. He backed out of the lot and headed north.

He hadn't meant to kill Rhonda. He had been working on the porch step and had come inside to get a broom. Somehow it just happened. It had been the same with the soldier twenty years earlier. The guy had been drunk and staggered into him in a parking lot outside a bar. The soldier started mouthing off about how he could take care of himself, wasn't afraid of anyone. Weaving on his feet, the guy pulled out a straight razor, waved it in the air, and then, based on some bizarre, booze-infused logic, placed the razor in Wallace's hand, patted it as if to make it disappear, and then turned and started to stumble away. Wallace never even thought about it. He reached across the soldier's shoulder and slit the man's throat. There was no remorse, no guilt. He even kept the razor as a souvenir.

Wallace switched on the radio and immediately lowered the volume on the bluegrass music that blasted through the speakers. He needed to think. The two-lane road was empty and dark but for an occasional southbound vehicle. He slipped another mint into his mouth.

Maybe if he hadn't killed that soldier it might have been different with Rhonda. She was eleven years older than he and had worked with his mother at the bus company before leaving to get into real estate. When his mother died, he fell apart and Rhonda took charge of things, helped him through it. He admired her strong character and forthright manner, and one thing led to another. They had been married thirteen years and, though Rhonda could be bossy and wanted nothing to do with the church, it had been a decent relationship. She became a successful broker. Wallace looked up to her. Then the plant closed and he lost his job in the mailroom. There was nothing else in town. He wanted to move, but she was making a lot of money and made it clear they weren't going anywhere. He spent his time keeping the house and doing maintenance work at the church.

Rhonda worked him over about it every chance she got. *"If I wanted a housekeeper, I could do a lot better than you,"* she would say. He didn't mind. He tried to joke about it, find ways to please her. But then came the late evening business meetings; the phone calls she took in another room; her cold, amused stares when he got up the nerve to ask her about them.

Well ... Rhonda wasn't so high and mighty anymore.

In the distance, he could see the flashing lights of a stopped police cruiser. He checked his speed. His gut tightened as he approached. In the cruiser's headlights, a female officer was conducting a sobriety check on a skinny, long-haired teenager with no shirt. Wallace grinned as he passed by.

There hadn't been any issues after he killed the soldier. It had been late at night, they'd been alone and it was just a coincidence he was walking by the bar. There was a blurb on the news; that was all.

He was still living at home and his only worry was that his mother might find out. He was uneasy around her for weeks. She always seemed to be able to read his mind, would know whenever he had done something wrong. And, even though he was twenty at the time, she would slap and scold him, take away privileges. *"You're still living in my house, you will obey my rules."* He wilted under his mother's attacks, would abide her cruel punishments and then pray with her. He worked hard for redemption and received such joy in her forgiveness. She never suspected a thing. It was the first time in his life he had been able to keep a secret from her and he was convinced that God had answered his prayers.

Things were different this time. Rhonda wasn't a drunken soldier stumbling through a dark parking lot in urban St. Louis where the potential for murder lurked around every corner. She was a well-known businesswoman. Someone would wonder why she hadn't shown up for her appointment, would try to contact her. Eventually, they would come looking. He didn't want to deal with that.

Now it was four a.m. and he was in the small town of Waterloo. Traffic was light. He passed a 7-Eleven where a group of construction workers with bags of fast food and large Styrofoam containers of coffee were getting back into a rusty, oversized pickup truck. A town police cruiser was parked against the building. Through the window Wallace saw a cop with a huge belly leaning on the counter stirring his coffee, talking with a female clerk with long blonde hair.

Wallace turned south and drove past Mud Lake and the Waterloo Recreation Area. Maybe he could say he had just gone fishing for a few days. People knew he did that from time to time. He could say she'd been at home when he left, he had no idea where she was. He thought of the couple who saw him coming out of the field. That could be a problem.

He glanced at the Bible lying on the seat next to him. His faith had saved him the first time and he knew it was his answer now. A couple days of prayer and he would know what to do. He had the time. He doubted the police were looking for him. And even if they were, what's the chance they would find him at a ratty motel in Michigan?

He put Rhonda's head on a moonlit stump and fixed up her hair with his fingers. He sat down in front of the stump, elbows on his knees, chin on his clenched hands. He turned the head slightly so they were face-to-face. Rhonda's eyelids drooped.

"You look tired," he said.

He reached into his shirt pocket, took out a roll of Life Savers, slipped one into his mouth. He studied the contours of Rhonda's face, her high cheekbones and full lips. The silver hoop earrings he had given her for Christmas glimmered in the soft light. She had always been a pretty woman. "I didn't plan to do it," he said. He shifted the candy around with his tongue. "The Lord's hand was in it. I know you're not a believer, but we are just His instruments." He glanced at Rhonda's torso lying next to the half-dug grave, took a breath between clenched teeth, and unconsciously stroked himself through his pants.

He stood up, paced back and forth in front of the stump. "I loved being your husband, Rhonda. Even the last few months when you had to go out so much at night, I was okay. Oh, I knew what you were doing. I knew. I prayed about it and I was okay. I was still proud to be with you.

"It wasn't my doing," he said. He sat down in front of the stump, picked up a handful of small dirt clods and tossed them one by one at Rhonda's face. He missed his mother.

Wallace was still driving through the countryside in the hazy gray light of early morning. He passed through a wooded area under a canopy of towering maple and poplar trees and past a farm with cattle lying in the field. Near the edge of a misty meadow, he spotted a one-room, clapboard church from another time. The neat black and white sign by the road read, The Church of the Holy Redeemer. He pulled into the parking lot.

Wallace got out of the truck with his Bible and tried the door, but it was locked. He walked down the sidewalk into an adjacent cemetery separated from the meadow by a low brick wall. The graves nearest the church had simple sandstone markers, many from the 1800s, but, as he walked further, the stones were newer and more elaborate. Near the wall, he found a memorial with a tall, granite cross and a plaque containing the script, *With the guidance of the Holy Spirit.*

Wallace knelt down. With both hands, he raised the Bible to the cross and closed his eyes. "I am forever your servant, Lord."

He hugged the Bible against his chest and stared at the gray sky. "I was a foolish man. I believed Rhonda's heart was pure, like mother's. I would have done anything for Rhonda. But you knew better. You knew, and your justice was swift."

Wallace hesitated, lowered his eyes. "And Lord, forgive me, but I am now filled with arrogant pride. I should be humbled to have been your servant, but, it's like the other time, Lord. I feel such joy, such passion." He swallowed. "And it manifests in disgusting, worldly ways. I've tried to stop, but I can't." He raised his eyes. "Help me Lord. I'm so ashamed."

And then the morning sun broke over the horizon and the cross was surrounded by a golden halo that seemed to grow in intensity before Wallace's eyes. His jaw dropped, his heart beat wildly. He thrust his Bible-clenched hands toward the cross and felt the Holy Spirit fill his body. When he thought he might burst, he began to jerk uncontrollably; from his tongue and from deep within his soul came a rolling tumble of glorious sounds spoken in the perfect language of the Lord.

As he drove back to the motel, Wallace was elated. The Lord had spoken to him. He didn't have to worry anymore. The Lord would protect him. The Lord would provide for his needs. And Wallace would be available, would serve whenever he was called. His hand would be guided by the supreme power.

He was tired, but suddenly hungry. He stopped at the convenience store at Waterloo. The female clerk he had seen earlier this morning was still on duty and she smiled at him as he came through the door. "Morning, sweety," she said.

He nodded, looked her over with a purpose he had never felt before. He smiled back and then spotted the ice-cream cooler. He bought a Klondike Bar and sat down on the curb in front of the store, peeled back the shiny wrapper and took a bite. A banged-up truck with the logo *Sal's Driveway Coating, Inc.* on the side pulled in and parked against the curb several feet away. Two twenty-something guys in dirty jeans and sweatshirts got out and hustled toward the door. "Get me a pack of cigarettes," one said. "I've got to hit the head." As they pulled open the door, Wallace checked them out like a cop on the beat.

Wallace slept for twelve hours, his best sleep in several days. He dreamed about the night in the potato field, how he had dug the grave with Rhonda's tarp-covered body lying nearby. He had intended to just push the bundle in, but as he dug he thought of the startled expression that remained on her face and he felt aroused. He wanted to see her again so he wouldn't forget any of the details. He unwrapped the tarp until the body was nearly freed, then yanked with both hands like a magician unveiling a trick. The tarp, still grasped in his right hand, fluttered off to the side.

In his dream it seemed so funny. He covered the body and ripped the tarp off again. "Abracadabra," he said and laughed. He looked at Rhonda's stony face, her partially shut eyelids, eyeballs gleaming in the moonlight. He kneeled down next to her and poked at the wound on her forehead. "Does that hurt?" he said. He stared at her for a long time and then stroked himself, shuddered. He ran his finger over the contours of Rhonda's face, down her chin and across her neck. And he thought of the soldier and the first time when he had reached across the man's shoulder and slit his throat, the gagging sounds, how the blood had gushed and splattered on the ground, how he had been consumed by that moment so many times alone in his bedroom, masturbating quietly, afraid of waking his mother down the hall. He knew the punishment if she found out what he was doing, had suffered it before, each time more severe and embarrassing. But he couldn't help himself, so he was quiet and, when the blissful moment passed, he prayed, asked God's forgiveness for disobeying his mother.

But his mother was gone and he had confessed to God and God had shined on him and called him into His service. Everything was as it should be now. In his dream, he watched himself slip the razor from his pocket, open the blade, and drag it lightly across Rhonda's windpipe. In the moonlight, a thin line appeared. He did it again and a little blood seeped along the length of the cut. He tried to calm his breathing as he smeared the blood across her neck with his thumb, but his adrenaline was pumping. He felt her throat with his hand, probed the muscle, cartilage, and soft tissue like a doctor checking a thyroid. In the soft spot just below her left ear, Wallace pressed in the angular tip of the razor and drew it hard and deep across her throat. Her neck gaped open and there was blood, but not the gush he had expected. He sliced again and Rhonda's head tilted awkwardly away from her body. The razor caught on cartilage and her vertebrae. And now, in his dream, he saw Rhonda's partially severed head in the moonlight and the subsequent strokes with the razor as he doggedly worked until the head came free and the necklace slipped off and pooled onto the ground in a shiny puddle. He woke up, his penis hard and tingly. He lay there in bed, eyes closed in half sleep, images of the dream and the moonlit night coming and going.

"Abracadabra," he said.

Wallace had a late dinner of steak, green beans, and potatoes at the diner. He was finishing when the blonde waitress hustled in to start her shift. She stashed her purse and was quickly tying on her apron when a surly-looking cook opened the kitchen door, glanced at the clock, and then called her in with his wagging finger.

"Sorry, Tony," she said as she went through the door. "I had a dead battery. I had to get one of the neighbors to start my car." The door closed as Tony's gruff voice took over the conversation.

Wallace picked up his Bible and his bill and went to the cash register. The brunette that had checked him out the night before gave him another pack of Life Savers and took his money, but then looked up at her friend who had come out of the kitchen. The brunette's eyes widened. "Did he can, ya?" she said.

The blonde brushed the question away with a swipe of her hand. "Pfff. Tony's a pussycat," she said. She turned toward Wallace and smiled. "Thought you'd be long gone by now." The brunette closed the register door, handed Wallace his change, and went to wait on another customer.

"I'll be around another day or so," he said.

The blonde nodded. "I'll keep the coffee warm."

Wallace went back to his room, stretched out on his bed, peeled open the Life Savers, and slipped two of the candies in his mouth. He switched on the TV, flipped through the local channels. The Tigers/Cubs game was in the last inning. A few minutes later he checked his watch—nine-thirty p.m. He turned off the TV, grabbed his keys and Bible.

It was a warm night and the sky was clear and bright. He drove slowly through the countryside with his window open, his arm resting on the jamb. He stuck his hand out and let the rushing air press against his open palm. It was fresh and made him feel alive. He didn't know where he was going or what he would do, but he wasn't worried anymore. He just had to be ready whenever he was called. And he would be.

He turned on the radio already tuned to the local bluegrass station. Wade Mariner and the Sons of the Mountaineers started into the song, "Anywhere is Home." It was one of Wallace's favorites and given his current circumstances, prophetic. Another message, he thought, another confirmation from the Lord. He hummed along.

He had been driving for an hour when he approached the turn to I-94. He knew he would pass the motel if he took the interstate west. The Foggy Mountain Boys sang "Crying My Heart Out Over You." Wallace pulled onto the entrance ramp. He had gone four miles when he came to a series of pylons and a lighted construction area. He slowed the pickup. As he approached the flagger and clanked over a large piece of steel covering a hole in the road, he noticed several hard-hatted workers gathered on the side of the eastbound lane. In the middle of the group was a sailor in his white uniform, dusting himself off. *That was odd.* He watched as long as he could, cleared the work-area, and continued down the interstate. Something wasn't right. He drove on but it kept niggling at him. He had to go back.

He made a U-turn at a crossover and sped toward the construction zone. He slowed the truck and strained to see. The men were all at work and the sailor was gone. Maybe he had been confused. Maybe it had just been some kind of weird vision. His hands wrung the steering wheel. He couldn't remember when he had felt so unsettled. A car behind him honked. Wallace accelerated. Just beyond the work area, the car sped past him.

And then in the distance, illuminated by headlights, the sailor walked along the side of the road. As the pickup approached, he turned and held out his thumb.

Wallace made it a point to never pick up hitchhikers. He had even braved an argument with Rhonda about it once. "You just never know what could happen," he had said. Now, in the dark and in the wash of the headlights, the sailor's white uniform gave an otherworldly glow. Wallace felt his adrenaline pump as he passed by and, although he hadn't planned to do it, he pulled the pickup off the road and stopped on the gravel apron. The sailor jogged to the truck. Wallace watched in his rearview mirror and felt a strange calm come over him.

The sailor pulled open the passenger door. Wallace turned down the music. "Hop on up here, young fellow," Wallace said. He took the Bible off the seat and slid it onto the dashboard.

The sailor glanced at Wallace and then at the Bible. He got in and closed the door. "Thanks for stopping," he said.

"Can't sleep again?" the waitress said as she topped off Wallace's coffee. It was two a.m. and the diner only had one other patron.

Wallace looked up from his Bible. "I'm getting ready to turn in now."

The waitress glanced at the book. "You a preacher?"

"No, not a preacher," he said.

The waitress looked at him as if she was expecting more.

"I'm just a servant of the Lord," Wallace said.

The waitress hesitated. "Well, that's nice. Good for you."

Wallace walked back to the motel. In his room, he stood in front of the mirror over the bureau. He leaned forward and checked his teeth in the reflection, then inspected the red streaks in his eyes. The razor and silver necklace lay on top of the bureau next to his keys and a half-eaten pack of Life Savers. He absentmindedly spun the razor like a top and tapped his fingers on the bureau until it stopped spinning. He pulled open the bureau drawer and took out the sailor's white-hat, put it on his head, and pushed the hat forward at a smartass cocky angle. He turned sideways, smiled at himself, saluted.

> "Abracadabra" is the second story in Russell Reece's
> **Mud Lake Trilogy**.

THE PLOTNIK CURSE

BY CARSON BUCKINGHAM

The day the strange little customer tottered into Neiman-Ames Jewelers was, if you asked Julius Neiman, the happiest day he'd had since venturing into the jewelry business some ten years previous.

If you asked Todd Ames, however, you'd hear a different story.

When the art nouveau revolving door whispered round on that fateful day, it carried with it a short, dried-up specimen of a female who looked more than a little bit out of place in the richly appointed store. Instead of the Neiman-Ames warm, welcoming smile, the sales staff favored her with expressions they normally reserved for roaches crawling through the pâté. One had to be so very careful about maintaining the *tone* in shops like this. They busied themselves in hopes that, if they ignored her long enough, she'd take her incompatible presence elsewhere before any of their better customers dropped in.

The woman made no move to depart; moreover, she actually had the temerity to browse. She studied the original Ecartes lining the walls, and the gold-inlaid Cocobalo jewelry boxes, and the Movado watches in the cases. She had just about circumnavigated the store when she stopped before the case occupied by the Neiman-Ames sapphire collection; all of which was for sale, but affordable by few. The little woman was systematically examining every item in the case, and the closer she came to the end of the display, the wider her smile grew. As

97

she studied the very last item, her mottled, apple-doll face broke into a full-fledged ear-to-ear, exhibiting a sparse scattering of crazily tilted teeth to the world.

Naturally, Julius Neiman chose that very moment to saunter in. He was an older man, semi-retired now, who only occasionally put in an appearance at the store. Previously, he'd been a successful stock broker for thirty years, three marriages, and one ulcer. As his third marriage came to an end and his ulcer found a new beginning, he left the brokerage firm and at the age of fifty-five, returned to college for the education in gems and collectibles that led to Neiman-Ames—again, with much success.

Julius had just passed the morning at a cutthroat golf game, which he had won, by the way, and he was feeling rather good about his swing, humanity, and life in general. That was why, when he saw that the odd little customer was not being served, he swept to her side as quickly as his portly frame allowed.

"Good morning, Madam. May I be of assistance?"

"Yeah. You the manager or the owner?"

"You are addressing both. Is there a problem?"

"Nope. I got a necklace I wanna sell, and the sign outside sez you buy jewelry."

The woman amused Neiman. A necklace to sell? He doubted that the piece of human flotsam before him owned anything of value. Why, just look at her—hair a rat's nest of a mess, ancient threadbare cloth coat worn over a faded housedress. And she wants to sell a necklace? To *this* store? Oh, it was just too delicious. He placed what he considered to be a professional smile on his face, but his eyes twinkled with barely suppressed laughter.

"What sort of necklace is it?"

"Chain's eighteen karat gold, and the stone is one of them padparadschas."

Neiman's eyebrow twitched. A padparadscha? The rarest of the rare orange sapphire?

"It's a big one."

"And how large is it?"

"A hunnert 'n five or six carats. I forget. Oh, and it's perfect, too."

Neiman could no longer contain himself. He began to giggle, then chuckle, then laugh as loudly as store decorum would permit. The woman seemed used to this reaction, and waited patiently until Mr. Neiman's merriment subsided.

"My dear woman," Neiman said, wiping his eyes. "Are you telling me that you have a perfect orange sapphire that is larger and better than the fine stone in the Museum of Natural History? That one is one hundred point eighteen carats and is regarded as the largest stone of its type and quality in the world."

"Don't matter. I got one bigger and better. You want it, or not?"

"May I see it?" Neiman was beginning to lose patience with this person. A joke is a joke, and this one had gone far enough.

"Sure. Got it right here in my pockabook"

"Of course you do."

While she rummaged through her satchel, Mr. Neiman winked at the three salespeople who had been following the conversation closely, while trying, and failing, to appear disinterested.

"Here 'tis. I knew it was in there somewheres," she said as she presented the worn velvet necklace box.

He plucked it from the stubby fingers with the positive notion that he would find within not a gem but a faceted piece of glass.

He whisked the cover open, and for a moment, he simply stared. The color drained from his face. He began to tremble. The contents of the box appeared, indeed, to be a huge, round-cut padparadscha.

After observing Neiman's reaction, the sales staff clustered around him for a better look.

"Is it ...?"

"It certainly appears to be," he replied with reverence. He turned his gaze to the woman. "I'll need to have my partner examine this, if you don't mind. We have a rather sophisticated gem testing facility on the premises, and I assure you that no harm will come to your stone."

"Sure, g'head."

Todd Ames was fetched from the back office, and thirty seconds later, stood gaping at the stone his partner held.

"I've already checked it with the loupe, Todd," Neiman said. "If this is a genuine stone, and I'm betting it is, it's flawless as far as I can see."

"And it ain't enhanced, neither. No heatin', no dyin', no treatin'," the woman added.

"Excellent! Excuse us for a moment, won't you?"

"Take your time, I'll wait," she said.

The two men placed the stone on their binocular microscope to test for clarity, and found that it was, indeed, a perfect stone.

Next they moved to the refractometer to determine the stone's composition and physical properties by measuring how the light passing though the gemstone is bent and then comparing that statistic to known stats for that particular gemstone. It tested positive as a padparadscha.

Finally, they placed it on their spectroscope to be certain that it was a natural stone, and it tested positive there, too.

The partners were awestruck. "What do you think it's worth?" Neiman asked Ames. In private, Neiman always deferred to Ames when it came to appraisals, since Ames had been in the business twelve years longer than he.

"Christ, Julius, what we have here is the largest perfect natural orange sapphire on the face of the earth. I mean, just a fine grade natural stone is worth thirty to fifty thousand per carat. This is a round cut, which makes it worth more, plus it's perfect. I'd say priceless, because what we have here is a stone that's worth at least fifty million dollars, and that's pretty damned conservative, considering that it's one of a kind."

Neiman whistled softly. "How much could we offer for it?"

"Did you not hear me? It's priceless!"

"Agreed, but she did come in here to sell it, Todd."

"She didn't mention a figure to you?"

"I never asked because I was sure that it would be a piece of glass. When it wasn't I was too stunned to think clearly."

"I can understand that completely," Ames said.

"What's the highest we could go?"

"Julius, I don't have that information on the tip of my tongue; you know that."

"Ballpark it."

"Five hundred thousand."

"We'll have to do better than that."

Ames sighed. "Look, Julius, I could probably go as high as two million if I were sure you were going to try to turn it over. Are you? Or are you going to put it on display with a 'Not for Sale' sign on it, like the Ming vases out there?"

"Don't worry about what I'm going to do with it, just buy it. And to put your mind at ease, Todd, we will sell it ... for the right price."

"I'm delighted to hear that. I'd hate to see a first-rate business turn into a nonprofit museum." Ames tore off a store check and pocketed it. "Don't get your hopes up, though, Julius. She knows all about this stone, including, I'm sure, what it's worth. We probably won't be able to afford it."

"Well, let's go and find out. Come on."

The little woman's face brightened as the men returned.

"Er, Miss ... eh ..."

"Plotnik. And it's Mrs."

"Ah, very good. Mrs. Plotnik, we would like to purchase this necklace from you. How much are you asking?" Ames inquired.

"Well, les'see ... I think prob'ly ten thousand would be fair."

Ames' eyes shot open wide at the same instant that Neiman's eyebrows disappeared into his hairline. "Madam, do you realize what you have here?" Ames asked. "We want to buy the stone, yes, but we certainly do not wish to be named defendants in a lawsuit for having cheated you. Could it be that you don't know the value of this stone?" The idea of becoming embroiled in litigation over anything purchased for the store was anathema to both partners.

"I know what it's worth, if you can even put a price tag on it. At least forty-seven mil, but I'm pretty sure the actual figger'd be a lot higher'n that."

"Then if you're aware of its worth, why do you want to sell it so cheaply?" Ames asked.

"I don't want it anymore."

"*You don't want it?*" the two men chorused.

"No, I don't. It comes with a curse."

"A curse?" Ames raised a skeptical eyebrow.

"A'course. Ya mean ya never hearda the Plotnik Curse?"

"No. What's the 'Plotnik Curse'?" Neiman asked.

"Mr. Plotnik!" she cried. There was total silence for just a beat, and then everyone exploded in laughter after being set up for and taken in by such an old joke.

Ames wrote out the check and handed it to Mrs. Plotnik. "I realize that this is a rather irregular request, Madam, but would you be willing to sign a document stating that you are fully aware of the value of the stone, that it was your uncoerced decision to sell it for this price and that the stone is, in fact, yours to sell? I will also need to see some form of photo identification. Your driver's license will do. Oh, and your Social Security card, as well."

"Sure."

"Fine. It will only take a moment to type it up and a member of the staff is also a notary, so we can get everything done right here."

Fifteen minutes later, Mrs. Plotnik laid aside the gold Cross pen and was on her way out the door, check in hand, amid smiles and cheerful goodbyes from the same sales people who had previously wished she would be a quick victim of spontaneous combustion. Hand on the doorknob, she turned, and with a small wave, said, "Good luck to ya," then was gone.

"What do you suppose she meant by that?" someone asked.

"Who knows what she means by anything?" Ames shrugged. "Who cares? We just made the deal of the millennium on a very rare gemstone."

"How much will we sell it for?"

"I don't know yet. I'll have to discuss it with Mr. Neiman first. Whatever we sell it for, it's certain that we'll make an astronomical profit on it."

When Ames strode into the back room, he found Neiman on the phone concluding arrangements for his annual six-week holiday vacation. The man always made it a point to be out of the country for Thanksgiving and Christmas, since he had no family left with which to celebrate.

"Well, that's that," Neiman said, hanging up the phone. "I'm off to Egypt the day after tomorrow. What kind of store expenses can you give me this time, Todd? I know I can get some terrific deals over there."

It vaguely annoyed Todd Ames that Julius Neiman, the senior partner in this venture, was both uninformed and unconcerned about store finances. "Why don't you just pick up what you want, and have the store reimburse you when you get back?"

"No, my boy. I prefer to have a budget to adhere to, and a store check gives me that. Plus, it prevents commingling funds, which our IRS friends deeply frown upon."

Todd fetched the store ledger and did a few quick calculations. "Since we got such a phenomenal deal on that padparadscha, I guess I can let you have eight hundred thousand for this trip, Julius. Good hunting." Where Neiman trusted Ames' gem expertise, Ames fully trusted Neiman's taste in buying. "And speaking of that, what's to be the price tag on it?"

"I really wouldn't want to see it go for less than forty-eight million."

"That's realistic, I suppose. We have a handful of customers who would be interested in it at that price."

"While I'm there, I'll look up Shaloub in Cairo. I may be able to sell it to him. I understand that he loans God money."

"If not, we could always consider Sotheby's or Christie's."

"Another option, certainly. See you in six weeks, Todd. Any special requests?"

"Oh, yes, as a matter of fact. Sheila has been dropping hints since last March about a carnelian and diamond necklace. You ought to be able to find a nice one over there for a decent price."

"Done. Have a Happy Thanksgiving, a Merry Christmas, et cetera."

"Oh, I probably will whether I care about it or not—Christmas, I mean."

"Come on, Ames, don't be such a Scrooge." When Todd rolled his eyes, Neiman said, "Christmas is still five weeks away. Maybe you'll feel more like celebrating when it gets a little closer."

"Right, Julius. Have a good time."

They shook hands and Ames was left with the padparadscha.

He parted the indigo velvet curtains and walked into the showroom. After a quick look around to be sure the store held no one but employees, he clapped his hands for their attention; a gesture the sales staff found annoying beyond description. It made them feel as if they were expected to sit up and beg. It also made them wish that Mr. Ames would roll over and play dead.

"Attention, please!" he called in a wasteful expenditure of syllables. "I'm entertaining suggestions regarding the best way to display the padparadscha."

Everyone had at least one idea. They walked it around the room, exposing the stone to a variety of lighting—incandescent, fluorescent, and daylight. Though it looked best in daylight, it would mean displaying it close to a door or window, which would raise the risk of robbery, so that was ruled out. Incandescent lighting made it look too red. Fluorescent lighting would work, but didn't really bring out all the rich, pink-orange colors of the stone.

They were stumped until Declan, the store's top diamond salesman, who was also well known in herpetological circles, mentioned the Lumichrome full-spectrum bulbs he used to light his snake enclosures. "It's as close as you can get to natural sunlight in a light bulb." He was dispatched forthwith to the nearest pet store to buy a supply of them, along with a fixture.

Inside of an hour the necklace was sparkling under Lumichrome lights, resting on ecru velvet, in a case by itself next to the register. Ames made it abundantly clear that if the padparadscha was not the best-guarded by day and the first to be safe-bound by night, that heads would roll, along with arms, legs, and a nose here and there.

In any other establishment, a stone that valuable would have been locked into a fully alarmed case. However, the ultra-rich patrons Neiman-Ames had cultivated over the years were not used to having to wait while someone fumbled for a key. They expected to touch and examine things up close immediately, and they were wealthy enough so that such expectations were met without question. In fact, so many valuable pieces were placed unprotected on shelves throughout the store that no children were allowed inside, no matter how rich the parent. Oddly enough, it was a well-respected rule among the clientele. There was never even the smallest complaint when the tastefully lettered sign reading "No Children, Please" was placed in the window.

Most of their regular patrons were too old to have young children anyway. They had grandchildren, though, and they utterly despised them. That always amazed Neiman, but nothing surprised Ames anymore. He'd dealt with the moneyed population for too long to expect anything but the unexpected.

The display hadn't been in place for two minutes before Mrs. McKay, a well-to-do widow, flounced through the door and homed in on the orange sapphire like a heat-seeking missile. "My my *my*! What have we here?" she demanded of the store in general. Ames heard her all the way out in the back office and came up front to greet her. He knew that neither Milane nor Charlotte could tolerate her. They were exceptional salespeople, but when Ruby McKay stepped through the door, sparks flew. Since Declan and Clark were occupied checking in a shipment, Ames waited on her himself.

"Good afternoon, Mrs. McKay. I see you've found our latest acquisition." He toyed with the idea of setting her up for the Plotnik Curse joke, but dismissed it. She probably wouldn't get it, anyway.

"What kind of a stone is that? Such an unusual color."

"It's an orange sapphire called a padparadscha. It's exceedingly rare, and we are now the proud owners of the largest perfect one in the world." He didn't think she'd buy it, but she had the biggest mouth east, west, north, and south of the Mississippi and the news of the stone would spread like caviar on toast points. Ames desperately wanted to sell the stone before Neiman returned and decided that he wanted to add it to his personal collection after all.

"Really! I've never seen one before."

"To see one near to this size, you'd have to visit a museum. Its perfection, its size, color, and cut all combine to render it nearly priceless. We're selling it for fifty-one million. Quite a bargain, really," Ames said.

"I assume it's set in fourteen-carat gold?"

Leave it to her to look at something of blinding beauty and focus on the metal that surrounds it. "It's eighteen karat gold." He was coming around more and more to Milane's way of thinking about this woman, whom she considered an "old crone with nothing better to do than make daily rounds irritating people." Off the sales floor, she certainly had a colorful way with words, and her description of Mrs. McKay was spot on.

Mrs. McKay spun a cursory glance around the store. "I'll be off, now. Just wait until I tell the girls about this!" she burbled. "They'll all be dying to see it, I assure you."

"That's fine. Have a nice day, Mrs. McKay."

"I do wish you'd stop calling me that."

"Beg pardon?"

"*Mrs.* It's not *Mrs.* It's *Ms.*"

"Of course. Ms. Goodbye now."

After Ms. McKay was safely outside, Milane snorted. "*Ms.* yet! An eighty-year-old biddy who wants to be called *Ms.* Can you beat that?" Milane had worked for seven years as a cocktail waitress before she was educated into the jewelry business and sometimes the "pub baby" in her rose to the surface before she could catch it.

"Milane!"

"Sorry, Mr. Ames. When it comes to her, I just can't help it."

"Well, work on it, please."

The rest of the day matched the next two in that literally hundreds of people, the well-to-do from miles around, poured into the store for a visual feast upon the padparadscha. But when they heard the price, they said, "Oh!" and quickly bought something else. Both days had record sales, but Ames was disturbed that there hadn't even been a nibble for the orange sapphire.

As it turned out, he should have been mightily grateful for the two days of excellent sales.

The third day began the period in the history of Neiman-Ames that Todd Ames would refer to as the "Black Christmas of '09." The store opened promptly at eight o'clock, as usual. At nine, the store was bustling with people—again, as usual.

At the height of the morning, on mornings such as these, Ames was often transported into a mild state of euphoria in which he felt that nothing could go wrong and the world was his crème brûlée. He was feeling precisely this way when the first uneasy stirrings began in the crowd—like a herd of wildebeests sensing a lion crouching in the shrubbery.

Something was not right in the store.

He scanned the crowd for a face he knew, and then moved quietly across the deep maroon oriental carpet.

"Mr. Fitzsimmons, do you notice anything strange in the air?" he inquired casually.

"It's not in the air, old man; it walks among us," he replied, inclining his head.

Had he said "strange?" That was hardly the word for the person standing in the middle of the showroom.

"Grotesque," maybe.

"Disgusting," absolutely.

But just "strange"? Never!

One really had to see him in person to truly understand. He looked as though he had been assembled by Dr. Frankenstein's apprentice, who was blind drunk on schnapps at the time. To start with, the man was severely humpbacked, an affliction that pushed his body floorward so far that his hands, complete with talon-like filthy fingernails, hung down past his knees. He had the standard number of eyes, although one was noticeably higher than the other, and protruded as if it were being prodded from behind with a poker. He didn't have a nose so much as just two elongated nostril openings flat against his face. To accessorize this look, he wore old and badly soiled clothing; a plaid jacket that looked as though it had been picked off the back of a draft horse and fit him about as well; and pants that were of indeterminate color and far too small. He had one short leg and wore improperly designed corrective shoes for it, which caused him to sway precariously when he walked and appear about to fall over when he stood still—all swimming in a hellish miasma of the most appalling body odor Ames had ever encountered.

But worse—worse than all that—he drooled.

It wasn't the subtle drool of the aged, nor was it the occasional drool of the infant. It was more like a faucet had been turned on somewhere in the deep recesses of his salivary glands with the shut-off valve nowhere to be found. The man sometimes used a dirt-caked handkerchief and sometimes the back of his sleeve to wipe it away, but it kept pouring forth and dripping on the carpet.

The large crowd of Neiman-Ames shoppers became a small crowd that became nonexistent in record time.

Ames forced himself to confront the man. "Good morning, sir. Is there something I can show you?" *Preferably the door*, he thought.

The little man shook his head, wiped his mouth, and began to weave around the store.

"If you're looking for a gift, perhaps I can help you." On the outside, Ames was a picture of tranquility. Inside, however, his stomach was spinning like a lathe at the man's abysmal lack of personal hygiene. All he could think of was getting him out of the store as quickly as possible. He'd already cost them, conservatively, close to three hundred thousand in lost sales from the people he'd chased away.

Ames would not be polite to the man much longer.

The undersized Quasimodo turned and grinned, revealing a mouth full of broken and decaying yellow and black teeth. "Abbalallaballalla llaaballala," he said.

Ames was convinced that his breath would remove paint, so he supposed it was actually better that the man couldn't speak.

The fellow covered his ears and shook his head.

Ames screwed his eyes shut and sighed. Then he looked down at the fellow again. "Deaf, too? Do you lip-read?"

The little man nodded, still grinning.

"Can you write?"

Another nod.

Ames reached for a pencil and pad and handed them over.

The man scribbled a quick note and handed it back. It read, in arrestingly beautiful penmanship, *I'm not here to buy anything. I'm here to stay.*

"What do you mean 'stay'?" You can't stay here! Didn't you see all the customers you drove away this morning?"

More scribbling and a wipe of the mouth. *There's nothing I can do about it. I have to stay. You have it now.*

"Have what?"

Top sheet torn off. More scribbling. *The sapphire.* As if that explained everything.

Ames thought back to the conversation with the strange woman who had sold them the stone. Meanwhile, the little man was writing again. *It comes with a curse, you know.*

The penny finally dropped. "Who are you?" Ames asked.

Scribble, wipe, scribble. Ames didn't really want to read the name on the paper, but forced himself.

Mr. Plotnik.

There was so much that made perfect sense now. No wonder Mrs. Plotnik sold the necklace for a pittance. No wonder she said, "Good luck" as she was leaving. No wonder ... no wonder ...

Ames was firm. "You can't stay here, Mr. Plotnik."

Scribble, scribble, wipe, scribble. Plotnik was firm, too.

Where the stone goes, I go. Want me to leave? Sell the stone or be damned, I don't much care one way or the other.

He then continued his trek around the store while Todd Ames looked dismally after him.

Over the next few days, they tried everything to get rid of Mr. Plotnik. Milane called the police, who put him outside. Later, he came back in again, and it became plain that continual summoning of law enforcement would only serve to finish the job Mr. Plotnik had begun and lead to complete financial ruin.

They tried begging, cajoling, threats, and bribery, but he would not be moved. Pass the stone on, was his response to their every effort.

A week passed. Word about Mr. Plotnik had traveled far and Neiman-Ames hadn't seen a single customer since.

"How the hell am I supposed to sell that damned necklace if you keep chasing away all my customers?" Ames raged.

Scribble, wipe. *So true. All right. One week. If it isn't gone by then, you'd better break out your paddle, because you'll know what creek you're up.*

"Wonderful!" he cried at Plotnik's retreating back. When the door whisked him onto the sidewalk, Ames sprang into action. "Charlotte, call *Ms.* McKay and tell her that it's safe to come in again. Ask her to tell as many people as she can. We're back in business—for a week, anyway. Milane? Please run down to Macmillan's and buy some subtle but effective air freshener."

By afternoon, the store was crammed with shoppers. Sales were good, but not good enough to offset a week of inactivity—not unless they could sell that necklace. So far, nobody had even glanced at it a second time. It was old news now. By Friday, Ames was getting panicky, and even though he'd be able to hear Julius screaming all the way from Cairo if he knew, Todd Ames, in front of God and the store's most prestigious customers, placed a ten-thousand-dollar price card, upon which he carefully lettered "This item is not returnable" next to the orange sapphire and went to lunch.

Upon his return, Declan ran out to meet him. "It's gone, Mr. Ames! It's gone! We sold it!" Ames was so ecstatic that he threw propriety to the wind and he and Declan did a little dance on the sidewalk.

"Isn't it great news, Mr. Ames?" Clark called from behind the counter.

"Glory hallelujah amen! Everybody take a two-hour lunch. I'll man the store."

Amid effusive thank-yous, something occurred to Ames. "By the way, who bought it?"

"Out-of-towner. Someone I've never seen before. Paid cash."

"Cash? How unusual. Well, no matter. What's important is that it's gone."

Business right up until Christmas Eve was booming. It was the best holiday season in the history of the store, even with that one slack week. Shipments were sold as fast as they were unpacked, and by the time the store closed on the night before Christmas, not a creature was stirring and the diamond case was completely empty.

Ames was the last to leave, as usual. He locked up, brushed the light dusting of snow from his Lexus, and headed home.

He found a station playing Christmas carols, and realized that Julius had been right after all. The Christmas spirit had finally found him. He had a lovely gift for his wife, too. The diamond and carnelian bracelet he selected for her was sure to look wonderful with the necklace Julius would be bringing back from Egypt.

Todd burst in the door, full of snowflakes and good cheer. "Merry Christmas, my love!" he called. Sheila ran to meet him and practically jumped into his arms. "Is that Dom Pérignon and prawn cocktails I smell?" he said, holding her close.

"It is, but I'll be damned if I know how you can smell them!" Sheila replied, grinning.

Dinner, beginning with the prawn cocktails, progressed through grilled quail, quinoa with sunflower seeds, arugula and radish salad, and raspberry granite for dessert. Two snifters each of a particularly fine cognac completed the meal, and in a soft-pastel glow, they retired for the night.

They awoke at eight to the sound of church bells heralding Christmas morning. After a quick breakfast, Todd and Sheila stood in the kitchen doorway, gazing at the tree.

"Last one plugs in the lights!"

They dashed and Todd lost. While he plugged in the lights, Sheila sorted out the packages bathed in the sweet piney aroma of their freshly cut twenty-foot blue spruce. She placed the gifts in one of three piles: his, hers, and ours. With their enormous circle of friends and close relatives, there was no gift shortage.

The tree burst into dazzling life. Todd came out from behind it and picked out his special gift from Sheila's pile and held it out. She tore at the paper with childlike eagerness and was awestruck by the bracelet within. "It's ... it's gorgeous, honey. Oh, *thank* you!" she whispered, eyes shining.

"Anything for you, dear heart."

She set the box carefully on the coffee table. The bracelet was already on her wrist and couldn't have looked lovelier. "Now here," she said. "Open your special present from me. But be careful—it's fragile."

After opening the gift, it was Todd's turn to be awestruck. In his hand was a small Matisse. Todd collected rare original artwork, and this piece would certainly be the new focal point in his present collection.

"Where did you *ever* ..."

"I've got connections," she said, laughing. "Now let's get that fireplace going and open the rest of the presents. And Todd, sweetheart? Thank you so much for the bracelet. I just love it."

He grinned and went to light the already laid fire, and then they turned their attention back to the matter at hand, spending the next hour slowly untying and unwrapping, oohing, and ahhing. Finally, they were down to their last gift each.

"I almost don't want to open it," Sheila said, "because then Christmas will be over."

"No, it won't. We haven't gone back to bed yet," Todd said, wiggling his eyebrows. "So who are these from?"

"My mother," Sheila replied. "Mine is huge. Wonder what's in it."

"I think I know what mine is," Todd sighed. "Monogrammed handkerchiefs."

"What can I say, honey? Mother never knows what to get for you, but she won't listen to a single suggestion I make." She patted his knee. "With your allergies, you can always use handkerchiefs."

"I suppose you're right." But he still felt that with all the money that old bag had, she could do a great deal better than six initialed cloth squares.

He opened the box.

Surprise, surprise.

Sheila opened hers. It was tightly packed with excelsior. She felt around a bit and found nothing. "Looks like this is going to take a while. This stuff is packed in so tightly I won't be able to get to the bottom without getting rid of some. I need a trash bag." Sheila jumped up, ran to the kitchen and back, and started stuffing excelsior into the plastic bag slowly, to keep it from getting everywhere. "Mother must have had some time on her hands."

"You have fun. I'm going to make us some hot chocolate," Todd said, shuffling through the litter of cast-off wrapping paper.

When Sheila finally stowed away all the excelsior, she was surprised to find that all remained at the bottom of the box was an ordinary sealed and padded eight-by-ten manila envelope.

The front doorbell rang.

"I'll go," Todd called, turning off the stove. *Happens every year. There's always one guest who just has to be early to the party.*

"How strange," she said, slitting the tape that held the envelope closed. She carefully slid the contents onto the carpet. "Oh, my heavens. Todd!" she called. "Come quickly!"

"Be right there," he called, swinging open the front door, with a hearty "Merry Christmas" on his lips.

Sheila was still calling to him from the living room. "You really have to see this to believe it!"

"I've seen it already," Todd muttered, hanging his head.

MIRROR MIRROR

BY CHANTAL NOORDELOOS

It was the year of our Lord 1852 when the old dragon mirror was broken, and that same year my family became the keepers of a secret.

I was the middle child of the Bellefleur family, and I have to admit that I was an un-extraordinary girl who often felt invisible. My mother was Master Bellefleur's second wife, and he was her second husband. They were both widowed and wealthy, and I believe they never married for love. I was a baby at the time of their wedding; my father died when I was still in my mother's womb. Mother valued family, and named me Sophie, after her own dear sister who died too soon, too young. The only real relation I had in the Bellefleur family was my half-sister, Constance. My older stepsister, Marie-Louise and I had little in common, and I don't think she ever saw me as a real sister.

Marie-Louise was everything that I was not. She was a true beauty with a strong will and a fiery temperament. I was a homely girl with mousy brown curls and watery blue eyes who barely spoke to anyone but the slaves on the plantation. Marie-Louise never liked my mother, which was understandable. She was five when her father remarried, and my mother brought a new child into the house.

I was seven years old when my mother died, which made me old enough to remember her, but not old enough to remember her well. I remember her death more clearly than I remember her life. As a young girl of seven it made quite an impact, seeing my mother bleed from her eyes, ears, nose and mouth, while she screamed about demons. Even now, as an old woman, I only have to close my eyes to relive that memory.

There are parts of her life that still stick with me, and I remember she was very unhappy at the Bellefleur Plantation. Life there was harsh, especially for someone like her, who wasn't born to it. I was too small to understand what real cruelty was, even though it was a regular way of life with the master. But as I grew older, and more able to form my own opinions, I became aware of his unnecessary brutishness. My eyes opened to the whippings and the torture long after my mother died.

The clearest memory I have of my mother was the day we sat together in her dressing room. The sun shone in through the windows, and for a moment I felt safe. At that age, I might not have known about the inhumanity of my father and his staff, but, even as a small girl, I felt something was "off" and rarely felt safe. My stepsister, Marie-Louise, liked to torment me with her cruel tricks, and it was difficult to get away from her. But that day in my mother's dressing room, I did not have a care in the world.

Mother combed my hair and put white ribbons in my frizzy locks. I hated my hair and wished I had beautiful smooth golden curls like Marie-Louise, or the strawberry-colored locks that my mother and half-sister, Constance, shared.

"You have my sister's hair," she remarked. "She had the same infuriating curls." Mother smiled, so I knew she meant well by her comment. "You have her kind heart too, my sweet Sophie."

"Did she give you the mirror?" I pointed my stubby finger at the large, ornate mirror on the wall. The frame was made out of gold, and it depicted two dragons at the top, glaring at each other among a spray of leaves. It was a beautiful mirror, but it also frightened me.

"It was my mother who gave it to me. My great uncle Jacques Aimee brought it with him to the Americas, and he gifted it to my mother. My great uncle lived in Paris, and he found the mirror in a market in Bourges. An old Jewish man told him he was Magi, skilled in the black arts, and sold him the mirror. It's supposed to be magical."

I gasped and examined the mirror as if it had changed somehow now that I knew it was magical, but it looked the same. "What does it do, Mama?" The idea of this enchanted mirror fascinated me, and played with my imagination.

"It is said that the longer one looks in the mirror, the longer one can maintain their beauty."

I looked at my mother, who was a real beauty, and then I looked at my own face. I wished I were pretty, too. That mirror could do nothing for me. I sighed wistfully, and my mother continued her story while she ran the brush through my hair.

"There is more to this mirror." Her voice now held a tone of conspiracy, and she bent over to whisper in my ear. "The mirror can see straight into a soul, and when that soul is wicked, the mirror will know." Mother placed her finger on the tip of my nose. "So you better be good, or the mirror will know."

Her words terrified me. The thought of a mirror looking into my soul provided me with nightmares for years to come. I just nodded, my mouth ajar, and my eyes big and round. *Marie-Louise better not look in this mirror*, I thought, *she is very wicked.* My beautiful stepsister, five years my senior, was known for her spoiled nature. She did not only play her mean tricks on me, but also on the servants, and most of all the slaves. She liked to get the slaves in trouble, and she enjoyed seeing them whipped, or worse. Mother often said Marie-Louise had the cruel nature of her father, and she worried that Constance would turn out the same. My little sister was only a year and a half old when my mother died. I am glad mother never saw Constance grow up. The Bellefleur hearts were colder than ice, and Constance was no exception.

Our plantation had a dark reputation, though that was something I only learned in my teens. Slaves feared it, and the masters from other plantations used ours as a threat. *"If you don't work, I'll sell you to the Bellefleurs."*

I feared my stepfather, and when my mother died, I felt truly alone in that house. My mother left me some trinkets, but my elder sister claimed the mirror. Marie-Louise loved looking in my mother's mirror, and each time I caught her looking in it, I wondered if the mirror could see her wickedness. If it did, it never seemed to do anything, and I wondered what the magic was for. I hoped that the mirror would punish her, or show her the true face that lay behind the beautiful blue eyes, soft lips, and button nose. But the mirror never punished Marie-Louise, and all it showed me was my sad little face.

Marie-Louise didn't even wait for my mother's body to grow cold when she claimed the mirror for her own. She had a fascination for mirrors, and hung several in her room, but she liked my mother's mirror best of all. She cried a few tears to Father, and told him she wanted the mirror to remember her stepmother. I cared very little for the mirror, and did not want it in my room. Yet at the same time, it bothered me that Marie-Louise would have something that belonged to 'my' mother. Her tears must have touched Father's iron heart, and he agreed that she should have it. A few days later, on the day of my mother's funeral, the large mirror was moved. It left an empty space above my mother's dresser.

I don't know why, but that space broke my heart. I did not, however, dare to speak out against Marie-Louise. I would like to say that my mother's death affected life on the plantation, but it seemed that mother was easily forgotten by everyone but me. Constance was too small to miss her mother, and hardly anyone ever spoke of her again. Her pictures were taken down and cleared away to the attic. Her dresses were stored away, and her room was cleaned out and redecorated. Sometimes I wondered if my mother ever lived in this house, or if I just dreamt her.

Our father remarried a week after mother's funeral. I was too young to understand, but I remember the servants whispering about shame, and how my mother's death was suspicious. Later, I learned that the first Madame Bellefleur died of the same symptoms, and only then did I, myself, become suspicious.

I liked our new mother. Father's new wife was a pleasant and beautiful woman. The servants said she was barely more than a girl. Of course, Marie-Louise felt no love for the new bride, and she was cold and callous to the young woman, but we instantly became good friends. I called her mama, and hoped that my kindness would make up for my sister's sharp tongue and disapproving glances.

Like my mother, the new Madame Bellefleur remarked on the cruelty against the slaves. She did not like to venture outside of the mansion too often, but when she did, she avoided the slave quarters.

I liked the slaves. They had so little, and yet they seemed to get happiness from the smallest places. Their lives were so different from ours, yet I somehow dreamed of being one of them. There was much love and warmth in those narrow slave quarters, and they all made me feel welcome. I loved to sneak out of the stuffy mansion and play with the children. The slaves knew games and songs that I never heard of, and they treated me as if I mattered.

"Come dance with us, Miss Sophie," they would say, or, "What a pretty dress you are wearing today, Miss Sophie. I love the ribbons in your hair." To reward them for their kindness, I would sneak bread and pastries from my plate, and share them with my friends.

There was one person I loved beyond all others; she was one of the oldest slaves on the Bellefleur plantation. Her name was Queenie, and when I was young I believed she was the oldest woman alive. I fantasized that the old woman was once a queen from a far away land. When I told her about my dreams, Queenie laughed and never confirmed nor denied my stories. Queenie was the only person who would ever speak to me about my mother. When I was sad, she would gather me up in her thin arms with her coarse dry skin, and hold me tight. I remember her rocking me back and forth and singing ancient songs to me. I knew the slave lullabies better than I did the songs of the white people.

Queenie was loved and respected by the other slaves. The old woman with her dark, deep-set eyes, and her black-gray wrinkly skin had lived on the plantation for three generations of masters. Age was the sort of thing people respected. No one knew how old she really was, not even Queenie herself, but she had been taken from Africa as a young girl, and still had distant memories of freedom that she would often share with me. She took special care of me, the little middle child, who for all her wealth, lacked love and affection.

I loved to listen to Queenie's stories, and as I grew older, they grew darker and more exciting. The story of the Ga-gorib was one of my favorites.

"What did he do, Queenie?" I asked, ten years old at the time, feeling a mix of dread and excitement tickle my stomach.

"Oh, he taunt people, little miss, he get right under der skins. 'Throw a stone at me,' he say. Natural, people can't resist the temptation. But the stone always fly back, knock the thrower into the pit an' the Ga-gorib gobble them up." I could picture the horrible Ga-gorib as he crawled down the well, his large teeth exposed. The thought alone made me shudder.

"Is the Ga-gorib the worst demon in Africa?"

Queenie looked at me with her deep brown eyes for a moment and she shook her ashen head. "No, chile. They worse demons, and they don't just live in Africa, neither. But you iz too young to hear dem stories," the old slave said. "When you iz older, mayhap one day I'z tells ya. Then I'z tells ya of the dark one, who lives in the mirror, and who seeks evil spirits." She took my face in her hands and looked me straight in the eye. I remember her coarse fingers, rough as wood, as if it were yesterday. "Queenie tell you one thing, chile ..." She paused and then spoke with hesitation in her voice, "You stay away from dem mirrors you sister is always looking at, ya hear? Dem's danger. Never get caught 'tween two mirrors, dat's what ole Queenie knows"

A chill ran down my spine. "Why Queenie? How can a mirror be dangerous?"

"Mirrors be magic, little one, that's why we's don' use em." Her grip on my face tightened. "Mirrors be of the dark ones; demon magic. Like to take your soul dem are." Then she let go of my face. *The mirror can see straight into a soul, and when dat soul is wicked, the mirror will know.*" My mother's words ran through my mind.

"My mother told me that her dragon mirror was magical."

"Dat one the worst of dem all."

I nodded and knew it was true. I knew it then when my mother told me three years before, but I knew it even more at that moment. "But Marie-Louise stands between mirrors all the time. She does it so she can see her hair in the back. Marie-Louise doesn't think mirrors are evil. She must have half a dozen mirrors in her bedroom alone. Should I warn her?"

There was a tormented look on the old woman's face, a look I could not decipher, and she sighed.

"She won't listen if you do, chile," Queenie said softly. "I'z too late for dat one, too late. In fact, ole Queenie think it too late for dat one at birth. Dat is a dark chile, that is."

I should have listened to Queenie, but I thought if I could warn Marie-Louise, I might get my stepsister to like me. That night, when the sun was setting in the sky, I walked to my sister's dressing room. She sat in front of the mirror while she brushed her curls and stared at her reflection with a dreamy expression. Her long lashes fluttered slightly when she became aware of my presence.

"What do you want?" Her voice was cold, and she rolled her eyes.

"Queenie says we mustn't stand between two mirrors," I panted. In the mirror, I could see my own image; my cheeks were crimson, and my eyes were round.

"What has gotten into you, silly child?" Marie-Louise snapped as she turned back to the mirror, and once again she brought the soft-bristled, horsehair brush to her long, honey-colored hair.

My sister took great pride in her hair, she brushed it a hundred strokes every morning, noon, and evening, and styled it to the latest trends. Her cold, gray eyes looked at me from her reflection, and I imagined that something inside the mirror moved. My sister held up her hand, and soft strands of hair fell down her palm like a golden waterfall, and there was a look of annoyance on her once placid face. I sensed danger. When Marie-Louise lost her temper, I was often the one to feel her wrath.

"I will not hear one word of it," she said strictly, as if she were a parent addressing her naughty child. "Bothering me, filling my ears with nonsense some dumb old slave told you." She turned around, and there was fire in her eyes, "You shouldn't talk to them, Sophie Annee Bellefleur. They are slaves. They are ignorant and disgusting. You have no business being near them."

I should have walked away right then, as I often did, but some stubborn streak in me made me stand my ground. Terribly angry, I wanted to defend Queenie, who meant more to me than my father and my sisters combined.

"Queenie's not dumb. Queenie says ..." I yelled. My cheeks and ears burned, and I threw all caution to the wind, which sent my sister into a rage. The look in her eyes frightened me; I had never seen her so angry before.

With a passion that made my knees weak, Marie-Louise threw down her hairbrush and flew at me, her manners and composure suddenly forgotten. Her mouth contorted in a cruel sneer. She looked like a demon to me.

"Queenie says, Queenie says," Marie-Louise parroted evilly while she pulled my hair. "If you are so keen to listen to slaves, why don't you become one?"

Her hands were strong and she was as swift as the devil when she dug her fingers into my curls. I cried in pain and struggled, but Marie-Louise was, in her madness, as strong as a grown man. She pulled my head forward and, when I looked to the side in my struggle, I saw the mirror. In it, I thought I could see the face of a man smiling wickedly. I screamed and tried to resist, but my sister pulled me out of the room and down the stairs. A few times I almost fell. Terrified, tears ran down my cheeks, and snot dripped from my nose over my lips. Her grip on my hair made my scalp sting. The violence with which my stepsister pulled me caused black spots in my vision. She dragged me outside. I could feel my dainty shoes slip on the stones.

We're heading to the barn, I thought. "Please," I begged. I wept, but she ignored my pleas. When we got closer to the barn, I smelled the hay and the manure. Marie-Louise flung me straight into the pigpen. It hurt when I hit the mud, and when I struggled to get up, I felt a strong hand push me down.

"You want to spend time with the slaves?" Marie-Louise screeched like a mad harpy. "We shall blacken you up nice and proper, so you look like one."

A cold, wet clod of muck hit me on the forehead, and it clung to my skin and hair. More muck followed, but whether it was mud or pig droppings, I didn't know. In my fear, I didn't even run away. I just lay there, curled up in the dirt, and protected my face from the barrage.

A shovel, I thought, *my sister found a shovel and wants to bury me.* I didn't dare to call out for her to stop, afraid I might swallow mud or excrement. Then I saw a shadow through the cracks of my eyelids— only it wasn't a shadow, it was Queenie. The old black woman had thrown herself in front of her young mistress and protected me with her body. Her callused hands and bony arms were a welcome softness. The hail of muck stopped and only then did I dare to look at my sister.

There were more people in the barn then. A large slave-driver named Jim-Bob gently took the shovel from Marie-Louise and calmed her down with a soothing voice. We both looked a fright, our faces, hair, and nightgowns covered in muck. While Jim-Bob ushered my sister away, Queenie fretted over me.

"Come now, Miss," she cooed in a sing-song voice as if talking to a babe. "Let Queenie take care of you. Clean dis here filth off your pretty face."

She guided me to the slave quarters, and I knew she did so to keep me away from Marie-Louise. With an old tattered rag and a bucket of clean water she started to wash away the worst of the dirt.

"There, there now" she soothed "There's a big girl." I sobbed softly, grateful for her presence. Queenie wiped my tears away and looked into my face. "You'll be all right, chile. It only be mud."

I knew she lied, even back then. I wouldn't be all right. This was a night I would always take with me. I feared my sister more than ever. Queenie pulled me on her lap. She did not mind the dirt, and wrapped her arms around me as she had done so many times before. Softly, she sang her lullaby and rocked me back and forth:

"Mammy went 'way—she tell me to stay,
And take good care of de baby.
She tell me to stay and sing disaway.
O, go to sleep, li'l baby.

The song and the darkness made me sleepy, and I felt my eyelids droop. There was the soft hum of the crickets in the fields, and Queenie's sweet old voice took away my fears.

"Do you miss your children, Queenie?" I asked drowsily.

"Every day, Miss," Queenie said with fresh heartbreak in her voice. "Every day. But I hardly knowz dem anyhow, and I has new children now."

There was strength in her voice, and I admired her.

"I has Tom, and I has Mamie, and Isaac." She named some of the slaves that were in her quarters. "And I'z takes care of dem as if dey my own, I surely do. And dey has little ones, and I'z takes care of dem, too. Whenever life takes things away, little miss, it replaces it with other things. Dey took aways my children, but dey gave me back you."

She smiled at me, and I smiled back, the tears still salty in the corners of my filthy eyes. There were curious faces all around us, children and adults looking at Queenie and me, but none dared come closer. I didn't mind. I felt at peace being rocked and sung to. But my peace was suddenly interrupted when my father stormed into the shabby little hut. Two of the large white slave drivers followed him.

"Where is my daughter?" he bellowed, and cracked a whip at any slave that got in his way. "Where is she?" The children screamed and ran from the great white ogres. He spotted me on Queenie's lap, and something came over him. He ran over and snatched me from her arms.

"How dare you?" He let the whip loose on the old black woman. "How dare you touch my child?"

"Please, Father," I yelled. I struggled in the grip of Father's left arm while his right wielded the whip. "Father, no! Queenie was only trying to help!"

But he did not respond to my cries. His arm was so strong that I thought he would squeeze the breath out of me. With a thrust he handed the whip to Boss Otis who, in turn, continued the whipping. Father took me home then, and I cried and struggled, but all to no avail. The guilt I felt for Queenie's punishment overwhelmed me.

Boss Otis punished Queenie severely for that night, and it took at least a week before she could walk and work again. In the house, no one spoke of the incident, and Marie-Louise carried on as if nothing had happened. I hated her for it, but I feared her, too.

About a month after the incident, I woke because I heard something stir outside of my bedroom. Carefully, I slipped from my bed and investigated the noise. To my surprise, I found Marie-Louise out and about. She walked as quietly as a thief through the hall and down the stairs. My curiosity piqued, I decided to follow her. The night was chilly. Autumn was fading into winter and the ground felt cold to my naked feet. I wrapped my arms around myself, rubbed my skin, and looked around.

In the distance, I saw a white shadow near the slaves' quarters. I followed, and found Marie-Louise crouched down behind a building. She peered into one of the shacks through a gap in the wooden slats. Fear rose in my throat as I neared my sister. The incident in the pigpen was still fresh in my mind. But, I was too curious to step away. Soft light illuminated the inside of the quarters and I could hear singing. It wasn't the sort of singing I'd ever heard before. The language was unfamiliar and so was the music.

I kept my distance from Marie-Louise and peeked through one of the cracks. Inside, some of the slaves had taken off their clothes and undergarments and were painted with something red. Their bodies writhed in a strange dance and one slave, who I recognized as Maisy, was holding up a little doll.

I wanted to get away then, afraid I would cause more trouble for the slaves, and took a few clumsy steps backward. My foot hit a twig and it snapped, which startled Marie-Louise, who cried out. Inside, the singing stopped. I heard the sounds of people running. Dark shapes fled the hut and ducked into others. My sister rose, furious, and she charged at me again.

"Why must you always spoil everything?" She slapped me with so much force that my teeth rattled. Then she lifted her night gown above her ankles and stormed off.

I stared after her, my hand on my cheek, and then I was startled myself by a nearby movement. I turned to see Maisy, fully dressed, as she skulked off.

"Maisy." The slave girl froze in her steps like a deer caught by a hunter.

"Please, Miss," Maisy said, her voice no more than a whimper.

"I won't hurt you, Maisy." I walked toward the girl. "And I won't tell anyone what I saw." I glanced at the little cloth doll in Maisy's hand. "What's that?"

Maisy hid the doll behind her back. "Nothing, Miss," she said forlornly. "Nothing but a little token to ward off evil, Miss."

"May I see it?" I knew it was unkind to ask her, but I was curious about what I'd seen, and I held out my hand. The slave reluctantly handed over the little white doll.

"It's funny." I examined the doll. "Is that my sister's ribbon around it?" An anxious nod answered. "Why would you ...?" I started to ask, but then I understood. It wasn't an evil spirit the slaves were trying to ward off; it was an evil person. *A very wicked girl.* A part of me wanted to scold her, to tell Maisy this was nonsense, but I couldn't.

The slaves had nothing to protect themselves from Marie-Louise's wrath ... nothing but this little cloth doll. I handed it back to Maisy.

"I won't tell," I said again, and then I ran off, back to my big house and my big bed, while tears ran down my cheeks. *She is a wicked, wicked girl.*

After the incident, Marie-Louise ignored me for a fortnight. She did not even grant me a single glance until one night, when she came into my room, and shook me awake.

I thought she was going to hurt me again, but there was something else in her face, a look of excitement.

"Why did you wake me?"

"Alice O'Connell told me that if you stand in front of a mirror on All Hallows' Eve, you will see your future husband." Marie-Louise tittered.

I had no idea what All Hallows' Eve was, and Marie-Louise seemed to know that, so she added: "All Hallows' Eve is some sort of Irish tradition that she learned from her father. Tomorrow night is All Hallows' Eve, so tomorrow night you and I will stand in front of your mother's mirror, and we will see who we are going to marry."

I didn't want to stand in front of that mirror, especially with Marie-Louise, but I was too afraid to vex her again. Instead of arguing, I just nodded and smiled the best I could.

"Tomorrow night, then," Marie-Louise said happily.

"Tomorrow night," I echoed.

The rest of the night, I did not sleep a wink for fear of the morning. All day I felt a lump in my stomach, and I told myself I was silly, *what could an old mirror do to me?* I remembered the face I thought I saw in that mirror the last time I looked into it, but brushed it off as my own overwrought imagination.

The fatigue from lack of sleep wore off when we arrived at the O'Connell plantation the next day. The O'Connell family decorated their house with carved pumpkins, some of which had impish smiles that leered at me, but there were some that looked so wicked, they made my stomach turn. The pumpkins were to ward off evil spirits, Alice assured me, and that made me feel a little better.

All day we played, just the three of us. Marie-Louise was kind to me for once, and I enjoyed the attention of the two bigger girls. We sang songs and told tales, and I don't remember if I was ever happier. Alice knew a lot of All Hallows' tales, and she told us the tale of Jack, who outwitted the devil three times, and was thus banned from both heaven and hell. Jack was cursed to wander the world for eternity with nothing but a light in a hollowed out turnip to guide his way. The story intrigued me, and I was an instant fan of the Irish tradition.

"It is to this man, Jack, that the hollowed-out pumpkins with the lights are an homage," Alice said wisely, with a face more serious than her thirteen years of age.

"Why do you carve pumpkins if he kept his light in a turnip?" I asked.

Alice looked at me for a moment, and thought, then she answered. "Because there are more pumpkins here, and they are easier to carve, I should think." She shrugged, and then pushed me over and ran away laughing.

My good mood faded when day turned to evening and the two older girls convinced father to let Alice stay at Bellefleur plantation for the night. The girls were intent to see their husbands in the dragon mirror. I secretly hoped they would forget about me, but they didn't. To my dismay, the two giggling girls stood by my bed that night, holding candles.

"Come on, sleepy head," Alice chirped with her thick Irish accent. "Let's go see if yer husband has a nose like a wee bonny pig."

Another round of giggles let loose and I got to my feet. We snuck off to Marie-Louise's dressing room while we held candles in our trembling hands. The flickering candlelight made the dark room eerie, and the mirrors in the dressing room reflected the small flames to infinity. It was Alice who stepped up first to the mirror. A giggle escaped her lips before she composed her face and chanted.

"Mirror, mirror, let me see, what bonny gent is meant for me."

We peeped over her shoulders, I stood on my tippy-toes to see.

"I see him, I see him," Alice cried with excitement.

"Where?" we asked in unison. I couldn't see anything but our reflections and candles.

"There." Alice pointed, and then added with a mock sadness, "Aw he's gone now ... such a pity you couldn't see him. He was very handsome. He looked a bit like John McKinna." Her face twisted in a mischievous smirk.

"Liar," Marie-Louise said vehemently. She was about to argue with the little Irish girl, but changed her mind. She pushed Alice aside. "My turn."

"Mirror, mirror, let me see, what bonny gent is meant for me."

There was a darkness in her voice that sent chills down my spine, and a gust of wind appeared out of nowhere. It extinguished several candles. I swallowed a scream and shuddered. Alice wrapped her arms around me. The room went darker and the few remaining lights gave the mirror a spooky glow.

We saw Marie-Louise and our own frightened reflections, but there was something else in the mirror, something that moved, swirled. It was dark and it moved around Marie-Louise's reflection, and then formed into a shape. I could see a tall, dark man. His skin was black— not a dark brown-black or bluish-black like the slaves. His skin was pure black like that of a starless night.

The eyes in the angular face were red. His smile revealed sharp fangs. Alice screamed and fainted. I tried to hold her body up, but she was too heavy. I could not stop trembling. The thing in the mirror reached out a hand to Marie-Louise. My stepsister slowly extended her own white hand, and was about to touch the shadowy fingers when someone pushed her out of the way. A chair hit the mirror and shattered the glass. Marie-Louise screamed bloody murder. I turned to see Queenie standing in the room with us, her chest heaving, her dark face flustered.

"Silly chile," she chided Marie-Louise bravely. "Silly chile messing with mirrors and demons. You stay away from dat now, ya hear?"

For a moment, Marie-Louise looked like a stricken child. Then she continued screaming. Her scream was so loud and so full of anger that it frightened Queenie, and the old woman ran from the room as if the devil himself were chasing her.

It took a while for Marie-Louise to get up. I half expected my father to come in at any moment, but he didn't. To my surprise, I saw Marie-Louise pick up the golden frame lined with long sharp shards, and run after the slave. I don't know what possessed me, but I ran after her. I followed her to the slave quarters, where she headed to Queenie's house.

"You broke my mirror."

"Marie-Louise," I said, but the fear made my voice soft and weak.

"You will mend this mirror!" Marie-Louise threw the frame in the center of the room.

The shards of glass tinkled with a soft melody. The other slaves, about five of them, most of them young children, were huddled in a corner, and looked at her in fear. Something evil was in that house with us. I could feel it, and so could they. Queenie stood to the side looking at her mistress defiantly. I don't know what it was about the old woman, but I could see my sister's temper start to boil. It was like that night at the pigpen, only worse.

"How would you like it if I break something of yours?" Marie-Louise screamed as she wrenched free one of the shards. Blood dripped down her fingers. With a fury and a strength that was fit for a devil, she jumped upon the huddled group of slaves, slashing out at all of them. I could hear them scream, and saw nothing but a flurry of movement and a mist of red. There was so much blood I felt queasy, and I screamed for it to stop. I wanted to run, but my legs refused to carry me.

Queenie tried to grab hold of Marie-Louise, but the girl was strong, too strong. I saw her swat the old woman away as if she weighed nothing.

When the slaves stopped struggling, Marie-Louise got back to her feet. She looked a fright. Her white night gown, pale skin, and honey-blonde hair were covered in blood. Most of it was the blood of the injured slaves, but I suspect some of it was her own. She dropped the shard of glass in front of Queenie's feet. The two women stared at each other, each filled with loathing that was almost palpable. I sobbed.

"Mirror Mary," Queenie hissed. She looked possessed, and I was suddenly frightened of her too. "You know who ya is? You is a demon chile, a bloody chile. Your name should be Bloody Mary." Insanity must have taken over as Queenie grabbed one of the other shards on the ground.

"Be with your mirror demons," Queenie roared. "I will send you to your mirrored grave."

She leapt at my sister, shard in front of her like a dagger. The point of the shard caught Marie-Louise in the throat and she gurgled. I tried to scream, but no sound came out of my throat. The sight numbed me.

Something happened to the shard and Queenie dropped it with a shriek. She waved her hand and blew on it. Marie-Louise tried to remain upright as streams of blood escaped her lips. Smoke rose thick and black, engulfing my wicked stepsister. Her gray eyes were bloodshot. I thought she would speak, but she disappeared in the thick black cloud. There was a sound as loud as thunder, and then the smoke vanished, taking Marie-Louise with it.

Queenie fell to her knees and wept. I wanted to comfort her, but I couldn't. Sounds came from all directions. Men ran into the shack. Two of them dragged Queenie away. She didn't protest; her eyes were empty. The injured slaves were also carried out. Later, I found out that two of the slaves died of their injuries. I was carried home too, and the last thing I noticed was the dragon mirror. It was whole again.

Three days later, they hanged Queenie.

I never saw Alice again, and I never heard any stories of that night from her or her family. No one believed me when I told them the mirror swallowed Marie-Louise. A story was fabricated to explain her death. According to the story, Marie-Louise fell down a well and drowned. No one outside of the family knew that stones were buried in my sister's coffin, that her body was never found.

The slaves that survived that dreadful night were sold to other masters. It was as if the incident never happened, just like the death of my mother never happened. We were silent about it, always silent. Perhaps the Bellefleur family believed their own lies.

The dragon mirror was placed back in the dressing room. It horrified me to see it there. None of the servants had any idea who gave the order to put it back, but no one dared come near it. The family didn't speak of it, but the servants did. They whispered behind their hands. Those who were very superstitious left the Bellefleur plantation altogether.

I made the mistake of looking in that mirror once. It was years after the incident, and I, by then, believed the Bellefleur lie, too. But when I got close, I saw my sister covered in blood, the same way she looked moments before she died. The sight of her made my skin crawl, and I gasped for breath. *This isn't happening,* I thought, *this can't be real.*

"Call my name, sister," an eerie voice whispered. "Call me."

A name popped into my head. I could almost hear Queenie say it.

"Bloody Mary," I muttered as if I were in a trance.

"Again, say it again," the voice urged.

"Bloody Mary," I replied obediently.

"Once more." There was a hunger in the bloodshot eyes, and something snapped me out of my trance. I screamed and ran from the room. It took me little effort to find some willing servants to help me cover the dragon mirror and bring it to the attic. There it will remain as long as I live.

A month later, all our other mirrors followed suit. My stepmother complained that she saw Marie-Louise stare at her from their reflections. She died soon after, from the same disease that struck the other Bellefleur brides. The mirrors were never returned.

I am an old woman now, but I still fear mirrors. Each time I see a reflection, I'm afraid my blood-covered sister will look back at me with those cold, dead eyes.

Sophie Bellefleur sighed. *I'm getting old.* She held a white sheet in her gnarled hands and placed it over the mirror hidden away in her attic. She patted it gently, awash in memories, then turned her back and sat at a small desk to finish her letter.

> *This mirror is the curse of my family, and I believe that we should bear it with dignity. Let this letter be a warning to all those who will guard it after I die. I have taught my children to fear the Dragon Mirror, and I hope they will teach theirs.*
>
> *Sophie Bellefleur*

Thirteen-year-old Melanie stood on the foldout stairs that led to the attic. She hated this place; it was dark and dusty and filled with her great-grandmother's old furniture, immobile ghosts lined up in a row.

"Come on, move." The voice below her belonged to fourteen-year-old Katie, her best friend and companion in mischief. It was Katie's idea to go to the attic to find the fabled magic mirror of Melanie's great-great grandmother.

With a slowness born of fear and caution, Melanie crawled onto the wooden floor. Dust particles flew around like tiny fairies and tickled her nose. Her hand trembled slightly when she turned on the light, and her heart felt tight with disappointment when she saw how little it truly illuminated. The light made the attic look more sinister by creating new, elongated shadows that led to dark, foreboding corners. Behind her, she heard Katie crawl into the attic. She turned in time to see her friend rub the dust off her knees.

"So this mirror, it's the original 'Bloody Mary' mirror?"

Melanie shrugged. "You read Sophie Bellefleur's letter." She waved the piece of paper with the neat handwriting. "She was my great

129

great-grandmother. Mom says they always kept the mirror, but no one ever dared to hang it in the house. It's a valuable heirloom, but it creeps out the family a bit."

Katie laughed, her voice shrill and unkind, and Melanie regretted telling her friend about the mirror. *That's my reward for bragging,* she thought. Katie always had such exciting stories, and when Melanie found Sophie Bellefleur's letter in her mother's belongings, she just had to share it with her friend. The legend of Bloody Mary could be traced back to her family, and that was too much for a thirteen-year-old girl to keep to herself.

"So where is this mirror?" Katie walked across the attic without any sign of fear.

Melanie looked around and pointed. With long strides, her friend approached a mountain of dusty white sheets and pulled them off.

There, on what looked to be an easel, stood a large mirror. It was a thing of beauty, with the two dragons sculpted in incredible detail. The sight of the thing made Melanie's skin break out in gooseflesh. The glass was still perfect, as if the mirror were brand new.

"You want to call her? Or should I?" Katie said.

For a moment Melanie thought she saw something move across the mirror's face, but she must have imagined it. *It's just a mirror.*

"I don't think we have to call her." Melanie wiped her nose with the back of her finger. She tried to sound calm, but her stomach did flip flops.

"Oh, come on." Katie gave her a small shove. "You can't have the mirror of Bloody Mary and not call her. I'll do it." Katie stood in front of the mirror, her face serious now.

"Katie, don't." Melanie felt a real sense of fear.

"Bloody Mary." There was a wicked smile on Katie's face.

Something in the mirror stirred. Melanie shivered and rubbed her arms.

"Bloody Mary."

"Katie, stop, or I'm going downstairs," Melanie threatened.

She pulled on her friend's shoulder. Katie spun around.

Melanie screamed.

Katie's dark brown eyes were covered by a milky skin. Her face looked thin and worn, haggard. There was an expression of absolute terror on Katie's young features.

"Katie?" Melanie whimpered. She watched in horror as her friend's lips moved.

"Bloody Mary."

THE NEXT KING

BY PATRICK DERRICKSON

Kelven Berhommer paced the heavily guarded camp. The sun had started its slow descent, dipping below the high stone wall that protected the Western Army's headquarters. The four Great Generals were meeting that night to pick Alludra's next king. As the most tenured general, Tomas of the West held the honor of hosting the conclave that chose the next monarch.

"We need more light over there!" Kelven snapped, pointing to a shadowy corner near the gate. "And why aren't those banners up?" The two soldiers following Kelven struggled to keep pace.

Kelven's patience was wearing thin. He had instructed the camp's servants to finish these menial tasks, but now had to use his own troops. Someone would need to pay for the disobedience. As the two soldiers hurried to complete the tasks, Kelven headed back to his small, one-room barrack. He needed to prepare as well.

He had just finished dressing when the watch announced the approach of the generals. Kelven hurried to inspect the honor guard before the guests arrived inside the compound. He saw movement at the bottom of the hill where a path of yellow torchlight guided the travelers to the main gate. Shadows flickered where the light barely reached.

Red and ocean-blue banners, swaying in a gentle breeze, decorated the walls and guard towers. The tang of the nearby sea hung in the air. Kelven greeted the generals while servants corralled their horses.

"Gentlemen!"

The men turned toward the speaker. More than one hand flicked to a sword hilt as Tomas approached, stepping from the shadows cast by the largest dwelling in the compound. Kelven saluted.

A blue silk tunic clung to Tomas's muscular frame. His black hair, neatly cropped, crowned the manicured beard that outlined his angular jaw. Tomas exuded confidence, power, and control. Kelven envied Tomas. One day, he would command such respect.

"Welcome, my brothers-in-arms. Tonight we feast, then choose our new king!" Even though Tomas grinned, Kelven noticed the other generals stood stiff and wary.

With a closed fist, Tomas covered his heart and cried, "For the Glory of Alludra!" The others mirrored his salute.

"Gregor of the North, welcome to the West." Gregor was a brute of a man, with wild black hair and rugged looks that bespoke the mountains he called home. His beard, unkempt even on this solemn occasion, was matted and gray with dust. His piercing blue eyes unsettled most men.

"Tomas," he growled.

Tomas moved down the line. Jory, from the South, was a thin, wiry man with shrewd eyes. His thin lips curled into a sneer. "Brother Tomas."

Tomas smiled, but there was no humor in his eyes.

Finally, Tomas reached Bron of the East. Kelven suppressed a grin. Bron was his father. As his only son, Kelven continued the proud military legacy of their family. From an early age, Bron instructed his son in his military training. A natural soldier, Kelven excelled at swordsmanship and strategy.

Although only twenty-two, he had quickly moved up the ranks under Tomas. Military life was a natural fit. Honor, loyalty, and order—Kelven thrived in the soldier's life. Besting a veteran soldier in a practice fight, he had caught General Tomas's eye. Impressed with Kelven's knowledge of military protocol, Tomas had promoted Kelven to second in command of the Western Army.

Kelven almost lost his composure when Tomas said, "Bron! The months have been kind indeed." Tomas's eyes grew wide as he took in Bron's midsection. Bron bellowed a laugh, and shook a meaty fist.

Of average height, Bron's girth was easily twice that of Tomas's. With the strength of two men, he wielded a double-bladed battle-ax one-handed with the ease of a rapier. A jovial man, laughter was always on his lips and humor in his eyes. Make him angry, though, and the last thing you would see would be a wicked, twenty-four-inch blade coming toward your face.

Of all the candidates, Bron was the clear choice. Easygoing and fair, his army loved him without reservation. Surrounding himself with strong leaders, his army had never suffered a defeat in battle.

"Come," Tomas said. "Let us eat and drink, and then decide the future of our kingdom." Kelven stepped aside. Tomas disappeared into the brightly lit doorway of his house. Bron followed immediately, but Gregor and Jory hesitated.

Leaning toward Gregor, Jory whispered, "Watch your back."

Kelven heard the exchange, and glanced at the two generals. He stood at attention until the men passed. Kelven nodded his head, and the sentries assumed their positions outside the house. Once inside, Kelven made his way toward the large dining room, located in the middle of the large building.

An oval table surrounded by chairs covered in plush cushions sat in the center of the sprawling room. Fruits from various parts of the kingdom were spread across the table. A handful of servants stood to the side, waiting to be beckoned. The aromas of spiced and roasted meat made Kelven's mouth water as he made his way to his post behind Tomas. The generals laughed when they heard Bron's stomach rumble.

"Gentleman, before we feast, please, refresh yourselves." With a wave from Tomas, the servants set pitchers of warm water and basins before the men. The generals washed the dust, accumulated from their long journey, from their hands and faces. Soft towels, warmed by firestones, were handed to each of them.

Once they finished, Tomas gestured for them to sit. Servants brought out large platters of freshly roasted meat and vegetables. Some held pitchers of water and wine, awaiting the guest's preference before serving.

Tomas raised his cup. "To King Juvian, may his soul find eternal rest." Tomas took a long sip. Kelven noticed the others did not share in the toast. His stomach tightened to see such blatant disrespect for their host. His gaze bore into Bron.

"Is there something wrong with my toast, brothers? Did you care so little for out late King?" Tomas asked.

Bron took a breath as if to speak, but just sighed. Tomas raised an eyebrow.

"Ah, I see. Gentlemen, I would not have invited you to my table to poison you. Tonight, I am not offended by your slight. Each of you, please choose from any dish or drink in front of you, and I will sample it."

Gregor moved first, reaching for the roasted pheasant. He tore off a leg, and handed it to Tomas, who took a huge bite. Warm juices dripped down Tomas's chin. He chewed slowly, looking at each of the generals. Wiping his mouth and hands, he asked, "Who is next?"

Jory selected pitchers of water and wine, and combined the two liquids in a goblet. He lifted his chin, his lips curling into a slight grin, and offered it to Tomas.

"With my blessing, oh brother," Jory said.

Shaking his head, Tomas took the goblet and downed the contents.

"And you, Bron? What would you have me sample?"

Bron contemplated the platters before him. He chose some roasted vegetables and an apple, handing them to Tomas. "I apologize, Tomas, but there is much at stake."

Tomas tasted the proffered food and smiled. "Do not concern yourself with this, Bron. It seems to be a common theme tonight. You wouldn't want to be the only one not participating in this foolery, right?"

His face red, Bron started to rise when Tomas placed a hand on his arm.

"Now, gentlemen, let us eat. Bron, your rumbling stomach is starting to shake the floor." Bron laughed, a smile creasing his broad face as he sat back down. He grabbed from the various platters. The other generals joined in, though more reservedly. Kelven's shoulders relaxed, his own tension dissipating.

"Where's the bread?" Gregor asked, scanning the table. Piles of venison and vegetables filled his plate.

Bron laughed. "Tomas doesn't eat bread. Never has for as long as I've known him"

Tomas raised his hands. "My apology if you feel the banquet is inadequate."

Gregor grumbled, but continued eating.

Kelven noticed Tomas made an effort to select from each platter. Light conversation about troop details and the kingdom's morale continued during the meal. Once everyone had their fill, the servants cleared the table and disappeared from the room. Only the generals and Kelven remained.

"And now, to the point of this meeting." Tomas looked at the faces around the table. "Is there anyone who does not want to be king?" The generals glanced at each other.

"I do not wish to be king," Gregor said. "I am comfortable in the North, surrounded by the snow and mountains." He eyed the other men.

Shrugging his shoulders, Tomas asked, "Anyone else?"

Jory laughed, and all eyes turned toward him. "I do not wish *you* to be king, Tomas. Can I choose that option?" He looked around at the taut faces. "I don't trust you. None of us do."

Bron squirmed in his seat, but offered no rebuttal. Kelven clenched his fists, swallowing the anger that threatened to cause him to pull his sword and gut the man that dishonored his general.

Tomas smirked. "And you would be the next great king, Jory?" he said in a low voice.

Jory looked hard at Tomas. "I would not *assume* to be a great king. But I would be a better king than you."

Tomas snorted and turned to Bron. "Bron, you are unusually quiet. What say you?"

Bron locked his fingers together and sighed. "You and I go back a long time, Tomas. My son is your second. I trust you with his life." His eyes bore into Tomas. "And yet, you are ambitious. You always have been. We all question if Alludra can withstand your ambition."

Kelven looked at his father in disbelief. Tomas and his father had fought together, had saved each other's lives countless times. That one sentence had betrayed their entire friendship.

Tomas glanced at each man. "Well, gentlemen, this was not unexpected. However, there were some surprises." His gazed rested on Bron. "Our goal here is to select our next king. Someone with the strength, wisdom, *and* ambition to lead our kingdom, to protect Alludra from the barbarian hordes at our borders. A king that allows the kingdom to prosper!"

Jory sniffed. "And you are such a man? You would have us expand our borders into the burial sites of the barbarians, inciting a war! Does that show wisdom? Does one show strength by swinging a sword, or knowing when to keep it sheathed?"

"Jory, you know those burial sites border some of the most fertile land in the valley," Tomas said. "And the barbarians haven't been above reproach. Just two months ago, we found signs of their tracks in our lands."

"Do we stay within our borders? How many scouting parties do we send out each month?" Jory said.

"I don't want another war," Gregor interjected, crossing his arms. "The towns in the north still haven't recovered."

Kelven recalled his father's account of that summer campaign twenty years ago. With so many young lives lost, the populace had shrunk by a third. Minerals critical to the kingdom could not be mined and shipped to the lower towns. King Juvian had paid a stipend to induce people to move north. But even silver could not attract enough people to replace the lives lost.

"Without the information those scouting parties provide, we won't know what the barbarians are up to. They *know* we're there. It's a deterrent from raiding the border towns." Kelven had been present during some heated battles over this same subject between Tomas and Jory.

"Gentlemen," Bron said. "Let's not rehash old arguments. King Juvian agreed with our current strategy. Those decrees remain in place until rescinded by a new monarch. What we need to determine here, right now, is who will be our next king."

Tomas stood. "I call for a vote. Besides Gregor, is there anyone else who does not wish to be king?"

When no answer came, Tomas nodded. "So be it. I nominate myself for king."

Rising, Bron said, "I nominate myself for king."

Kelven was torn between his loyalty to his general and his love for his father. However, if Tomas were selected king, Kelven would assume command of the Western Army. He had worked his entire life to lead an army. To be like his father.

Jory slowly rose, pursing his lips. "I nominate Bron."

Kelven could not hold back his gasp this time. He had expected Jory to nominate himself. Tomas shrugged, looking toward Gregor.

"Well, Gregor, it comes down to you. If you don't want to be the next king, whom do you select?"

Gregor cocked his head to the side, sighing. "I nominate Bron as the next king."

Kelven found it hard to focus. His father, the next king! Kelven should be happy for him, but disappointment flooded his body. He had been so close to commanding the Western Army. He breathed deeply to calm his nerves.

"Well, gentlemen, I guess that's settled. I am disappointed you all think so little of me." Tomas stepped in front of Bron, and gripped his forearm. "Hail Bron, the next King of Alludra. May your reign be long, wise, and prosperous." Bron nodded, lips pressed together.

Tomas raised his goblet. "To Bron Berhommer, the next King of Alludra!"

Draining it, Tomas tossed the goblet on the table. "Gentlemen, I'll take my leave now. Please feel free to eat and drink as you wish."

Tomas turned to Kelven.

"Please see to the generals' retinue. Announce the decision tonight to the men, and then have the signal fires lit to spread the news."

"Yes, sir."

Tomas's face softened. "Enjoy some time with your father, and report to me in the morning."

"Yes, sir," Kelven replied. He didn't feel like celebrating.

When Tomas left, Kelven walked up to the generals. Jory smiled. Gregor just grunted. Bron embraced him quickly. "Kelven, you accounted yourself well tonight. We'll talk later."

Bron turned to face the other men. "I need to get back to start the preparations. Stay if you wish."

Jory shook his head. "Kelven, get our horses ready. I don't want to spend another moment here."

Kelven saluted the generals, and within minutes, they were gone. He spoke with the watch commander before leaving. He needed sleep. The meeting with Tomas in the morning would not be pleasant.

Two days later, Jory held a meeting with his senior staff. While eating, they reviewed the camp's provision status. The aroma of fresh baked goods and pungent cheese filled the room.

"Commander Fray, what are the levels of our winter stores?" Jory asked. He popped a warm, buttered biscuit into his mouth.

"Sir, some of the stores are near their ideal levels. The root vegetables from the North are at maximum. The wine and ale supply will be at capacity with the shipment due next week. Our local crops and cattle ranges are at sufficient levels. However, we are still short grain from the Western farms. We have enough supplies for four months. Unless we receive additional shipments, we will need to start rationing."

"What does rationing get us?"

"Bread only, served once a day. We can get by, but it is not ideal."

Jory took a deep breath and sighed. Tomas was showing his true colors again. This was the third time this year grain shipments had been late. With no king officially on the throne, Jory couldn't escalate this issue. Complaining to Bron would only show weakness. With Bron's son Kelven ready to assume command of an army, Jory needed to tread carefully. He didn't want to give Bron any ideas that the current generals needed replacing.

"Commander, get some riders together to deliver a message to General Tomas. They'll need to leave tonight."

"Yes, sir."

Jory's stomach churned. He took a sip of spiced wine to cover the bitter taste in his mouth. A sharp pain pierced his chest. He sprayed the half-swallowed wine on the table, dousing the reports. He gripped the chair, his knuckles turning white. Men rushed toward him, while Fray called for a healer.

"General, what's wrong?" a man cried.

Jory tried to speak, to breathe, but the pressure in his chest was unbearable.

The soldiers heard a loud pop, and blood shot from Jory's mouth. The white of his eyes turned red. With a gasp, he slumped into his chair. Blank eyes stared back at the shaken men.

The healer arrived, shoving the men aside. "Move, you idiots!"

The healer grabbed Jory's head, moving it from side to side. Placing one hand on the general's chest, the healer raised her holy symbol, shaped like an oak leaf, in the other. Her voice rose and fell as she chanted to her God. After a few moments, she collapsed to the floor, unconscious.

The men stared in shock. She had never failed to heal before.

Fray peered at the blood dribbling down Jory's chin.

"Poison! He's been poisoned!" Fray pointed to silver streaking through the bright red blood staining Jory's shirt.

Commander Fray turned his head toward the soldiers. "Send riders to the other generals. Tell them General Jory is dead."

Gregor followed the tight, winding trail up the mountain. The cool wind whipped through his beard, whisking away the sweat from his three-hour climb. Raising his hand, Gregor stopped the group for a short rest. Some bent over, catching their breath. Others leaned against the mountain, drinking from water skins.

Gregor was in his element. Born on this mountain, he grew up exploring every crevice. The tallest mountain on the southern range offered the perfect view of the plains of Alludra. One could see for miles. It also held a signal pyre.

Once a year, Gregor would visit each of the signal pyres. It gave him a chance to check on the soldiers so far away from the main army. But getting to hike up the rugged mountains several times each year was the true reason for his tours. One day, he would retire here. Maybe even take a wife, have a family.

Looking at the sun, Gregor realized he only had a few hours of light left. He didn't want to be on the trail when darkness came. While he would not have an issue following the trail in the dark, his soldiers would find it difficult. He nibbled on a travel biscuit. Noting its bitter taste, he tossed it over the side of the trail. Gregor took a swig of water, and ordered the troops to continue their ascent.

Within a few steps, Gregor staggered, suddenly dizzy. The bitter taste was stronger now, and he struggled to breathe. His chest felt as if it was squeezed in a vice. The soldier next to him noticed he'd stumbled, and moved to steady him. Reaching out, Gregor gripped the soldier's outstretched arm. He licked his lips, the metallic taste of blood in his mouth. Catching his foot on a rock, he lurched toward the edge of the trail. Gregor heard muffled shouts, but couldn't focus. The sky spun.

Then he was flying.

The wind whipped through his hair. He saw the snowcapped mountains above him recede until he slammed into the side of the mountain.

Tomas was inspecting his troops when a cry from the guard tower alerted the camp to approaching riders. Grim-faced soldiers wearing uniforms from the Southern Army dismounted and approached him. Kelven put his hand on his sword. Something was wrong.

One of the soldiers saluted. "General Tomas."

"Yes, soldier?"

"We come bearing grave news. General Jory collapsed two nights ago. He's dead."

"What? Don't you have a healer in camp? Couldn't she save him?"

"The healer said General Jory was poisoned, and it was too late to save him. The poison moved swiftly." Kelven stiffened. Poisoning was a coward's way to kill a man.

"Who is in charge now?" Tomas asked.

"Commander Fray, General Jory's second, has assumed command of the Southern Army." The soldier's voice cracked. "We have sent riders to King-Elect Bron as well." He looked tired and worn.

"I am sorry for your loss. General Jory was a fine leader." Tomas studied the soldier's face. "Is there anything else?"

"Yes, sir." The soldier's hesitation irritated Kelven.

"Well, out with it!"

"Sir, Commander Fray would like to know when the shipment of grain will be sent to the Southern Army."

Tomas threw him a scornful look. "Your general is dead, murdered it seems, and your commander wants to know when his grain shipment is coming?"

"Yes, sir," the soldier whispered.

Tomas shook his head. He motioned to some servants. "Care for the horses and get these men food and drink." Turning back to the Kelven, he motioned for him to follow.

As soon as they entered Tomas's house, Kelven said, "Sir, what do you make of this?"

"Well, we all have our enemies. Jory was well liked though." Leaning against the table, Tomas crossed his arms.

Kelven clenched his fists. "I'll double the guard around the camp perimeter, and tell the men to report anything unusual to their captains. We'll question anyone who hasn't been in camp more than three months."

When Tomas nodded, Kelven turned to leave.

"Kelven, your father can take care of himself."

"Yes, sir, I know." Kelven tried to keep a blank face.

"Let's make sure nothing happens here."

"Aye, sir," Kelven replied, and hurried to carry out his orders. He went to talk with the soldiers from the Southern Army.

They weren't much help. They hadn't been present when Jory died, and only overheard bits of conversation from the healer. Jory had grabbed his chest and collapsed. The healer saw silver in his blood, and concluded he had been poisoned. Kelven left to find his captains.

While discussing the camp's guard rotation, sentries announced the arrival of more riders. Soldiers from the Northern Army reined in exhausted horses.

Tomas greeted the soldiers, who bore shocking news. While climbing, Gregor had fallen over the mountain trail to his death. Uneasiness swept over Kelven. Gregor wouldn't have just fallen off a mountain; his mountain skills were legendary.

Concerned, Kelven appointed a contingent of his most trusted troops to guard Tomas. News of the deaths flew around camp, putting everyone on edge. Kelven made his way to the barracks housing the messengers. He needed more information.

The group of men looked wretched. Kelven would have felt the same if Tomas had died. He sat at the table, shadows dancing on the soldier's faces from the candlelight. Light and shadow. Life and death.

One of the Northern soldiers uttered something to his counterpart from the Southern Army. When Kelven glanced at him, the man chuckled and looked away.

"What's so funny?"

"Why, nothing Commander."

Kelven stepped forward and lowered his voice. "This will be the last time I ask you, soldier. What is so funny?"

The soldier sniffed. "We thought it curious that our beloved generals are dead, and yet the general most disliked seems unaffected."

Kelven backhanded the man out of his chair. Shouting, the other men stood and reached for their swords. Before their hands touched the hilts, Kelven had his sword out and pressed into the soldier's chest.

"One should be careful with words. They can be as sharp as a sword. And just as deadly."

The other soldiers backed away, leaving their trembling comrade alone. Kelven lifted the man's chin with the point of his sword.

"Now, soldier, tell me what you know about General Gregor's death."

The soldier did not provide any new information. Gregor's death seemed to be accidental, but he had grabbed his chest before falling off the mountain. Could Gregor have been poisoned as well?

Heading back to his quarters, Kelven considered the soldiers' accounts when he heard shouting from within Tomas's house. Noticing the guards missing from their posts, Kelven drew his sword and rushed inside, heart racing, fearing he was too late.

He skidded to a stop when he saw Tomas swinging his sword at Nom, his personal cook. When Nom looked at Kelven, Tomas thrust his sword through Nom's chest. The point exploded through Nom's back. Blood sprayed from his mouth, misting the air. With a gurgle, he collapsed to floor. Tomas pulled the sword free. Shocked, Kelven found his voice.

"Guards! Guards to the General's house!"

Pounding feet and the clanging of steel announced the arrival of the soldiers. Kelven rounded on them, waving his sword.

"Why weren't you at your posts? The General was attacked!"

The soldiers stared past him to the body leaking blood on the floor.

"Kelven, it's my fault," Tomas said.

Kelven spun around. "Sir?"

Tomas nodded. "I wanted to have a quiet dinner. When Nom arrived, I sent the guards away. When they left, Nom pulled a dagger and nearly gutted me."

Kelven saw the red streak on Tomas's arm. "Go get the healer!" he ordered a soldier. The man ran raced out of the room. Kelven approached Tomas, but was waved away.

"I'm fine. I fought stouter men before you could walk."

The healer arrived and pushed Tomas into a chair. Garbed in the traditional blue robes of her Order, she flipped the long braid of her hair over her shoulder. Dressing the wound, she offered a silent prayer to her God. Her holy symbol, dangling from her neck, glowed briefly. The healer's faced flushed with color.

"You'll be healed within a few minutes. Until then, keep the arm still so it mends without a scar." When Tomas nodded, she left.

"Guards, wait outside. Kelven, we need to talk."

Kelven poured them both some wine. Tomas stood, staring at him, holding his sword.

"Sir?" he asked.

"Kelven, I need to know whose side you're on."

"Side, sir?"

"Jory was poisoned. Gregor had an accident, but was probably murdered as well. Then tonight, I am attacked. I need to know if you knew your father was behind the assassinations of the generals." Tomas pointed his sword at Kelven's chest.

Kelven staggered. "Sir, I would not betray you. My father could not be behind this!"

"And yet, Jory and Gregor are dead, and I was attacked in my own house."

Kelven opened his mouth to respond, and then closed it. From Tomas's point of view, it did seem suspicious. But his father would not stoop to such cowardly acts. He had taught Kelven about honor and duty, especially to one's king.

"Why would my father want to kill you? You have known him most of your life. There has to be another explanation."

"I have known him a long time. I thought I knew him, anyway. The night of the conclave proved otherwise. You were there. You heard what he said."

Kelven remembered. It troubled him to remember how his father disrespected his general. But it made no sense. Why would his father want to kill the other generals?

"So, did you know your father would send someone to kill me?"

Kelven shook his head. "What reason would my father want to kill you, or the other generals? He is the King-Elect. Jory and Gregor voted for him."

"Kelven, who has the most to gain in my death? Who is next in line to lead this army?"

Kelven's eyes narrowed. He didn't like where this was going.

"Sir? If you died, then I would assume command until the King assigned a permanent general."

"And?" Tomas prompted.

"Then I guess I would have the most to gain if you died. But I swore an oath of honor and duty to you."

"You see, Kelven, even though Bron was elected King, the other generals still lead the armies. And if the King doesn't trust the generals, or have Alludra's best interest at heart, they can become a thorn in his side. They are also one step from the crown. By removing his chief rivals, he can appoint those he favors. You being his only son, and already second in command ..." Tomas trailed off.

"I have not forgotten my oath, sir," Kelven said.

"I believe you, Kelven. I have to think about our next steps, so please keep this between us for now."

"Yes, sir."

Tomas sheathed his sword and sat, fingering the goblet of wine. "Make sure the other messengers leave first thing in the morning. I don't want them around in case they're spies."

"Yes, sir."

"That is all for tonight. Make sure my guard is in place before you retire."

Kelven walked out into the warm night air. This had turned into the worst day of his life.

Bron slipped from his bed, trying not to wake his wife. They had entertained some of the largest landowners well into the night. He made his way into the dining area, looking for a snack. He spied a plate of pastries on a side table. Henry, his personal cook for the past twenty years, knew he liked to snack after a long night of revelry. Spotting some of his favorites, he put one in his mouth and poured himself some spiced wine. He grabbed the plate and relaxed in his chair.

King Bron. It was pleasant to the ears. He had worked hard to get to this position. The landowners in the East owed much to his leadership and protection. The fertile land provided an abundance of food, and the wine from its vineyards was the best in Alludra. He thanked the Gods he was given such an opportunity. When he was king, he would share his good fortune with the rest of the kingdom.

Thinking of Kelven, he smiled. His son had done well for himself. Granted, he'd had a great teacher, but the drive to attain his position had come from within. Just like his father. Although only twenty-two, Kelven was ready to lead a Grand Army. Bron's smile darkened when his thoughts went to Tomas. They had campaigned together over the years, moving up almost at the same time.

It became a competition between them.

When the impossible happened, and two general's appointments became available, King Juvian selected Bron and Tomas. Tomas had wanted the East region, but King Juvian told him the West would be his. He'd wanted Tomas close to him, to keep an eye on his new general.

Bron remembered how they were appointed generals nearly at the same time. Both of the generals died within days of each other. While not too old, it appeared their hearts had given out. Not unlike Jory and Gregor.

Bron frowned. In fact, both occurrences had much in common. That old, nagging feeling about Tomas was back. He would have to do something about him.

Bron finished the last of the pastry and rose to return to bed. As soon as he stood, the room swam. He gripped the table to help balance himself, but his strength left him. He collapsed, his head hitting the cold, tiled floor. White light exploded in his head. He gasped for air. Blood oozed from his eyes and ears. Through the bright pain in his head, his thoughts went to his old friend. *Tomas, what have you done?*

Bron convulsed one last time, and then lay still.

Shouts of riders approaching mustered the stronghold. Kelven raced to the entrance. When he saw the East banner, he gripped his sword to steady himself. The riders brought the gravest news of all; King-Elect Bron was dead. He had suffered a severe brain injury after a fall. Tomas gripped Kelven's shoulder.

"I'm sorry, Kelven. Your father would have made a fine king."

Kelven just nodded. He couldn't speak. His father, once suspected by Tomas, now shared the same fate as the other generals.

The heat of the sun intensified the dryness in his mouth. Colorful banners snapped in the warm salty breeze. The colors of Alludra unwavering, even under the stain of death. When he looked back to Tomas, realization set in.

"All hail King Tomas!" he cried. All those present knelt. "All hail, King Tomas!" they chanted.

When they rose, Kelven flew into action. His duty to protect Tomas replaced his shock. Addressing the troops guarding Tomas, Kelven said, "You are now the King's Honor Guard. Protect him with your lives. If something happens to him, you'll wish you'd died!"

Unable to sleep, Kelven stared at the dancing shadows on his ceiling. Tradition required the crowning of the new king on the night of the new moon. That was only eight days away.

It was customary for the large landowners and most successful merchants to welcome the new king in person. Although gaining favor with the new monarch was important, it was the deals between the upper echelons that really attracted the large crowds. With money to spend, the attendees enticed swarms of minor merchants. Controlling the influx of people created its own problem in the capital city. And it fell to Kelven to solve.

Kelven stared at the shadows dancing across his wall, thinking of his father's burial that he would miss because too many lesser affairs of state needed his attention. Collaborating with the Clerics to perform the crowning ceremony, getting the taverns in the city provisioned to welcome the influx of supporters, and assigning guard duties topped his list. All regions would be providing supplies for the celebration, which had to be recorded and distributed. Troops arrived from each army to help control the populace during the three-day event. Also needed were the appointments of the new generals to lead the four Grand Armies. Typically, the second in command would succeed, but the King could appoint anyone.

The reminder of his father's death still stung. He couldn't lose anyone else. He blinked back tears. He didn't have time to grieve, but, by the Gods, he would avenge his father. Why was his father killed? Who wanted him dead? Was Nom the mastermind of this plot? He was just a lowly cook, in service to the Western Army.

The cooking staff had been questioned extensively. A couple more harshly than others, yet nothing was found. But something nagged in the back of his head.

His stomach growled, interrupting his thoughts. Due to a late night meeting, he had missed dinner. He surveyed his room. A pot of stew sat on his table next to a bowl of fruit. Last night's dinner. It was cold, but he still ate it. He thought of his father, dunking large pieces of bread into a stew pot, while his mother smacked his hand away.

Buckling his sword and dagger, he left his room to clear his head. Walking the stronghold in the early morning calmed him. Kelven breathed in the cool, salty air. The sun was just peeking over the horizon as he checked the camp. He heard the servants preparing for the coming day and the light clang of armor as guards changed posts.

As he passed Tomas's house, a small figure detached itself from a shadow, and slunk away. Alarmed, Kelven sprinted toward the figure, drawing his dagger. He grabbed the hood and yanked backward, the blade of the dagger pressed under the person's chin. "Who are you?" he demanded.

A trembling voice replied. "Nadine."

Kelven recognized her. She had been with Nom for years. He remembered one of his captains interrogating her. She appeared shy and withdrawn, but now he wondered if that had been act.

"What were you doing behind the General's house?" he hissed.

Nadine quivered, but remained silent.

"I asked you a question!" His hand clenched, tightening the hood around her throat.

"I—I was looking for you."

"Me?"

"I know who killed your father and the other generals."

Her words rocked him.

"Please, come to the cook's quarters. It's quiet there. No one will hear us." Kelven didn't relax his hold. "Please, sir, there isn't much time."

The fear in her voice stirred his emotions. He gestured with his dagger for Nadine to move. Entering the small building, the sharp smells of fresh spices hit Kelven. Herbs hung from the ceiling beams. Several small plants in containers rested on the window sills. Metal pots were stacked neatly on the table, next to a small pile of tools used to repair them.

Nadine gestured to a seat at the table. Kelven shook his head. He preferred to stand, in case she tried something. Leaning against the table, he recalled something his father had taught him. Show a nonthreatening stance, but stay coiled like a snake, ready to strike. He gestured with his dagger for her to sit.

"Nom was my father." Tears welled in her eyes. "General Tomas recruited him to be his personal cook after eating at the inn my parents owned. When my father declined to join his army, my mother disappeared."

She sagged in the chair. Tears rolled down her cheeks, collecting on her chin, before tumbling to the bare floor. Freckles dotted her pale face. Her green eyes were wet with sorrow. Red, curly hair framed her dimpled cheeks. At a different time, he would have found her gorgeous. When he looked at her now, he saw the pitiful offspring of a murderer.

"My father was devastated. But when General Tomas told him that it would be a shame if something happened to me, he realized he didn't have a choice. But that bastard knew more about my father than he admitted." Her eyes flashed with anger. "While he had a knack for combining spices, my father's first love was alchemy. He had been apprenticed to a Master Alchemist, who sometimes delved into the darker arts. They made potions, poisons, and charms—anything, really, if you could pay for it. He made a name for himself."

Kelven felt sympathetic, but quickly shrugged it off. No matter what Tomas might have done, it did not give cause for Nom to murder his father.

"He struck out on his own, and was soon successful. However, he had a change of heart when he met my mother. They were inseparable. He no longer wanted to exploit weak-minded people. So, he took his alchemy knowledge, applied it to cooking, and opened an inn."

"Is that what you wanted to tell me? Your family history?" Kelven snarled.

"No! I wanted you to know that my father was forced to do things he wouldn't have done otherwise. He didn't have a choice!"

"He had a choice! He chose to betray those he swore to serve. It looks like his daughter his following in his footsteps." Kelven pointed his dagger at her.

"You're not listening! General Tomas didn't want my father to cook for him. He wanted my father for his alchemical ability. He had plans."

"What kind of plans?"

"General Tomas knew a little about alchemy, and provided some rare ingredients to enhance my father's work. One such item was a basilisk egg."

Kelven's eyes widened. Basilisk eggs were rare and cost a fortune. They were mostly used in poisons.

"Using the basilisk yoke, he created an untraceable poison that could be activated by a specific reagent. This poison would turn blood into liquid stone, killing the victim within seconds." She stared at Kelven. "I did not know, nor was I ever told, of his intentions of using this poison. You must believe me. Tomas killed my father, too."

Kelven struggled to breathe, gripping the table to steady himself. If what Nadine said was true, then Tomas had poisoned the other generals.

Poisoned his father.

Kelven flushed with anger. Tomas was an honorable man, a great leader, loyal to the kingdom—everything he wanted to become.

"That is a likely story. It tells me you want to shift the blame from you and your father onto the next King of Alludra. Just by its utterance, such an accusation is punishable by immediate death!"

But if what she said was true, then Tomas had killed his father, the true King of Alludra. But why? Just to become King? The other generals said he was ambitious, but murder?

For several moments, neither spoke. Nadine hung her head, sobbing. All the military training he received over the years did not prepare him for this moment. Breathing deeply, he tried to expel the rage and hurt through clenched teeth.

"If I believe you, what proof do you have? It's your word against a well-respected general and the King-Elect. You are just a serving girl whose father tried to kill General Tomas, and provided the poison that killed the others."

That killed my father.

"My father always thought Tomas would kill him one day. He hid a small amount of the poison in case of that moment."

Nadine went to the large herb cabinet and withdrew a small stone container. When she removed the lid, Kelven noticed a waxy stopper designed to keep liquid from escaping. Taking an apple from the bowl, Nadine placed it on a plate, and tipped the stone container until a clear, viscous liquid dripped out. When the poison touched the apple, nothing happened.

"Now watch." She placed a piece of crusty bread on the plate, and poured another drop. This time, when the liquid touched the bread, its color changed to silver. The bread dissolved.

Kelven's dagger fell from his hand. Clanging to the floor, it shattered the silence. He couldn't believe Tomas would kill his father, or the other generals. But here was the poison, proof that it existed, in Tomas's camp.

His eyes focused on Nadine, whose tear-streaked face now showed pity.

"You were fooled like the others," she said.

Something snapped inside Kelven, fueling the hatred he now felt for Tomas. His life no longer mattered. Nothing mattered now but to avenge his father. To kill Tomas.

Kelven remembered the times spent following his father around the Eastern Army's compound, absorbing all the interactions between the soldiers. He heard his father's voice in his heard. *Sometimes, Kelven, even the most complex problem has a simple solution. Sometimes, the simple answer is right in front of you.*

Looking at the plate, and then to Nadine, a plan formed in Kelven's mind. He thought about the consequences. Timing would be crucial; it needed to be done before Tomas left for the crowning. He had four days.

"Nadine," Kelven said. "I need your help."

She looked at him in amazement. "My help?"

"Yes. And when this is finished, you will leave this army and go back home. I never want to see your face again."

She nodded. "Anything."

The next couple of days flew by. Overseeing the transfer of power of the other armies to their second in command and finalizing Tomas's move to the capital city took most of Kelven's waking hours. Supervising the day-to-day operation of the Western Army proved the easiest. He was certain to be named general once Tomas left for the Capital. Kelven was so well liked among the officers, each wanted to prove worthy to be his second in command.

Kelven dragged himself to his quarters, hoping to sleep. He unbuckled his sword belt and flopped on his bed, still in his clothes. Something crinkled under him. Rolling over, he saw a folded note partially tucked under his blanket. He broke the seal and flipped it open.

He took a deep breath and read the note. Only three words. But three powerful words that would change his life forever. *It is ready.*

Kelven rose and poured himself some wine. He read the note again. He touched the note to the candle's flame, setting it on fire. It flared brightly, shriveled, its ashes floating away in the slight draft. Just like his father's life.

The next day, Kelven updated Tomas on the Western Army. Tomas grinned. "I don't know what I would do without you, Kelven."

He gestured to the report in his hand. "Everything seems in order. You have done a wonderful job." The smile left his face. "Your father would have been proud. You'll be a great general; you've earned the right."

It took all of Kelven's willpower not to betray his thoughts. *You will soon pay for my father's death.* "Thank you, sir."

Tomas gestured for the servants. "Well, it has been a long morning. Let's have some food. Kelven, please join me. I heard the new cook prepared my favorite, roasted quail."

"I'm sorry, sir, but if you don't mind, I'd like to check on the shipment of grain leaving for the Southern region today. It's already late, and I want to make sure there are no issues." Two girls passed him. One in particular, carrying a decanter of wine, caught his eye. She filled the goblet in front of Tomas.

Tomas waved his hand. "That's fine." He sipped from his goblet. "You really need to start delegating better. You don't have to do it all yourself."

Kelven nodded. "Yes, sir. With your leave, sir." He had turned away when Tomas gurgled behind him.

Kelven spun around. Tomas clawed at his throat, his eyes bugged as blood leaked from the corners.

"For my father!" Nadine screamed, knocking Tomas to the floor. Pulling his sword, Kelven leapt toward Tomas.

The point burst through Nadine's chest, spraying Tomas with blood. He pulled Nadine off Tomas, yanking his sword free. "Go get the healer!" he ordered the other girl. She ran screaming from the room.

Kelven bent over Tomas. "This is for *my* father, you bastard," he whispered.

Silvery blood bubbled from Tomas's mouth. Kelven watched the life leave Tomas's eyes. A whimper drew his attention away from the dead man.

Nadine lay in a heap on the floor, struggling for breath. He avoided her pooling blood and knelt beside her.

"Wha—wha—why?" she whispered.

"You knew Nom made the poison for Tomas. And you did nothing to stop him from using it on my father. You must atone for my father's death."

But she couldn't hear him. She was already gone.

Guards and healers burst into the room. The two healers used every prayer they knew trying to save Tomas, but it was too late. Surveying the scene, the guards listened as Kelven recounted what happened. It was a horrible day for Alludra.

As he left the house, Kelven smiled. Alludra needed a king, and he knew just the man.

HOME IMPROVEMENTS

BY BARBARA ROSS

Molly stroked the shiny enamel paint onto the kitchen cabinets, working carefully to avoid streaks. She'd selected the color, a beautiful pale yellow called "Moonlight," after numerous trips to the hardware store. At Target, she'd purchased inexpensive curtains and placemats to match, imagining how peaceful and calm, how together, the dirty little kitchen would look when she was done.

She'd throw dinner parties—they would have to be small—in the tiny living-dining room next to the newly redecorated kitchen. But who could she invite? Certainly, her friends Nancy and Cat who had been so loyal through everything. Perhaps now even their husbands would come. And Mom and Dad—Dad trying so hard to be hearty and upbeat, and Mom with that line across her brow that signaled both worry and sadness. Not much of a guest list. She would have to make some new friends.

They met on the first day of their junior year in college. Molly was flying high—just back from a coveted internship at a magazine in the City, dean's list, with a bevy of girlfriends. She was unattached after her high school romance had finally broken its moorings and drifted away. Jim was ten years older, back to get an education after a stint in the Army and a period spent "trying different things." He was a business major with a focus in sports management. Molly thought he was a practical, grown-up man.

They were friends of friends, part of the same extended gang. Molly felt Jim watching her. His attention warmed her. He was generous, creative, and fun. When the time came, he wooed her with drives along the Jersey shore, Broadway shows, and fancy restaurants; so different from the dates her girlfriends went on with broke college boys their own age.

Even then he was Jim. He drank a lot, but they all did. It was college, after all. Drunk or sober, Jim had a way of dominating the conversation, believing his opinions were truth, seeing demurrer as a challenge. When he argued, his face glowing red, Molly's girlfriends rolled their eyes and slunk away, but Molly just loved him more. She loved the way she, and she alone, could distract him with a well-formed question or soothe him with a subtle touch. She believed she had a unique ability to love Jim, to run interference for him in a difficult world, and that made her feel proud.

During their senior year, the San Francisco Forty-Niners offered Jim a job selling luxury boxes to corporations. He proposed. Molly added education courses to her already heavy load and began to look at education schools in the Bay Area. She didn't go back to New York or to a magazine job. She had found her truest talent in loving Jim.

Her parents were appalled. "Why don't you just live with him, for God's sake?" her father demanded. "See how it goes." But Molly didn't want to go to the west coast as a girlfriend—and besides, something deep inside her suspected this might be the last time in her life she would have a clutch of friends to precede her down the aisle.

Once her parents saw she was adamant, they gave in and demanded a big wedding with all their friends at the country club. Molly played along, enjoying her moment as the center of attention, nagging Jim to supply the names of family and Army buddies for the guest list. His brother and his brother's wife were the only ones to RSVP. Molly discreetly asked their college friends to sit on the groom's side so the church wouldn't look so unbalanced.

In the middle of the ceremony, Molly's mother burst into noisy sobs that couldn't be passed off as tears of joy or even heartfelt sadness at losing a daughter. Jim's brother showed up late and refused to make a toast. Nonetheless, they were the first of their friends to get married, and the college gang was still intact. The reception was a rousing success, with almost everyone drinking and dancing well into the night. Only once did Molly overhear someone making a bet about how long her marriage would last.

They moved to San Francisco, taking an apartment in Pacific Heights. While Jim started work, Molly fixed up the place, determined to turn its blank white walls into some semblance of home before she started her masters at the University of San Francisco in the fall. She found a dining table on the curb one trash day and hauled it up the narrow apartment stairs. She couldn't believe her luck. The table was a perfect cherry oval that would seat eight comfortably. She poured her life into the table, stripping, sanding, staining, waxing, picking up mismatched chairs wherever she could and recovering their seat cushions. She pictured herself sitting at the table eating and laughing with Jim and their new friends.

When school started, Molly invited guests over, choosing very carefully from the people she met at school, women closer to Jim's age than hers and their husbands or boyfriends. She prepared the meals with a budding cook's care. All went well at first. The husbands were fascinated by Jim's behind-the-scene stories about the Forty-Niners, just coming off their fifth Super Bowl win. But as the evenings wore on, Jim became louder and more monopolizing. The new friends headed for the exits. There were never any return invitations.

Still, Molly looked back on that era in the Heights as a golden time in their marriage. On the weekends in the off-season they wandered through the shops in Sausalito, drove to see the sea lions in Monterey, walked among the towering redwoods in Muir Woods. Jim worked so hard to please her on these outings, it felt like they were still dating.

When Molly graduated and got a teaching job, they celebrated by buying a townhouse in Santa Clara. The summer before her job started, she began remodeling in earnest, tackling things she never would have tried in the rental. Jim was never much for home maintenance, so Molly was the one who became proficient with the power tools required by her various projects.

Molly did the work around the house and the shopping and cooking. Jim took care of the household finances, the bills, the taxes, insurance, and their savings. He used a computer program to manage their money and often pointed out with delight how well their 401K investments were doing, or how much they had saved in taxes by buying the townhouse.

As Molly finished remodeling each room, she chose new furniture with great care, though she kept the dining room table she had worked on so hard and loved so much. The townhouse had an open plan design, and many nights Molly sat at that table grading papers while Jim watched sports—sometimes it seemed like any sport, with the TV turned up full volume, yelling at the screen with each missed point.

"They'll fire you, you know," she said quietly one evening when he reacted to a loss by an obscure college basketball team with a particularly graphic string of expletives.

"I never bet on football, babe," he answered. "You know that. Just blowing off a little steam."

Jim was often tense now. He'd been promoted to selling ever more complex corporate sponsorships and the Niners' poor seasons and ownership controversies didn't help. He was drinking too much. Molly knew that. On nights when he entertained clients, she would lie in bed and hear the car turning into the driveway, taking the corner too fast, then the fumbling at the lock. She'd hear him in the bathroom, the long, strong stream of piss hitting the bowl or more often not, Jim sighing with relief.

Sometimes on these nights, he would lurch into the bedroom. Her stomach, already tight with tension, would clamp into a ball. More often, he turned on the TV, took another beer from the refrigerator and dozed off on the couch. Waking early for her job, Molly turned off the lights and blaring TV, closed the cabinet doors, and sometimes even the refrigerator door that Jim left hanging open. She roused him at the last possible moment, rushing to her car as he lumbered off to the bathroom to shower and shave.

In spite of the drinking, Jim seemed to be doing well at work. When wives were invited to corporate events at the park, Molly searched his colleagues' faces for signs of pity, but never saw any, and their relationships with Jim seemed comfortable and friendly.

Molly kept her friendships at work now, too. She was smarter than to bring anybody home. When the subject of babies came up, as it did from time to time in the teachers' lounge, she would laugh and say, "Why would I? I already have a child at home."

When it came, it was a surprise—a job, a better job, with the New York Giants. They were going home. The money they made on their townhouse in Santa Clara enabled them to buy a house in Montclair, close to the stadium and to Molly's new teaching job in Cedar Grove. The house they chose was awful, as only a house built in the 1970s can be, but it was near a park and came with a quarter acre of overgrown backyard.

Molly threw herself into the renovation, determined to finish before she began her job in the fall. The kitchen was ripped out, and, while the professionals installed the maple cabinets, granite countertops, and gleaming stainless steel appliances, Molly completed as much of the rest of the work as she could. After taking a class at Home Depot, her final do-it-yourself job was replacing the broken automatic garage door opener on the attached double-bay garage, another new luxury. Installing the opener turned out to be easy, but the garage door showed its age, sometimes leaving a gap of inches at the bottom, other times coming down with a crash and buckling at the seams. Molly spent hours adjusting its pulleys and rollers to get it just right.

On the Saturday of Labor Day weekend, they held a barbecue to celebrate the completion of the work. In addition to Mom and Dad, Molly invited her extended family, aunts, uncles, cousins, and their children as well as the two college friends she'd been able to reconnect

161

with. Cat had just made partner at her Manhattan law firm and Nancy was pregnant with her third child. When Molly had been the first one married, creating a home out of the apartment in San Francisco, she'd felt like the first out of the gate, firmly ahead of the pack. Now she was falling behind.

The house was a hit. Everyone ooohed and ahhed. "You should have seen it before." Her mother's voice was filled with pride. "Nobody could've seen its potential but Molly."

"And so big," said her aunt, appreciatively, "a master and three additional bedrooms. You'd better get busy if you're going to fill them up!"

Molly didn't say anything. She'd put Jim's office with his beloved computer in the little room off the foyer. Upstairs, she selected one of the spare rooms for her office. In another she created a bright guest room with twin beds, in case anyone should stay over. She decorated the third spare room in a masculine plaid and, without any discussion, unpacked Jim's clothes into its bureau and closet. "Because you come home so late," she said. What she meant was, "because you come home so drunk." He hadn't touched her in over two years. There would be no children filling up these bedrooms.

The cook-out went surprisingly well. They had hot dogs and hamburgers, corn on the cob, and plump Jersey tomatoes. Drinking beer and asking Jim questions about the Giants, the men moved back and forth between the barbecue and the den where the college games played on the new flat screen TV. Finally, though, in the late afternoon when Texas Christian upset Oklahoma, Jim howled in rage and pushed the new TV to the floor with so much force the screen cracked. The crowd thinned quickly after that.

Everyone said, "We love the house," or something like it, giving quick hugs as they left. Molly took some solace in that. This is what she lived for, to create order where there was none, to bring beauty to neglected places. But even as she gazed in satisfaction at her work, somewhere, nagging, was the knowledge that transforming the stage set was easier than rewriting the play.

162

Early on a Saturday afternoon in January, Molly opened the front door and grabbed the mail from the box. Jim was at the stadium. The Giants were in the playoffs the next day and the biggest of the corporate sponsors had to be wined and dined all weekend so they could be induced to spend even more money next year.

As usual, there was very little mail, just reams of catalogs and junk. Jim paid all the bills online and no one got any personal correspondence anymore. But today was different. In a pink envelope was an invitation to Nancy's eldest's fifth birthday. Molly wouldn't go, she had enough of other people's children during the week, but the string of Xs and Os scribbled in a girlish hand at the bottom of the invitation touched her. Molly was seized with a desire to buy the child a special gift.

She drove to a toy store on Bloomfield Avenue. It wasn't a route she often took, but she'd passed the store once with Jim and remembered it. Inside, Molly picked out a hand puppet, a beautiful princess dressed in a lavender cape and flowing pink gown. "Some little girl will love this," the proprietor said as she wrapped the present in pink paper and tied it with a lavender bow. Standing there in the toy shop, Molly was overwhelmed by a longing she'd never before allowed herself to fully feel.

Driven by the same purposeful momentum that had propelled her to the toy shop, Molly stopped next at the UPS Store to package the gift and send it on its way. She filled out the shipping form, including the required name, address, and phone number.

"Mrs. Davis," the clerk said, squinting at her writing. "While you're here, do you want to pick up the mail from your box? Your husband hasn't been here in a long time and it's overflowing."

Molly stood stunned as the boy handed her two plastic bags full of envelopes. In the car, she tore through the bags like a wild animal, overwhelmed by the scores of utility bills and credit card notices. There were at least a half dozen letters from the IRS and as many from their mortgage company. She was shaking so hard, she could barely drive home. At the house, she made the turn at their mailbox, put her car in park, opened the door, and vomited into the drive.

That night Molly didn't sleep, tossing and turning before finally getting out of bed at two. She checked Jim's room, but his bed was not slept in. At three, she padded downstairs and paced through the dark house. Finally, the hum and grind of the new garage door opener broke the silence. Molly waited for Jim to stagger through the door.

Minutes ticked by. Molly opened the door from the kitchen to the garage. Jim was slumped against the seat in his car. Somehow, he had made it home, but no further. He'd passed out before he'd even managed to turn off the engine.

Molly stood in the doorway for a single beat of her heart.

She flipped the switch. The garage door closed with a satisfying thunk.

She shut the kitchen door, stuffing a towel into the gap where the door met the floor. She went back to her bedroom, opened her windows wide to the cold January night and fell into a dreamless sleep. She awakened at dawn, closed the bedroom windows, removed the towel from under the kitchen door, and called 911.

Her friend Cat was a stalwart, even bringing in tax and bankruptcy specialists from her law firm, but there was nothing to be done to save the house. No mortgage payment had been made since the closing, and the IRS was demanding to look at filings going back five years.

It didn't really matter. Molly couldn't afford the mortgage payments on her teaching salary, and Jim had stopped paying the premiums on their life insurance years before.

With Cat's intercession and the bank's permission Molly sold her perfect house and all the furnishings, including the beautiful dining room table, to a grateful couple with two little girls, just transferred back from overseas. She settled the mortgage and sent the rest to the IRS. On the day of the closing, she backed her car out of the garage, closed the big double door for the last time, and drove away.

Molly pushed herself off the floor. Her foot had fallen asleep while she applied the Moonlight yellow to the last cabinet door, and now her leg threatened to buckle under her. The hallways of the Passaic apartment building were grimy and smelled of curry, borscht, and rice and beans, but Molly was determined that when you opened the door of her little apartment, you would find sanctuary from the ugliness outside.

She limped to the threshold, stamping her foot to wake it, and turned to survey her work. Beautiful. Even without the curtains, with the hardware off and the cabinet doors open, the change was dramatic. The dark little kitchen was now urban, chic, sophisticated. Molly leaned against the door frame and sighed, dreaming of pale yellow dishes, square, with an Asian touch, stacked in the glass-fronted cabinets.

MISSING

BY JM REINBOLD

Detective Chief Inspector Rylan Crowe and Detective Sergeant Rolly Burke parked in front of the Mortimer house. The downstairs curtains were drawn, the drive empty.

Burke shut off the Ford Mondeo's engine. "No one home, looks like."

"They're at home," Crowe replied. He fished in his inside jacket pocket for a cigarette that wasn't there. "The shoe is Evie's. Smythe got confirmation from them not ten minutes ago." He hadn't smoked in a year or more, but with the clock ticking away on Evie Mortimer, the urge clawed at him, like he'd never quit. Haunted him like a ghost in his brain.

"I expect they've had more attention than they can bear. A missing child brings on the helpful and unhelpful in droves."

"No need to disturb them," Burke said. "For the moment."

"Right," Crowe agreed. "Smythe's volunteer is the first order of business."

They stepped from the car into a warm, pleasant morning. While London boiled in a July heat wave, Somerset and the rest of the Southwest enjoyed ocean breezes and temperatures in the mid-70s.

They found Detective Constable Smythe, the officer in charge of the grid search, in a portable pavilion set up inside the walls of the

167

Mortimers' garden. Smythe had a map of Brightworthy and the land surrounding the village spread out on a picnic table. Grid-blocks on the map had been marked through, some crossed with two colors indicating the areas had been searched more than once.

Smythe handed Crowe a sheet of paper. "The volunteer's details, sir."

Crowe scanned the report, what little there was of it, and sighed.

"Absolutely squeaky," Burke said, reading over Crowe's shoulder.

"Indeed." Crowe handed the report to Burke. "And where is Mrs. Cicely Willington, age seventy-five?"

"This way, sir. The old dear's tucked up over here."

Crowe and Burke followed Smythe to a sunny patio where Mrs. Willington had been billeted in a lawn chair with a steaming cup of tea and the daily crossword.

"Nice work, Smythe," Crowe said.

Smythe's eyebrows did a little bounce. "Thank you, sir." He made introductions and left them to it.

"Mrs. Willington," Crowe said. "Thank you for your assistance."

"You're quite welcome, Chief Inspector. I'm glad to be of help. It's not often I get out in the field anymore."

Intrigued, Crowe asked, "Are you a retired police officer?"

Mrs. Willington, small-boned, her feathery gray hair swept back like wings on both sides of her head, reminded him of a mourning dove.

"Oh, goodness, no," she replied. "Nothing as official as that. I've been a civilian volunteer for years with the fire brigade and the village watch, but you know," she said, massaging her elbows, "time catches us up."

"Well, we're grateful you felt up to it today. Now, can you tell me exactly how you came to find the shoe?"

"Of course I can, Chief Inspector—though it is a bit of a mystery. I've been over it in my mind and I cannot for the life of me figure it out."

"What can't you figure out?" Crowe knelt beside her.

"How I missed it the first time. Constable Smythe gave me that area because of my balance problem, you know. The ground isn't rough or bumpy back there."

"Yes," Crowe said, "Go on."

"It must be old age," she said, shaking her head. "I'm going gaga and not even aware of it. I passed that tree on the side closest to the garden wall. I looked closely, I know I did. There was nothing there. I made my way back and forth, back and forth, the way one's supposed to do, across the alley to the neighbor's garden wall. My attention didn't waver; I was most careful. I started back to report to Constable Smythe that the area was clear and it was then I saw it, that little pink shoe shining like a beacon. It couldn't have been there before."

In some agitation, Mrs. Willington gripped the arms of the chair and pulled herself forward.

"It would have been impossible to miss it. Yet, clearly, Chief Inspector, I did miss it. And it is only because I went back that way that I saw it. I could have gone on down the alley. I almost did. But something made me go back to the Mortimers' garden wall. I've no idea why." She shook her head and eased herself back into the chair.

"Whatever the reason, it's our good fortune that you did. Now, can you tell me what time that was, Mrs. Willington?"

At Crowe's praise, she perked up immediately, eyes bright as a sparrow's. "Of course, Chief Inspector, I noted the time particularly. Because of the shoe, you know." She fiddled a small notebook from her pocket, followed by a pair of brightly colored reading glasses that she positioned and repositioned on her nose as she turned pages in her book. "Ah," she said at last. "I've got it. It was eight-thirty this morning, precisely."

"And when did you commence searching that area?"

"At eight o'clock on the dot."

Crowe thanked Mrs. Willington profusely. She was glowing like a peach as he and Burke walked back to the car.

"What do you make of that?" Burke asked. "The old girl's not gaga. Sharp as a tack, if you ask me. Two previous grid searches in an area that small, they wouldn't have missed a flea." Burke sipped from his carry-cup and made a face. "Nasty," he declared. He cracked open the door and dumped the cold coffee into the gutter.

"The same thing you're thinking, I expect," Crowe replied. "If Mrs. Willington didn't put the shoe there—and I don't believe for a minute that she did—who did?"

169

"And why? If she didn't put it there and she'd didn't miss it on her first pass, then it had to have been put there *while* she was searching the area. And the place crawling with police."

"That's the million dollar question, Rolly." Crowe flipped open his tablet and logged in to his e-mail. "Has Waverly sent the MAPPA search?"

Burke checked his mobile. "Yeah. And it's not good news. There's a Level Three sex offender recently moved into the area"

"Who?"

"Arthur Tuttle. Lives in Williston."

Arthur Tuttle's registered place of residence squatted atop a ramshackle automotive garage. An open stair attached to the L-shaped end of the building led to the flat-roofed, low-ceilinged, waste-board affair. The look of the place made Crowe's skin crawl.

"He ain't up there, mate."

The voice sounded close, but Crowe saw no one.

"Police. Show yourself."

A man wearing a mechanic's coverall, pushing a tire in front of him, emerged from a door beneath the stair. No wonder they hadn't seen him, Crowe thought. He'd probably stayed hidden until he was certain they were looking for Tuttle and not him.

"What's your name?" Burke asked. "Let's see your identification."

"Keep your hair on." The mechanic shot them an aggrieved look.

"Get on with it," Burke snapped. "We haven't time to mess about."

"Keith Rickey." He leaned the tire against the stair before extracting a greasy-looking wallet from oil-stained coveralls. He handed Burke his license.

Scrawny, with nicotine-stained fingers and teeth, Rickey stank of strong tobacco and petrol.

Burke smiled benevolently. "We're looking for Arthur Tuttle. He gave this location as his address."

"Gotten himself into it again, has he?"

"What do you mean by that?" Crowe asked.

Rickey made a show of lighting a hand-rolled, unfiltered cigarette and took a long drag. He exhaled tendrils of smoke through his nose, pausing for effect, then sucked them back in.

"I know what he done. They say that type don't quit, even if you cut off their goolies."

Crowe pulled up a picture of Evie on his mobile and held it up in front of Rickey. "Have you seen this child here?"

Rickey paled. "No!"

"Would you tell us if you had?" Burke asked.

"Sure I would," Rickey said. A look of understanding that turned to outrage spread across his face. "What, you think I'm like him?"

"He lives with you, doesn't he?" Burke asked.

"I don't live here. What do you take me for? Tuttle lives up there. He's a lodger." Rickey jerked a thumb at the stairs. "Where you was going when I saw you."

"You know what he's done and you rent to him?" Crowe asked.

"Not a crime. Besides, there ain't no kids 'round here. Better he's here than in some neighborhood."

"Well, Mr. Rickey, we'll see for ourselves whether your friend is here or not." Crowe moved toward the stairs.

"Look it, he ain't here. He's got a job he goes to."

"Where?" Burke asked.

Rickey muttered something unintelligible under his breath.

"Sergeant Burke," Crowe said, "ring DI Waverly. Have her bring a team to Mr. Tuttle's flat. Make sure you're here to let my officers in, Mr. Rickey. If you're not, they'll break down the door."

"Now that we understand each other," Burke said, pulling out his mobile. "Be a good chap and tell us where to find Tuttle."

"He works at Peterson's News & Tobacco. Down this alley, cross, and turn left. You can't miss it."

"For your sake, I hope you're telling the truth." Crowe paused. "And, Mr. Rickey, do not alert Mr. Tuttle that we're on our way."

Rickey glowered at them. "Don't you be threatening me. He'll be there all right. And he ain't my friend."

As they started down the alley, Crowe heard a gob of spit hit the ground behind them. "Against the law," he said over his shoulder.

"Isn't everything?" came Rickey's sour reply.

171

Peterson's News & Tobacco had a steady stream of foot traffic.

"Blimey," Burke said. "What're they selling to get business like that?"

Crowe laughed. "I'd wager Peterson, if there is a Peterson, has a betting shop or some such set up in the back."

"No doubt," Burke said. "Look at the windows. They've painted the glass."

They crossed the road and went into the shop. The front was a maze of off-kilter spinners stuffed with newspapers, sporting magazines, and racing forms. Beyond these, Crowe saw racks of fitness and men's magazines. Burke directed his attention to a portable partition at the back with a hand-lettered placard on the door stating: **Adult Videos ~ Under 21 Not Allowed**.

Tuttle stood at a counter to their left. Embroiled in a verbal altercation with a couple of customers, he had not yet noticed them. With a derisive wave of his hand, he dispatched the disgruntled pair. When he saw Crowe and Burke, his face twisted in disgust.

"Not my day today. No, it bloody isn't," he muttered.

At the counter, Crowe reached for his warrant card.

"Don't bother," Tuttle said. "You could hardly be more bloody obvious."

Crowe winked at Burke. "We've been made, Rolly."

"Nice place," Burke said. He nodded toward the back where a group of men clustered around a display of adult magazines. They glanced uneasily over their shoulders.

Tuttle needed a shave. His hair and his shirt both wanted washing. In vivid contrast to the rest of him, Tuttle's hands were like a woman's—small, soft, and finely manicured. His nails shone like little moons from a recent buffing.

"I've been expecting you lot. You've got that tot's face plastered all over the county and her mum weeping and begging on telly."

"Shut it, Tuttle," Burke said.

Tuttle snorted. "You can't solve your little problem with me. I've got an alibi." He thrust out his jaw. "I was right here at my job and my employer with me, not to mention any number of customers will recall I handled their transactions."

"Do your friends have alibis?" Crowe asked.

Tuttle laughed bitterly. "Friends? What friends? You lot have made my life a misery. Can't get what I need no more and that's a fact. My life's a ruin and no mistake."

"We've been to your flat," Burke said.

Was that a flash of panic Crowe saw in Tuttle's eyes?

"You've no right to toss my place."

"Unfortunately, for you," Burke said, "because of your previous convictions, we can search your place any time we feel there's a need."

"And arrest you," Crowe said. "If we think you're lying to us or holding back information that would lead to the recovery of Evie Mortimer."

Tuttle's face had gone gray.

"She's your type," Burke said. "Are you denying it?"

"Let's look at your history, Arthur," Crowe said. "Violent, predatory pedophile ..."

"Shut your mouth," Tuttle hissed. "You're putting a target on my back."

Crowe noticed the men in the back had moved closer as their exchange with Tuttle became more heated. Burke held out his phone, displaying Evie's picture. "Oy, you lot. Any of you seen this little girl? Around here? Anywhere?"

They shook their heads and mumbled "no," "never seen her" as they retreated through the partition door.

Burke turned back to Tuttle. "Should I have a look?

Tuttle's mouth twisted in a mocking smile. He sniggered. "It's filthy, but it ain't illegal."

Crowe slammed his fist on the counter. "Released from prison three months past. Moved to the Williston area three weeks ago. Surprise, surprise, little Evie Mortimer goes missing. And here we are, Arthur. Here we are. Wanting answers, Arthur. Answers only you can give us."

Tuttle gripped the edge of the counter, his face so close to Crowe's that Crowe nearly gagged on the man's breath. Earlier, he'd wondered about the crusty white residue around Tuttle's lips. Now he could see it was dried froth from chewable antacids used to treat the sour stomach causing Tuttle's halitosis.

Crowe held out his phone so Tuttle could see Evie's picture. Tuttle stared, then seemingly without realizing what he was doing, reached for the phone. Crowe pulled back. Startled, Tuttle jerked his hand away.

"I swear, I never seen her except on telly."

Burke's mobile rang. He answered, then turned to Crowe and shook his head.

Tuttle grinned broadly. "You got nothing on me!" he exclaimed.

"Where's your guv?" Burke asked. "Let's get your so-called alibi sorted."

"He's not here," Tuttle said. "He has business elsewhere."

"You let him know," Crowe said, "he's got business at Killingsworth Constabulary within the hour. If he doesn't show, we'll be back for you."

"Oh," Burke said. "Our lads send apologies for the mess."

Tuttle gritted his teeth.

"I do hope you're not thinking of doing a runner," Crowe said. "That turned out rather badly for you the last time."

Burke smiled pleasantly. "Do yourself a favor, Arthur. Take us to Evie and we'll put in a good word on your behalf."

"Haven't got her," Tuttle spit out the words. "And you claiming I do won't make it so."

"Your name hasn't been mentioned in connection with Evie Mortimer." Crowe flipped open his mobile. "Yet."

In the Incident Room at Killingsworth CID, DI Waverly removed a snapshot of Evie Mortimer from the evidence board and replaced it with a portrait taken recently by a professional photographer.

"Evie has heterochromia iridum," Waverly said pointing to the girl's eyes. "In other words, she has one blue eye and one brown eye. It's a significant distinguishing feature. You couldn't see it on the other photograph, but it's unmistakable in this one."

"Well done, Waverly," Crowe said. Evie Mortimer had wispy red-gold hair, shoulder length. Slightly parted lips revealed baby teeth. In the picture, she was wide-eyed. Crowe thought she looked surprised. Her features were burned in his memory. He could see her with his eyes closed. Last night, he'd dreamed of her, but she'd had his sister's face.

He turned to Smythe. "Have you found anyone who saw Evie leave with her family or return with them?"

"A couple across the street saw them pull in Sunday night, but couldn't say for sure if Evie was with them."

Crowe wrote on the evidence board.

"How about the caravan park where they say they stayed?"

"The manager can only confirm that the Mortimers' caravan was there the entire time. We're running the license plates of vehicles that registered around the same time."

Burke leaned back in his chair. "You don't believe the parents' story, guv?"

"Not entirely, no."

"Sir," Waverly said. "A Mr. Peterson stopped in to alibi Arthur Tuttle. But, it's only a partial alibi."

Smythe snorted. "Did you hear him going on about that scum, Tuttle, like he was a Boy Scout?"

"The search of his place turned up nothing," Waverly said. "There's nothing to connect him to Evie Mortimer. He's under surveillance."

Smythe made a face. "Peterson's News & Tobacco is a front for porno. Ten to one, Peterson's one of them."

Waverly frowned. "It's no good moaning about it."

Smythe took a deep breath. "It's Tuttle. You mark my words."

"Waverly, what does the forensic lab say about the shoe?" Crowe asked.

"Nothing yet, sir."

"We can't discount Tuttle," Smythe said. "He was part of larger ring that supplied custom orders."

"We're not discounting him," Crowe said. "Waverly, coordinate with the Yard's Pedophile Unit. If they pick up anything in their surveillance, I want to know about it immediately."

"Yes, sir." She looked down at her keyboard and grimaced. "Ugh," she said. "The thought of it turns your stomach."

Crowe tapped the evidence board. "Evie's been missing forty-eight hours. Her mother appears to be the last person to have seen her. We found no forced entry of the Mortimers' home. Nothing has turned up on CCTV security cameras. The dozen reported sightings have all been false."

Crowe secured a picture of the pink shoe to the timeline. "And, as you all know, we've had no viable leads until today."

Waverly flipped through the Mortimers' statement. "Here it is," she said. "Karen reported those shoes missing, along with a green tulle sparkle-skirt, a yellow flower petal top, and a lion-head hat on the day Evie went missing."

Crowe drummed his fingers on the desk. "The clothing that Karen reported missing, what do you make of that?"

"Doesn't make any sense," Waverly said. "If someone took her out of her bed, why stop and dress her in a get-up like that? And, if the kidnapper didn't dress her, why take it along?"

Burke whistled softly. "Playtime."

"Spot on, Sergeant," Crowe said. "Other than the shoes, those clothes were for playing dress up. They were in her toy box."

Waverly closed her eyes and sighed. "Evie dressed herself."

"Yes," Crowe said. "I believe she did." He stood up. "Sergeant Burke and I need to have another talk with the Mortimers. And let's do another canvas of the village. Someone, somewhere, knows something, saw something, or heard something. We just haven't found them."

Karen Mortimer answered the door. When she saw them, her eyes narrowed and her mouth formed a hard, tight line. Crowe didn't flinch. He asked to come in and she grudgingly stepped aside.

The lounge was a shambles. Newspapers, cups, glasses, and take-away cartons littered every surface. Karen wedged herself into a space between an arm of the couch and a jumble of boys' sport socks and Y-fronts.

"Sit, if you can find a spot."

Crowe and Burke moved stacks of posters from two chairs and sat facing her. Gaunt-faced and puffy-eyed, Karen looked as if she'd lost weight since Crowe had last seen her, and she'd been skinny as a twig then. She wore dirty white shorts and a pink sleeveless top. She hadn't bothered to put on a bra and when she turned to roll the loose socks into balls, he could see the slight swell of her breasts.

With an exaggerated sigh, Karen shoved the clothes aside and grabbed a packet of cigarettes from a side table. She shook one out and tapped it on the side of her hand before lighting it.

"What do you want, Chief Inspector?" She took a quick, anxious drag.

What did he want? He'd expected her first question to be: Have you found her?

She held up her cigarette. "I've started smoking again."

"Karen," Burke said, "do you have any idea how Evie's shoe came to be under the tree outside your garden wall?"

Karen Mortimer looked confused. "What? ... I don't ... It must have fallen off when she was taken."

"How can that be, Karen?" Burke asked. He smiled encouragingly. "That area was searched twice before and the shoe wasn't there."

"It's obvious, isn't it?" a man's voice interjected. Karen's husband, Malcolm, came into the lounge. "Someone put it there."

Unruffled, Burke said, "Spot on, Malcolm. Do you know who that someone might be?"

"How the devil would I know who put it there?"

"There aren't that many possibilities given the short window of time and the fact there were police all around your house when the shoe appeared."

Malcolm gaped at them. "Now, just a minute!" he exclaimed. He began to pace. He turned on Crowe. "You think we had something to do with Evie's disappearance? You think we put the shoe there to make it look like ... look like ..."

"Look like what, Malcolm?"

"I don't know," Malcolm stammered, "like someone carried her off."

"Your words, Malcolm, not ours. Now, tell us about the shoe."

Malcolm snorted. "This is outrageous!"

"Don't be an idiot, husband dearest. We're suspects. We've been suspects all along, isn't that right, Chief Inspector?" Karen stared at Crowe steadily, silently challenging him.

"Unfortunately, that is why we're here."

Malcolm glared at them. "Get out!"

"We'll speak with the two of you again soon, Mr. Mortimer," Crow said.

As they stood to leave, the front door opened and Ian, Evie's older brother, dashed in and skidded to a stop. He looked at his parents, then from Crowe to Burke. He mumbled a hello and headed for the stairs.

"Ian," Crowe said.

The boy stopped midway up the stairs.

"We know someone put Evie's shoe under the tree, but it would have been impossible for that person to put the shoe there without being seen, unless that person was already here and was known to the police. Did you put Evie's shoe under the tree, Ian, or do you know who did?"

"No," Ian said firmly and ran up the stairs.

Outside, Crowe saw a dark-blue, unmarked police vehicle parked opposite the Mortimers' driveway. Smythe and Waverly had started re-interviewing the neighbors. He and Burke would revisit residences where no one had been home during the first door-to-door.

Burke tugged at his tie and loosened it, then shrugged out of his jacket. He regarded the sweat stains on his shirt and harrumphed.

"Well, so much for that," he said, and pulled the jacket back on. "I'll take this end of the village shall I, guv, and you the other?"

Two hours later, at the next-to-the-last house on his list, Crowe found an elderly Mr. Ashford and his dog, a sprightly Jack Russell terrier, pottering about in the garden. He'd had a bad reaction to some medicine, he said, and had stayed a few days with his daughter in Williston. Fingers crossed, Crowe showed him Evie's picture. The old man took the photograph and held it at arm's length, scrutinizing.

When he nodded and said he'd seen the Mortimer children, Crowe wanted to kick up his heels.

"The brother was in a confab with two boys about his own age, I reckon. They were in the front garden, if you can call it a garden, of the old Rutherford place. When they see us out and about, they want to play with Fezziwig."

"But not on that day?"

"No. Didn't wave. Didn't even look. The brother followed the two boys inside and the little girl went with them."

"How long did they stay inside?"

"Dunno. I didn't stop. None of my business."

"Did you see them again after that at any time?"

"Wasn't home again until today, as I said. Saw the news about her on the telly. Poor little mite. Hope you find her."

"We're doing our best," Crowe said. "Can you show me where you saw them?"

"Of course, just there," Ashford said, directing Crowe's gaze up the street to the right. "Third from the corner. You can't miss it. Been lowering the property values on this street for years."

There was a sight line, but no direct access between the Mortimers' home and the Rutherford house. DC Smythe's contact card was still stuck in the door. The other houses in the street had tidy, attractive front gardens. Here, the grass, suffocated by weeds, struggled to grow. The paint peeled. The shades on every grime-covered window were drawn. Ramshackle, Crowe thought, that was the word for it. He went up the cracked walk to the front door and knocked. No answer. He knocked again loudly. Nothing.

He pulled out his mobile and rang Killingsworth CID. Waverly answered and he requested she check the name of the property owner. He waited while she looked it up. "Be certain he has the keys with him."

Crowe followed a foot path to the back of the house where he found a cramped yard littered with broken-down furniture, a cracked aquarium, and a heap of broken boards, metal fittings, and broken glass. He picked his way through the refuse and peered into the aquarium. Open to the weather, rain had turned whatever was left inside to a foul-smelling sludge. Crowe wrinkled his nose. A couple of dilapidated lawn chairs sat on a concrete slab—a parody of a patio—at the bottom of the back steps. In a window well, Crowe noticed a broken window, large enough for a child to crawl through. He went up the steps and tried the door. Locked.

Thirty minutes or so later, a car horn tooted. Crowe rounded the side of the house and saw a middle-aged, unshaven, white man stepping out of DC Smythe's car. The man walked over to Crowe.

Crowe displayed his warrant card. "Detective Chief Inspector Crowe. And you are Mr. Rutherford, the owner?"

"Right. What's this about?"

"Do you live in this house, Mr. Rutherford?"

"Not no more. I let it out."

"To whom do you let it?"

Rutherford stared at Crowe as if he'd spoken an incomprehensible language.

"The name of your tenant, please, Mr. Rutherford."

Rutherford frowned, scratched the stubble on his chin and ran his fingers through his halo of uncombed gray hair. The question seemed to have flummoxed him.

"You collect the rent, do you not?"

"You needn't take that tone. Give me a moment."

"While you're thinking, could you tell me the last time you had contact with your tenants?"

This question seemed to further confuse Rutherford. Crowe suspected the man hadn't been to the property in a donkey's age.

"Barrett, maybe," Rutherford offered. "Might be Barstow."

"You'll have it written down somewhere, I'm sure," Crowe said.

Rutherford was having a good look around.

"The back is worse," Crowe said. "I'll be amazed if the neighbors haven't complained."

A vein pulsed in Rutherford's neck. He cleared his throat and spat. "How much is the fine?"

"I'm not here in that capacity," Crowe said tersely. "A three-year-old girl has gone missing. Evie Mortimer's her name. She lives at number 10 Birdbrook Lane. She was seen outside this house two days ago, right before she went missing."

"Why didn't you say so? No need to be so hush-hush about it. You want to look around, help yourself. You'll get no argument from me."

"Evie and her brother were seen going into this house with two other children." Crowe showed Rutherford Evie's picture.

"I don't know nothing about that. There ain't no children here. Whoever told you that has got it wrong."

"Unlock the door, please."

Rutherford trudged up the steps. The lock turned, but the door stuck and he had to force it back, dislodging a pile of uncollected post.

"Perhaps, we can discover the name of your tenant," Crowe said. He picked up a handful from the pile, sifted through it, tossed it aside, and picked up another handful.

"There's nothing but advertisements here. All of it addressed to Occupant. Did this person receive no post at this address?"

"How would I know?"

"Who did you rent to? A family? A single person?"

"A bloke."

"This bloke, any luck in recalling his name."

"Blackwood, maybe."

"He signed a lease didn't he?"

"We had a verbal agreement."

Rutherford stepped back through the open door. Crowe followed him and saw the Ford Mondeo coming up the street. Earlier, while waiting for Rutherford, he'd called his Sergeant for assistance. Burke parked and joined Crowe and Rutherford on the porch.

"Sergeant Burke, this is Mr. Rutherford, the owner."

Crowe turned to Rutherford. "Please wait in the Sergeant's car until we're finished."

Burke settled Rutherford in the backseat of the Mondeo.

Back on the porch, he watched Rutherford talking animatedly on his mobile. "Looks a bit dodgy to me."

"He's hiding something."

Half a dozen steps into the hall on the threadbare runner, they stopped abruptly. Crowe wrinkled his nose at the musky, armpit-like odor. "What is that smell?"

181

Burke shook his head. "No idea. Strong, though. Whew!"

They peered into rooms on either side of the hall. Brittle paper shades kept the rooms in shadow. Crowe felt along the doorframe for a light switch. He found one and flipped it on. The bulb was low wattage and provided only a dim light. But it was enough for them to see the cracking plaster walls, the narrow floorboards, a couple of tatty throw rugs, a sagging couch, and a pair of rickety chairs. The lot of it looked like it had been picked off the street. Empty soda cans, crumpled cigarette packets, and other trash were scattered about. They found a similar scene in the room across the hall.

They moved on to the back of the house. In the kitchen, an Indian take-away meal had been set out on the table and abandoned untouched. Crowe saw the end of a receipt sticking out from beneath a flattened paper bag. He pulled it free and read out the date. The food had been purchased the day before Evie Mortimer disappeared.

Burke raised an eyebrow.

"Take Mr. Rutherford to CID. Maybe that will improve his memory."

Crowe looked around the kitchen. No dishes. No pots and pans. In the pantry, he found a door with the knob missing, the hole plugged with a wad of newspaper. An open padlock hung from a hasp. Crowe tugged at the paper plug. The door opened easily onto steps going down into the darkness of a cellar. He felt inside the door for a light switch—found it and turned it on. Crowe descended cautiously. The hair on the back of his neck prickled; he felt a tremor in his bowels, a chill up his spine.

The basement was empty. Not so much as a shelf or a workbench. A thick coating of dust on the floor showed scuff marks and footprints going every which way. Crowe saw a narrow path in the dust. It appeared something had been dragged from one side of the cellar to the other. He followed the drag path to another set of steps that led to the hatchway doors he'd seen earlier at the back of the house. He swiped away the cobwebs in the doorway, ducked his head, and went halfway up the steps. He pushed at the doors and lifted them easily.

A short while later, Burke returned.

"Something happened here, Rolly." Crowe pointed to the hodgepodge of footprints. "Something was dragged out through those doors."

As they returned to the stairs, Crowe noticed something under the bottom tread. He used his pen to nudge it into the light. Burke pulled a latex glove from his pocket and picked up the chalky, white lump.

Burke made a face. "Oy, what a stink."

"Bag it," Crowe said. "And get a Scenes of Crime team out here."

Late that afternoon, when they returned to Killingsworth CID, Crowe was surprised to find Karen and Ian Mortimer waiting for him. Ian insisted on speaking with Crowe alone. Karen reluctantly agreed.

"I'll be right out there." She pointed at the visitor's area where they'd been sitting.

In the Interview Room, Crowe smiled in what he hoped was a warm, encouraging way.

"What is it you wanted to see me about?"

Ian sighed. "I've done something stupid." He paused. "I didn't mean for it to happen. It's just that sometimes I want to do stuff and not have to watch her, but mum always has a headache. She has to lie down a lot."

"Go on."

"I got up early. I wanted to watch telly. But Evie woke up, too. She wanted breakfast and she needed to be changed. Mum wouldn't get up. I think she took one of her pills."

Crowe's heart beat faster. "What happened?"

"I took her diaper off her and dressed her."

"Did you dress her in the sparkle-skirt?"

"Yeah. She's loves that stuff. And that goofy lion hat mum-mum bought her. Then I toasted a jam thingie for her. But she kept pestering me to take her outside to play. I didn't want to, so I got the baby alarm and put it on her so I could tell where she was." He reached in his pocket, pulled out a plastic receiver with an antenna and laid it on the table. "The other part's a pink teddy bear."

Crowe picked up the receiver and examined it.

Ian looked the picture of misery. "Someone forgot to latch the gate. That's how she got out. I tried the alarm over and over. It didn't work. All I found was her shoe." He pushed his chair back and stood up. "That's all I know."

"Sit down," Crowe said. "Did you throw Evie's shoe over the garden wall?"

Ian hesitated. "Yeah."

"Why didn't you tell your parents?"

Ian looked away and began scraping at his thumbnail.

"Well?"

Crowe let the silence stretch.

"Your mother has to be told."

Ian's head snapped up. "You can't tell her!"

Crowe brought Karen Mortimer to the Interview Room. She looked as if she hadn't showered or changed her clothes in days.

"Is something wrong?"

Crowe heard the apprehension in her voice. He took his pen from his pocket and fiddled it between his fingers.

"We now know how Evie's shoe came to be outside your garden wall and who saw your daughter last." He let that sink in. "It was Ian who threw Evie's shoe over the wall the morning it was found."

Karen stared at Crowe. "What?"

"The morning Evie went missing, Ian said he tried several times to wake you, but couldn't. He thought you might have taken a sleeping pill."

Karen's face flamed scarlet.

"He'd gotten up early to watch telly by himself. But Evie got up too and wanted him to play with her outside. He dressed her, then fixed her something to eat, put a child locator alarm on her, and let her play in the garden by herself. Sometime later, he went looking for her and she was gone, except for the shoe. He tried to find her with the locator device. When he couldn't, he panicked and hid the shoe. When the searches began, he waited for an opportunity, then threw it over the wall."

It took Karen a moment to fully grasp what Crowe had told her.

"The child locator alarm?" She shook her head briskly. "It isn't Evie's. It was Ian's. He walked in his sleep when he was little. If he moved thirty feet from the receiver, it started beeping. We haven't used it in years."

"He couldn't get a signal and thought it was broken."

Karen put her face in her hands.

"I have more questions I need to ask Ian," Crowe said. "And I'd prefer if you were present this time, Mrs. Mortimer."

Karen stared at her son. "Well?"

Ian looked away and began scraping at his thumbnail again. "I'm sorry, mum."

"Sorry won't half do, now will it?"

He didn't answer.

"Ian," Crowe said, "can you tell me what you and your sister were doing at Mr. Rutherford's house the day before your sister disappeared?"

"Where's that?" Ian asked.

Crowe described the location.

"Oh," Ian said. "We walked past it plenty times. But we never stopped."

"You never went there? Never talked to anyone?"

Ian shook his head. "No one lives there."

"What's this got to do with Evie?" Karen asked.

"Ian's not telling the truth. He and Evie were seen going inside." Crowe had the boy's attention now.

As Karen took in her son's reaction to Crowe's accusation, her demeanor changed. "Ian! What have you done?"

The boy looked as if she'd struck him.

"Who were the two boys and why did you follow them into the house?" Crowe asked.

Ian said nothing.

"Answer!" his mother shouted.

Ian winced. "Just some kids. They were with their mum."

Crowe asked again, "Why did you follow them in?"

185

When Ian shrugged, his mother twisted his arm. The boy cried out. Karen glared at him. "Tell it," she said. "Right now!"

"Stop it, mum! I didn't mean for it to happen. It wasn't my fault!"

"What happened?" Crowe asked.

Ian hung his head. "They said the guy their dad worked for had snakes and lizards and stuff in there. I said I didn't believe it. And they said they'd prove it."

"And were there snakes and lizards?"

"Yeah."

"What happened when you went inside?"

"We were looking at the cobra. One of the kids started tapping on the glass. The cobra stood up and started striking at him. That's when the guy ran down from upstairs."

"What did he do?"

"He was yelling and swearing. I grabbed Evie and we ran. I don't know what happened to the other kids. I guess they got in trouble."

During Ian's revelation, Karen sat open-mouthed, stunned.

"What were you thinking, Ian?" She turned to Crowe. "Do you think these people took Evie?"

"I don't know," Crowe said. "We're looking for them. Ian and Evie may have seen something they shouldn't have."

"Oh, dear Lord, do you think Ian's in danger, too?"

Ian started to cry. Crowe felt for the boy. He'd been in a similar situation himself, years ago. He put a hand on Ian's shoulder. He wished he could tell him it would be all right.

Crowe sat in his office at Killingsworth CID reviewing reports. He'd had another short, terse call that morning from Detective Chief Superintendent Parker-Bowles wanting to know why after ninety-six hours Crowe and his team had failed to find Evie Mortimer or recover her body. The public and the media, Parker-Bowles informed him, were snapping at their heels wanting information, answers, and he had nothing to give them.

Two days after Rutherford had identified his tenant as Terence Banks, Banks and a man named Dawson had been taken into custody.

Rutherford, as Crowe suspected, knew more about the goings-on at his property than he wanted to tell. Banks had refused to speak without a solicitor. Smart fellow. But Rutherford, facing a charge of obstructing a police investigation, had revealed that Banks was a reptile smuggler. Rutherford, for supplying the "safe house," got a cut of Banks' profits on the illegal sale of the animals. Both vehemently denied any knowledge of Evie Mortimer. Crowe shut down his tablet and turned to his Sergeant.

"Banks isn't your run-of-the-mill reptile smuggler. His clientele are connoisseurs. Not satisfied with your average deadly viper. Generally speaking, he's a loner. But, based on what Rutherford let slip, I suspect he had a special order that required more than one man, hence, Dawson."

Burke leaned back in his chair. "You think they're lying?"

Crowe shook his head. "No. I believe they're telling the truth or as much of the truth as you can ever expect to get from that sort. When you think about it, Rolly, it doesn't matter what the Mortimer children saw, because Banks and Dawson vacated the property immediately with no intention of ever returning. They guessed, and rightly so, that Ian and Evie would keep quiet because they knew they'd get into trouble."

"We're back to nothing, then," Burke said.

Crowe heard the disappointment in his Sergeant's voice. The whole department had been working around the clock to find Evie. And now it seemed their only real lead had dried up. They had failed to find her. Failed to turn up one clue to her whereabouts. Crowe steepled his fingers and gazed at the ceiling fan that turned lazily overhead. "Unless something else happened."

"What are you thinking, guv?"

"It's unlikely we'll get much more from Banks or Dawson at this point. We need a different approach. Locate Dawson's wife and bring her in for questioning."

A few hours later, Tina Dawson sat in Crowe's Interview Room.

"After Banks chased the children away, what happened?"

"The bastard gave my boys a good shellacking. Not that they didn't deserve it. But that's my job, not his. He had no right."

"And then all of you left the house, is that correct?"

"No. I took the boys home. Dawson was to come home after he helped Banks with a delivery."

"What time was that?"

"I don't know. Some time that night."

"But Dawson didn't come home. Why was that?"

Tina looked past Crowe at the door. "I want to go. I've done nothing. You can't hold me."

"If we find out that this business has anything to do with the disappearance of Evie Mortimer and that you could have given us information that would lead to locating her and refused to do so, you'll be spending your time in the same place they're going."

Tina tried to give him a tough stare. She wasn't good at it. Crowe thought she didn't really have it in her.

"If it was one of your kids missing four days and you had no idea where he was, don't you think you'd want someone who might offer a lead to come forward?"

Tina's eyes misted over and she sniffed a bit. That put her right where Crowe wanted her. Whatever else she might be, she wasn't a neglectful or uncaring mother. Crowe handed her a tissue packet.

"Thanks," she said and blew her nose. "You know right where to twist the knife, don't you? Your job, right? I'll tell you then, but I don't know how it could possibly help you."

"Just tell me," Crowe said. "Let me decide."

Tina took a deep breath. "When Dawson called later that evening, he said they had a problem. A serious problem. I left my boys with my mum and went over there. When I got there, they were packing to leave—lock, stock, and barrel. When Banks found out that Dawson called me, he lost his mind. I thought he was going to murder us."

"What did Dawson tell you, Tina?"

"I've said too much all ready. Banks will kill me if he finds out."

"Banks is in prison. He can't hurt you."

Tina looked hard at Crowe. "One of those things got away. And before you ask, I don't know what it was. Dawson didn't tell me. He wasn't half making sense anyway. Banks was having fits. They were running about outside trying to find it, but they were afraid to draw attention."

"And they didn't alert the police because it was illegal. They might have done so anonymously."

"Dawson might have done that, Chief Inspector, but Banks isn't that kind. He'd cut and run, and the less said the better. As much as I hate to say it, Dawson is weak. He needs someone to follow and he never picks the right one." She shook her head sadly.

"Do you know what Banks was keeping locked up in the basement?"

"What? No. I didn't know there was a basement."

Crowe believed her. He told her to go. Her kids were raising hell outside in the hall, but as soon as they saw her they settled down and fell into line behind her. He watched as they disappeared into the stream of people coming and going from Killingsworth Constabulary.

That night, alone in his office, Crowe massaged his temples and forehead, attempting to ward off a headache. On top of everything else, he now had a second crime on his hands: an escaped reptile, species unknown. Probably poisonous. Loose in a village. The local Constable, Priddy, had been alerted. Crowe had contacted a herpetologist at a nearby college, who had agreed to help them locate the thing, if it could be located. Needle in a haystack, Dr. Wakefield had said. But he was game. He realized the danger. On a hunch, Crowe described the white, chalky stuff he and Burke had found in Rutherford's basement. Wakefield said it sounded like it could be a urate—reptiles excreted nitrogen in the form of uric acid, which could be excreted dry—but he'd have to see it to be sure. Crowe drummed his fingers on the desk, damning the slowness of the forensics lab.

He could not shake the feeling that the Mortimer children's visit to the Rutherford house and Evie's disappearance the very next day were related. It was the strongest lead they had. He had shared his theory— what little of it there was—with his team. On the surface, the connection between the two events appeared tenuous, but it was the only thing that made any sense.

A few days later, at seven o'clock in the morning, Crowe was surprised and fearful when the police dispatch alerted him to an emergency call reporting a snake in a swimming pool at a private residence in Brightworthy. When he arrived at the house, a glaringly modern glass and metal monstrosity, there was no answer at the front door. After a quick look around, he found a path and followed it to the rear of the house. On the way, Crowe rang his Sergeant and then Wakefield.

At the back, he found a distraught woman and Constable Priddy standing near the terraced steps of a kidney-shaped swimming pool. Crowe identified himself and joined them, gazing into the sparkling water. What he saw there, lying at the bottom of the pool, deeply shocked him. He reckoned the pool to be at least fifty feet long. The snake, an albino Burmese python, stretched nearly half its length.

The middle-aged woman, wearing a white bikini, was soaking wet and shaking uncontrollably. Both she and the Constable appeared mesmerized.

"Constable Priddy," Crowe snapped.

The young officer jerked to attention. "Sir."

"Have you called Animal Control?"

"Yes, sir, they'll be here directly." He swallowed. "I'm to keep the snake from leaving the pool until they arrive."

Crowe eyed the creature. It hadn't moved. He knew a bit about pythons. They were crack swimmers and could stay submerged for as long as thirty minutes.

"I'll assist you," Crowe said.

The young officer looked much relieved.

Crowe nodded toward the woman. "Report, Constable."

Priddy flushed. "Sorry, sir. It's just that ... well ... as best as I can make out, Mrs. Trevanian came out at approximately six-thirty for her morning swim. She dove into the water at the other end of the pool and swam a couple laps before she noticed something on the terraced steps at this end. She had her glasses off and couldn't see clearly what it was from that distance. She moved closer and at that point the snake raised its head and she realized what it was."

Mrs. Trevanian groaned. She stared at Crowe, her eyes glassy bright. "It raised its head and looked right at me." She hugged herself tightly, but her body still shook. "I couldn't believe my eyes." She squeezed her eyes shut, as if trying to rid herself of the memory.

"It started to move, to uncoil." She made a strangled cry. "My god, there was no end to it. I couldn't scream. I couldn't move." She clapped a hand over her mouth. "And then I did scream. I know I did. And then ... I don't remember. Everything's a blur. But somehow, I got out."

Crowe saw her scraped knees, the abrasions on her thighs. She'd made it to the side and hauled herself out.

"And the snake?" he asked.

She pointed. "Down there, where it is now. Where I was." She began to cry.

Crowe slipped off his jacket and draped it around her shoulders. He led her away from the pool and settled her on a lounge chair while Constable Priddy kept an eye on the snake. If the python tried to leave the pool, Crowe had no idea how they would stop it. The only things at hand were two long-handled skims used for removing leaves and debris from the surface of the water. They would hardly do, except perhaps as a way to herd the snake back into the pool. Crowe was doubtful even of that. The python at the bottom of Elspeth Trevanian's pool was at least twenty feet long and, even though the water magnified its size somewhat, Crowe had no doubt the creature had to weigh upward of two hundred pounds.

"Sir," Priddy called, his voice shrill. "It's moving!"

Crowe urged Mrs. Trevanian's to go inside. Then he grabbed the skims and hurried to where Constable Priddy stood at the edge of the terraced steps.

Crowe handed Priddy a skim. "Stand well back. Pythons are fast and dangerous if threatened."

As the snake's head broke the surface of the water, they retreated to what Crowe hoped was a safe distance. The python stared at them a moment, eyes cold and expressionless. Then it swam toward the steps.

The snake's body undulated as it sailed through the water and Crowe could not help but admire the grace with which the creature

191

swam. Its massive size made its agility even more amazing. Confronted by Crowe and Priddy, the snake halted, raised its upper body, and extended its flat, blunt-nosed head. Its forked tongue flicked out, tasting the air between them. Crowe stepped forward and pressed the skim against the creature's neck. Its head whipped around and, in an instant, it lunged at Crowe. He scrambled back. The snake hissed, its mouth wide open. Crowe hit it with the skim pole.

"Priddy," he shouted. "I'll take this side, you take the other."

Hesitant at first, Priddy found his courage and came forward, his skim at the ready. Crowe felt for him. Police school couldn't prepare you for something like this.

"Together now," Crowe said.

They advanced on the giant serpent, shouting and beating at the ground. For an instant, Crowe feared it wouldn't yield. Then, with another fearsome, open-mouthed hiss, it whipped its massive body backward into the water and dove to the bottom of the pool. As Crowe and Priddy leaned on their skims breathing hard, adrenaline pumping, a man lugging a large plastic crate and a snake hook came onto the patio.

"Brian Steele, Animal Control."

Crowe identified himself and Priddy.

"Where's the snake?"

Priddy pointed to the pool. Steele walked to the edge. "Jesus God!" He looked from Crowe to Priddy. "Bloody hell. You might have warned me."

Priddy colored. "Sorry."

Steele hitched up his trousers. Squinting at Crowe, he scratched the back of his sun-browned neck. "I'll call for a stun gun."

"Look out!" Priddy shouted.

The snake surged out of the water and over the shallow steps, forcing them to leap aside. In seconds, a third of its body had already reached the terrazzo tiles on the patio, while the bulk of it still slithered past them.

Steele signaled Crowe and Priddy. "When the tail comes by, grab it and hold on."

Priddy looked at Steele as if the man had lost his mind.

"I know what I'm doing," Steele said. He held up the snake loop. "I'll get this around her head, and then we'll get her into the crate."

Crowe watched as the python continued to move toward the patio. With a shock, he realized that Mrs. Trevanian had not gone inside. He shouted and waved his hands. She saw the snake moving toward her and began to scream.

Steele, who apparently had not seen the woman when he arrived, looked up, startled.

Mrs. Trevanian, still screaming, jerked open the door to the glass-walled sunroom that let onto the patio and fled inside. Crowe heard the door slam and the lock click.

"Now!" Steele shouted. They grabbed the snake's tail and hung on while its massive body whipped back and forth as it tried to shake them off. A second later, it lunged at them.

Crowe felt the snake's power as its muscles rippled and bunched and knew they were in trouble. As Steele advanced on its head with his noose, the snake rolled away. The heaviest part of its body, nearly a foot in diameter, struck Crowe and sent him sprawling. Priddy, knocked off balance, threw out an arm to steady himself. But, with nothing but air to hold on to, he lost his footing on the wet tiles and slid under the snake's head.

"Priddy!" Crowe shouted as he leaped to his feet.

Lunging with unbelievable speed, the snake struck, sinking its teeth into Priddy's face. Priddy screamed, eyes bulging in panic. A heartbeat later, the snaked heaved its body onto his shoulders.

Crowe heard a shout. Wakefield had arrived and was running to assist Steele. As they strained against the python's weight, the herpetologist took hold of the snake's head, while Steele tried to prevent it from coiling around Priddy. A minute later, Crowe saw his Sergeant come through the gate.

The snake was still gaining ground. Crowe grabbed at the torch in Priddy's utility belt.

As if reading Crowe's mind, Wakefield said, "It's no good trying to beat it loose. See if these people have any whiskey."

They were all grunting with the effort of holding off the python and Crowe feared if he let go, the tide of the battle would turn against them.

"Damn it, man!" Wakefield shouted. "Get moving! Get as much of the stuff as you can! Hurry!"

"Rolly!" Crowe shouted, breaking the spell riveting Burke's attention on the grotesque scene. "Find some whiskey!"

"And call for an ambulance," Steele shouted after him. "This man needs care!"

Crowe heard pounding. Burke shouting. More pounding. Then a crash and glass breaking. At every opportunity, the snake pulled its body closer, attempting to wind itself around Priddy's chest.

"Hold her back," Steele said through clenched teeth. "She'll suffocate him."

The snake bunched its muscles and squeezed. Priddy squealed, followed by an awful strangling sound as he clawed helplessly at the snake's head.

"Steady on!" Wakefield shouted.

Crowe heard desperation in Wakefield's cry, but he also heard Burke shouting, "Got it!"

Wakefield loosed his hold on the snake and Burke took his place. Wakefield snapped a skim pole in half. He grasped the snake's head, prying at its mouth with his fingers. Seconds ticked by and Wakefield couldn't budge its grip on Priddy.

"Bloody hell," Wakefield muttered. His biceps bulged and the ligaments in his forearms strained with the effort. Then, in an instant, the snake's jaws parted and Wakefield thrust the piece of skim pole in the gap.

"Here!" Wakefield shouted. "Hold this. And mind you don't let it slip."

Burke grabbed the rod. The power of the snake's jaws had already begun to crush the hollow metal tube. Wakefield opened a bottle and began pouring the whiskey in the snake's mouth.

Crowe looked at Steele. His face showed the strain of holding off the monster. Sweat trickled into Crowe's eyes. They were all exhausted.

"Hang on, guv," Burke said. Crowe nodded.

Priddy was ashen, eyes glazed, arms limp. "Priddy," Crowe said, "can you hear me?"

"Unconscious," Wakefield said. "Mercifully." He grabbed another bottle and poured. The snake's mouth opened. Its head reared back.

"Now!" Wakefield shouted. "Drag it back!"

For a moment, Crowe thought the snake wouldn't budge, then it uncoiled, lashing from side to side. Finally, staggering under its powerful body, the four of them hauled the monster away from Priddy. With Wakefield controlling its head with a noose, Steele, Crowe, and Burke, positioned at intervals along the snake's body, managed to keep it prone. Crowe saw the bulge at the same time as the herpetologist.

"Ate recently," Wakefield said. "Something large by the look of it."

"Sergeant," Crowe said, holding out his hand.

Burke handed him the child locator device.

"Fresh batteries?"

Burke nodded. Crowe pushed the button that activated the transmitter.

They heard a muffled *Beep! Beep! Beep! Beep!*

Banks finally spilled on the python. He'd stolen it from a breeder in France. The job should have been a piece of cake. But it wasn't. From the start of it, nothing had gone right. His regular man had been bitten, nearly killed. He'd had to take on Dawson at the last minute. It was his bad luck the snake had started to shed while they were smuggling it into England. Painfully uncomfortable, the twenty-foot albino burm was aggressive and hungry. Banks had told Dawson how to contain it, how to take care of it, had given him precise instructions. But the lazy git hadn't done as he was told. And the snake, to no one's surprise except Dawson's, had escaped. Pushed through the unsecured cellar hatchway doors and disappeared into the night and the lush gardens of Brightworthy.

"And you didn't report it because it was stolen, is that right?" Crowe asked.

"That's right." Banks laughed without mirth. "I'm no fool."

"That monster killed a three-year-old child. Dawson, to his credit, is devastated. But you, you care nothing about that, do you?" Crowe did not try to hide his disgust.

Banks stared steadily at Crowe.

"That snake was worth £42,000. I had a buyer. And now, because of that toerag Dawson, I have no snake, no money, and you've clapped me in irons."

Crowe persisted. "You could have reported it anonymously. Why didn't you?"

Banks' eyes narrowed, a half smile tweaked his lips. "Now, where's the fun in that, mate?"

DESPAIR

BY SHAUN MEEKS

Frank held her in his arms, felt her drool down the front of his shirt as he picked up what had come out of her head and tried to put it back in. He rocked her back and forth, tears streaming from his eyes. He looked over at the ruined car, his daughter still buried inside, then down at his wife. He leaned over and kissed her forehead, begged her to be okay. In the distance, he heard wailing sirens and told her help would be there soon; told her to hold on.

Then, he awoke, arms empty—just like his life.

Slowly, Frank got out of bed. He saw that it was only four in the morning, but he knew it was time to abandon sleep. His wife and daughter had been dead for seven months and, since then, he hadn't had a decent night's sleep.

He walked down the hall to the kitchen, almost lost his way at first. He had to remind himself that he was not at home, that he had followed his brother's advice—no, his insistence—that he move into the old family house where they had grown up. Frank's brother, Stephen, a psychiatrist, told him that it would be therapeutic to get out of the home that he had shared with his wife Donna and daughter Alicia. He said it would help to leave those memories behind and instead surround himself with those of his childhood. Yet, after two days in the old house, his memories and dreams always came back to his wife and child.

The good memories were far and few between, but the bad ones lurked around every corner, haunted him. The worst were those last moments he'd spent with them before they were taken to the morgue.

Frank sat down in the cold kitchen and looked out the window as the snow fell. There were no neighbors near him, nothing outside but woods and the guesthouse that his father built when Frank was ten. Stephen had told him that the solitude might help. Not a day had gone by that he didn't feel tears streaming down his cheeks; sometimes they lasted from the moment he woke until he went back to bed. Other times, as he lay in his empty room, he would stare at the ceiling and wish he could feel Donna's head on his chest again, smell her freshly washed hair. Then he would cry himself to sleep and meet the horrible dreams again.

It was his fault they were dead. That's what Stephen didn't know, couldn't see. The reason Frank could not let go of them was not just love, but guilt.

He went to the fridge and pulled the coffee from the freezer, decided he was going to stay up and get on with the day. To do that, he would need a good helping of caffeine, though he was sure sooner or later he would turn to the whiskey in the cupboard. Lately, it was the only thing he enjoyed.

He brewed a pot of strong coffee, poured a cup, and headed toward the porch. If he sat out in the cold, watched the snow fall, and just absorbed the grandness of the world, it would be enough of a distraction from his dreams and his guilt. He slipped on his boots and coat and went out into the crisp air. He sat in an old chair his father had made and tried to forget.

He thought of his dad, a man bigger in memory than he had been in life. He looked up to his father, someone who was strong, good with his hands, and had been there for his family when they needed him. If Frank fell out of a tree and cut himself or bruised his body, his dad was there to make him feel better. He would give him a hug, tell him to buck up, and everything would be better. He could fix anything. Frank wished he was more like him—though his father never had to see his child pulled from a car in more than one piece.

Again, his mind went back to them. He hated that he couldn't move on, wasn't able to get past his loss and his failure. He should have been protecting them, saved them from what had happened. Time and time again, he wondered if he hadn't been lazy, if he had just gone out to pick up Alicia from piano practice like Donna asked, would they all be together. Would they be alive or would he have died with Alicia?

He can hear his wife reminding him to get Alicia, while he sat at the laptop writing a new story for some unknown magazine that only fifty people would ever read. He didn't even look up from the screen when he told her to do it for him, that he was in the middle of an important piece. She reluctantly went, and thirty minutes later he heard the squeal of tires and the impact of two cars. He stood up from the desk, looked out the window, and saw their car buried into another, a woman lying on the ground—a woman wearing Donna's dress.

The memories came in waves and Frank held back the tears that burned his eyes; hated himself. The darkness loomed overhead and he wondered if he should wait for the sky to lighten up or if he should just get on with the inevitable. The sun was still below the horizon, but he thought he might as well get started dulling his senses with booze. Fuck etiquette.

He went back into the house and stopped dead in his tracks. Were his eyes playing tricks on him? The coffee mug nearly slipped from his fingers as he stared at the tricycle that sat near the stairs. He hadn't brought it with him. In fact, a month after he buried Donna and Alicia, Stephen had come over and removed it, as well as other things that belonged to them. Clothes. Toys.

And yet it was there. Not just there, but looming in the hallway, a ghost of his daughter's past. He took a tentative step toward it, not sure if or how it could be real, but he needed to touch it. His heart raced as he moved a shaky hand toward the red handle bars with the white grips and streamers. Then, just as his index finger was about to make contact, he heard laughter.

Alicia's laugh.

The cup fell. He looked up at the ceiling where the sound had come from.

"Alicia?" He moaned. His legs felt shaky and weak. He called her name again, but there was no other sound. He looked back down at the bike, mocking him, and he ran away from it, out the door and into the snow.

Panic overcame him. There was no way that bike could be there, or that he could hear Alicia's laughter. He had lost it, had gone nuts. Leaving the house he had bought with his wife and going out to the middle of nowhere, with nobody there to help him, was stupid. The dreams, the memories, and the guilt had made something in his head break. He backed away from the house, tripped, and fell in the snow. For what felt like an hour, he didn't move. He sat in the snow and looked at the house as if at any moment, an apparition was going to appear—the ghosts of his dead family.

Nothing came.

He waited awhile longer, then stood up and made his way back to the house. He tried to tell himself that maybe he wasn't going crazy, that it was just the remnants of a nightmare and stress getting to him. He was sure that was the answer. He didn't want to believe that he had lost it, or worse, that it was a ghost. Those were childish thoughts.

He walked up the steps to the porch, moving slowly, taking deep breaths. He tried to convince himself that there was nothing there. It was like the time he had gone into the woods with Stephen as a kid and thought he had seen Bigfoot. He had just watched a show about mysteries and the supernatural, so of course when he had gotten to the woods, he had seen the hulking Sasquatch. Stephen had told him on the way that it would be cool to see one, that he had heard rumors that the woods near their house was home to a colony of Sasquatches. That was all he could think about on the hike. Every shadow, any movement he saw, his mind told him it was the legendary monster. He went home swearing up and down that they were in the woods and they would eventually come and get them.

It was the same with the tricycle and the laughter. He hadn't been able to stop thinking about Donna and Alicia. It was the power of suggestion. He was sure that's what Stephen would tell him, if he had come to the house with him.

And, as he peeked over the porch rail and looked into the house, he saw he was right. There was nothing there; just the same hallway and stairs that he had always known. He shook it off, not thinking about madness any longer, only that he had too much on his mind. He wondered if he should go to bed after all, try and sleep and give everything a rest.

It was all he could think to do other than drink.

When Frank opened his eyes next, it was two in the afternoon and he was thankful to have had a somewhat peaceful rest. No nightmares followed him down into his subconscious, just a sweet and relaxed darkness. He felt more rested than he had in months.

He was also hungry.

Frank headed back down to the kitchen, thinking of eggs and bacon as he passed the living room. He was just in its doorway, when the television turned on and began skipping through channels. Frank stopped dead in his tracks. He turned to look in the living room, and watched as the television jumped from station to station. The changes were rapid, the voices and images a blur, until it finally stopped on a channel that couldn't exist.

The television played a memory of Frank's, one from long ago, from happier days. Alicia was on the screen, looking down at the birthday cake in front of her, eyes wide in amazement. She was transfixed by the candles. Around her, people sang a terrible rendition of Happy Birthday. Then, Donna leaned in. "Make a wish, darling," she said. Frank put a hand over his mouth. Donna turned to him and smiled. "I can't believe our little girl is five," she said, and then turned back to Alicia as she sucked in a big breath and blew the candles out. And, as she did, the television turned off.

"No," he cried to the lost images of his family. He ran into the living room, dropped to his knees in front of the darkened screen, and touched it softly. "Please don't leave again. Don't leave me alone."

He spoke to the dark television, but nothing more happened. It didn't come back on. After hours passed, Frank stood up, walked over to the couch, and sat down. He stared at the screen, then at the ceiling and wondered what was going on. First he had seen the tricycle, and then videos of his family had come on the television. He had never believed in ghosts—but what if? What if his wife and daughter had found him?

"I miss you, Donna. And I miss my little girl," he whispered to the walls, hoping for something in return, but the house was as empty as he felt inside.

He lay down on the couch, curled up in a fetal position and watched the dark screen in case they came back. He imagined what it would have been like if they had lived. How his wife would have looked each morning, the sun kissing her face. He loved the idea of growing old with her, but that could never happen.

Frank also thought of Alicia, growing up, trying new things and succeeding in anything that came her way. He saw her move from a child to a teen to an adult. He could picture her clearly as she became the woman he wished she could still be, become a doctor or lawyer or even an artist. He saw her sitting by a husband she loved and children that echoed her own face. He wanted nothing more than to see the child he had helped make, that he had loved and watched die, get a chance at life.

He closed his eyes and fell asleep again, mentally exhausted and depressed.

In his dreams, it happened again.

He sat at the computer, going over paperwork that could have waited, and left Donna to go and get their daughter. He stared at the screen that filled him with stress, and heard the screeching of tires outside. Then there was a sound of metal crushing against metal and Frank knew it was close. He stood up from his chair and looked out the bay window at the front of the house and saw the car. *Their* car.

The next moment, he was beside the wreck, saw his wife on the ground, head impossibly twisted, blood everywhere. He went to her, lifted her into his arms, and saw that parts of her head were still on the asphalt. He started to scoop them up and attempted to put her back together. He looked down at her face, one eye rolled in the back of her head, the other spread across her bloody cheek.

"You just hang in there, darling. It's okay. It's not that bad."

From behind him, from inside the car, he heard his daughter. She cried and coughed hoarsely, called out for help. He held Donna close to him and turned to look at the car. It was gone. And he found his arms empty. He looked down to where his wife had been and saw his hands were stained red; globs of coagulated blood and bits of hair coated them. He looked up and saw the street was empty. Almost empty. His wife and daughter stood a few feet from him, pale and ruined. They began to move their mouths, as though they were trying to speak, but nothing came out, yet he could read their lips.

Your fault.

The dream repeated itself over and over while he slept, and when he woke up, he felt worse than when he had gone to sleep. He sat up, curious as to what time it might be. Did it really matter? The house he had grown up in had become a prison, a place where time seemed to lose all meaning and the ghosts of his old life found a way to bleed through.

Frank realized he needed to talk to someone, and there was only one person he could think of. The same person that had told him to leave his home and return to the place he had grown up.

Stephen.

He looked at the wall clock and saw that it was only ten-thirty, which seemed like a reasonable time to call. Using the old house phone, he dialed his brother's cell number. He was glad to hear his brother answer on the second ring.

"Frank?" Stephen's voice, calm and deep. So much like their father's voice.

"Stephen. I think coming to the farmhouse was a mistake."

"What's wrong?" Concern in his voice, as always.

"I'm ... seeing things. And I'm having horrible dreams. It's Donna and Alicia. I can't get them out of my head. I heard ... I think I heard Alicia laughing."

"That's not possible, Frank. I think you know that. You're grieving. You have to let it all out. You're letting things build up and if you don't let them out, you will feel like you are going insane. You know you can't bottle it up, right?"

"I know, but ..."

"No buts, Frank. I'm not talking here as your brother. This is my medical advice. These things you think you are seeing and hearing, they're no more than your subconscious trying to fight against what's bothering you. Loss, guilt, mourning. It all adds up and if you don't let them come out, it will only get worse.

"But it hurts so much, Stevie. You don't understand. The dreams are as bad as always, but these other things—I don't know if I can take it. I hate being alone. Maybe I should come back to the city, go to one of those groups at the church?"

"You have to trust me. I'm only trying to give you the best advice. You need this, Frank. You need to let all of it go and only then will things get better. Going back to the city, to the house you shared with them, is the worst thing you could do. Those meetings they have where everyone goes around the room and tells their sad stories do nothing to help. They only make you think more about what you've lost. You know that I graduated top of my class, that I had the best marks and was even offered a job as a professor. I know what I'm talking about. What you are doing is a lot like what the monks in Tibet do. You have gone back to nature, embraced solitude and escaped the memories that haunt you. That is how you will heal, Frank. Now, I better go. I need to finish some paperwork. Love you, little brother."

"I love you too, Stevie." He hung up, but felt no better. He wasn't so sure about his brother's assessment, though he hoped it was true, that it would all get better.

A few hours later, after he made some food and thought the worst of the day was over, Frank went to the living room, deciding to kill time by watching TV. He thought of how much he used to love doing the same with Donna and Alicia. They would make popcorn, split it into two bowls, then Alicia would lie on the floor and he would sit on the couch with Donna, watching a show or a movie, laughing together. Sometimes Donna would squeeze next to him if the show was a bit scary. He wondered if those memories of his old life with them, reliving them after they were gone, were helpful or hurt him more. Either way, they were his memories and he wasn't sure he could escape them.

He sat on the couch, a drink in one hand and a whiskey bottle on the coffee table, and turned on the television. He took a deep breath, worried that, when the TV came on, the home videos would still be there, but they weren't. Instead, he watched old reruns of an '80s sitcom that he never used to like. It had not improved with age. Still, it was better to watch something dumb and mindless than to think about anything else.

The show bled into another, then to another. After the fourth one ended, infomercials followed, but he didn't change the channel. Instead, he poured another glass from the nearly empty bottle and continued to watch. A man and a woman that looked like plastic versions of real people talked excitedly about some product that was both new and improved. The audience feigned interest. Frank was pouring another drink when he noticed a change in the air. He wasn't sure what it was. He paused, listened, but it wasn't a sound. It was something else.

A smell.

Frank breathed it in, tried to figure it out. It was so familiar, something he had smelled a thousand times but couldn't put his finger on what it was. There was sweetness to it, not sugary but more like perfume. Donna's perfume. He looked around the room, stumbled to his feet and felt the effects of the alcohol when he did. He swayed and grabbed hold of the couch to steady himself. Once he regained some control over his body, he tried to find the source of the scent.

The room was dark, lit only by the television, and there seemed to be nothing there with him, at least no sign of what could be making the room smell of Donna's perfume. He remembered the day he had bought it for her, a birthday present, and it quickly became her favorite scent. Whenever they went out for dinner, on a special date, or when Donna decided she was going to try to seduce him when he came home from work, she wore it. As he smelled it, Frank was flooded with memories of her.

Her lips.

Her hair.

The way she smiled when she flirted with him.

All the things that made him love her.

Slowly, he moved away from the couch, squinting through the darkness as he went. He stubbed his toe on the leg of the hulking couch. He cried out and he fell, crashing to the floor, his head bouncing off the carpet. Frank began to moan, made a move to get up, but couldn't find the strength. He fell back to the floor defeated, and as he lay there, still smelling the perfume, a foot appeared beside his head. He gasped, seeing the high heels that he recognized right away as the one pair of expensive shoes that Donna had owned. He looked up, wanting and needing to see if it was her, if Donna had come back for him. There was someone standing there wrapped in shadows. He knew it had to be her.

'D-Donna?" he whispered, his head full of pain. The figure above him, the ghost of his wife, leaned toward him. Before he blacked out, he caught another whiff of her perfume. He felt cold fingers caress his cheek, and then he was lost to the world.

He woke up, head throbbing, body aching, from hours spent on the hard floor. Sunlight spilled into the room. He winced at the brightness and stood up. Frank tried to remember the night before, how he had ended up on the floor, but his memory was a haze. The television was still on, tuned to a useless talk show, people laughing at dumb jokes as the host went on and on about her amazing guests. He shut off the TV, and when he did his hand knocked something off the stand.

What the hell is going on? he thought, looking at the engagement ring lying on the carpet. It was Donna's, a diamond set in white gold filigree. He picked it up. It was real. The previous night leaked back into his head. He remembered the perfume, the woman standing next to him and ...

Did she touch me? Donna touched me. She left the ring for me.

Frank took the ring and carried it to his bedroom, placed it on his pillow, and stared at it, sure that if he took his eyes off the ring, it would disappear as the tricycle had. But it stayed. Even when he left the room and came back, it was still there.

Over the next week, other objects showed up from Donna and Alicia. A shoe, a picture Alicia had drawn him for Father's Day, photos that had been lost, a necklace, a dress, a doll. Frank collected them all and put them on the bed with the ring. He heard laughter coming from the walls, feet running up and down the hall, his name whispered from thin air. Sometimes he laughed, other times he cried, as his mind slipped further away. Some days he spent hours talking to the room as though his wife and daughter were there, sharing stories and letting them know how happy he was that they were close to him.

The nightmares continued to haunt him, but when he woke from them he felt as though his family was close by. He spoke to them, told them how glad he was to have them back, how sad and lost he had been since they left. Soon after, he would find an object, a sign that they heard him.

He ate less and drank more as the days passed. He did not bathe or change his clothes. None of that mattered. What did a shaved face and clean clothes mean when his wife and daughter had breached the space between the living and the dead to be with him again? Nothing outside the walls of the house mattered any longer.

Frank fought off sleep as much as he could, not wanting to revisit the nightmares. He stayed awake to hear his wife's and daughter's laughter, sometimes a disembodied word or two. He heard Alicia call out "daddy" over and over again from one room, her voice full of excitement. He ran to chase her down, only to find no one there. He called out her name, as though she was playing hide and seek with him, until he found her favorite hairpin and added it to his collection.

The next day, after less than two hours sleep, Frank woke up and waited to hear the sound of one of them; a laugh, a giggle, footsteps, anything, but nothing came. He walked around the house, calling to Donna and Alicia. Nothing.

In the kitchen, he made himself breakfast, a handful of nuts and a pint glass of whiskey and ice. Outside, the wind howled, slapping the windows with snow and ice pellets. Other than that, the house was quiet and still. Frank downed his drink in four quick gulps and dropped the empty glass into the sink where it clinked against the others. Returning to his search, he moved from room to empty room looking for his ghostly family. Nothing.

He went to the bedroom, to look over the collection of the items he'd already found. He felt cold pain stab his chest, the same pain he'd felt as he watched Donna and Alicia's coffins lowered into ground.

The bed was empty.

"Where are they? Where is it all?" He cried out to the empty room. "They left that for me! Who the fuck stole it?"

Frank stormed through the house. He screamed, demanded the return of what was stolen. Called out to his family. Pushed the television over; it shattered on the floor. He looked under the wall unit. Nothing. He tore the drawers out of every dresser in the house. His feet cut on broken glass, his hands torn from punching walls, he rooted through cupboards and drawers, only to come up empty-handed.

He took his father's fire ax from the basement and destroyed the house. Vowing to find the stolen things, his screams echoed through the empty rooms.

Sarah sat back in her chair, eating popcorn and listening to her Mp3 player as one of her favorite singers screamed about what it was to burn. She nodded her head to the music, looking across the room now and then. Everything seemed normal. Then, as one song ended and the next began, she noticed something.

Or the lack of something.

"Shit." She ran to the room where her boss was napping. "I think we have a problem."

She watched as he jumped out of bed. He'd been extremely excited the last few days. She doubted he'd slept at all. The whole thing was strange to her—his attitude, his idea to run an experiment on his brother, and even the experiment itself. Part of her thought it was crazy and mean. She had trouble understanding how he could put his brother through such horrible trauma, yet she never spoke up about it. She was a second year student in University, had little to no money and what Stephen was offering for the job was enough to last her an entire semester. He also said he would give her a letter to present to her professor that would get her extra credit. He claimed he was well respected at the U of T. So, despite her misgivings and how she felt about the doctor himself, she went along with it. A girl has to eat after all

"When did this happen?" he asked as he walked into the room.

"Only a second ago," Sarah told him. She'd been too busy with her music and own thoughts to be sure. But, it couldn't have been that long since she last looked.

He leaned toward the bank of screens and saw nothing. Nothing wasn't good.

"Get out the laptop, look at the footage, find out where he went, if he left the house. He couldn't have gone far; his car is still there."

Sarah did as she was told.

Stephen sat in the chair, his eyes moving over the monitors showing every room in the house, including the front and back doors. There was no sign of his brother anywhere and the last thing he needed was for Frank to stumble on him and Sarah in the guesthouse. Stephen had invested too much time and money for things to go wrong now.

Shortly after his brother's family died, Stephen came up with an idea—a study on the process of grief. He had an idea for a paper based on forcing someone to face their grief, the ghosts of the people they had lost, both real and imagined. He wanted to see if they cracked or if they were able to cleanse themselves of the sorrow they held so tightly to. Stephen knew that Frank suffered not just from the loss of those he loved, but also from guilt. His brother blamed himself for their deaths. That guilt was making it impossible for him to let go.

So Stephen turned the old family house into a set piece, a place to run an experiment. He placed speakers in the walls, hidden cameras in every possible space, built new hidden doors into rooms so that he or his assistant could get in and out unseen.

The next step had been helping Frank remove all the items from his house that reminded him of what he had lost. Stephen took them to use in his experiment.

After he set up the guesthouse as a lab, he ran camera feeds to the main house. Then he went to work on his brother. Once he'd convinced Frank to return to the house they grew up in, Stephen knew things would fall into place.

And they had at first. Frank was breaking down, coming apart from the sights and sounds, along with the lack of food, sleep, and the addition of alcohol that Stephen himself kept replenishing. It bothered him a bit to see his brother slip further and further away from reality. He observed the small cracks in Frank's sanity turn into fissures.

209

Finally, when the things Frank had collected on the bed went missing, he completely lost it. Through it all, Stephen watched as Frank talked to things that weren't there and cried day after day. Stephen made notes as his brother crumbled bit by bit. It bothered him, but, he reminded himself, he was doing it for science; doing it so he could help others.

And, it would make him famous.

That was a benefit too. It would show the teachers that failed him and the industry that denied him a job. They would see his paper, the study he had done, and know that they were wrong about him. Frank had no idea that his brother never finished school, that he wasn't a licensed psychiatrist. Frank didn't know that Stephen's professor had called him unstable and said that his personality bordered on sociopathic. Stephen knew they were wrong, knew they couldn't see his genius. But once they read the paper based on his research, they would see him differently. Stephen was sure that, once he showed how extreme grief could drive a person beyond reason and how a mind would bend, his professor and the entire industry would look up to him as a leader.

But now, with his brother missing, the experiment was incomplete. He had removed the items that Frank had collected and cherished to see how he would react. When his brother went on a rampage, fulfilling Stephen's expectations, he made notes, then went to lie down and told Sarah to wake him up if anything changed.

"I don't see anything," Sarah said, closing the laptop. She sounded worried. "One minute he was in the living room, the next he was heading to the kitchen, but never showed up. I don't know where he is, but he didn't leave the house."

"Great!" Stephen leaned back in his chair, considering his next move as he watched the monitors. There was nothing to do but wait. Frank had to show himself. But, after two hours of nothing, he knew they had to go find him. "Grab the Taser. If you see him, zap him."

"Am I going in alone?" Sarah asked. She sounded more than a little afraid. "The last time I saw him, he had an ax and was screaming like a madman."

"I'm going in, too. If he only sees you he won't feel safe. He trusts me."

They put their coats on and trekked from the guesthouse to the main house, fighting the wind and snow. They kept their eyes on the door as they approached in case Frank came at them. Stephen thought that if Frank saw him, he would immediately calm down, drop the ax, and ask for help. Frank trusted him.

They entered the house, slow and cautious, dropped their bulky coats by the front door, and then moved down the hall.

"Give me the Taser," Stephen whispered. Sarah handed it over. "Follow me."

They walked as lightly as they could on the squeaky floor. They both knew the layout of the house. As they came to the living room, Stephen stopped and turned to Sarah.

"If he's in there, I'll try and talk to him and—"

Warm liquid sprayed Sarah's face, got in her eyes so that she had to shut them. It stung a bit and she rubbed at them with the balls of her hands.

"Wh—what is this?"

She stopped rubbing her eyes and opened them. Her boss stood in front of her, his mouth wide open—as was the left side of his body. When he had turned to her, Frank had come from his hiding spot, the doorframe of the living room, and buried his ax between his brother's neck and shoulder. Sarah heard bones splintering as Frank pulled the ax free. Her boss dropped to the floor and a blood-splattered Frank moved toward her. She backed away, hands up, crying as she pleaded.

"Please ... don't hurt me ... it was his idea ... not mine!"

Frank paid her no mind. He swung his ax and lopped off her head. He watched as it flew through the air, hit the wall, then bounced once on the floor. Her hands, comically, went to her blood-spouting neck for a second or two as though searching for her head, and then she fell forward.

Frank leaned down, caressed her cheek, and smiled.

Frank sat on the couch, watching another sitcom, happy to be with his wife and daughter again. He stroked Donna's shoulder and kissed her cheek, listening to his daughter laugh at a dumb joke from the show. The sound of her laughter brought a smile to his face. He couldn't remember the last time he'd felt so good.

"This is so nice," Donna said. "I love to spend this kind of time with you."

"Same here. I missed you guys so much. I'm glad you're back. Both of you."

Frank looked down at his daughter who was on the floor, lying on her stomach, her feet in the air. She chuckled again at something funny, then turned back and looked at Frank.

"I missed you too, daddy. But if you and mom can hold it down, I want to watch this before I have to go to bed."

"Sorry, cutie," he said. She was such a sweet girl. His eyes moved from her, back to his wife who rested her head against his shoulder.

"Can you stroke my head?" she asked.

"Sure." He moved his fingers through her hair, not bothered by the blood and smell. He looked past those things, seeing only her beauty, not that it was his dead, rotting brother. When he looked down, he only saw her beautiful figure, not the insects and maggots that moved around in Stephen's open chest. Nor did he see that his daughter was actually Sarah, her decapitated head balanced on her back, mouth open, empty eye sockets alive with hungry movement.

All that he saw was his family.

And he was happy to have them back.

SISTERS: A FAIRY TALE

BY LIZ DEJESUS

The King's son, seeing five or six pearls and as many diamonds falling from her mouth as she spoke, fell in love with her. Thinking that such a gift was worth more than any ordinary dowry brought by another, he carried her off to his father's palace and there married her.

Gift. It was meant to be a gift but in reality ... it was a curse. Blow after blow, pain exploded in every part of Fanny's body.

Her vision swam. The threat of tears stung her eyes.

Please, she so desperately wanted to say. Any word would suffice if only it would make him stop. His handsome face was contorted in anger. He looked more like a monster than a king. The man of her dreams was now her worst nightmare. Three years they had been together and all she had to show for it were countless bruises, a cracked rib, scars on her back, and a shattered heart she was certain would never heal.

"Speak! Speak, goddamn you," Frederick shouted.

Fanny opened and closed her lips and tried to say something, anything to stop Frederick from causing her even more pain. But all that came out were sobs and tears. She swallowed some of her tears and it felt as though she had shoved shards of glass down her throat. Every time she spoke, a flower or a precious stone would fall from her

213

mouth. Titania, the Fairy Queen, had failed to think about the price Fanny's throat would pay as a result of her "gift." Stones had sharp edges. Roses had thorns. Fanny preferred to spend her time reading books in silence. It was the only thing that gave her time to heal. She chose her words carefully and sparingly.

He had other plans.

Her *loving* husband ... the beloved king of their realm. King Frederick.

He grabbed a fistful of her hair and pulled on it until she stood. Fanny whimpered as she felt each strand strain beneath his grasp. He dragged her onto the bed and shoved her down. Fanny yelped as her head struck the headboard. She saw a clump of her dark-brown locks tangled in her husband's hand. Frederick threw them to the floor. She touched the top of her scalp; there was a bald spot.

"That was the sole purpose of our marriage. You give me the precious gems that fall out of your pretty little mouth and I make you a queen. Now speak."

I can't. Fanny desperately wanted to say those words. She longed to make him understand how much pain it caused her every time a thorny rose or a sharp-edged stone traveled up her throat, ripping flesh from the inside as it traveled through her body.

She closed her eyes and remembered ...

"Call me Freddy," he whispered the day after they met. She smiled and said his name. A diamond fell out of her mouth. His eyes widened in astonishment.

Frederick slapped her across the cheek with the back of his hand and grunted with frustration. Fanny's vision swam. A shock of pain bloomed over the left side of her face. As she braced herself for the next strike, she heard a faint hiss. Her heart jumped. It was a familiar sound, one she hadn't heard in many years. Fanny remembered it with a mixture of terror and love. Not exactly comforting, but it was the next best thing. Fanny then heard soft footsteps.

Elda, my sister.

Fanny turned her eyes to her husband and smiled. Her smile turned into a giggle. It was the first time in months that she felt a surge of hope rush through her.

"What's so funny?" he asked.

Fanny pointed at him and with her other hand drew an imaginary line across her neck.

Today, you die.

As soon as the thought came to her, a dozen snakes crawled into the room through the open window. Pale lemon. Emerald green. Ruby red. Their bodies landed with loud slaps on the stone floor; they made their way toward the king. For the first time since she met him, she saw the look of fear in Frederick's eyes. He took a step back and then tripped over his own feet. He fell on his back and pushed himself away until his head touched the wall.

The reptiles took their time. Frederick muttered a prayer and kept pushing himself back, as though the wall would magically disappear and allow him to escape. A sapphire blue snake was the first to reach him. It opened its mouth wide, revealing pale pink gums and tongue and two needle-sharp fangs. It coiled and sprang onto Frederick's neck. He screamed as he tried to pull the snake from his throat. Then, they all bit him and didn't release their deadly grips until they had injected their poison into his veins.

He rolled his eyes at Fanny and whispered, "Forgive me."

Fanny stifled a sob. A part of her wanted to forgive him for what he had done to her, for all the years of abuse she had suffered at his hands. But, how could she possibly forgive all the agony he had put her through? Had he shown her any kindness or mercy, she would've given him everything. Love. Trust. Loyalty. Respect. Along with every precious stone that fell from her lips. She would've gladly given it to him had he truly loved her.

Frederick grimaced. Then his face turned bright red. He took one last painful breath and died.

Moments later, a pale hand appeared on the windowsill. In crawled Elda, with the same stealth and grace of the reptiles she commanded. Her skin was deathly pale, dry and cracked. Her lips were thin, and her teeth pushed forward from years of having snakes and toads crawling out of her mouth. Elda, her sister. Her savior. She walked toward Fanny, stepping over Frederick's corpse.

"Sister, it has been too long." Her voice was dry and gravelly.

Fanny nodded in response.

Several baby snakes crawled from Elda's mouth and slithered around her neck until they made themselves at home in her long, salt-and-pepper hair. Several dozen snakes coiled around her feet.

Elda avoided making eye contact with Fanny as she spoke. "Still unable to control what comes out of your mouth, I see. No matter. Come, let's leave this dismal place."

Fanny gazed at her dead husband, at the vacant stare of his hazel eyes. Her life here was over. Even if she could prove her innocence, none of the villagers would accept her as their ruler. She was a peasant turned queen. She would be dead either way. Her best chance lay with Elda. Her sister extended her hand to Fanny, and Fanny took it.

"Good, we have work to do." Elda grunted as she helped Fanny stand.

Confused, Fanny frowned.

"We're going to kill the Fairy Queen," Elda said.

Fanny shook her head and pulled her hand out of Elda's grasp. Kill Titania? Was she mad? The Fairy Queen was immortal.

"I need you, Fanny."

Four ruby-colored baby snakes slithered out of her sister's mouth. Red for love. Red for blood. Red for lies. Who knew?

"I can't do this alone," Elda whispered.

Fanny had a hard time believing that.

Elda took a deep breath. She stomped her foot and sneered. "I can't believe you're going to make me say it. Fine. I don't *want* to do it alone. I need you by my side, Fanny. Please."

Fanny reconsidered Elda's offer. Maybe she could convince her to forget her plan to kill the Fairy Queen. Perhaps they could start a new life together—someplace peaceful where they wouldn't be bothered, where they could be alone, two sisters under the same roof once more.

Fanny nodded. For better or worse, their lives were tied to each other.

"You are so very pretty, my dear, so good and so mannerly, that I cannot help giving you a gift." For this was a fairy, who had taken the form of a poor countrywoman, to see how far the civility and good manners of this pretty girl would go. "I will give you for a gift," continued the Fairy, "that, at every word you speak, there shall come out of your mouth either a flower or a jewel."

Fanny quickly ran to her chambers. She grabbed a small leather pouch filled with silver and gold. Fanny had stolen coins whenever Frederick wasn't paying attention. Always one at a time, so he wouldn't notice that they were missing. She wanted to pack a few other things— her favorite dresses and some jewelry—but decided against it. Elda and Fanny shoved Frederick's body underneath the bed. It wasn't the best plan, for she knew the servants would soon come to empty the chamber pot and tidy the room.

"Let's go, Fanny," Elda hissed.

Fanny grabbed two hooded robes. Probably not the best disguises, but they would have to do. Elda put on the brown robe and waited as Fanny slipped on the navy-blue robe. She put her coin purse in her pocket and put the hood over her head. Now she was ready to leave.

As they walked among the villagers, Fanny pulled her hood down so it covered half of her face. Together, they snuck out of the village. She soon realized that no one was looking at them. No one cared. No one gave a damn who she was ... or wasn't.

Elda was silent until they were a few miles away. Where she hid her snakes ... Fanny didn't want to know. She was just glad that no one had seen any of Elda's pets on their way out of the village.

They found a tavern and sat in a dark corner to eat. Fanny tried not to look at Elda as she ate her meal. Her sister's face was misshapen. Elda caught Fanny's eye just as she looked away.

"I wasn't as lucky as you. The curse ruined my teeth and my skin. You thought losing your voice was tragic? I would gladly trade places with you," Elda said.

Twenty-nine baby snakes fell from her mouth and crawled into her hair.

Fanny could only hope that no one in the tavern had seen.

"Snakes? Hair?" Fanny whispered. Two pearls rolled out of her mouth and fell on the wooden table.

Elda wasted no time. She snatched the pearls and slipped them into her pocket. She smirked in response to Fanny's question.

"It took some time, but I learned how to control some of the creatures that come out of my mouth. At least now, I'm not vomiting up a giant toad every damned day. On a good day, all I get are little snake eggs. Those are tasty."

217

"Teach?" Fanny asked. A bright orange topaz fell onto the table. Before her sister could take it, Fanny took the precious gem and slipped it in her pocket.

Elda chuckled, a sound like dry leaves rustling on the forest floor. She tapped the side of her head. "Teach yourself. It's all in your head."

Fanny frowned. It couldn't be that simple. Elda had to be lying ... it wouldn't be the first time.

They continued to eat their meal in silence. A mouse skittered past them. Elda stepped on it and snatched it up. Fanny covered her mouth and tried not to gag. Elda cocked an eyebrow, as if daring Fanny to make a comment. She took the tiny mouse and dangled it over her pocket. A black snake poked its head up, opened its mouth, and swallowed the terrified mouse.

"This is my lovely pet, Mora. Isn't she beautiful?" Elda cooed as she rubbed the snake's head with her thumb.

Fanny gave her a tight-lipped smile and nodded.

Oh God. What have I gotten myself into?

After their meal, they left the tavern (it was surprisingly mouse-free). Elda explained what she wanted Fanny to do. The plan was that Fanny would go to the Enchanted Forest, near the Fairy Realm, and scream until the Fairy Queen arrived to rescue her. Elda would wait in the shadows and pounce when the queen least expected it.

Fanny frowned at her sister.

"I know what you are thinking, sister," Elda said. "Why would she come to your aid?"

Fanny nodded.

"Because *you* are her weakness. That *abomination* happens to be in love with you, with every fiber of her immortal being."

Love?

The word echoed through Fanny's mind. Why would Queen Titania love her? She was no one. Nothing. Less than nothing. The air around her was worth more. Love? Why would anyone care for her? Her own husband had not loved her. The only reason he married her was because of her so-called gift. Her own mother often called her an unlovable creature, unworthy of a kind word or gesture. Fanny never truly understood why her mother mistreated her. She suspected that it was because she was more like her poor father.

Fanny shook her head and stopped walking.

Liar. Why are you lying to me? She wanted to scream those words at Elda. She had to be toying with her. Otherwise, why would she have said such a thing? Fanny crouched and with her index finger wrote the word LIAR on the rich, brown soil. She stood and pointed at her sister.

"Is that what you think of me?"

Fanny nodded in response.

Elda shrugged her shoulders and continued to walk. Fanny remained still and watched as her sister walked away from her. As if what she said, did, or thought were of no great consequence. Fanny covered her face with her hands and fought the urge to scream in frustration. She ran her fingers through her hair and looked up at the sky. Perhaps the answers to her problems would be somewhere in the clouds. She wished to be struck by lightning and end her pitiful, useless life.

"Are you coming or what?" Elda shouted from a distance.

Fanny thought of Queen Titania. She wondered why such a beautiful creature would waste her time loving her. Why bestow such a strange gift upon her? Was she really worthy of love?

Perhaps, yes.

At that moment, something shifted inside Fanny. The crack inside her heart closed just the tiniest bit. She wasn't sure why, but it was enough to get her walking until she caught up with her sister.

"Enough daydreaming. Time for your big opening scene," Elda said.

As they got closer to the Fairy Realm, Fanny saw creatures hiding among the trees and bushes. Pixies and fairies giggling behind the cerulean and amethyst wild flowers. A gnome watched them from a treetop, his dark brown eyes following them as they passed.

Doomed, they whispered.

The wind carried that word to Fanny and left it hovering above her head as Elda dragged her deeper into the forest.

Elda hid in the bushes and waited. Fanny wasn't sure what to do—follow her sister's command or ask the Fairy Queen for help, if by some miracle she appeared. Fanny cried for help several times, spitting out pearls in the process. After a few minutes of waiting, she thought that perhaps she was wrong, that she was a fool for deluding herself into thinking the Fairy Queen would ever come to her rescue. Then a gust of wind moved the tree branches in a soft, rhythmic whisper. They spoke to her. Fanny closed her eyes and listened intently.

She's coming. The trees had delivered their message. The queen would arrive shortly.

A small tornado formed a few feet away from where Fanny stood, throwing leaves and dirt in every direction. In a swirl of air and glitter, Queen Titania appeared. She was more beautiful than Fanny remembered. She had long, strawberry-blond hair that cascaded off her shoulders in luxurious waves. Her eyes were cornflower-blue. Her skin was pale like ivory with a sprinkling of powdery gold. Every inch of her exposed skin sparkled in the light as though the sun was doing everything in its power to illuminate her. The queen's lips were small and full. They were stained pink, as if she had just finished eating a bowl of cherries.

"Fanny? What are you doing here?" The Fairy Queen crouched and caressed Fanny's cheek. Her eyes traveled all over her face as though trying to read a map.

Fanny's eyes darted nervously from side to side. She was unsure of where Elda was now that Titania had appeared. The queen grinned and gave Fanny a playful wink.

"Worry not. I know where she is. No harm will come to me or you," Titania whispered.

Fanny wanted the queen to promise that she wouldn't hurt Elda. After all, her sister had saved her from Frederick.

Queen Titania stood to her full height and in a loud voice said, "Show yourself, Elda. Do you send a mewling kitten to kill a lioness?"

Elda emerged from the shadows surrounded by a dozen snakes. Titania raised an eyebrow. She didn't look surprised, merely amused.

"This is your last chance, Snake Witch. Walk away and I will spare your life."

"I will not walk away. What I want is for you to lift this curse from me. Fix the damage you and your magic have done."

"What of your sister? You brought her to draw me out of my realm."

Elda shrugged her shoulders and glanced at Fanny. Her eyes were vacant. There was no love in them for her or anyone. "I don't care what you do with her. She served her purpose."

"Which is precisely why I cursed you in the first place. You don't care about anyone but yourself. Very much like the snakes that continuously slither out of your mouth."

"I don't care? I wasn't the one who abandoned Fanny and left her to be abused by her husband." Several snakes twisted their way out of Elda's mouth and dropped to the ground.

"All she had to do was whisper my name and I would have taken her from that miserable place. But she's here now, no matter the circumstances," Titania replied.

Fanny pushed herself up and stood beside the Fairy Queen. She figured her chances at survival were higher with her. She wanted nothing to do with their quarrel. All she wanted was her freedom, to be left alone and have time to heal from her wounds. She hoped to one day speak without it causing her pain.

Elda let out a series of hisses and high-pitched shrieks. Fanny covered her ears and shuddered at the inhuman sound. Within moments, snakes appeared.

Fanny gasped. *Oh my God.*

Hundreds of snakes covered the forest floor and surrounded Elda. She had a triumphant smile on her face. She probably thought she had won the battle. Fanny turned her gaze to Titania. The Fairy Queen narrowed her eyes at Elda and gave her a small grin, as though Elda were a naughty toddler having a temper tantrum and not a full-grown woman hell-bent on revenge.

Does she not understand that Elda wants her dead?

"You forget who I am, Elda. I'm no mere mortal. I am Queen Titania, Ruler of the Fairy Realm. I am the Summer Queen. And I am that which rules over the warm seasons. Do you know what I am, Elda?"

Elda frowned.

"The sun," Titania whispered.

Her eyes changed from bright blue to a brilliant yellow-orange. Her blond hair burst into flames as though she were a phoenix. Titania conjured a ball of fire in each hand. It was as if she spent all of her time containing her power within herself and she finally had the chance to unleash it into the world.

Fanny locked eyes with Elda.

Please don't do this! She mouthed the words, still too afraid to speak.

Elda's face hardened, as though Fanny had made the most unreasonable of requests.

She won't stop. She'll never stop until the queen is dead.

Elda hissed a command at her snakes.

"Your choice has sealed your fate, Elda," the queen said.

The snakes moved as one, rippling over one another like a giant, multicolored wave. Titania took a tiny step back, as if caught by surprise by their speed. The queen waved her hands and, with a delicate flourish, she created a massive wall of fire that surrounded her and Fanny.

I'm going to die.

Titania hissed through clenched teeth, "Close your eyes, Fanny."

Fanny pressed herself against Queen Titania's back and waited.

At first, Fanny could only stare. If the queen was going to die like this, someone should witness it. But then the glow started. A pure white light, emanating from Titania's skin, enveloped the snakes. It quickly grew too bright to bear and Fanny turned away. Behind the Fairy Queen, she saw her own shadow dark on the ground, the bright light all around. Soon, even that became too intense. Fanny closed her eyes tight and even then saw dancing flames of red and blue behind her eyelids.

There was no heat. Whatever the queen was doing, she wasn't allowing it to hurt Fanny.

A few more seconds passed, and the dancing lights on Fanny's eyelids died down. She risked a peek, and though she still saw her own shadow dark on the ground, the burning light was gone. In a circle around them, the green of the forest had been turned to a scorched brown. The grass, trees, and shrubs had vanished. A stone's throw away, everything was normal in the forest.

Afraid to turn around to see what had happened, Fanny stared at her shadow. She moved her arm, but the shadow didn't move. It remained still, burned into the exposed dirt.

She realized what the Fairy Queen had done. For a moment, in a small, twenty-foot area of her own forest, the Summer Queen had unleashed the terrible power of the heart of the sun itself.

Fanny finally turned around. Titania stood exactly as she had before, but the snakes were gone. In front of her, Elda lay on the blasted ground. Another burned-in shadow stretched out behind her. She was burned black on every exposed surface. Her arms were thrown up over her head, but then she opened her eyes and the pupils glowed white in stark contrast to the rest of her body. She brought her arms down and Fanny saw the backs of her arms and hands were still pale white.

Titania bent over Elda and stretched out her hand, a single finger extended. It began to glow again, that terrible bright white. Fanny flinched. Elda glared, hatred in her eyes. Then the Fairy Queen spoke. "This is your last chance. Give up revenge and spite, and accept your place in the Order of Things. Or be unmade."

"Do your worst," Elda spat.

"So be it," Titania whispered.

Titania cupped one hand over the other until they formed a small circle. She called upon her magic and created a tiny ball of fire.

Fanny looked on the scene in silence. She didn't dare get between the two of them. All she wanted was to survive the ordeal unscathed. She was neither good nor evil. What did it make her then? Wicked? Was that what she was now? Even Elda, who was foul and temperamental, stopped Frederick from beating Fanny to death. It was for Elda's own selfish purposes, but a part of Fanny hoped that perhaps it had been out of love. Had it been the other way around, would she have done the same? Would she have stopped him, or would she have simply walked past knowing that it had nothing to do with her?

Titania took a deep breath and launched her attack on Elda. Fanny screamed and covered her face rather than watch Elda burn to death.

"Bluebell," Titania cried. Within moments, a tiny light-blue fairy appeared before the queen.

"Yes, Your Majesty?"

"Take her bones and dispose of them," she commanded.

"Where do you want me to take them, Your Majesty?" Bluebell asked.

"I care not," Titania said.

Bluebell gave her a deep, reverential bow and zipped away. Within moments, he gathered Elda's bones into a sack and vanished. All that remained were the black burn marks on the ground. The grass was gone and the soil resembled soot. Fanny wondered if she would ever be able to smell clean air again.

Titania took a deep breath and waved her arms over her face. She magically changed into a dress as pale as the moon. Her skin was clean and pearlescent. Not a trace of ash or soot on her. It was as if she had never fought with Elda. As if she hadn't burst into flames and set Fanny's only relative on fire. Now she had no one. She was truly, completely alone.

I'm sorry. I'm so sorry. She said that to herself over and over as she fell to the ground. She sobbed until her throat burned and her sides ached. Fanny's hands hovered over the charred soil where Elda once stood. More tears stung her eyes. She should have said something. Anything.

"Fanny?" Titania whispered as she gently touched her shoulder.

She gasped and turned around.

Titania knelt before Fanny and lifted her chin using her index finger. Fanny refused to meet the queen's gaze.

"Please look at me," Titania whispered.

Fanny shook her head.

"You are the only one in the whole world with the power to hurt me. You didn't know that ... did you?"

Fanny glanced at her. Words. So many pretty words. What had words ever done for her, other than cause her pain and grief?

"I didn't know," Titania said. "I swear to you that I didn't know you were suffering. But I didn't go looking for you either. I didn't want to know if you were happy with him. I was furious and devastated ... that you had chosen him."

I didn't know I had a choice. Why would a beautiful queen want to be with me?

"I heard that," Titania said.

Fanny's heart skipped a beat. She hadn't spoken, there was no pain, and no blood. Yet, she had finally been able to communicate.

"Please stay with me. I swear on my life that I will keep you safe and let no one harm you."

I'm so tired. I just want to rest.

The Fairy Queen held Fanny's hand. "Then let me be your sanctuary."

Once more, Fanny was surprised that she had been heard. She could get used to this. She sighed and then looked at her sister's remains one last time. Always so angry, even before Titania had cursed her ... so much rage for someone so young. Fanny wiped her tears away and stifled a sob. She didn't even understand why she was so upset. Elda was awful to her while they were growing up.

"Stay with me," Titania said.

"Why?" Fanny whispered. A tiny, red rosebud fluttered out of her mouth.

"Because ... I want to keep you safe," the Fairy Queen said.

Titania was the sun and Fanny was nothing but a minuscule star.

The queen sighed. "You're not going to make it easy for me, are you? My dear Fanny, you want me to admit it? Is that right? Say it out loud?"

Fanny turned back to Titania and looked into her brilliant blue eyes, like the sapphires that occasionally fell from her mouth. She frowned, unsure of what she wanted. Did she want the Fairy Queen to admit she loved her?

"Your silence has forced my hand, my dear," Titania whispered. "I love you, Fanny. Please stay with me ... for as long as you like and I promise I will keep you safe."

Safe. That word echoed through her mind like a feather floating gently in the air.

Fanny gave the queen a warm smile and a single nod.

"Do you want me to take away your gift?"

Can you do that?

"I could try."

Titania gently placed her hands on Fanny's throat.

Fanny's eye widened with wonder as the Fairy Queen's hands began to glow with a warm, yellow-orange light that reminded her of sunset. At first, she felt lightheaded. Then her lungs began to burn, and she gasped for air as her vision blurred. Fanny clawed at Titania's shoulders as she struggled to breathe.

Titania let out a strangled cry and quickly stopped, pulling her hands from Fanny's throat. Fanny dropped to the ground, taking in deep, ragged breaths and coughing.

Titania carefully guided Fanny's head until it rested on her lap; she combed her fingers through Fanny's dark-brown hair.

I don't understand. Why didn't it work?

"Oh, my love. I'm afraid that too much time has passed. My magic has become embedded within your body."

What is going to happen to me? What will I become?

Titania remained silent. Fanny wondered if these were questions without answers. Or perhaps Titania knew the answers but didn't want to tell her.

What am I?

Bluebell followed the queen's command. He took Elda's bones and disposed of them in a swamp. It was the furthest place he could think of—far, far away from the Fairy Realm. He waited until the sack sank beneath the murky water. Only then did he allow himself to leave. He felt as though he had accomplished his task.

Elda's favorite pet, Mora, was the one that rescued her from her watery grave. The black python gracefully dove into the water and retrieved the sack that was filled with Elda's bones. It curled and uncurled itself as it made its way to the surface with its prize held tightly in its jaws.

Mora dropped the sack on the shore and pushed it further inland until both were out of the water. She pulled every bone from the bag, and then snuggled close to her mistress. Mora summoned some of her life force to share with Elda. It wasn't much, but it was enough to ignite a magical spark within Elda's charred remains.

It took several days, but Elda's body slowly repaired itself. Her body twitched and pulsed until she was whole once more.

"Mora," Elda whispered.

Mora stirred from her nap and kissed Elda's cheek with her forked tongue.

Elda's face hurt from smiling, but she was truly grateful to have another chance at life. Another chance at revenge. Her thoughts turned dark as she plotted and schemed.

I will kill her if it's the last thing I do.

THE FLOWERING PRINCESS OF DREAMS

BY DOUG BLAKESLEE

Bent trees with limbs of blackened bark, knotted, and covered with globules of thick, amber sap blocked his path through the woods. Obstacles and impediments to his freedom, they blocked his route of escape, roots tripping and sending him sprawling to the soft, springy beds of moss that carpeted the ground. His dark gold fur was matted with sweat and morning dew brushed from the flowers along the path. Sharp eyes darted back and forth looking at the shadows and into high branches. Sensitive ears twitched at the softest of breezes, at a mere rustle in the dappled undergrowth. Scents of prey, blood, and meat invaded his nose, along with the delicate perfume of flowers and the dank smell of the old forest.

Seeking her. His mistress. His keeper. The Flowering Princess of Dreams. His nightmare. Bushes, with oval leaves of apple red and banana yellow rustled ahead. He crouched, waiting to spring. The buck leapt from the concealing foliage, head and horns high, looking at him with blank black eyes.

Eddy ...

Justin hefted the .30-30 to his shoulder, focusing down the iron sights at the buck. *Six points. Perfectly legal. Easy as pie.* He exhaled and pulled the trigger, letting the rifle recoil against his arm, listening to the shot echo down the canyon. The deer staggered and pitched over, crashing against a Douglas fir, scraping off bark in its death throes.

"Hot damn, man! Got that sucker with one shot!" Eddy put down the binoculars and gave him a gapped, green-toothed grin. He took a swig from the open bottle of Coors.

"That was a good piece of luck. And stop drinking! That ranger comes back, he'll give us both a fine. Your parole officer will freak the hell out if you get busted." Justin shouldered the rifle and headed down the hill, keeping one hand splayed for balance, feet slipping on the loose scree. His prize had stopped moving, succumbing to the neck wound.

"You worry too much. That dude ain't coming back," Eddy said. The bottle clattered against the rocks.

"Pick that shit up, man."

"Whatever. Not like anyone cares."

"You're an idiot at times, little brother." Justin glanced back. *How can we be related?* Eddy was shorter, stocky but not fat, the perfect wrestler's build. Shaved head, too-wide mouth, and too-small nose. His left bicep sported a green and red tattoo of a devil girl, complete with pitchfork, tail, and horns. The tattoo, obtained after a night of binge drinking, was on display due to Eddy's sleeveless, red-stained wife-beater. Justin's brother had barely worked a day in his life, coasting along by selling pot to local college students and taking the odd taxidermy job when the mood took him.

Eddy snorted, but picked up the bottle, tossing it into the cooler. "And you bitch too much." He skidded to the bottom of the ravine. "Christ. That's a big damn buck."

"A hell of a lot bigger than it looked down the sights." Justin leaned his rifle against a tree. "Let's get this thing cleaned and dressed."

His brother pulled a boning knife from his belt. "I've got this."

Justin had to admit, Eddy had a talent for skinning and dressing animals. The shelves in their late parent's garage once contained over a dozen stuffed animals, carefully preserved along with a pile of furs as hunting trophies. *If only he would get serious about going straight.* Eddy's drinking and pot smoking had increased in the year since the death of their parents. With the sale of the house, his living conditions had taken an appalling turn. He now lived in a small apartment by himself in a community where the cops were called weekly for domestic violence and gang activity. Twice, Eddy had called, asking to be bailed out for a disturbing the peace or public intoxication.

"Done." Eddy stood up, wiping the knife off on his jeans, smearing them with streaks of red. A pile of intestines, lungs, and other organs lay off to the side, with the heart and liver in the now open cooler. "No way we're getting this carcass back up that hill."

"The ravine cuts down to the river. We can find the trail back to camp from there. Only a couple miles tops."

"Dude, where the hell are we?" Eddy dropped his end of the branch. The buck hit the ground with a dull thump.

Justin lowered his end. "Christ. The trail disappeared," he said, surveying the steep slope of bare dirt, broken logs, and upturned stumps. "The rain washed out the path." The sun hung low in the sky, hovering over the edge of the surrounding mountains. "No way we can climb this or go down." Below, the river roiled and foamed, brown with spring melt and run off.

"Fuck. Does that mean we have to go back?" Sweat covered Eddy's brow. A dark streak ran down the back of his shirt.

"Yeah. There's a spur about half a mile back. Steep, but we should be able to do it."

"Middle of goddamn nowhere, aren't we?"

"That covers half the forest. Take days to walk the hell out of here if you get lost."

"Good."

"What do you mean?"

Without warning, Eddy shoved him. Justin pitched forward, stumbling toward the broken edge. His hands and arms flailed as he tried to regain his balance. Boots slipping as the dirt crumbled, he yelled, "What the hell?" Eddy shoved him again and then there was nothing but air, dirt, and the river.

"Later, dude," Eddy shouted.

Justin coughed and puked into the shallows of the river, expelling the dirty water he'd swallowed. He tumbled in the white water, carried by the swift flow of the current. His hands squished in the mud on the banks; rough stones scraped against his battered and bruised flesh. Justin groaned as he crawled up the bank, shivering in the cooling evening air. Blood flowed from cuts on his cheek and brow, one eye was swollen shut, and his left leg dragged. *Why Eddy? Why?* He struggled upward, seeking shelter in the trees from the wind and cold. Justin knew the answer. *The money. It's always about the money. Enough to make him happy. Solve his problems. Until he spends it all.* He laughed bitterly, wincing at the pain shooting up his leg. Nausea threatened again and darkness blurred his vision. Dry heaves shuddered through his body, his stomach contents long gone, swept away in the river.

Footsteps. Soft, deliberate, footsteps. A pair of delicate, pale-yellow feet, speckled with mud, stained green from too many walks on wet grass, stepped into his vision. *That's gotta hurt on the rocks. Why is she wearing a green dress?* The smell of daffodils, roses, and orchids wafted in the breeze, tickling his nose, soothing the pain.

"Oh my," said the lilting voice, soft, silken, and smooth. "What do we have here?" Clothing rustled in response to movement. The hem of a diaphanous, pale-green robe came into view. Vines of dark green and brown wound around the fabric with red, orange, and gold roses, yellow tulips, and white orchids sprouting in random patterns.

"Help," Justin said.

"Help? There's a price for help."

"Please ..." He craned his neck to look up and failed, the side of his face sinking into the mud.

"Since you asked nicely." She clucked with annoyance. "Your leg is broken. You will be no good to me if that is not healed."

No good? He winced as a thin covering of bark scrubbed on his face, roughly tracing over the cuts, leaving a warm goo in passing. Warmth flowed down his face and into his limbs, as if he were immersed in a pool of mud, heated to just the right temperature.

"You must learn to accept the pain. I love you, my beast."

"What?" Fire erupted in his veins, replacing the warmth, turning his blood to a molten and searing fluid. He screamed.

"What's goin' on? We had a deal."

"Yes. You have delivered him to me as promised, but not undamaged. I'm upset, Eddy."

Justin heard the scuff of boots and opened his eyes. Firelight. Flames dancing and flickering through the haze of pain. *What? Where?*

"Sorry, but I had to take that chance. 'Sides, he doesn't look that hurt." More scuffing. "Those bruises will go away. Why does he look ... hairy?"

"His current form doesn't suit me. I need a hunting beast, not a hairless monkey."

"Oh."

"Now, Eddy, about the contract?"

"You want more?" his voice raised a notch.

"You promised him to me, unharmed and unspoiled. I can smell other women on him."

"So what? He slept with a couple of girls, big deal. Bastard was always boning chicks."

"Tsk. I have needs and you agreed to meet them." More bark rubbed down Justin's back, stroking the short, fine fur. "But, he's a fine specimen, so I shall not request more."

Fur?

"Then I get my reward?"

"Oh yes, Eddy. As promised. Beauty and adoration. Those were your demands, no?"

"Yeah. I wanna be like him. Always getting the girls and skating through life."

"That's ... not ... true," Justin said. His arms moved slowly. Heavily. The golden fur ruffled as he pushed up. His vision focused on the two figures, standing on the other side of the campfire. Eddy and the tall lady. Flesh stained yellow. Blotches of dark brown painted randomly along her arms and face. Long cattails sprung from her scalp, the fluffy heads swaying as she turned toward him. Thin vines of pale green, no thicker than his pinky, wrapped around her chest to form shirt and sleeves.

"It is! You were always the favorite one!" Eddy sneered. "Now, you ain't shit."

"Calm, Eddy. Be calm." She smiled at Justin, rows of green thorn-like teeth showing between thin lips of yellow. "It's good to see you recovering, my pet. I shall give your brother his due reward and then we shall be off."

Eddy grinned. "Maybe we could hook up after this?"

"No, Eddy, that would not be wise." She reached toward him, tore off the wife-beater, and touched his bare chest. "Here is my blessing, Eddy. A gift of the wild to make you admired and beautiful."

"Hey, that's warm ..." A spot of green grew on his chest, expanding to cover him in seconds. "What's going on?"

"Eddy ... don't ..."

"Don't worry, my pet. The prettiest of roses spring from the waste of animals."

Eddy grabbed his head; his hands came away with clumps of hair. "Hey, my hair!" Lines of brown and yellow streaked through his now dark-green skin, twisting around in swirls and loops, tattooing a knot-work pattern as they went. Eddy's eyes grew wide as knots of bark erupted along his arms. Knees. Elbows. Shoulders. Wrists and ankles. The bark encased him in an inflexible sheath. "Oh god! What the hell's going on? This wasn't our bargain!"

"I'm making you beautiful. Like your brother. Like you asked."

"I'm a freak."

"No, Eddy, you are beautiful. I shall place you in my garden and adore you. My servants will take care of you, as they do all my pets. Each spring you will bloom. A moment of perfection until winter comes." Her eyes glimmered as she took in the transformation.

Branches and boles sprouted from Eddy's head and chest, small limbs with green buds. Bark crept up his neck, then over his mouth and nose. Eddy's eyes stared at Justin, wide with horror and accusation before disappearing. Only faint features of his face remained on the tree.

"I'm sorry, Eddy."

"Oh, my pet. Don't be sorry." Her bark covered hand stroked his face. "Truly, he is now beautiful. From such base material comes the most precious of jewels. Others will look upon him with envy and desire, but will know that he is mine and only mine. Just like you."

"Who are you?" His voice sounded odd. Muffled. Slurred. Strength flowed back into his limbs. *Why are my arms so hairy?* His claws dug furrows in the earth. Wind ruffled the fur on his body. His eyes fell upon the carcass of the deer, hung from a nearby branch, blood dripping from the decapitation. Plop. Plop. Plop. *God, that smells good.*

"I am your mistress. Eddy gave you as a present, in honor of my name and in payment for making him beautiful. I am the Flowering Princess of Dreams. The Haunter of the Bright Woods. The Keeper of Wild Fragrances."

"Hungry."

"Eat, my pet. Consume your fill and then we shall return to my realm. My tamer of beasts anticipates and awaits your presence. In time, you will worship me and join us in the great hunts."

Justin stood up. Claws splayed from the great pads on his feet; his tail swished back and forth in the dirt. A thick, rough tongue licked across his chops. He stumbled toward the carcass, lumbering and swaying to keep his balance. Clawed fingers tore into the hide, slicing off slabs of meat, shoveling them into a hyena-like muzzle of sharp canines, chewing and swallowing and gulping down the slick, juicy morsels. *Eat. Food.*

His mistress' hand slid across the golden fur. "You are a magnificent beast. Aren't you?"

He loomed over her. Half again as tall, twice as wide. The Beast rumbled and knelt to ground as she scratched between his ears.

She stepped from the woods, smiling at him as if to a child. "Bad Beast. Running away from me."

He crouched down. Arms curled. Legs tense. Ears back. His tail swished across the grass in short, fast sweeps. A growl rumbled from his throat.

"Have I not given you purpose? A new life free from care and worry?" she asked, her voice full of disappointment and reproach.

"Not Beast."

Her cherry-red eyes narrowed. A soft sigh escaped between pursed lips. "Too much spirit. How disappointing." Vines and runners, two fingers thick, whipped from the trees. Grasping. Entangling. Binding.

He bit and clawed at the restraints. Seeking freedom to run and escape. A long mournful howl issued from his throat.

"My poor Beast." A rose-scented hand rubbed across a rough cheek. "More discipline. Structure. Order. No need for thinking or will. All I ask for is your obedience."

Vines strained to hold him in place as he recoiled from her touch.

"I give you so much love, my Beast. All those good things. A kind mistress rewards her Beast. It hurts me to punish you." A tear of amber sap oozed down her cheek, idly brushed away by a floral green fingertip. "I'm ... very disappointed in you, but I love you. Even as you misbehave, my love grows."

His body dug a furrow into the earth as the vines dragged him back into the woods. Mud and leaves caked his fur. Ticks and chiggers crawled and nipped and burrowed under the golden pelt.

"I won't leave you alone, my Beast." She gave him a soft smile and gestured to the tree that grew in the center of manicured clearing. Silver bark gleamed in the fading sunlight. "Think of it as a family reunion. You remember your brother?"

He remembered. Lost memories. Hidden and blocked, no longer. A low puppy whimper. His ears drooped and tail curled up. With a jerk, the vines hauled him to his feet, toes brushing along the top of the grass. Facing the tree. Facing the features molded into the bark.

Lips like the petals of violets, soft and fuzzy, kissed his snout. "I forgive you, my Beast. For now, I will leave you here, but know that I will return in the morning to bring you home."

"Please ..." he coughed out.

"Goodbye, my Beast." She faded into the forest, the scent of roses and freshly tilled earth lingering in the air.

Eddy ...

The Beast howled.

THE SEMI-AQUATIC
BLUE BAKER OF BORNEO

BY JUSTYNN TYME

The turpentine sloshed down my pantalets and pooled around my feet in shimmering swells. Then it silently trickled over to the base of the salad bar and dripped down into some vacancy underneath the grocery store. Although my gyrating eyes followed his every gesticulation, I remained motionless like a deerfly in a headlock. There was no mistaking that it was Mister Mysterious with that sheen, black pompadour towering over his big, bushy, black eyebrows that rested on top of two hideously round walleyes. Those eyes were the most gauche aspect about him. They appeared to shift closer to you, as if they were part binocular. This was accentuated by his rather unique taste in clothing. His stylish seven-piece suit made of a bright-blue, simulated afghan fur; his four-foot, neon-yellow, nylon necktie; and his bright-red, fuzzy shoes were the embodiment of his derangement. I can remember the first time my eyes were seared by their intensity, as if it were yesterday.

Norwood, Ohio 1991

Like an episode of *This Is Your Life*, it all came rushing back. I was sitting in the dentist's chair getting a haircut while waiting to have my teeth cleaned. Doctor Stranger and I were idly discussing the sumo-wrestling event we had both attended. The doctor made some incendiary remarks about the Dutch wrestler, I.K. Bonset, of whom I was quite a fan. I regret it now. But, in a moment of illogicality, I splurged out some personal remarks about his refrigerator. I condemned it for being as "old as hell" and something about it frying lard, hatching eggs, and curdling milk, which must have caused his "mental deficiency." Furthermore, I said, "No reputable dentist would cut his own hair in the middle of a cleaning, where the gaping mouth of the patient would catch every falling follicle." Moreover, I may have mentioned his "shirt was ugly, his shoes moldy, and that he had the hair of a newborn," and possibly something about his wife having "hideously large elbows and feet the size of cantaloupes."

I must have struck a nerve because when I regained consciousness, I was laying in the street in a pool of my own drool, with my knees against my chest and my rear pointing toward the heavens. It was then Mister Mysterious just happened by and came to my assistance. He helped me to my feet and quickly set about seducing me with his pulsating eyes and his velvety, French overtones. Had I known the awful truth, I would have pinged his IP.

"No, no, this is not good. You have been beaten and maltreated. Do you know what ill wind has overtaken you, my befuddled buckeye? I must say this is highly unusual, a fine specimen such as you floundering in this alleyway. A nod to the odd, indeed."

"I don't have a clue what happened. I was getting my teeth cleaned in there and, next thing I know, I'm out here splayed in the street like a toad hopper. I always expected to find myself in the streets, rebuffed by society, but not for several more years. Why is it dark?" I asked, nursing my groggy head.

"You must have lain here for several days by the state of you. You're quite the monkey flower, good sir. The place thus is vacated, and recently, by the disorder of the waiting room. Magazines scattered all over."

"What is this sticky, goopy goo all over my head?"

"Fluoride, I might assume by its pale color and appearance. I must say, in this waning light the pink tones are very enticing."

"Huh?" My head was nearly clear, but the cut of his giblets was playing havoc with my senses.

"... and those teeth! Have they always had a pastel green hue? Very reminiscent of Picasso, Degas, or Rothko. Truly magnifique! May I hire you?"

"I am just a lousy, stinking pot-walloper. Could you use one of those?" I still pondered the moldy hue of my teeth.

"A duck-walloper maybe, but no, never ever a pot-walloper. Although for you, I have other plans. More theatrical with fine—but not fair—pay, and the most parsimonious of benefits. And yet, every day is a vacation! Agreed?" Those eyes of his were pulsating again as they peered deep into the creases of my brain.

"Sounds interesting, but I don't know. I have never been ... theatrical."

When I awoke again, I was on stage in a large, flamboyantly decorated wooden box with a hot spotlight trained on me. The heat from the light caused little wafts of steam to rise up from the fresh layers of fluoride. I could not be sure, but I think my teeth were still bright green, considering the audible gasps from the crowd when Mister Mysterious pointed to my mouth. Much to my embarrassment, I was wearing only a loincloth and tassels. On my feet were two large, aluminum buckets, each jingling with a gray, viscous like substance. Then, like a fork in the forehead, I knew what he meant by "theatrical." I can hear that crass carny pitch echoing through the ivy halls of my maltreated mind.

"Come quickly, one and all! Feast your eyes on the bewildering nature of this beleaguered creature. The Freak from Friesland. Society rejected him. Nature abandoned him. Science too scared to study him. Gaze upon the oozing pink fluoride that dribbles from his brain. Squirm at the sight of his thirty-two chlorophyll-filled crowns. Ogle his tantalizing tassels and lurid loincloth. Two free tickets to any youngster who can chuck a buck into the buckets of fish pudding he calls shoes! Step up folks, only a dollar to step inside."

My ears curled in horror when my nostrils recognized the scent of French dressing, which brought my daydream to an abrupt halt. I came to a disturbing realization as the cool, reddish-orange glop cascaded down my face onto my shoulders. I was enveloped in a glaze of salad dressing and croutons from the salad bar. How did that happen? It was starting all over again. It was a disastrous predicament, too, for French dressing was an irresistible lure for Mister Mysterious. Yet, with my face obscured by a reddish-orange globular hood, there was no recognition as he danced toward me that I was his runaway thrall. On the other hand, was he dancing the cha-cha across the dairy department because he knew it was me? After all, reddish-orange is reminiscent of florid pink. I was frozen by the horror of it. Do I stay and risk being recognized or do I run away? A pang of panic abused me as I felt my hand suddenly wilt. The frozen peas now pouring out of my hat made such a clatter as they bombarded the floor tiles. They sounded so much like missiles over Macedonia that I nearly croaked like a frog.

If Mister Mysterious caught me here today, my wife, Beebe, The Beanbag Lady, would never know what happened to me. I paused a moment to recall if I had left the light on in the pantry. She might well believe I had decided to stay in the pantry for the rest of my life. I could never let her feel unloved again. That was his crime against her, the fiend. We vowed when we escaped over a year ago, it was our last time. We would never be captured alive again. What was Mister Mysterious doing here alone, so far from home, idly shopping? Certainly not looking for asparagus tips or corn plasters. It had to be a ruse.

There was salad dressing and thawing peas all over the floor. I would surely be doomed if I tried to flee. That's when I saw it—my out—the bacon bits, a full tray of them. I mustered up my courage and expelled my panic in a raucous, primal eruption. I vociferated like a loon under the moon. Wrenching the bacon bits bin from the salad bar, I flung them through the air. The bacon bits ricocheted off the ceiling and fell like hail all over him. In that instant, I leapt into the cooler case and slithered over the edge with a splish. Huddling behind the cooler, I stuck my nose above the rim to see if he was looking. He was. They all were. A dozen doddering old geezers, so dumbfounded they were dropping fruits and vegetables all over the floor. I still did not see any recognition in his expression. So, in full resolution, I embarked on my great escape.

As a man made mad, I scampered into the cutlery department of the grocery store. I paused for moment to see if they had a spoon seven to ten feet long—it was his only weakness—but there wasn't one. I peered toward the produce department but he was no longer there. A sigh of relief almost escaped my lips when I saw him again. I could not believe my poached eyes—now in the floral department, the rotter was in hot pursuit of me. Did he really not recognize me? Did he think I was new quarry for him and his silly sideshow?

With all the subtly of an earthquake, I pulled away part of the shelving with a vigorous jerk. Spoons, forks, and other cutlery hurtled in every direction. I jammed the dislocated shelving across the aisle between us. Now he could not know in which direction I would flee. One in four chances to choose correctly. There was also a doorway next to the hallway. It went straight into the forbidden backrooms of the grocery store. So that's where I went; one in five was far better odds.

On the other side of the doors, there was a dark corridor filled with groaning sounds of strange machines and giggling women. I could see nothing but two tiny, bright squares at the end of the hallway. For a moment, I thought it might be two televisions. I hoped it was a creature double feature, Gamera and Gog. Then the memory of my second escape exploded in my skull. The thought of it was so ghastly, my feet started to Frug. My arms swung back and forth limply. My head buzzed and my eyes spun wildly. I could not suppress a burbling shriek. The knees of my trousers caught on fire and I fell to the floor. I was there again—

Helsinki 1999

I was modeling for a painting in the studios of Bam van Boozle. He had convinced me, for the right price, to wear a ballerina's costume and a magnificently feathered American Indian headdress. I inquired as to why he chose this odd ensemble.

"It is the new arithmetic!" is all he would say, but he said it in several tones. Then, after some coaxing, van Boozle had me cram my feet into a couple of watermelons and cover them with candy-cane-colored hosiery. I began to fear he was a Dadaist, and there was no telling what van Boozle might suggest with a willing model. This was quickly battered out of my brain by the ferocity of his vision.

"NO! NO! NO! You must not have runs in the stockings, fool! Do it again! Do it again, and again, and again until you get it right. It is the new arithmetic and it needs to be precise, and concise, and nice. Nice. NICE!"

So, for nearly three hours, I attempted to squeeze those bulbous melons down the red and white nylons without causing a rip or a run. All the while, van Boozle screamed at me to do it faster and faster. If I were not a fugitive from a freak show, I would have dinged his door. Eventually, after seventy pairs, I was able to force the watermelons into the feet of the stockings and then slide my feet inside without disaster. When I heralded my victory, van Boozle laughed and gestured toward the curtains.

Someone had been filming the whole bizarre event from behind the curtain. It was Mister Mysterious and he was laughing, too. I had not only been discovered, but also tricked, trapped, and traumatized.

"Oh, my wonderful little green pupa, you are extra-ordinary. I have inputted your voyeuristic film into the digital dimension where it has already earned enough to fund my little pixilated show for the next several years. You shall never vacate my slip and slide. Come now, my pungent Rubenesque puppet, we are late for your personal appearance tour of Finland. Five hundred stops in five hundred days. Agreed?"

Then I heard it, and I was zapped back to the present like a laser beam. The door creaked behind me and I froze mid-flail. Paralyzed, I listened fearfully. Then a tiny voice came echoing down the hall.

"Hello? I can't find the capers. Hello? Is anyone there? Hello? I lost my coupons in my pantyhose. Hello? Hello? I am looking for the capers. I need one small jar, just a little one, a few ounces. If I leave my shoes in the hallway, will they call my name over the intercom? Hello? I saw you come in here. Why don't you answer the telephone? Hello? Hello?"

It must be some little old lady, a hundred and thirty years old and completely out of her silvery-blue brains. Thankfully, she interrupted my terrible memories and I pressed on before Mister Mysterious decided to come in and check for himself. I slapped at my knees with a paddy whack to put out the flames. Then, moving gingerly but swiftly, I headed toward the bright squares. Pushing through a set of mottled-blue swinging doors, I found myself in an odd lobby. It was as spotless as a hospital, yet there was not a crumb of food anywhere. I heard the groan of an anchor chain. Startled, I hurried through the length of this weird stockroom. There were people milling around, bumping into walls, falling down, laughing like hyenas. A man came walking up to me and put his finger in my ear. He called me "Bo Bang Joe Joe" and handed me his tie, and then disappeared into the teetering mass. I put on his tie, but quickly realized it was broken; the knot had come apart above the neck.

I was tracing the sideboard when a penny-packer linebacker zipping past leapt off a motorized lazy boy and tackled me. We went crashing into a pocket of nonplused people. He quickly stood, helped me up, and dusted off my clothes.

"Sorry, my good man. I thought you were the president of the penny-pinchers. Natural enemies of ours, you know. Very devious, those penny-pinchers. Always pinching the pennies we're packing. If you see a penny-pincher, call my mother. The number is pressed into your forehead, I'm afraid. Metal plates were a bad idea. I told them so, but do they listen? No, they do not. Not a word."

This penny-packer bulldozer didn't even bother to stop talking before he turned and rode away. His words trailed off, mingling with the cacophony of other disembodied voices. The next thing I heard reminded me of the matter at hand.

"Clean up in aisles seven, eight, and nine."

I remembered Mister Mysterious, but there was no way he would know where I was, because even I didn't know where I was. I've always dreamt about what it would be like going behind those *Employees Only* doors at the grocery store. Yet, I never imagined anything like this. Where does all the food come from? Is this what all the employees do when they come back here? Do they restock insanity in here? Do they somehow adopt strange personalities that cause them to stagger around laughing hysterically? Another voice that came over the intercom sounded like it belonged to a mutated thug.

"CSR please dial one one one. CSR dial one, one, one." Suddenly, a mongoloid of authority appeared and screamed at me to pave the way. I attempted a query, but more loutish giants came out of the woodwork. I could tell from the glint in their eyes that they intended to punch me in the brain. So I ran like a whirlwind through the twisting and turning halls of burning barrel fires until I hit a dead end. There was nothing but a miniature door, which could only belong to a cabinet. I was frantic, and the thought of Mister Mysterious creeping up unseen haunted me. Were those hideous trolls sent by him? As the ruffians galumphed closer and closer, I flung open the little door and bounded inside, slamming it closed in their faces. Sitting inside was an employee munching on a kielbasa. The high-pitched squishing, squirting, and squealing noises that came out of that kielbasa as she gnawed on it were frightening. The juices spurted across the room, staining my clothes.

As they wrenched and rattled the door from the outside, I furtively glanced around. It was only a closet—a large, empty closet with nothing more than a broken swivel chair, mushrooms growing on the walls, and a sloppy employee. Then I caught a hint of fresh air coming from the ceiling. I stood on the chair and pushed my nose over the ledge. There was the street in front of the grocery store. I craned my head in every direction to see if anyone was lurking about. I could see no one. After considerable strain—tearing the rear out of my pants—I crawled out.

I had finally found my way out of the grocery store and away from Mister Mysterious. The street was quiet, almost deserted. I did not know how many hours, days, weeks I had roamed those backrooms. It was surely long enough for Mister Mysterious to have given up. There were four grocery stores, one on each corner. I was no longer sure which store I had gone into or come out of. I rested on the sidewalk trying to regain my composure. I had escaped his clutches and if I could just make it home, I would be safe. However, before I could decide which way to go, I was accosted by a blaring car horn, which startled me. This precipitated a hideously loud woman to lean out of her apartment window and shriek something terrible while looking right at me!

"Aha! I see you! I see you there! Yes! Yes! Yes! I see you! I can see you!"

My nerves liquefied and drained away with my resolve. Like a deranged, four-legged ostrich, I ran down the street yelping loudly in sheer panic. I sought a safety zone, but I didn't know where I was going or where I should go. I no longer knew the official bird of the Solomon Islands; I was utterly screwed. That woman, that miserable old crone, must have been working for Mister Mysterious. He was clever like that, leaving the area but paying off anyone who would take the money to watch out for me. They might even have followed me ... damn it! I let out a grisly, protracted wail.

I was so hysterical that I never looked back to see if that old woman or some lackey was stalking me. I could feel my wits redoubling. Wait! It dawned on me that I had come to town on my little yellow riding mower. I had dreams like this, not remembering where I parked, not remembering what vehicle I had driven, and now it was all coming true. Then I remembered my keys. I pressed the horn button and a horn blared from far off somewhere. That horn sounded awfully familiar. The horn that scared me, it was my own. Again, the horn was followed by that old prune yelling out the window. She was crazy! Thank god, she's madder than the mad hatter and certainly nobody's stooge.

"Hey! Mister Forkfinger!"

It was a voice out of the silence, an unfamiliar voice calling an unfamiliar name. It was a girl from inside the tanning salon.

"My name isn't Forkfinger."

"Oh, well, what the hell happened to you? You look like shit, man."

"Tell Mister Mysterious he can suck eggs, because he won't get me!"

"Say what, dude!?!" She gave me such a look that it made my sock twitch.

"Sorry, I ... there's this crazy man that's after me and I had a freak-out in the grocery store because he almost caught me. That's why I look all disheveled."

"Yeah, crazy guys are always after me, too. But, man, you don't just look messed up. You look like a reject from Candy Land. Maybe you should come in here and have a shower and a tan. Nobody's here but me."

"Really? Thanks. I could use a shower and ... a tan, I guess."

"Sure, come on in. The showers are over there behind the curtains, but use the one on the far right. I haven't cleaned the other ones yet."

"Thanks!" The thought of curtains made my other sock twitch.

"My name's Tabitha, but most people call me Tabby, or Tab like the soda. What's your name, fella? Just in case you're an escaped convict and I gotta call the cops."

"Pete. Pete Pocketsock and I'm no escaped ... convict."

"Yeah, I can see that. I'm Googling you. You should really reconsider your digital footprint, guy. You got some freaky stuff out there."

"Yeah, well, it's me but ... I ... I don't want to talk about it." I hadn't really considered ... holy crap, the internet, but I was too tired to care.

"Tanning booth two is ready when you're done, Pete, and don't forget to cover your junk when you go in there." She winked when she said it.

"Oh, thanks, thanks very much!"

I got in the shower and the warm water felt soothing as it washed away the dried salad dressing, the dirt, the grime, and the tension of my ordeal. But as long as Mister Mysterious was in the area, we would never be safe. I could not know who was or wasn't working for him, so I would have to be on my guard. Maybe even Tabitha was, and when I came out, Mister Mysterious would be there with that cheese-eating grin of his. A vision of serenity flashed across my mind: My lovely wife, Beebe, at home, waiting for me. The sun streaming through the windows bathes her in golden hues as she relaxes on the couch watching *One Step Beyond*. It's funny all the things that come to mind for no apparent reason.

Meanwhile, in a diner not far from the tanning salon, a man in hazard-orange angora overalls, a blood-red silk shirt, and a bright-blue Sherpa hat with three-foot ear flaps sits in a booth. Two grotesque, baby-like men sit across from him. They speak in low moans so that people glance over suspiciously. When those curious people look over, Mister Mysterious or one of his goons—both named Jackson—hands them carnival flyers promoting a new act. Otherwise, they wait … impatiently.

"What can I git ya honey?" the waitress asks. Her nametag reading "Flo" teeters on her tired bosom.

"Coffee!" Jackson yells.

"Coffee and pie," the other Jackson whispers.

"Pie and coffee and corn nuts!" the first Jackson yells.

"I would like a ten stack of cheesy scrapple and toast," requests Mister Mysterious. "Three eggs—one hard-boiled, one over hard, one poached. The shells should have an Easter motif. A cut biscuit and a bowl full of creamed orange juice. Please, we're in such a tizzy." His walleyes rolled around in a gleeful orbit.

"That's a tall, strange order. Cost ya extra, peppy."

"By all means, madam, brandish burnt offerings and bullrings!" His mustache trembled with merriment.

"Bullring?" asked Flo, unsure of his quizzical jibe.

"CHARGE!" yelled Jackson

"CHARGE!" yelled the other Jackson and Mister Mysterious tittered with a solitary finger resting on his pursed lips.

As I walked from the showers to the tanning bed, I thought about ... the chair. Some memories are like that. I am just minding my own business and bang, pow, zoom, a deeply repressed memory comes rocketing up. They can knock me down sometimes. Doctor Rizo Goff III once said it had something to do with undeveloped keratin. Mister Mysterious had abused me with that chair and I hated that chair with a passion. I had managed to escape his clutches yet again. I needed a safe place to hide out, and so I had made my way to Austria.

Austria 2003

"Secluded. Private. Completely wired, debugged, with running water and machine washable. Homely meals and easy access a plus. Apply at once."

It was a humorous butchery of the English language, but it appealed to me for some reason. So I walked the several miles to review the lodgings. The proprietor, Mister Newgarden, was a little old man with a hideously bulbous nose. One could not miss that nose—whenever he said something witty, he would jiggle it with his finger.

"Is the place still for rent?" I asked when he answered the door.

"We all live alone!" he sputtered. He then gestured for me to go deeper into his dwelling. We walked through a long hallway with walls made of cork, which I noted were growing thicker the further we went. It was as if he had carved this room right out of a giant cork. We came to a large rubber door, which prompted me to ask why the room needed a rubber door.

"It is so the authorities cannot break in and arrest you for living alone, my friend, nor can you escape your fate. It is only available to the most special personas." He fitted the key in the lock and pushed the door open.

"There is a light switcher behind the door. Would you mind turning it over? There is nothing in the room but a chair, and I have a dead fear of chairs."

"Sure. Right behind the door you say." I stepped into the dark room and behind the door. I placed my hand on the wall, feeling around for the switch.

"Ah! I found it, Mr. Newgarden." As I grasped the toggle, the door bonked shut. Briefly startled, I took my hand off the switch, which was followed by a scraping noise. The light switch slid down the wall to the floor. I flipped the toggle switch and didn't notice any difference, but when I looked up at the ceiling there was just one tiny LED bulb about the size of a pencil eraser. Gradually, my eyes grew somewhat accustomed to the light, although it was very dim.

"Hey, quit screwing around and let me out! Let me out!" However, the only response was a low titter that seemed to come from the ceiling. I plodded around the room until I found the chair and sat down. Before I could relax and consider my plight, the chair threw me to the floor. A nightmare in the making, I heard that tittering again and then the chair slowly slid across the floor. Was it looking for me? Was it possessed? Was it Newgarden? Suddenly, the chair squealed violently across the floor until it rammed me. I fell and rolled across the room. I got up and started yelling, hoping someone could hear me.

Dark day after dark night, I was incessantly bullied by that chair, and always accompanied by that ethereal tittering. I don't know how long it had gone on, but one day, it just stopped. The door slowly creaked open and there stood Mister Mysterious. As I lay there, a malnourished shell of a man, he came to me and said in a voice so sweet and tender. "Oh, my dear potboy, I have found you and saved you from this indelicate depravity. Come along, I will feed you, roust you back to robustness, and care for you carefully." Mister Mysterious lifted me gently off the floor and did not let me go until my legs were steady.

The weeks that followed were some of the best of my life. Mister Mysterious was almost like a second father to me, truly a Scrooge reborn. One day, he came to me and gently put his hand on my shoulder.

"Potboy, my potluck, you have brought me much tenderized transport and you have returned to such voluptuous vigor that I am more than plump with pride. I have a surprise for you, a little something to embody the enjoyment I get from you. A little something that will commemorate in celebration of our special friendship." With that, he put his arm over my shoulders and we walked to a line of carny boxes that were nestled together. The backdoor of one had been, lovingly and festively decorated. He motioned for me to go inside with a gentle nudge and pat on the back. I climbed the stairs with my mind full of wonder and sweet imaginings.

I stepped into the carny box, which was dark except for the sliver of light coming from the split in the curtain. Mister Mysterious followed me in and sat at his podium at stage right. I looked at him quizzically and he handed me a thick, rustic oak branch. It had been polished smooth, and had my name engraved on it. I held it up feigning triumph when the curtain flew open and I stood stunned before a cheering crowd.

"Greetings friends! Before you stands a man reborn in murk! A gentle soul turned savage by an irrational fear! Feast your eyes on raw brutality like nothing you've seen before. Behold, if you dare, The Awestruck Autocrat from Austria!"

I stood there, dazed and dejected, for he had duped me again. But what was the act? Then the side door opened and two goons pushed in a chair. When I saw it, I broke out in a cold sweat. As if possessed, it came toward me completely unaided and the fear from the black room came flooding back. It was ... that chair! My grip tightened around the stick when I heard the tittering. Mister Mysterious had been behind everything. The chair rushed at me at every opportunity. With my sanity gone, I swung and swung and swung, defending myself with such rancorous passion the crowd howled with delight.

I must have dozed off, because the shock of that recall woke me up. There were no lights, no heat, and not a sound in the tanning booth. I cursed myself because I had blacked out again. Did she sell me out? When I fell asleep, did she see her opportunity to lock me in a box and leave me to be collected by Mister Mysterious? I pushed the lid and it propelled upward with a bang. I breathed a momentary sigh of relief. I looked at myself in the mirror. I was slightly ruddy. That was fast, I thought, but was glad to see I was back to normal. I tiptoed quietly back to the lobby and peeked around the corner. The place was eerily quiet.

"Coast is clear, Pete." Tabitha sprang out from behind the counter.

"Well, I ..."

"It's all good, dude. I could've burnt you to a crisp in there if I wanted, and you would've never known the difference. You fell asleep, you dingus. Ever heard of something called cancer? Yeah, I saved your life."

"Uh, thanks ... I mean, thank you very much. It's been one of those days."

"No problem. You can repay me by coming over here and giving me a Johnny Rocket."

"... but I'm married!"

"You spazasarus! You're cute, I'll give you that, but what kind of chick do you think I am? You come in here all freaked out looking like a moron from Mars and expect that to turn me on? Drive me wild? Who married you? Lady Haha?"

"Sorry, I haven't been thinking straight lately."

"Yeah, yeah, Mister Pocketsock. Now come over here and gimme a Johnny Rocket, aka a big punch to this surveillance machine. This thing is jammed and I wanna show you something. A nut job came in here looking for you while you were asleep in the coffin."

"Why are you looking after me like this? Have we met before now? Are you a friend of Beebe's?"

"I can read people pretty good. Call it a woman's intuition. You are as weird as they come, but you're harmless enough. Okay, here it is, about an hour ago. Watch this and tell me if this hipster dingle is a friend of yours or not."

I watched the screen intently. A man skipped into the tanning salon wearing purple velvet shorts with shocking pink suspenders and those same red fuzzy shoes. He was carrying a towel and a picture of a little yellow riding mower.

"Hello. Are you the cooking and tanning expert?" he asked in his strange dialect. He showed Tabitha the picture of the yellow riding mower. She set her huge melons on the counter and looked at the picture.

"Yeah, I've seen that tractor around. About a week ago, WPPO ran a warning about some Dadaist who was making a spectacle of himself. He was riding on that same mower!" She became naturally defensive because the strange man in the fluffy, fuzzy red shoes was now squeezing her melons.

"You like doing that, don't you?" she chided.

"Yes. I love the feel of fresh cantaloupes," he said in his highly expressive way tracing the veins with his fingers. Tab, Tabby, Tabitha took out a five-foot kitchen knife and sliced both melons in half with one swipe. Mister Mysterious smiled as his eyes glazed over; they shared a cantaloupe on a cold and cloudy morning.

"I haven't seen the little yellow mower around lately. You might want to check across town. I heard a report involving a weird tractor. Might be the same one."

"Where, pray tell, is this incident coincidence?" he asked. I didn't have to see his eyes to know they were throbbing in and out.

"Not far from here, Ukulele Street I think it was, or Kayak Avenue. Either one, they are practically next to one another. I can draw you a map if you need it."

"Okay, on my hand! And, may I pay you for more information, if you should see this funny little tractor and its night rider?"

"Um, no. The Sheriff says I can't take any money from strangers anymore. Apparently, its unscrupulous behavior to sell tickets to an underground rave and not tell people it's really a policemen's ball. God, I cleaned up that year. Dumb stoners, haha."

"Burrr-nakysaky! Very well, peachy girl, I will venture across the town then and again. Thank you, Pinkachu!" And with that, he left the screen.

So, Mister Mysterious had been around, and he or someone else had followed me. I stood gaping over Tabitha's shoulder, my mind clicking. I needed to get out of here unseen and back home. How could I get my yellow tractor back with him closing in? Mister Mysterious could be hiding around the next corner, if he'd found it already. On the other hand, he could be waiting around any corner like a Freedonian thug ready to christen me like a sailor the moment I walked out. The gears in my brain were really grinding now. A plan was coming together.

"I have an idea. Give me that phone." I dialed feverishly.

"Hello! Axco Gas Station and Towing ... if you need gas we have a buyers beware special, only ten cents a gallon, and if you need a tow, the first nonstop fifty feet or fifty thousand miles are free. Onslow Olsen speaking, but you can call me Onslow or Olof or Ollie. How can I help you? Oh! Vintage urinal cakes, two for a dollar. How can I help you?"

"Ollie, it's me Pete ... Pete Pocketsock."

"Hey, Petey Pete! What's up buddy?"

"I need a favor. I need you to tow my little yellow tractor behind the tanning salon on Pumpkin Pie Avenue, and I need you to kind of park it so I can steal it."

"What the hell? Steal it? You crazy!?! I got Brittney here and she's waiting to have a good time."

"Yes, Ollie, I am crazy, because you know who is after me?"

"Mmmmm!"

"Yeah, him! Somehow he's found me."

"Ok, give me ten minutes."

"Thanks." I hung up the telephone. Then, without saying a word, I took Tabitha into my arms and she gazed at me with those big, mudpuppy eyes. I leaned in close ...

"If my cabbages weren't zip coded, I could easily fall in love with you. But my shoes are too tight, so I must be going ... my life is in danger ... and danger is not my middle name. It's Peggy."

"Ha! Go, ya goonie! Run like the girl scouts are after you, you mad, crazy fool."

I stood at the salon's back door. After a few minutes, I heard the shrill beeping as Ollie backed up into the alley and then the clinks and clanks of him dragging my tractor off the flatbed. Ollie walked back to the street when Brittney pulled up in her beamer steamer. Ollie hopped in and they drove away. I slunk out to my tractor and started it. I started slowly to see if Mister Mysterious would suddenly appear and attack. He didn't. I hit the nitro with impudence and rocketed down the alley.

As I blasted down the long alley, trashcans ricocheted off the walls, leaves and debris flew all over the place. This alley was at least three miles long with a few cross streets. I exploded across busy traffic lanes in a hail of sparks. There was no way he could catch me now. A few more blocks and I would be on the Rhubarb Pie Parkway—the desolate road that lead home. The sun was cresting; the afternoon almost gone. I would be home just in time to catch the late summer light illuminating my dear wife. How she must be worrying. I only went out for sour cream, but that was several hours ago. I knew her resolve; she would wait there for eternity, that's how much she loved me. I would fight until my knees turned purple, that's how much I loved her. We rescued each other from the insidious clutches of Mister Mysterious, and, of course, we lived in ambiguous fear. Still, we were meant for each other and we were meant for more than being mere eye candy in a sideshow attraction, titillating turtle-lipped rubes.

I could see my house rising above the trees in the distance. I checked the rearview mirrors. There was no one in sight. I gripped the wheel tightly and pressed on because I had thought I wasn't followed to the tanning salon and I had been. I rattled down Rhubarb Pie Avenue, pressing the pedal to the rusted metal to get home before the rain—a storm was blowing in, making the trees sway.

Elsewhere, in a rundown gas station somewhere in the continental United States, a strange man was about to harass the cashier. This man wore a billowing, pink-velvet three-piece suit with a shocking purple and red polka-dot dress shirt and a white bow tie. This odd fellow was also wearing the fluffiest, fuzziest red shoes anyone had ever seen. It was, of course, Mister Mysterious—and he was trying to buy a particular riding mower at the gas station.

"Hello, are you the happy cashier?" inquired Mister Mysterious. He stood motionless, his eyes pulsating.

"Look, weirdo, I told you before we don't sell little yellow riding mowers and we ain't never sold any riding mowers, not at all!" But Ollie, the cashier, could not convince him otherwise. Ollie was highly irritated now because his girlfriend, Brittney, was waiting in the back room. She was itching to go all the way this time. She cracked the door open to peek out every two minutes, but the stranger was still there. Truth be told, Ollie couldn't wait either, but it was more than his job was worth to chuck this guy to the curb and crush his teeth into the pavement. Ollie wasn't at all like that in real life—it was just a scene from the movie "Armenia X." He happened to think of it because this wacko was really getting up his nose.

"I need a trailer hitch too, Mitch," Mister Mysterious exclaimed in his unusual halting manner as his fuzzy red shoes bounced around beneath him.

"That's it, Freakazoid Floyd. You're getting your ass handed to you." Ollie bounded over the counter in cinematic style. Grabbing Mister Mysterious in a headlock, Ollie forcefully dragged the stiff body of Mister Mysterious out the doors.

"Leaping Leeks! Now listen here, my good surly goon! I am in the midst of a transcendental transaction and you are interrupting my inquisition!" Mister Mysterious shouted as he flailed about like an octopus in the octagon.

Out in the parking lot, Ollie dropped Mister Mysterious like a sack of paraffin and locked the doors. Ollie threatened to call the police if Mister Mysterious tried to come back into the store. This did not phase Mister Mysterious one bit. He simply rolled his eyes, waggled his head, and jitterbugged back to the carny bus that was waiting for him. Ollie, finally sure the weirdo wouldn't return, called to his girlfriend.

"He's gone, Brittney, we can get it on now." Britney crept out of the backroom with a mop and bucket. As they held the mop handle, Ollie patiently explained how to mop the floor with cold, scummy water in such a way that it didn't stink or make someone slip and fall. Brittney found it highly romantic because her boyfriend was revealing to her a janitorial secret. She smiled as Ollie held her close and they sloshed the mop back and forth, rearranging the black smears.

I shut off the engine and paused in the driveway a moment. I sat there listening to the natural silence. Taking a moment to settle myself, I closed my eyes and let the wind blow around me. I then watched the birds flit from bush to bush. A few red squirrels, drunk on summer, raced past and some hip pigeons strutted by. I was home. I hopped off my little yellow tractor, spit-polished the hood, and threw camouflage over it.

I climbed into the lift and hoisted myself the eighty-eight feet to the house. It was a beautiful place, once an abandoned water tower, now our dream home. Beebe was home, sitting where she was the happiest, on the couch with one of her books. Her favorites were books on cultivating the powers of the mind. So far, it had done her little good, but I loved her just the same, fully functional brain or not.

"Hi, Kewpie doll, I'm home!" I leaned on the doorframe for a minute to shake off the stink of fear. I needed to play it cool. I certainly didn't want Beebe to know how close I had come to being caught. She wouldn't admit it, but it would be a miserable existence without me. I sat down on the couch and started rubbing her feet. I decided I was going to lie like a red-headed menace.

"I think you were right, maybe we should move. Head down to Key West, Florida. It's nice down there, and they have some of those bridges you love so much." Beebe did not speak, but just looked at me with those big, beautiful eyes. I knew she was concerned, so I hugged her gently, and lied about there being pudding in the refrigerator. I needed a toe curler in the worst way, and I went to the kitchen to make one.

As I was shaking my drink—two parts pickle juice, three parts gin, and a sugar cube—I was considering the severity of our situation. Mister Mysterious had a knack for knowing the impossible and it would not be long before he showed up on our doorstep. Eventually, I got lost in thought, listening to the rain rattling down the rainspouts. The lights flickered a bit, and then there was a knock at the door.

I opened it, not expecting it to be him—but it was. Soaking wet, Mister Mysterious stood on the landing in a drab trench coat and woolen trousers, with a sinister scowl plastered on his face. It was unfit weather to be skulking about and we both knew it. After a long awkward silence, he plunged through the door and began to yell and shout. Releasing a tirade about the gaudiness of Mozart and the inconsistencies of my grout, he climbed up my curtains and blubbered curses at me. I tried to settle him down, in the hope of overpowering him, but he ran off in a huff. I chased him through the house as he sang songs of his gypsy caravans and admired my astrolabe. I had finally driven him over the edge.

"I am wearing average, laymen's clothes for Pete's sake and I am seething in my own skin! You are my golden gaff and I can't let you get away from me."

Pulsating with a combination of fear and fury, I knew this had to be a final showdown. He was trying to destroy our love and repeal our freedom. I had to act and act quickly. I put on my oven mitts and chef's hat. I began feigning a weird kind of pantomime baking, while running over scenarios in my head. I must have imagined five thousand ways of crippling him before I decided on the best-laid plan. Just as I had built up enough moxie to attack him, a window broke behind me. I whirled around just in time to see the two Jacksons poke their elephant guns through the window, but they were not aiming for me ...

BANG! BANG!! BANG!!! BANG!!!!

"NO!" I screamed as I watched my beautiful wife Beebe explode in a cloud of buckwheat. Something broke inside me. If I didn't run now, I would be a victim of his tyranny forever. I called up my geese-fighting skills, flung Mister Mysterious into the oven, and hurled myself off the front porch into the dark, damp night with a squawk. I hit the muddy ground with a splash. Stunned, I scrambled to my feet and looked up. Mister Mysterious was smiling down at me. Obviously, he was just as glad I wasn't dead. I didn't wait to see if I was hurt, I just ran. Like a twelve-legged penguin, I ran, tripping and falling with every step. With rain and tears blinding me, and muddy ruts sucking at my feet, I bolted into the forest. It was all just so goddamned awful. I howled like a Comanche banshee until I lost my voice. First my heart, then my mind, and now my voice, all gone, I was losing everything bit by bit. All because the goddamned show must go on.

The moon was high in the night sky when I staggered out of the woods, exhausted and half starving, into an all-night bakery on the edge of town. I plunked down the buck and quarter I had earned fighting geese in the park and bought a day old loaf of asiago cheese bread. I had just walked out of the bakery with my knob of bread when I heard the baker loudly call ...

"You get no bread with one meatball!"

I could smell something in the air, something familiar. There was a lingering stench of rosewater on the wind. Then a thought detonated in my head and I fell to the ground. I spent several minutes flailing around, trying to regain my senses. My trousers were twisting into terrible, spiraling wrinkles, while my broken necktie had inexplicably wound itself around a parking meter. My shoes flew off and were scattered along the street with the laces totally dislodged from them. Luckily, my socks were still intact, but were steaming or smoldering in some fashion. My shirt was over my head, and my head was jutting out of a broken seam. I could not see where my knob of bread had fallen, but either my underwear had become horribly knotted or I was reclining on my bread.

Before I could fully assess the situation and pull myself together, an ambulance screeched to a halt with a frightening hiss and two medics ran to my assistance. They snipped off my tie just the below my collar and helped me to my feet. After a few minutes of rearranging my clothes into a respectable manner, one of the medics decided to rearrange my face as well. The big, baby-faced brute drew back his clenched fist and dotted my eye.

When I regained consciousness, I was hanging upside down on the docks, probably some five hundred miles away from the bakery. I was soaking wet right through my rumpled clothes, and I was painted blue. I could not see the medics, only several men—obviously fishermen—all waiting in line to have their pictures taken with me. However, as soon as I could seize the attention of someone, I asked where my knob of bread might be. My innocent question was met with an indignant response. When a salty, surly sailor hurled a handful of squid bait at me, it splattered all over my face. This was the response to my question, no matter whom I asked.

After many weeks of this and several deliberate inquiries about my knob of bread, I heard his velvety accent over the dissonance of disgruntled dockhands. He had come at last. Then I knew Mister Mysterious had found me for the last time. After he inquired about my well-being, I was loaded onto a truck and driven to a riparian carnival. Once there, I was placed in a dusty tent half-submerged in a large tank of water, which housed a large brick oven to which I was cleverly attached. I was instructed to make bread five days a week, for eight hours each night. Apparently, I am now referred to as ...

FANFARE

"Come one, come all. That's right, brave naysayers. Step right in to see the strange, the bizarre, the bewildering, and all that it entails. Gentlemen, are any of you man enough to kiss a fish? That's right, kiss a catfish, only a dollar. Ladies, would you rather punch a dunce? If you make him wince, you'll get a chaffinch! Would you care to see a man wrestle a tree, or a woman shave her feet? Take your pick and step right in. That is not what you came to see though, is it? Of course not, folks! You came to see the newest exhibit at the Sacrilegious Circus of the Strange. So step up, ladies and gentlemen! For just a dollar or two, see the indigene of Indonesia, who was plucked from the night sky and buried deep in the jungles of Malaysia. Feast your eyes on the preposterous and the anomalous.

Behold! The One! The Only! Semi-Aquatic Blue Baker of Borneo

As I kneaded the dough, I realized I had been right. I would not try to escape again. I had nothing left to live for now, except to create my breads, my wonderful artisan breads. It's nice to make decent money again, even if it is against my will.

THE TAIL OF FATE

BY ERNESTUS JIMINY CHALD

The Double Happiness Chinese Restaurant, located on the southeast corner of Verikosto Boulevard and Main Street, had been one of downtown Garnetsville's most popular dining establishments since it opened in the mid-seventies. Its proprietor, a Chinese immigrant named Ming Ming, had long dreamt of opening a Cantonese restaurant, and he couldn't have hoped to find a more ideal location than the small town of Garnetsville. When Ming, his wife, Ming Mei, and their two infant daughters—Ming Qing and Ming Jiao—moved into the small apartment above what was destined to become their restaurant, they were the first Asian family to take up residence in Garnetsville in the town's nearly two-hundred year history. The Mings were pleasantly surprised by how warmly they were received by Garnetsville's primarily Caucasian residents. With a population of fewer than seven hundred, Garnetsville was small enough that the arrival of a Chinese family seemed to lend the town a note of the exotic that it had previously been lacking.

The passing of Ming's father in Hong Kong made Ming the recipient of a substantial inheritance, and, armed with that money, he leased the vacant storefront beneath the family's apartment and began the arduous process of transforming that empty space into the restaurant he'd always dreamed of. Although Garnetsville was

259

legendary for its stone trade, Ming insisted on having pillars of the finest imperial gray granite, expertly carved and polished, imported from China, and installed in front of the building along with five-clawed dragon and Shishi statues. In the entryway to his restaurant, he erected a massive fountain that was soon filled with Chinese bubble-headed goldfish, and, eventually, the wishes of small children who clamored to drop coins into its clear water.

Upon entering the restaurant proper, diners were greeted by a large golden statue of the Buddha, the patina of whose belly was dulled over the years by the wishful rubbing of passersby. The restaurant's interior was equally as impressive as its facade, with the subdued lighting of Chinese lanterns strung from the ceiling, and intricately carved statuary of imitation ivory and jade standing atop silver-mink marble pedestals. The feeling of stepping out of the run-of-the-mill confines of Garnetsville and into a far more exotic locale was complimented by the restaurant's sound system, which was rather sophisticated for its time, and through which diners were treated to a beguiling soundscape of traditional Chinese Erhu music.

Although the restaurant was ready for its Grand Opening nearly a month earlier than slated, Ming waited to open its doors until the nearest Lucky Day arrived to officially unveil his actualized dream: The Double Happiness Chinese Restaurant. It was a great success from the start, with residents from Garnetsville and neighboring small towns, unable to resist the allure of Ming's exotic cuisine, filling its tables morning, noon, and night.

Ming himself performed a variety of roles at the restaurant: he greeted patrons at the door and led them to their tables, smiling broadly and bowing at folks as they entered; he also took orders and conversed warmly with diners, explaining the dishes to them in broken yet enthusiastic English ("Yes, ah Char Siu is bah-bah-kyoo poahk we soav wiss ah Chai-nees ah vetch-ta-boh and ah fwied wice. It is ah ved-dy tays-tee! Yoo wiw like."); he also worked the cash register and mirthfully handed fortune cookies to satiated customers as they left his establishment, dutifully repeating his mantra: "OK, thank yoo foh' ah din-ning at ah Dub-bow Happi-ness, OK. Come ah-gain!"); he helped Mei out in the kitchen when things got busy—frying potstickers, grilling vegetables, and washing dishes with gusto; and he personally delivered food to the doorsteps of his patrons when delivery orders came through on the telephone.

As the weeks turned to months, the months turned to years, and the years turned to decades, business at Double Happiness showed no signs of letting up and continued to boom. The restaurant became a Garnetsville staple. Adults who had grown up dining there with their parents were now dining there with their own children. To celebrate the restaurant's thirtieth anniversary, Ming decided to take his family on a greatly deserved vacation to Hong Kong. Thus, it was with a joyful smile on his face that Ming hung a handwritten sign in the restaurant's front window: "Closed for Vacation. Re-open in 2 weeks." He gazed out the window and was pleased to see how much Main Street had grown since he'd been there. Construction was underway all along the block as new businesses—clothing boutiques, record shops, book stores—sprouted up on what seemed like a daily basis. He was excited to see Garnetsville growing and prospering around him, and about the business all of these new attractions would generate for his own establishment.

Little did Ming know as he locked the doors of the Double Happiness Restaurant the night his family left town that the three decades of success his dream had enjoyed would soon be coming to an abrupt end.

The Ming family returned from their trip to Hong Kong two weeks later in bright spirits. As much as they had loved spending time in their homeland—the sights and sounds of the bustling city Ming and Mei had grown up in and loved, and which Qing and Jiao were finally able to experience for themselves—they were happy to return to what they had come to regard as their true home: Garnetsville. The family pulled their '77 Buick Estate Wagon into the garage behind their building early in the morning, and, after enjoying a scrumptious Dim Sum breakfast (featuring steamed har gow, biluochun tea, chicken congee with zha cai, and salted duck eggs), made their way down to the kitchen where Mei, Qing, and Jiao prepared for the morning rush. Ming flicked the restaurant's iconic neon "Double Happiness" sign on, removed his handwritten vacation notice from the window, and unlocked the restaurant's doors. He whistled an old Guangdong folk tune blithesomely whilst methodically laying Chinese zodiac placemats and silverware upon each table, waiting for the day's first customer to arrive. He waited while feeding the goldfish in his fountain. He waited while dusting the artwork hanging from the walls. He waited while polishing the golden Buddha statue. He waited further while stacking new inventory (boxes of rice candy, tea, candied lotus seeds, fortune cookies) in the display case beneath the front counter. He waited for the day's first customer to arrive ... and he waited.

But the day's first customer never came.

Minutes rolled into hours, and, before Ming knew it, noon had arrived, and not a single soul had set foot in his restaurant. What's more, the phone had not rung with a single carry-out or delivery order. Ming lifted the telephone receiver to his ear and listened to its dial tone to make sure it was in proper working order, which it unquestionably was.

Confuzzled, he headed into the kitchen to speak with Mei (who was idling away the hours playing Mahjong with Qing and Jiao). They looked at their Western calendar to make sure it wasn't a holiday of some sort. It was not. They tuned in to their small transistor radio to listen for emergency broadcasts. There were none. The Mings, thus, were at a total loss as to why, for the first time in thirty years, their restaurant was completely deserted.

Exasperated, Ming cursed loudly—"Aiya! Puk gaai! Ding!"—and stormed out the front door onto Main Street. It was there that Ming's eyes were first met with the source of his sudden misfortune. Directly across the street from his establishment, a new restaurant had opened—a restaurant with a flashier façade (massive imperial gray pillars that dwarfed his own; more intricately carved shishi and five-clawed dragon statuary; a more ornate Chinese water fountain), and a much larger, more impressive neon sign: The Triple Happiness Chinese Restaurant. Livid, and in a state of utter disbelief, he crossed the street and peered through the front window of this new restaurant. The décor, like the name of the restaurant itself, was very similar to that of his own establishment—too similar, Ming felt, to chalk up to pure coincidence—only everything within seemed to be better, newer, more elaborate. Ming's outrage was exacerbated by the fact that, as far as his peering eyes could see, tables at the Triple Happiness Restaurant were filled to capacity.

Revolted, Ming spat a thick gob of saliva on the asphalt as he crossed back over to his own restaurant, which he was suddenly forced to view in a different light. Paint was chipped and flaking off all along the Double Happiness façade; his imperial gray pillars looked grimy and weather-beaten; entire sections of his neon sign were burnt-out or flickering. He couldn't help but feel a deep sense of shame when comparing his aging restaurant to the new one that had just opened across the street.

Ming stormed into the kitchen of his restaurant and explained the irksome development he'd just discovered to his family in rapid, wrathful Cantonese. Mei, Qing, and Jiao couldn't bring themselves to believe that such an absurd turn of events had actually taken place until they walked out into the dining room and saw the Triple Happiness restaurant with their own eyes. Immediately, the Mings began to strategize over what the most logical course of action should be. Ultimately, it was decided that Ming himself would walk across the street and calmly talk with the Triple Happiness proprietor in order to reach a resolution of some sort to their current dilemma. Surely, it was reasoned, they would realize what a lousy business move it was to open their establishment directly across from Double Happiness. So Ming grabbed his hat, made his way across the street, and entered the Triple Happiness restaurant.

The minute he stepped through the door, he was overwhelmed by the tantalizing scent of the food being served at this rival establishment, and realized that the flashy exterior of Triple Happiness was the least of his problems. He didn't even have to sample his competitor's food for himself to realize that it was far more delectable than the meals that Mei had been preparing the past thirty years. As he flared his nostrils and deeply inhaled the aromas permeating the air around him, his stomach began to growl wantonly and his mouth watered. Nevertheless, he remained undaunted and strode right up to the front counter, behind which sat a young, attractive Chinese woman.

"Welcome to Triple Happiness, sir," she said mirthfully. "Dine-in or Carry-out?"

"Nei-ther," Ming shot back at her. "My name is Ming. Let me speak to man-ager."

"Yes, of course, sir," she replied, rising from the stool upon which she sat and motioning for Ming to follow her toward the back of the restaurant. "Right this way."

As Ming followed her, his eyes scanned the restaurant's lush décor. Though he didn't wish to admit it to himself, he realized that Triple Happiness was everything he'd ever wanted Double Happiness to be—and then some. It was a masterpiece of bilateral symmetry. The walls were covered on opposing ends with beautiful works of art—ink paintings, ornate pottery, and antique weaponry. Ming felt utterly vanquished seeing every seat in this rival restaurant filled with customers that two weeks before had been his own.

The hostess led Ming through a large oaken door labeled "Employees Only" and down a hallway leading to a small room in back that was furnished with an antique trestle desk, a set of plush club chairs, and what appeared to be a fine replica of a nineteenth-century Oriental rug. Seated behind the trestle desk was a middle-aged Chinese man who appeared to be in the midst of reviewing important paperwork of some sort.

"Mr. Chang," the beautiful Chinese girl began. "... this is Mister ..."

"Ming," Ming interjected, his face twisted in a contemptuous scowl. "I am ow-nuh' of ah Chai-nees res-tau-rant ah-cross the street."

Chang gazed up at Ming bemusedly, and motioned for his hostess to take her leave. The minute Ming heard the door latch shut behind him, he attempted to dispense with the English altogether and began speaking in frenetic Cantonese but was quickly interrupted by Chang.

"Forgive me, Mr. Ming, but I am from Shanghai and do not speak Cantonese. My English, as you can see, is superb, however."

Ming, taking this as a personal jab, felt his blood begin to boil but maintained his composure. He took a deep breath and softened the scowl on his face. When Ming spoke next, he spoke slowly and deliberately, carefully running his wording—and the pronunciation of each word—through his mind in an attempt to give Chang the impression that his grasp of the English language was much greater than he knew it actually was.

"This is ah some place yoo have op-ened here, Mis-ter Chang. If on-ly you had op-ened it in an-oth'er part of town, I would not have cause foh com-plaint. How-ev-ah, I am ahf-raid that op-ening yoh res-tau-rant di-rectly across the street from mine shows an ex-treme lack of foh-sight on yoh part."

"In what way?" Chang responded, the expression of bemusement on his face giving way to a look of smug superiority. "My restaurant has been packed ever since we opened last week."

"Yes, this is be-cause my res-tau-rant has been closed while my fam-ily away on va-cation. Do you rea-lly think that two ah Chai-nees res-tau-rants can thrive with-in such close prox-imity to each other in such a small town?"

Ming waited for a reaction of some sort from Chang before continuing, but Chang continued to stare at him silently with that smug, smirking expression on his face, so Ming continued.

"The Dub-bow Happ-iness Res-tau-rant has been here foh ah thir-ty years now, Mis-ter Chang. Gen-erations of families have grown up eat-ing my food. It is a Gah-nets-ville sta-poh!"

Chang nodded, still wearing a smug, borderline condescending smirk on his face.

"I understand and sympathize with your concerns, Mr. Ming, however, I must disagree with your assessment of the situation. You see, the fact that your restaurant has been here for so long—and has held such a monopolizing grip on the local Chinese food market—only means one thing: the people of Garnetsville are clamoring for a change—something different from, and more adventurous than, the regular old Double Happiness fare, that is."

If Ming's blood had simply been boiling before, here it turned to steam. His hands clenched into rigid, white-knuckled fists deep inside his jacket pockets, but he kept himself together knowing that fist-fighting wasn't going to rectify anything.

"Allow me to show you something," Chang continued, rising slowly from his chair amidst a tiny cacophony of creaking wood and settling leather. He walked across the room and drew open a set of heavy black curtains revealing a one-way glass window through which they had a panoramic view of the bustling Triple Happiness dining room. Before continuing, he took a moment to gaze beamingly at his restaurant like a parent watching his child win a prestigious award.

"Look at those tables, Mr. Ming, and tell me what you see."

Ming gazed at his rival's dining hall with a mixture of covetous awe and rancorous contempt, his fists clenching ever tighter within his pockets.

"Allow me to tell you what we are looking at when we gaze out into my dining room, Mr. Ming: We see a busy restaurant. We see every table filled with satisfied customers, many of whom, I assume, you may recognize as former patrons of your own restaurant. Is that correct?"

It was correct ... and Chang's cocksure attitude and lack of respect infuriated Ming. It took every ounce of restraint he could muster to prevent him from attacking Chang where he stood.

"Garnetsville is a very small town, Mr. Ming. And, perhaps, you are correct. Perhaps this town may not be big enough for two Chinese restaurants. If that is the case, though, Mr. Ming, I don't think that there is any question regarding which restaurant is going to thrive here. The people of Garnetsville have clearly already made their choice."

Unable to bite his tongue any longer, Ming turned to his rival and exploded, hissing, "Yoo wiw not get a-way with this, Mis-tah Chang! Mah'k my words: Yoh restau-rant will not succ-eed here like mine has. I wiw see to that!"

For the first time since Ming had entered that back room, the look of complacency vanished from Chang's face and was quickly replaced with an expression of unconcealed contempt.

"That, Mr. Ming, sounds like a threat," he fumed, pausing to size Ming up from head to toe. "And, from the looks of you, it would appear to be a threat that you could not possibly back up. I do not take to your threats kindly."

At that moment, the door to Chang's office burst open and a gorgeous Chinese woman—even more beautiful than the hostess who had greeted Ming at the door—informed Chang that he had an urgent phone call. After assuring her he'd be right there, he turned to face Ming once more, and flashed a derisive smirk at his rival. "Well, Mr. Ming, I'm afraid it is time for you to leave. It was certainly ... interesting to meet you. I have a feeling that we shall meet again someday."

Chang bowed lightly in Ming's direction, and then motioned for him to exit through the open door of his office. A million quips, curses, and reproachful jabs swirled through Ming's brain, yet he couldn't bring himself to utter another word. Instead, he exited Chang's office and walked shamefully back through the Triple

Happiness dining room, the sights and sounds of its satisfied diners fanning the flames of wrath that threatened to consume him as he made his way out of the restaurant and crossed the street to inform his family that war was about to be declared.

Back in the Double Happiness kitchen, Mei, Qing, and Jiao listened, appalled, as Ming recounted the details of his meeting with Chang. A thick vein throbbed along his left temple as he spoke. He couldn't sit still, and paced back and forth between the kitchen and empty dining room, muttering all sorts of vile cacophemisms under his breath ("Diu la sing! Hui sik see la!").

In the weeks that followed, the Mings did everything they could to compete with the Triple Happiness restaurant. They lowered the prices of everything on their menu, and posted large hand-painted signs in their front window announcing new specials. Periodically, a customer or two would saunter in off the street; however Ming needed only to glance out his window to see patrons virtually swarming his rival's establishment. Mei did everything she could to comfort and inspirit him, persistently telling him that Triple Happiness and its success was just a novelty and a fad, and that, over time, his previously loyal customers would return ... but nothing seemed to cheer Ming up. He grew increasingly sullen, and began snapping at Mei and his daughters over trivial matters, as though the sudden inevitable demise of Double Happiness was their fault. And, to a certain extent, deep down, he truly did place a lot of the blame on them. He had been inside his rival's establishment and had gotten a whiff of the food being served there. He'd seen the satiated faces of the Triple Happiness diners, their foreheads and upper lips glistening with perspiration as they gormandized themselves on Chang's delicacies. There was no question that the food being prepared by Mei, Qing, and Jiao was substantially inferior to the Triple Happiness fare.

As weeks grew into months, the rivalry between the two restaurants began to exact a heavy toll on Ming. His hair was turning gray at an alarming rate, and his face had begun to grow haggard and sunken. Most days now found Ming seated before the front window of his restaurant, gazing across the street and scowling as he beheld the smiling faces of customers that used to be his as they exited Triple Happiness with carry-out bags, chopsticks, and fortune cookies in their hands.

When customers did patronize Double Happiness, Ming took every opportunity he could to slander Chang, spreading false and malicious rumors to anybody who would listen. Among the many lies Ming fabricated and attempted to perpetrate against Chang was that the beef served at the Triple Happiness restaurant actually came from neighborhood cats that Chang and his staff collected each night. The folks that were gullible enough to believe this preposterous untruth were aghast when word had gotten around Garnetsville—as word is wont to do in such a small town—that Mr. Chang had been witnessed prowling the streets late at night, a burlap sack in one hand and a bloody cudgel in the other. As word is also wont to do in such a small town as it travels from one mouth to the next, the stories of Chang's nocturnal cat-hunts grew increasingly graphic and more stomach-churning, with Chang being depicted as a sadistic monster who often left his cudgel at home in favor of tearing live cats apart with his bare hands, and returning home with the bloody burlap sack slung over his shoulder, filled with the mutilated remains of countless neighborhood cats.

These rumors gained a bit of steam as they circulated, as reports of missing housecats did seem to be on the rise. Perched in what had become his usual spot—directly before the front window of his restaurant peering across the street at his rival's establishment—Ming did notice what he perceived to be a slight drop in his competitor's volume of customers. He smiled with callous satisfaction as he saw patrons slowly trickling back to dine at the Double Happiness restaurant. This, however, was not enough for Ming. A man of deep-seated pride, he would never be satisfied until his rival's establishment had been shut down entirely and shut down for good. Chang's very presence offended Ming's honor, and he yearned for vengeance.

As he finished dinner one muggy August evening, Ming decided to help himself to a fortune cookie. He had never really been a fan of them himself—Ming was more of an almond biscuit kind of guy—so on the rare occasions when he found himself developing a craving for one, he was always quick to indulge. As he tore open the fortune cookie's plastic wrapper and snapped the cookie in half, he concentrated intensely on his rivalry with Chang, and fantasized about a day when he would come downstairs to open his restaurant and find a large "For Lease" sign posted on the front window of the Triple Happiness restaurant, its imperial gray pillars hauled away for scrap, and its eye-catching neon sign dismantled and removed. He drew the folded strip of paper from the crumbled remains of his cookie and read his fortune:

"Seize the tail of Fate before Fate seizes your tail."

Ming knew precisely what needed to happen, and, at that moment, in a flash of diabolical inspiration, he knew precisely what he needed to do to make it happen.

Later that evening, he snuck out of bed—careful not to wake Mei (a notoriously light sleeper)—and silently made his way downstairs and into the kitchen of his restaurant where he retrieved a large trash bag. He then made his way to his garage out back where he grabbed a smaller utility sack, inside of which he loaded a flashlight, a set of screwdrivers, and a few other odds and ends, before hopping on his bicycle and taking off down Main Street. The night was silent and humid, and, as he rode off in the dark, Ming ruminated over how much Garnetsville had changed since his family had moved there. Even within the past five years, it had changed so much, and, up until Triple Happiness opened, in Ming's opinion, it had been changing for the better. New businesses seemed to be popping up every day all over town as old ones became obsolescent or extinct entirely. Construction tarps seemed to be up on every other building all along Main and Verikosto. Garnetsville was a town in transition.

Six and a half blocks away, he arrived at his destination—the Garnetsville Animal Shelter. Parking his bicycle alongside the building, Ming crept around back and easily scaled the tall chain-link fence leading to the shelter's rear disposal area. Stealthily, he approached two large commercial-grade trash receptacles, both of which were emblazoned with large orange stickers reading "Caution: Hazardous Waste Storage Area. Restricted Entry." Opening the first of these receptacles, Ming nearly gagged as the repugnant stench of death seeped out into the humid August air.

He covered his mouth with his handkerchief and proceeded to laboriously dig through each of these receptacles, both of which were filled with the corpses of recently euthanized animals. The first container was filled predominantly with canines, although he was able to extract a plastic bag from the bottom filled with what appeared to be several litters of stillborn kittens that had been crushed beneath the corpse of a large Saint Bernard. In the second container, Ming hit pay dirt, for it was chock-full of dead felines. He filled his garbage bag to near bursting with dead cats, slung it over his shoulder, and made his way back over the chain-link fence and to his waiting bicycle, upon which, under the cover of a black Garnetsville night, he rode off into the shadows to enact his odious plan.

It was eerily quiet as Ming rode past the gates of Saint Lazarus Cemetery. He shuddered at the realization that he was utterly surrounded by death. Death filled the ground around him, and it filled the sack on his back. The only living thing in sight or sound was Ming himself. The thought of being placed in a coffin and buried beneath the dirt caused his forearms to horripilate. At sixty-two years of age, how much longer could he really have left to live after all?

Taking a shortcut through the back alleys of Verikosto before rolling down Main unobserved, Ming ultimately arrived at his destination—the Triple Happiness restaurant—and parked his bike several yards away in the alley near the back entrance. Once on foot, he withdrew his flashlight and approached the building cautiously. Shining his flashlight through a small basement window, Ming was able to ascertain that the room he was peering into was being used as an inventory room. He reached into his utility sack and retrieved a flat-head screwdriver, which he then used to pry the window open. A faintly perceptible snap was heard as his screwdriver dislocated the window's wooden frame and latch. Although no audible alarm sounded, Ming, fearing that he may have triggered a silent alarm, knew that he had to move fast. He lowered himself through the window and leapt to the floor of the inventory room with remarkable agility for a man of his age, dragging his sack of dead cats down with him. His goal was to make his way to the Triple Happiness freezer and replace all of the beef contained inside with the cat carcasses he'd collected. He would then disconnect the power to the freezer and place an anonymous call to the police before the restaurant opened for the day to report a cadaverous stench emanating from the building. When they arrived to investigate, they would discover that the ghastly rumors that had been circulating throughout town about Chang were true—he had, in fact, been serving neighborhood cats to his patrons. There would be no way for the restaurant to recover from such a grisly discovery, and Chang would, indubitably, find himself in prison. Ming derived a great sense of grim satisfaction at the thought of Chang being hauled away in handcuffs while he smiled victoriously at his rival from across the street through the window of the Double Happiness restaurant.

He made his way out of the inventory room and quickly ascended a small flight of stairs that led to a doorway down the hall from what he knew to be Chang's office. From there, he cut a sharp left and entered the kitchen through a set of swinging aluminum doors. The freezer door was visible along the back wall of the kitchen, and Ming wasted no time in propping it open with a nearby broomstick and setting himself to work. Lucky for him, the freezer wasn't fully stocked, so he didn't have much beef to remove before he could begin stacking dead cats along the shelves.

Rather than tossing the cats along the shelves willy-nilly, Ming took the time to stack them in a neat, orderly fashion—to lend the preposterous notion of a freezer filled with cat carcasses an air of plausibility. As soon as his trash bag was emptied, he meticulously filled it with all of the beef that had previously been stacked neatly on the freezer shelves. The thought actually occurred to him as he stuffed the last slab of beef into his bag that he could serve it later at his restaurant while watching Triple Happiness being shut down from across the street. As he rose to make his getaway, Ming was startled by a voice from behind him, and froze in his tracks.

"Mr. Ming," the voice said, with an air of smug indignation. He didn't even have to turn around to know that it was the voice of Chang himself. When he did turn his head, he saw the figure of Chang standing just outside of the heavy steel freezer door holding a monk's spade, which he immediately recognized as one of two such spades he'd seen hanging on the walls of the Triple Happiness dining room.

"It seems as though you just couldn't leave well enough alone, could you?" Chang asked calmly, that look of smug supremacy that

Ming had despised so much worn across his face. "Spreading false and vindictive rumors about me is one thing ... but breaking into my restaurant in an effort to sabotage my business is a crime for which you shall not be forgiven. Perhaps spending a few hours in my freezer before the police are alerted will give you some time to contemplate the error of your ways."

When Ming saw Chang's left hand reaching to yank away the broomstick he'd used to prop the freezer door open, he quickly sprang to action, grabbing the tail of a dead cat and whipping the carcass at Chang with all of his might. The cat caught Chang unaware, striking him in the face and causing him to drop his monk's spade. Ming lunged out of the freezer toward the weapon and the two became entangled in a struggle to gain possession of it. As they rolled about the floor tussling over the weapon, Chang reached into his pocket and withdrew a box-cutter, the blade of which he drove forcefully into Ming's side. In desperation, Ming opened his mouth and bit down on the tip of Chang's nose, causing him to scream out in agony and loosen his grip on the monk's spade. Their scuffle temporarily interrupted, both men leapt to their feet. With the weapon's pole firmly gripped in his hands, Ming flashed a sadistic smile and spat out the tip of Chang's nose.

Sensing a decisive advantage while his rival clutched at his nose in an attempt to stop its profuse bleeding, Ming let out a bloodcurdling battle cry and vaulted toward Chang with the monk's spade, causing Chang to back himself into a corner. Chang quickly took possession of a meat cleaver that was lodged in a nearby cutting board, and began swinging it furiously at Ming who used the pole of the monk's spade to deflect its blows.

The battle quickly spilled out from the kitchen into the dining room with both men exchanging blows and parrying each other's attacks. The sounds of Ming and Chang engaged in fatal warfare could be heard out on the street as night gave way to daybreak and the battle raged on. Tables were upturned—plates and glasses smashing cacophonously to the floor—while the two bitter foes struggled to gain dominance in the skirmish. Chang hurled his meat cleaver at Ming and the blade caught him on the shoulder, distracting him long enough for Chang to retrieve the monk's spade's companion from the wall. Mutually armed now, the two men went at each other with mounting fury, each landing minor blows here and there.

The floor was soon slippery with the blood of both combatants, and it became abundantly clear that both men would not be walking away from this entanglement with their lives intact. It was now kill or be killed. A pivotal point in the battle came when Ming was able to chop Chang's left hand clean off with a single devastating swing of his monk's spade. The hand fell to the floor with a loud thump, and its fingers continued to twitch for several moments before curling up lifelessly where it had landed. The force behind Chang's attempted attacks was visibly diminished with the loss of his hand, and, although the color was slowly draining from his face, and the swings of his spade grew increasingly sloppy and erratic, he continued to advance on Ming with an impressive degree of pertinacity.

A fierce slice delivered across Ming's forehead caused a steady stream of blood to trickle down into his eyes, obscuring his vision, and giving Chang a momentary advantage, which he willfully seized upon, driving the razor-sharp edge of his monk's spade deep into Ming's momentarily unprotected abdomen. When Chang yanked his gore-bedrabbled spade away from his opponent's belly, it brought chunks of stomach muscle and viscera with it, which Chang scraped off against the floor. Seeing the tide of this battle turning away from his favor, Ming leapt at Chang in utter desperation, and the two began to grapple with the poles of their spades interlocked. Chang was able to maneuver his handless left arm around the back of Ming's neck, locking him in a chokehold. Ming dropped his spade, withdrew the flat-head screwdriver from his pocket, and began to drive it in and out of Chang's ribcage with murderous abandon.

Weary from blood loss and the rigors of mortal combat, Chang's legs gave way beneath him, sending both men crashing out through the restaurant's front window amidst a cascading shower of shattered glass. They landed in the Chinese fountain out front and continued to struggle against each other as the water quickly turned red with their blood. By pure chance, the position of both assailants had shifted during their fall, leaving Ming with a decisive advantage on top of Chang. He merely had to push his weight against Chang to force his head underwater, and within a matter of minutes, Chang's body ceased to struggle and stopped moving entirely. Ming watched as the bloody bubbles stopped rising from Chang's mouth and the water grew still around him.

Victorious, yet mortally wounded, Ming rose from the fountain with great difficulty, and stood above Chang for a moment, glaring at his lifeless body. A small crowd of passersby had gathered along the fountain and stood aghast at what they had just witnessed. Nobody attempted to impede Ming's path as he stepped out of the fountain and staggered groggily into the street, struggling to stay upright on spaghetti-legs.

He made it halfway across the street before collapsing on the warm asphalt with a heavy thud. A thick pool of dark, uncoagulated blood developed around his open abdominal cavity as Ming Ming drew in his final breath, mere footsteps away from his restaurant's doorstep. Before that final breath had been expelled, Ming gazed down the block and saw that construction had ended on one of the new buildings at the corner of Verikosto Boulevard, and its construction tarps had been removed to reveal the facade of Garnetsville's newest dining establishment: The Quadruple Happiness Chinese Restaurant.

RIGHT-HAND MAN

BY WELDON BURGE

The two remaining crème donuts were as hard as a bull's ass, and the coffee was this side of motor oil. It was time to make another run to Dunkin' Donuts—as soon as it got dark and he could slip out unnoticed. At the donut joint, there was also a restroom and a pay phone. The restroom was a godsend.

He hated to recon his targets.

Francis "Flash" Conwright sat at a second-floor window of a dark, vacant house, holding high-powered binoculars to his eyes with one hand and a cell phone to his ear with the other. It was a burner phone and he had no intention of staying on it long. He watched another seemingly empty house across the street, five doors down.

"I don't know. Something doesn't smell right."

"What's the problem?" Solly Ventura asked.

"Intuition, I guess. I can't put my finger on it, but something doesn't add up. I have to trust my intuition with these things. Saved my ass more than once." Conwright sighed. "I'm getting too old for this shit, Solly."

"What are you talking about? You're only forty-two and in the best shape of your life!"

"I'm eating donuts and crap food and drinking coffee by the friggin' gallon. I haven't worked out in weeks."

275

"So? You're sweating your ass off, you probably smell like a syphilitic Tijuana whore, and you're bored beyond belief sitting in that room. I know it's the least favorite part of your job, but it's a necessary evil. You know that. How long now?"

"Three days. You're right. I'd kill for a shower. It's so hot in here, I've got perpetual swamp-ass. I'm dying to get this over with, just to get reacquainted with air-conditioning."

"Look, don't start doubting yourself. You're the best in the business—"

"—and getting older—"

"I don't want to hear that shit. You've got years yet. Hell, you're at your prime. Listen to me. Don't doubt yourself."

"I hear you, Solly," Conwright said. But he had plenty of doubt. He never ate tons of junk food during other recons. Something had changed. He had changed. Was he getting soft? "Listen, let me call you back in about an hour."

Conwright ended the call and pocketed the phone; he'd toss it down a storm drain later. He watched the tall man standing guard on the lawn in front of his target house. The guy obviously didn't care if he was conspicuous or not. But, why would he care? The entire development was under construction and there currently were no residents. The perfect sanctuary for a mobster in hiding. Conwright didn't recognize the thug, but he knew the old man, Cartanza, was in the house.

Vito Cartanza had been an enforcer in the Jersey mob most of his life, moving up in the ranks until, at the age of eighty, he finally found religion and turned state's evidence. The Jersey families didn't take kindly to this and had already attempted twice to take out Cartanza. The feds offered to put Cartanza into witness protection, but the old man didn't want to go into protective custody. Instead, he fled New Jersey with four of his henchmen, ending up in a house in a new real estate development in Paradise, PA, just outside Lancaster. Amish country. Rolling farmland. Horses and buggies. A slower lifestyle.

What was bothering him? Not like he hadn't faced similar scenarios in the past. He already knew the layout of the house from building plans. Had scoped out the neighborhood, knew the ins and outs of the construction crews now building houses on the far side of the development. No obvious obstructions other than the four men protecting Cartanza. Challenging perhaps, but certainly not problematic.

When the sun went down, he slipped out the back of the empty house.

"Are you sure the old man's there?"

"I saw them bring him in two days ago," Conwright said. "Four goons and the geezer. Two guys at a time guarding the house, front and back, working shifts. Cartanza's got to be there."

Conwright took another bite from the chocolate-covered donut, cradling the pay-phone receiver against his shoulder. He stood in front of the donut shop, watching the darkened, vacant parking lot. Not many folks buying donuts at eleven o'clock on a hot, steamy July night.

"So, what do you want to do?" Solly asked. "You can bail at any time, no hard feelings. Or, I can renegotiate the contract more to your liking, if that changes anything."

Solomon Ventura was Conwright's liaison with the mob, had known him since their early days in South Philly. Whenever the Philly mafia needed a clean hit with no family ties, Solly made the arrangements with Conwright. Solly had ties with the right people in Jersey, as well. The politics of the Cartanza situation, dealing with the Jersey mob, required a special tack—precisely the situation for which Conwright was most suitable. The Philly boys wanted nothing to do with it, of course.

"I'll need to take out the four guards to get to the old man," Conwright said. "What can you do for me?"

"Financially speaking?"

"Yes."

"I can swing five Gs a head, on top of the hundred Gs for Cartanza. I think the Jersey guys would go for that."

"What else can you do for me?"

"How so?"

"Can you tell me anything about these goombahs?" Conwright asked. "I don't know all the Jersey boys."

"Describe them."

"The one guy chain-smokes. Tall guy, probably the most observant of the bunch, seems to be perpetually on edge. Kinda bald, big ears. Lots of tats on his arms and going up his neck. Doesn't seem to talk much with the others. But also seems to be the one giving all the orders."

"Sounds like Benito Arturo."

"Benny the Artist. Heard of him. Real sleazebag."

"I'm surprised he's there. Benny doesn't go for the bodyguard thing. He must owe Cartanza big time."

"Advice?"

"I'd take him out first, if possible. He's pretty badass. You don't want to get anywhere near him. He'll rip off your arms and beat you to death with them."

"OK. There's a short guy, kinda overweight. Looks like he'd rather be somewhere else, like he could fall asleep at a moment's notice. Dark goatee, nose like a warthog. Older than the others."

"That's gotta be Louie Barcola. He's been with Cartanza for decades, an old friend. He's slow and not that bright. Shouldn't present any problems for you, though."

"A thug, built like a brick shithouse, arms wider than his head. I haven't seen much of him. Light hair, kinda long. Constantly combs it. Probably spends a lot of time in front of a mirror."

"Hmm ... could be Nicky Suffo. He used to be a boxer, and the mob owned him. If it's him, he's been breaking legs and smashing kneecaps for the past few years. Younger guy?"

"Probably early thirties."

"That's Suffo. He can kill you with one punch, so don't get within arm's length. Suffo is kind of a younger version of Cartanza, started as a mob grunt but with higher ambitions. Not sure why he would side with Cartanza, unless he really respects the codger. What's the fourth guy look like?"

"Rarely comes out of the house. Every time I've seen him, he's been right next to the old man. Doesn't look like mob material. Relative maybe?"

"How old is this guy?"

"Mid-twenties, maybe."

"Nah, Cartanza's kids are in their fifties," Solly said. "Describe this guy."

"Light hair, clean face. Not a goon like the other three, not the build."

"Hmmm ... sounds like Cartanza's right-hand man. Cartanza has some health issues, so maybe this guy handles the medicines, the food, and such. A nurse. Not much of a threat."

"OK, thanks, Solly. You'll check into the extra payment for the goons, let me know?"

"Sure thing. Listen, don't jump on this if you're still having doubts. Hear me? I don't want to lose my best hitter."

As soon as he entered the room, Conwright knew he was in trouble. Louie Barcola, the fat, slow one, stood opposite the door, gun raised. Stupid, stupid! How could he have let this toad get the jump on him?

"What the fuck you think you're doing here, Ace?" Barcola waved his gun toward the bedroll on the floor, the junk-food wrappers and empty coffee cups.

Conwright made a quick scan of the room. Despite the darkness, he was pretty sure he'd left nothing suspicious out in the open. The binoculars were in his back pocket. No guns left in the room. Still, what did Barcola know?

"Look, I don't want no trouble, man," Conwright said. "I'm just squattin' here 'til somethin' turns up. I been outta work for months. Wife kicked me out. Just tryin' to get by, ya know?"

"Yet, you can afford Starbucks coffee," Barcola said, nodding to the empty cup on the floor.

Damn! He only went to the Starbucks that one time.

"Look, man, I panhandle during the day, crash here at night. I know I'm trespassin', but I ain't causin' no trouble. And I don't want no trouble."

"How long you been here?"

"Coupla days. You want me to move on, I'll move on. I was lookin' to hitchhike to Philly anyway."

Conwright started toward his bedroll as if to collect his gear, but Barcola waved his gun again, motioning him to step back.

"Maybe I'll just call the cops," Barcola said.

"Man, you don't wanna do that. Just let me go, OK?"

"Or, better still, just put a bullet in your head."

Conwright forced his voice to sound terrified. "C'mon, man, I ain't done nothin'. Just let me pack up and go. You won't see me again, swear to God." He started toward his gear again.

"Hold it there, buckaroo."

Conwright stopped, stared at the man, waiting for the next move. He still wasn't close enough. But Barcola's hesitation was promising.

"Nah, I think I'll shoot you," Barcola said, stepping forward, closer, close enough, "and worry about it later."

Conwright slapped the gun from Barcola's right hand with his left hand, striking the pressure point just above the wrist to break his grip. Simultaneously, he punched the man's left ear with his cupped right hand—a practiced maneuver that usually burst the eardrum or at least caused enough inner-ear trauma to drive an assailant to his knees. As Barcola lost his balance, Conwright yanked a length of garrote wire secreted in his sleeve, looped it around that thick neck, and used Barcola's own weight as he fell to cinch the wire around his throat. Barcola fought for breath, flailing and grasping at empty air, until, with a sharp tug, Conwright crushed the hyoid bone, sealing the man's doom.

He dropped Barcola to the floor, uncoiled the wire from the dead man's throat, and allowed it to recoil on the spool in his sleeve. Conwright stared at the frog-eyed face, the eyes already filming. The garrote was efficient, but not enjoyable. What he could have done with a handheld circular sander and a little more time, peeling Barcola's cheeks, taking off only the top epithelial layers where the nerve endings were the keenest. Maybe even grating his porcine nose down to the cartilage. Or maybe use a filet knife and slice those meaty jowls to the bone. It would have been far more fun—and far better than the goon deserved. Conwright could have also gleaned more information about the specific layout of the house and Cartanza's defense plans—if only he'd had time to play.

Time, however, was precisely what he didn't have.

The circumstances demanded a change in strategy. The others would miss Barcola. If they had sent Barcola to the house, that meant they were probably aware of his presence. They would send someone

280

else to investigate. Not good. He'd have to take action far earlier than expected.

Conwright pulled the binoculars from his back pocket and stepped to the window, then hesitated. Had a glint on the binocular lens given him away? Something must have alerted them. Had they seen him come or go earlier? Or did they patrol the neighborhood and just happened to come upon his gear?

Staying in the shadows, he looked out the window without the binoculars. Arturo stood on the front lawn of the home down the block, hands on hips, staring in his direction. Arturo lifted something to his ear—

—and a raking, static-filled sound came from behind Conwright, startling him. The sound came from a small device attached to Barcola's belt, a walkie-talkie of the sort often used by construction workers.

Arturo's voice, thick and venomous, came from the small speaker. "What's going on, you idiot? You've been up there for over an hour."

Conwright unclipped the device from Barcola's belt.

"Talk to me, numb-nuts!" Arturo growled.

At first, Conwright thought to mimic Barcola's voice. But, he'd already made at least one stupid mistake, not securing this room. How many other dumb mistakes had he made?

"Talk to me!"

Conwright clicked the button a few times, on and off, on and off, on and off.

"Sweet Jesus, you don't even know how to work the damn thing!" Arturo said. "If you didn't find anything, get your lardass back here. Now!"

That gave Conwright some time. He hoped it was enough.

Conwright worked his way back to his car, parked just outside the development next to an abandoned gas station. The car looked like a derelict and fit in well next to the run-down garage. He was sure there were no active security cameras on the building. Popping the trunk, he pulled out the gear he thought he'd need for the job, gear that would not hamper him or slow him down if things didn't go well. He had to act fast before the other goons found Barcola's corpse.

It would be so much easier to take out Arturo and Suffo with a sniper rifle, simply by positioning himself where both guards were simultaneously in range. Of course, the gunshots would alert those in the house and make things difficult. But, Conwright had never become proficient with a sniper rifle—largely because he abhorred sniper killings, much like he abhorred hunting. The thought of killing a deer from a distance—detached from the event, the deer not even aware of his presence, taking down the unsuspecting beast without even a confrontation—seemed cowardly to him. Too safe, too antiseptic. But, here he faced two trained killers before he could even enter the target house. What now? He had no time to strategize as he'd hoped. He had to move before they realized they had a problem.

When construction started at the new development, sewer and waterlines, electrical cables, and other utilities had been the first to go in. The streets were paved, largely through empty lots, and streetlights had been installed. There was a streetlight just past the target house, fully illuminating the front yard where Arturo now stood, smoking a cigarette. No way for a frontal attack, so Conwright worked his way to the back of the house where he assumed Suffo was stationed.

Conwright crouched at the back of an adjoining house, scoping out the situation. From there, he could see lighting in the rear rooms, probably where Cartanza was holed up. And the flickering fluorescence of what was certainly a television. A gas-powered electric generator had been placed near the back door—Cartanza had the only electricity in the neighborhood.

Suffo stood at the back door, staring up at the moon.

Conwright heard Arturo on the walkie-talkie, trying to contact Barcola again, his voice getting louder as no response came.

"Suffo, get your ass over here!" Arturo yelled from the front yard.

Suffo grumbled, then disappeared around the end of the house. That was the break Conwright needed. He sprinted across the lot and melted into the shadows at the back of the house, working his way to the generator. He ducked behind it as Suffo returned to his position. The thug cursed under his breath, "Fuckin' Barcola. How the shit am I supposed to baby-sit Barcola and watch the house at the same time? Pain in my ass."

Conwright used the chugging hum of the generator to mask his movement as he approached Suffo from behind, his KA-BAR serrated knife in his right hand. Suffo became aware of him just as Conwright jammed his left hand over Suffo's mouth, tilting his head back. Before Conwright could slide the blade through Suffo's exposed throat, Suffo clenched a massive hand around Conwright's wrist, nearly breaking bone. Conwright suppressed a scream as the KA-BAR dropped to the ground. He shifted his weight, pulling harder on Suffo's head until the man's center of balance tilted him backward. Suffo still grasped Conwright's wrist, and he felt the agony of grinding bones in his hand as he too began to fall. Both men hit the ground.

Suffo was faster than Conwright expected, releasing his grip on Conwright's wrist and rolling aside, quickly bringing himself up on one knee. Conwright tried to do the same, but Suffo landed a devastating kidney punch. The pain was immediate and excruciating.

"Arturo!" Suffo yelled.

Now on his back, Conwright reached for his ankle holster, but couldn't pull up his pant leg before Suffo landed another punch directly to his stomach, driving the air from his lungs and doubling the pain in his abdomen.

"What the hell's going on?" Arturo rounded the corner of the house, gun drawn.

"This asshole tried to take me out," Suffo said. The ex-boxer stood, looking down at Conwright writhing on the ground. "You know him?"

Arturo stepped closer, gun pointed at Conwright's head. "Nope. Never seen him before."

"Just shoot him, get it over with," Suffo said.

"Can't do that, you idiot. We need to find out who he is, who sent him."

"Isn't it obvious?"

"No, it's not fuckin' obvious. We need to question him. 'Bout time we had some fun around here."

There was the crack of a gunshot, a muzzle flash at the back door of the house. Arturo staggered backward, a dark stain blossoming on his chest.

Suffo said, "What the——?" before another gunshot, a bullet this time punching a hole through the side of Suffo's head and blowing a chunk of skull the size of a lemon out the other side. Suffo tumbled to the lawn next to Conwright.

Arturo still stood, an expression of disbelief on his face as he looked down at his pulsing chest. Another shot and Arturo's head exploded; he dropped to the grass as well.

Conwright looked toward the door, expecting a bullet himself. In the frame of the door was the kid, the one Solly had called "the right-hand man," Cartanza's personal aide. He looked even younger than he had in the binoculars, clean-shaven and boy-band attractive. The kid held the handgun to his side, smiling at Conwright.

"So, Mr. Conwright. We finally meet. Sorry these two thugs caused you such distress."

What the hell? Conwright thought.

"May I call you Flash? Please, Flash, come into the house. Let's get acquainted." He lifted the gun. "But no funny business or I can make things very difficult for you."

Conwright's wrist throbbed, and he felt like his left kidney had exploded, judging from the pain in his lower back. How much damage had Suffo done? He could be bleeding internally, for all he knew.

He stumbled through the kitchen area, trying to maintain his balance, the kid with the gun behind him. He noticed the refrigerator, connected by a cable to the generator out back. Several cables snaked down the hall, he assumed to the living area where Cartanza now resided. He wondered if they also had running water and a functioning bathroom. Considering Cartanza's ill heath and age, most likely.

"I guess you already took out Barcola, huh?" the kid asked. "I was the one who suggested he check out the house. You see, I've been expecting you."

"How?"

"How did I expect you? Simple. The man who hired me also hired you. I've known all along that you were hired to kill Cartanza. But, it's not quite what you think." The kid chuckled, and it was that little laugh that bothered Conwright the most. Why hadn't the kid put a bullet in his head? None of this made sense.

Although the rest of the house was presumably empty, the kitchen, adjoining bathroom, and dining room (now acting as a living room) were well furnished, with electrical cables running every which way. Cartanza sat in an armchair in front of a large, flat-screen TV, watching an old episode of "The A-Team." Only Cartanza was no longer capable of watching or hearing anything. His eyes bulged from his bloated, purple face; his black tongue protruded from his dark lips—a leather belt had been tightened around his throat.

"All the comforts of home, wouldn't you say?" the kid asked.

Conwright glared at him. "What's this about?"

"Like I said, I knew you were coming, knew you were here. As soon as you arrived at the house and I heard Suffo grappling with you, I took care of Cartanza. That was the plan, you see. You've been the real target all along."

"And the other two?"

"Also in the plan, although I'd hoped you'd take them out before I had to. I must say, I'm disappointed with your performance so far. I expected more, considering your reputation."

"It's been a fubar day, what can I say? Are you going to tie me up, cuff me, or what?"

Then Conwright saw it—just a glint, a fraction, of fear in the kid's eyes. His captor, despite his bravado, was keeping his distance.

"Take your clothes off," the kid said.

"You're kidding."

"Not at all. I know you're carrying, and I have no intention of letting you use any of your weapons. So, take it all off."

"Just kill me now, junior. I'm not playing your games."

"No games. No games at all. Just precautions. You see, I've been paid to detain you, not kill you."

Conwright cocked his head. "What's this really about?"

"Like I said, you've been the target all along. You're a hard man to lure out into the open, Mr. Conwright. My employer has been tracking you for years. When Cartanza became a potential hit, my employer—"

"Just who is your employer?"

The kid ignored the question. "My employer had an opportunity to hire you to take out Cartanza. What better way to draw you into the crosshairs?"

So, Conwright thought, whoever was behind this had mob connections, knew to contact Solly Ventura to contract him. Had to be someone who could fund a contract on Cartanza, someone tied to the Jersey mob—yet also someone who could hire this weasel to capture him.

"I want you nude," the kid said. "Now. Everything off. I'm not supposed to kill you, but I can certainly put a bullet where you wouldn't want one."

Conwright sighed and started to undress. He dropped his clothes in a pile next to Cartanza's chair, and then stripped off his various holsters, sheathed knives, and other killing devices (including the garrote and a pouch of shurikens). The young assassin was most impressed with Conwright's Bernadelli .22, a palm-sized handgun Conwright had positioned in a holster between his shoulder blades, easy to pull from the back of his neck—and generally missed in a pat down. The Bernadelli was Conwright's preferred firearm.

Conwright stood naked in front of the kid, arms outstretched. "Unless you want to check the crevice of my ass, that's it. Now what, junior?"

"Sit. On the floor. Legs crossed."

Conwright sat. As he did so, he glanced around the room, weighing his options. "You got a name, kid?"

"Actually, I kinda like 'The Kid.' Has an outlaw feel to it, wouldn't you say?"

"This isn't the wild west, kid. This is Amish country. We're not gunslingers."

The kid nodded. "Maybe not gunslingers, but certainly killers."

"You really don't know what you're dealing with, do you?"

The kid smiled, tipped the gun. "Inform me."

"Remember in the news, the Atlantic City Slasher, killed a dozen hookers? They never caught the guy. Or the Baltimore Strangler?"

"Man, that's old news, happened a decade or so ago. So what?" The kid's eyes narrowed. "Wait, are you—?"

"Catching on, junior."

"No way, man. A serial killer? And a hit man? BS. Pure BS." The kid laughed.

"Even hired guns take vacations. A little R and R. On the job, I don't kill unless I get paid. But, on my own time, well ..."

"Bullshit!"

Conwright shrugged. "Let's just say I have unique skills and experience. For example, I can imagine attaching jumper cables to your scrotum and giving you the thrill of your short life. Plus some fun and games with strategically placed drops of hydrochloric acid. I can hear you screaming. But, of course, that would be way too much fun. I don't mix business with pleasure, and I'm here on business. So, more than likely, I'll take the boring route and just put a bullet in your head."

The kid laughed again. "Aw, man, you're killing me here! I'm the one with gun, dipshit. You're sitting with your nuts on the floor. Your career ends tonight, old man." He pulled a cell phone from his pants pocket, punched in a number. "Yeah, I have him here now. He's not going anywhere. No. Arturo and Suffo roughed him up a bit. I had to take them both out. Yeah, Cartanza's dead, too. No. No problem." He finished the call, and then smiled at Conwright. "He'll be here soon."

"Then what?"

"Oh, I think he wants to take care of you himself. Some revenge thing. I hope it's fun to watch."

"I'm sure it will be," Conwright said as he grasped an electrical cable on the floor next to him and yanked with all his strength, sending spikes of pain from his injured kidney through his spine. The cable snapped taut against the back of the kid's ankles, toppling him backward to the floor. Conwright sprang from his sitting position, straddled his captor, and drove his flat, open hand into the kid's throat, punching his larynx, causing spontaneous gagging. Conwright ripped the gun from the kid's hand, jammed the gun into the side of his knee, and fired one shot. The kid howled.

Conwright put his lips next to the kid's left ear. "What's the plan?" he asked.

The kid sobbed, his eyes wide.

"What's the friggin' plan?" Conwright repeated.

"He wants to kill you himself."

"Why does he want me dead?"

"I don't know! Can't you see I'm bleedin' here?" the kid cried out.

287

"I noticed."

Conwright jammed the gun under his jaw.

Tears welled in the boy's eyes, sweat beaded on his forehead. He shook uncontrollably. Conwright had to get him to talk before he passed out.

"Did Solly put you up to this?"

The kid looked thoroughly bewildered.

"Solly?" Conwright repeated. "Was it Solly?"

"Who the shit's Solly? Dude told me his name was Hanson."

"Hanson?" Conwright couldn't remember anyone named Hanson from his past. Probably an alias.

"Yeah, Hanson. That's all the fuck I know, man. He set the whole thing up. And, right now, I wish to hell I never met the stupid—"

"So, you met him? What did the guy look like?"

"What? I don't know. Little guy, like an accountant or something."

"Dark hair?"

"No hair. The dude was bald."

Not Solly, then. Who could this be?

He pressed the gun deeper under the punk's chin—

"Wait! Wait! No—"

—and put a bullet straight up through his brain.

Conwright stood, wiping blood from his face with the back of his hand. "Tough business for rookies, kid." He tossed the gun to the floor.

He got dressed, pulled the Bernadelli from its holster, and sat in the chair opposite Cartanza's corpse.

And waited.

Conwright pointed his Bernadelli directly into the man's face. Hanson, or whatever his true name was, had strolled into the room liked he owned the place, his face beaming. But the smile instantly dissolved when he saw the kid dead on the floor and Conwright sitting in the chair holding a gun.

"Never send a child to do your dirty work," Conwright said.

The man glared at Conwright, hatred and malice in his eyes. The kid was right. He was a puny, balding guy who looked everything in the world like an accountant, someone who hovered over a desk for much of his life crunching numbers and perusing spreadsheets.

"You're Hanson?"

The man said nothing.

"Why do you want to kill me?"

"You killed my fiancée."

"I've killed a lot of people."

"Josephine Hunnicutt."

Conwright couldn't place the name. It must have been a hit, not one of his "pleasure" kills, for Hanson to attach him to the killing. He hadn't hit many women over the years. Probably not a mob thing. More likely a jealous lover or ex-husband. But he was always better at faces than names. If he had a photo—

"She was to testify against Marco Gabretti, just two weeks before our wedding. She witnessed his assassination of Brian Macauley, one of the leaders of the Irish mob in Philadelphia. I guess Marco decided he didn't want her to testify ... so he hired you."

Conwright could remember the Gabretti trial. But he couldn't remember the hit, couldn't remember the woman at all. Was his memory really getting that bad?

"You bastard, you don't even remember her!" Hanson vibrated with anger, clenching his fists at his sides.

"How long ago was this?"

"Nine years."

"Well, there you go! You can't expect me to remember that far back."

"You destroyed me. Took away the only love I've ever known."

"Nothing personal, I assure you. Strictly business."

Hanson's face reddened; a vein throbbed on his forehead. "You *killed* her! Of course it was personal!"

Conwright shrugged. "That's what I'm paid to do. Let me remind you, you apparently paid me to kill. You paid the weasel on the floor over there to kill. You're no different. You have no moral high ground."

"I'm nothing like you. I despise you, you son of a bitch. I want to see you die in the worst possible fashion. Slowly. Painfully. And then I hope you roast in Hell."

Conwright shrugged again. "Tell me if I have this straight. You're a bookkeeper for the Jersey mob, and the boys told you to fund a hit on Cartanza, right?"

Hanson said nothing.

"So, you called Solly Ventura and asked for me specifically. I don't know how you figured out Solly was my liaison—"

Hanson grinned. "I have my connections. Took me years to develop them, years to track you down."

Conwright nodded. "But, once you contracted with Solly to have me hit Cartanza, you then contracted with the kid to take me out."

"No, not take you out. I wanted that opportunity."

"Do I have the story straight?"

"Think you're smart, don't you? You're not so smart."

Conwright nodded again. "I was a little sloppy this time around, I'll admit. And my gut told me something was screwy with this set up. But I never figured on you."

"So, I assume you're going to kill me now," Hanson said. He crossed his arms, glaring at Conwright. "It will bring you no satisfaction, you know."

Conwright smiled. He stood, felt a twinge of pain in his lower back again, but the pain had lessened. Maybe he was getting older, but he was still resilient.

"You clearly misunderstand me," he said. "This is a business. I'm a businessman. I don't kill unless I'm paid to do so. There is no profit in killing you." He moved closer to Hanson, making circles with the gun in his hand. "Oh, I did kill one man who refused to pay me, refused to honor our contract. Thoroughly unprofessional. I viewed it as writing off a bad debt."

Hanson's eyes never left Conwright's face. He remained silent. Conwright sensed the hatred growing like a parasite on the man's soul.

"I've killed in self-defense," Conwright continued. He took another step closer to Hanson.

"Is that why you killed the kid? In self-defense?"

"No, he was part of the contract. You paid me to take him out, same as the others. Unfortunately, your boy took them out before I had a chance, even Cartanza." Conwright sighed. "So, you owe me $10,000, for Barcola and the kid."

"Well, I'm not part of the contract, correct?"

"True."

"And since I'm not foolish enough to attack you while you're pointing a gun in my face, I'm not an immediate threat to your life."

"Not immediate, no."

"So, you cannot kill me in self-defense."

"Right again. I have no intention of killing you. By the way, are you right-handed?"

"What?"

"Are you right-handed? It's not a tough question. Most people are right-handed. I was just wondering if you are."

"I'm right-handed, yes. But—"

Conwright thrust his Bernadelli into Hanson's right shoulder, angling the barrel up under the armpit, and rapidly pulled the trigger four times, exploding muscle, tendons, nerves, and cartilage, shattering the rotator cuff and the head of the humerus.

Hanson dropped to the floor, screeching like a skewered pig.

"Extensive corrective surgery and you'll eventually regain some use of that arm," Conwright said. "A little physical and occupational therapy, you may be able to hold a cup of coffee. Someday."

Hanson's eyes, just a moment before brimming with hatred, were now wide with fear and agony.

Conwright crouched next to him. "My advice. Drop it. You're still alive. Cherish what you have, while you have it. This hatred will only consume you."

"Bastard," Hanson hissed.

"Now see, you still haven't learned the lesson here. Just remember that there are other parts of your body that can take a bullet without killing you. Other parts that can be hacked off or blown away. Please keep this in mind if you harbor any thoughts of striking out at me again. Oh, and don't forget you owe me ten grand."

As Hanson writhed on the floor, Conwright used the kid's cell phone and anonymously reported a shooting to the police. He pocketed the phone; he'd dump it later. He also picked up the kid's gun to dispose of. Then, he walked out the front door of the house.

Conwright knew, as he always knew, that he would have to watch his back.

ULTIMATE BETRAYAL

BY JOSEPH BADAL

CHAPTER 1

"You cut yourself with that knife and I'll never forgive you."

David Hood chuckled, placed the kitchen knife on the counter next to the tomatoes he'd been cutting, and turned to look at Carmela. Five feet, eight inches tall, still model-perfect, with long legs, raven-colored hair, and classic Mediterranean features. "Nothing's going to get in the way of our night out," he said. "This is one anniversary we're going to spend together."

Carmela stepped into David's arms and tilted her head. She combed her fingers through his salt-and-pepper hair. "You know you get better looking every year. Kiss me, you handsome devil."

"With pleasure."

"Yuck! Daddy's smooching Mommy," three-year-old Kyle shouted in his bullhorn voice.

"Don't be a pain," his five-year-old sister, Heather, told her brother.

Carmela laughed and whispered, "I owe you a kiss."

"You owe me more than a kiss," David said.

She walked over to the kitchen table where Kyle and Heather worked on a puzzle.

"I'd better get changed," David said as he unknotted his tie.

"Before you do that, would you get a jar of carrots for the children's dinner?"

"Sure," David said.

"Can we come?" Heather asked. "Can we, Daddy?"

David knew the kids would slow things down; they'd want to explore the basement, play hide n' seek. "Next time, guys," he said.

David descended the worn, wooden stairs to the concrete basement floor. Two inches taller than the six foot clearance, he bent slightly. He shook his head as he looked around the basement of his one hundred-year-old Bethesda home. *What a mess!* he thought. Two rusted bicycles, broken-down lawn furniture, dried-out garden hoses, coffee cans full of nails and screws, a wooden icebox he'd sworn he would refinish someday. *I've got to clean out this place,* he thought for the thousandth time. He crossed to the old fallout shelter a previous owner had installed during the paranoia of the Cold War. Now Carmela stored her canned fruit and vegetables here. He smiled at the sounds of Heather and Kyle's voices—music to his ears—drifting down from the kitchen.

David flipped the light switch, turned the shelter's door handle, and stepped inside. The weighted door closed behind him with a soft *whoosh*. He selected from a shelf a jar of the carrots Carmela had put up from her vegetable garden, turned, and took a second to enjoy the quiet of the ten-by-ten shelter. The cellar's stone exterior walls, combined with the shelter's rebar-reinforced concrete, made the room a suburban fortress. He always found comfort down here, especially after a manic day at the security business he'd founded six years earlier.

He reached for the door handle, but it was suddenly, inexplicably beyond his reach. Before his mind could process an explanation, he was thrown back. Thudding glass jars crashed on and around him; shelves cascaded on his head and shoulders.

"What the ...!" David groaned.

Then, terror seized him. Even within the shelter's thick walls, he heard the full roar of an explosion. The little room swayed. The *whoomp* of the blast was all too familiar. He'd heard and felt enough of them years ago in Afghanistan. He placed a hand against a side wall; struggled to his feet. His mind whirled as he attempted to make sense of it. He tried to deny what he knew from instinct and experience had occurred—an enormous explosion had rocked his home.

The room went suddenly black. The shelves he'd carefully built for Carmela now lay in a scatter of glass, fruit, and vegetables.

David shouted, "Carmela!" He took two steps and pushed the shelter door handle. It wouldn't budge. Through the door's small Plexiglas window he saw dim light streaming into the cellar from where a solid wall should have been. Plaster, brick, stone, and insulation fell in a fog of dust. His three-story Colonial home was falling in on itself. Debris blocked the shelter door and obliterated what little view the window had provided.

Once the death throes of his home subsided, funereal quiet returned. David's hands trembled. His heart beat against his ribs as though trying to escape the confines of his chest. He'd never felt this kind of fear. "Carmela!" he screamed. "Heather! Kyle!" The only answers he got were the sounds of his own voice reverberating off the shelter walls.

David pushed on the door again. It wouldn't move. Bracing himself, he slammed his foot against it, over and again, to no avail. Primordial shrieks echoed off the walls, while a feeling of horrendous grief swept over him. He heard the shrieks, but couldn't seem to connect them to himself. Trapped inside the shelter, he threw his body against the door until, bruised and battered, he had no more strength. He collapsed in a corner and waited for help—his mind filled with images of his wife and children, and what the explosion might have done to them.

Time passed in slow motion. David could barely keep his eyes open—light-headed, sleep seduced him. He knew lack of oxygen had begun to affect him. He stretched out and gasped for breath, as he felt the blanket of unconsciousness creep over him.

CHAPTER 2

Rolf Bishop rubbed his hands together and tried to force himself to be calm. There was only one man left from his old unit in Afghanistan. Thirteen men were now dead. David Hood the only survivor. With Hood out of the way, there would be no one left to threaten him. Bishop rose from his desk chair and paced the length of his spacious Georgetown home office. He relished the room's opulent décor—the Persian carpets, the collection of first editions in the floor to ceiling bookcases, the antique pool table, the sculptures and paintings. Until he'd served in Afghanistan he could never have afforded any of these things. The war there had changed everything. He was a colonel back then—a warlord.

He stopped in front of his ego wall and looked at the framed citations and photographs of him with presidents and generals and corporate bigwigs. He was on top of the world. But one man could bring it all down.

The ringing of the telephone interrupted his musings. He spun around and walked back to his desk, sucked in a huge breath, and then let it out slowly as he dropped into his chair. He closed his eyes and ran both hands through his white hair. The phone rang for the fifth time before he snatched up the receiver and pressed it to his ear. "Bishop!" he blurted, louder than he'd intended.

"It's done," a man said.

"You're certain?" Bishop asked.

"Watch the news," the man said and hung up.

Bishop stared at the receiver for a moment and then replaced it. He picked up the remote and switched on the wall-mounted television to his right. He scrolled through the local channels until he found one that covered the story of an incident in Bethesda. The television newswoman talked about an explosion that had leveled a house and apparently killed four members of the Hood family.

"My God!" Bishop muttered. "An explosion! One damned bullet could have done the job and the idiot blows up the guy's house and kills his whole family!" He slammed the palm of his hand onto his desk and cursed. Forced himself to breath slowly. After a few seconds, he calmed down, placed his elbows on his desk, and lowered his head into his hands. Hood's family was collateral damage. *It's over*, he thought.

CHAPTER 3

Chicago Police Lieutenant Shane McDonough was into his third Budweiser at McNally's Tavern when a CNN news report on the television behind the bar caught his attention. An explosion in Bethesda, Maryland had destroyed a home and killed a woman and two children. A guy named David Hood had survived the blast and was now in a Bethesda hospital. McDonough put down his beer and asked the bartender to turn up the volume on the television. He listened to the rest of the report and then dug into a pants pocket, pulled out a twenty-dollar bill, and dropped it on the counter. He left the bar, walked the two blocks to his tiny Brookfield home, and went into the second bedroom where he kept his computer. It took him less than an hour to confirm that the David Hood from the television news report was the same David Hood who had saved his life in Afghanistan ten years ago.

McDonough reflected on that day in Helmand Province, his first week in-country with his special ops team. They'd been ambushed and he had taken an AK-47 round in the thigh. Under heavy enemy fire, David Hood had run to him, lifted him onto his shoulder, and carried him to safety. Hood had been wounded in the process. That bullet wound had earned McDonough a trip back home. And David Hood had earned McDonough's lifelong gratitude and respect.

A wild thought came to McDonough. What if he got the old special ops team together for a reunion in Bethesda? God knows, McDonough thought, Hood could benefit from having former comrades-in-arms around him at this terrible time.

McDonough called an old friend, Billy Hanson, from Chicago, who was still in the Army and assigned to the Pentagon. He told him about the explosion in Bethesda and the deaths of David Hood's family members. He told him what he had in mind, gave him information about his old unit, and asked for the contact information of the men who had been in that unit in 2003.

"I'll get back to you," Hanson told him.

McDonough hung up the phone and wondered how long it would take Billy to get the information he'd requested. While he waited, he called the information operator in Maryland and asked to be connected to the Bethesda Police Department. After being transferred three times, he was put through to a detective named Roger Cromwell.

"What can I do for you, Mr. McDonald?" Cromwell said in an uncooperative tone.

"It's McDonough. I'm a detective with the Chicago Police Department. I'm calling about the explosion at the Hood residence."

There was a brief pause on Cromwell's end of the line and then the Bethesda detective asked, "What's your interest in the case?"

"I served with David Hood in Afghanistan a decade ago. I wouldn't be here if it weren't for him."

"His family *would* be here if it weren't for him. The bastard killed them."

"Bullshit!" McDonough blurted. "There's no way David Hood would do such a thing. Do you hear me?"

Cromwell had hung up.

McDonough barely had enough time to think about what Cromwell had said when his telephone rang.

"Yeah?" he barked into the phone.

"Having a bad day?"

McDonough recognized Billy Hanson's voice. "Sorry, Billy," he said. "You could say that."

"Well, I'm about to make it even worse. I started checking on your old unit. There were fourteen men in the unit when you were assigned to it. Three of them were killed in Afghanistan. One more died a few years back—car wreck. A sergeant named Robert Campbell disappeared after rotating back to the States in 2004. You're not going to believe this. His body was found in a 55-gallon drum floating in the East River in New York City. Of the remaining nine men, I found eight in the Veterans Administration database."

"Were they getting medical benefits?" McDonough asked.

"No," Hanson said. "Death benefits. Relatives had applied for burial benefits for the men."

"Jeez," McDonough said. "All eight of them?"

"Yeah. But this is where it gets *really* weird. Every one of those guys died in the last thirty days. All under suspicious circumstances."

"Suspicious?" McDonough said.

"Yeah. They were all murdered."

CHAPTER 4

David opened his eyes and tried to focus on his surroundings. The only light seeped around the edges of blinds on his right. He was disoriented. Then a door opened, letting in bright light that back-lighted a woman in a nurse's uniform.

"Where am I?" David asked.

"Bethesda Hospital."

His mind spooled back to the fallout shelter in the basement of his home. There'd been an explosion. "My family? Where's my family?"

The nurse walked to his bedside, touched his arm, and said, "I'm sorry, Mr. Hood."

"No-o-o!" David screamed. "No-o-o!"

He saw the nurse move to the intravenous rack on the other side of the bed and turn something. He suddenly felt sleepy. Then a thought came to him as he felt himself drifting off: If he'd brought Heather and Kyle with him to the fallout shelter, maybe—

When David woke he found a florid-faced man with a road map of broken veins on his nose and cheeks staring down at him. The guy smelled of cigarettes and a faint aura of booze. He introduced himself as Detective Roger Cromwell.

It had taken only a few seconds with Cromwell for David to realize the cop had already convicted him of murdering his family. If Cromwell succeeded in getting him arrested and thrown in jail, he would never be able to find the real murderer.

He'd been in the hospital for less than a day when his father-in-law, Gino Bartolucci, came by. Gino still lived in Philadelphia where he'd been a mafia don until he retired a decade ago. He had the distinction of being the only Philadelphia capo who hadn't been killed or gone to prison. He'd gotten out of the business just in time. The old don was in his mid-sixties, short and squat, with a huge belly, and ham hock hands that would have looked too big on a man half-again his size.

Since he'd regained consciousness in the hospital, David had ridden an emotional roller coaster that took him from lows of deep and abiding sorrow to heights of raging fits of anger. He cried and then ranted about revenge. The nurses had tried to sedate him but he had refused medication. Gino's appearance only concentrated David's anger and subordinated his sorrow. The old man's eyes were black— like shark's eyes—and despite his father-in-law's sadness, he could see in Gino's eyes something more than just grief. Gino had an old world need for vengeance.

"I need to get out of here, Gino," David said. "The cops think I killed Carmela and the children. It won't be long before they try to charge me. And whoever killed Carmela and the kids—" David's voice broke. He swallowed and after a few seconds said, "They had to be after me, not them. I'm an easy target here in the hospital."

"You sure you're okay to leave the hospital?"

"I'll be a whole lot better if I'm doing something constructive."

"What do you need?" Gino asked.

"Clothes, a car, some money. I'm going to find out who murdered my family."

Gino added, "We're going to do that together."

David felt as though he was about to break down. "I've got to ... bury ..."

"Carmela's sisters are handling everything. Services will be on Saturday. Four days. We—"

A thirty-something, wiry man wearing a suit entered the room. The guy was medium height with short brown hair and chiseled features. Gino moved toward him, blocking his path.

The man stopped. "I'm looking for David Hood."

"Who are you?" Gino demanded.

"I'm going to reach for my wallet and show you my ID."

David watched the man, who somehow looked familiar, show Gino a badge, and say, "I'm Shane McDonough. I'm a Chicago detective and I served with David in Afghanistan."

"Damn!" David said. "Shane. My God, it's been ten years. I didn't recognize you. What are you doing here?"

"I've got a story to tell you," McDonough said, "that might shed some light on the explosion at your home."

Shane McDonough told David and Gino what he'd learned from Billy Hanson at the Pentagon.

"All murdered?" David asked.

"That's right. All during the past thirty days. You could have been the ninth."

"What the hell is going on?" David asked.

Gino and Shane stared at David. Neither of them had an answer.

"You're still alive," David said. "You were part of our team."

Shane shrugged. "I was with the team only for about a week before getting wounded. They shipped me back to the States right after my first mission."

Gino cleared his throat and said to Shane, "That tells me something went on in Afghanistan after you left and while the rest of the team was still there." He started pacing and then asked, "Were there any other men assigned to your unit?"

"No," David answered. "Other than Shane, and the three guys who were killed over there, we were an intact unit for almost eighteen months. No replacements came in."

"Who did you report to?" Gino asked.

"No one, really," David said. "I mean, we had a Captain who was our team leader. He reported to some guy in Kabul. I heard his name one time. But I don't recall it now."

"It was Bishop," McDonough said. "Rolf Bishop. His name was on the orders that medevaced me back to the States."

"Sonofa—" Gino went to the window and stared out.

David looked at Gino's back and said, "What's the matter?"

Gino turned. "You know who Bishop is?"

"No," David said.

"Nope," Shane said.

"You guys need to watch the news. About a month ago, the President nominated Rolf Bishop to be a new Deputy Director at the CIA."

"So?" Shane said.

"You don't find it suspicious that the guy who commanded your unit in Afghanistan was nominated to a high position in the CIA about the same time the murders of your former teammates began?"

Shane said, "Are you saying Bishop is behind these murders? That's a hell of a big leap to take."

"Are you aware that Bishop is a multimillionaire?" Gino asked.

"So what?" David said.

"How's a career Army officer become world-class wealthy?"

"Maybe he had a rich uncle," Shane offered.

"Yeah, maybe," Gino said.

CHAPTER 5

With driving instructions in hand, Shane left to drop off his rental car at Baltimore-Washington Airport, where Gino and David were going to pick him up. Gino sent his driver, Carlo, to a men's shop to buy David some clothing.

Alone with David, Gino asked, "Are you sure you're feeling all right?"

"Besides a headache and cuts and bruises, I'm fine."

Gino nodded.

"Why didn't you have Carlo follow Shane to the airport? It was almost as though you wanted to get rid of him?"

"I did want to get rid of him. At least for a while, so we could talk. I think Bishop might have been dealing drugs while in Afghanistan."

David squinted at Gino. "Come on, Gino. How could you possibly know that?"

"Because Joey Cataldo, the head of the New York Family, bought drugs from someone in Afghanistan during the time your team was there. Cataldo had a contract with the government to ship bodies from Afghanistan to mortuaries all over the country. Drugs were put in those caskets. I attended a meeting Cataldo hosted in 2003 in New York City for the heads of all the families. I declined to participate. That's why I retired. It was go along with the drug scheme, retire, or get eliminated."

"How do you know Bishop was involved with smuggling drugs?" David asked.

"I don't. But the drugs came to the U.S. in 2003 and 2004, when the Afghan War began. Bishop and your special ops team were there then. Bishop's a rich man who may or may not have a rich uncle. Someone's wiping out the former members of that team. Why? Maybe because that *someone* believes one or more of the men on that team knew what he was doing.

"That's a lot of maybes."

"It is. But I know how to find out for sure."

CHAPTER 6

After Carlo returned with clothes for David, Gino sent him to keep the nurses busy at the station down the hall while David dressed. Then he and David walked to the emergency exit stairs at the end of the hall and went down to the parking lot. Carlo joined them a few minutes later and drove to the airport to pick up Shane.

Shane twisted around in the front passenger seat of Gino's Lincoln Navigator and looked at David and Gino in the backseat. "Why are we going to New York City?" he asked.

"I gotta meet somebody," Gino said.

"Who?"

"Carlo, pull over," Gino ordered.

As soon as the vehicle had stopped on the shoulder of the New Jersey Turnpike, Gino pointed a finger at Shane and said, "Outside!" He got out of the car and waited for the detective to join him.

"Here's the deal," Gino said. "You're a cop; that makes me very uncomfortable. The only reason you're here is because David vouches for you. But that doesn't make me any less uncomfortable. You want to go along for the ride? Fine. But you ask any more questions, I'll dump your ass on this highway." Gino stared up at Shane and waited for a response.

Shane finally said, "I'd like to ask one question, if that's all right."

Gino tilted his head and looked at Shane as though he thought the detective was stupid. Then he nodded.

"Is what I'm about to get involved in going to put my pension in jeopardy?"

"Absolutely!"

Shane looked down at his feet and took in a deep breath. "Ah, hell," he muttered. "I'm in."

Fifty-year-old Joey Cataldo, the New York *Capo di tutti capi*, sat with one of his bodyguards at a corner table at the back of *Il Stazione* Restaurant in Manhattan and waited for Gino Bartolucci. The restaurant was one of Cataldo's "legitimate" businesses. He looked at his image in the mirrored wall and swept his hands through his thick, graying mane of hair. He was vain about his looks, and his wavy hair had always been a part of his vanity. He knew he was a handsome man—the women had let him know that even before he had power. He was tall—six foot four—and still powerfully built.

When Joey saw Gino enter the restaurant, preceded by a linebacker of a man who Cataldo knew was the old man's bodyguard, he stood, buttoned his suit jacket, and waited respectfully. The bodyguard carefully scanned the room and then stepped aside to let Gino move to the back. Despite Gino's short stature and large belly—bigger by at least two belt sizes since Joey had seen him last—the old Don still exuded power. While Gino walked toward him, Joey stared at Gino's hands. They were the biggest Joey had ever seen on a man Gino's size. He thought those hands could snap a man's neck with ease.

They exchanged greetings in Italian and embraced. After the further formality of introducing their bodyguards to each other, the two Dons took seats at the table while the bodyguards moved to a table at the front.

Joey and Gino spoke cordially, even affectionately to one another. Joey expressed sadness about Carmela and Gino's grandchildren's deaths. They talked about old times, joked about characters they both had known. Their dinner included five courses, lasting two hours, and not a word of business was spoken.

It wasn't until their waiter had brought espressos that Gino got down to business.

"Joey, we talked earlier about my sweet Carmela's death, about my grandchildren. I know you would do anything you could to help me find the *seppia* who killed my angels."

"Of course, Don Bartolucci. You know I'd personally rip the bastard's heart out. But, naturally, I would leave that honor to you."

"Well, maybe you *can* help me. I believe the man who killed Carmela and my grandchildren was really after my son-in-law. I also think the same man has killed many other people who were in Afghanistan during the time my son-in-law served there. And I think I know who that man is. But there's one thing I can't figure out—the reason for the killings. I figure this man has something big to hide. I want to know what that is."

"Don Bartolucci, you know I'll do all in my power to assist you."

"One of the men who served with my son-in-law in Afghanistan disappeared here in New York back in 2004, just two days after he left Afghanistan."

Joey was confused. "Don Bartolucci, 2004 was a long time ago." After a beat, he added, "What would I know about such a thing?"

Gino nodded. "Sure, I understand and I'm not saying you know anything about it. But the guy's body was found a couple months later in a 55-gallon drum. This is a little strange ... you agree?"

Joey nodded. "Don't sound like any random mugging I ever heard of. But that's years ago."

"Right!" Gino paused, then said, "Even more interesting, the drum the guy was found in had a familiar logo painted on it: Atlantic Waste Disposal. I racked my brain trying to remember why I know that name. And then it hit me. That was one of your companies."

Joey knew there were dozens of bodies packed away in drums all over the eastern seaboard. The body Gino was talking about could have been dumped by any one of hundreds of wise guys connected with any one of dozens of criminal organizations. Hell, he had disposed of three guys in the same way himself, including one around 2004.

"What is it you want me to find out?" Joey asked. "You know nobody's going to step forward and admit they killed this guy."

"All I want to know is why this guy was hit," Gino said.

Joey asked, "What was the name of the dead guy?"

"Robert Campbell," Gino replied. "Sergeant Robert Campbell."

Joey felt a sharp pain in his stomach. He hoped his expression hadn't changed. He couldn't believe Campbell's name was resurfacing after so many years. He'd ordered the hit on Campbell as a favor to his business partner in Afghanistan—the guy who'd been supplying him with heroin. Joey excused himself and walked into the men's room at the back of the restaurant. He paced the floor and considered his options. He could promise Gino he would try to help him, and then do nothing. But he knew the old man was no dummy. If Gino found out he'd been lied to, he would be a dangerously unhappy man. He could claim ignorance. Or he could tell the old Don what he knew. And have Gino in his debt.

Joey wet a paper towel, pressed it to his eyes, and returned to the table.

"Don Bartolucci, I gotta tell you I'm uncomfortable about this ... matter."

"Why's that, Don Cataldo?"

"You see, I know who killed Campbell."

"You gotta be shittin' me."

"You're aware of my former connection in Afghanistan. We met about that in 2003. My only contact with the supplier had been this Robert Campbell. I suspected all along that Campbell was just a messenger boy for the real brains behind the operation. One day, I got an e-mail message telling me the price of the next shipment of heroin coming to New York was going to be discounted in return for a favor being done. The favor was that I kill Campbell, who thought he was coming to New York to pick up payment for the dope. The real reason he was sent to the city was to get whacked."

"Who sent you the e-mail?"

"I never had the guy's name. He used a code name."

"How did you make payment for the ... goods?"

"I shipped cash to a bank in Switzerland. All I had was an account number."

"Do you have records showing the amounts and dates of the deposits to the Swiss bank?"

Joey hesitated. This was the moment of truth. With this information, his life would be in Gino's hands. He either trusted the old Don or he didn't. He met Gino's gaze and made his decision.

"I can get that information to you. I assume it will be for your eyes only."

"You assume correctly," Gino said.

"Call me tomorrow morning."

"Thanks, Joey," Gino said. "You been a big help." He stood, and Joey rose with him. The two men embraced.

"Joey," Gino whispered.

"Yeah?"

"Take my advice. Next time, put some bowling balls in the drum before you dump it in the river."

CHAPTER 7

Rolf Bishop's driver pulled the Audi S7 into the garage at the back of the townhouse. Bishop entered the house and hurried up the stairs to his second-floor office. He flipped on the lights, and again read part of the report his personal assistant had prepared. *David Hood's wife was born Carmela Bartolucci. Her father, Gino Bartolucci, was one of seven crime bosses in the U.S. until his "retirement" in 2003. Supposedly, his only business activities today are legitimate. Included is a list of all of Bartolucci's known businesses and addresses.*

He scanned the list of Bartolucci's residences and businesses. They were all in Pennsylvania or New Jersey. He'd already learned that Hood had left the hospital in Bethesda. His gut told him he had probably found refuge with his father-in-law.

Bishop pulled his cell phone from his jacket pocket and dialed the number for his hired killer. He passed on the information about Bartolucci's relationship to David Hood. "You find Bartolucci," he said, "you'll find Hood. No mistakes this time. I want Hood eliminated."

After packing an overnight bag, Bishop called his driver's cell phone and told him to be ready to leave in fifteen minutes. He went to his office, printed off a copy of the speech he had to make tomorrow night, and placed the speech in his briefcase. This speech in New York City to the delegates at the G-8 Conference would be his formal introduction to the international community. This was a huge moment in his career and his life.

David took the elevator down to the lobby of the New York City hotel where Gino, Shane, and he were staying. He picked up a newspaper at the front desk, walked to the coffee shop, and ordered a cup of coffee and an English muffin. The front page of the newspaper had an article about the G-8 conference in New York City. He knew his security firm had a number of clients attending this meeting. At least ten of his employees would be working the conference. He thought about calling his operations manager, Frank Sampson, to make sure everything was set up. But he knew Frank would, as usual, have everything in order. Besides, he had other things on his mind.

He read the article and stopped when he saw that Rolf Bishop was scheduled to speak at the conference. David dropped a ten-dollar bill on the table, took the newspaper, and returned to his room. He found Gino and Shane sitting in front of the television.

David waved the newspaper at them and said, "Guess who's in the city."

Gino and Shane simultaneously answered, "Rolf Bishop."

"How'd you know?"

"It's all over the television," Shane said.

Gino pulled out a sheet of paper from an inside jacket pocket. "I called a friend of mine this morning and wrote down this information he provided. Your company still have clients in Switzerland?" he asked David.

"Yes," David said.

"Is *Banque Securite Swiss* one of them?"

"Yes. We do business with most of the Swiss banks."

Gino reached over and handed David the sheet of paper. On it was the name of the bank and what appeared to be an account number at the top. Below that were two columns, one with dates and the other with dollar-denominated amounts. At the bottom of the page was a single sentence reading: *On the dates shown above, the corresponding dollar amounts were deposited in the account number shown.*

"What is this?" David asked.

"It's a list of deposits made by a friend of mine to an account in that bank. The payments were for heroin shipments sent from Afghanistan to New York City in 2003 and 2004. All we have to do is find out who owns that bank account. If it belongs to Rolf Bishop, then we'll know he had motive for murder. I've been thinking about the reason for all these killings. I think Bishop realized that, when the President appointed him to the CIA position, there would be a background investigation conducted. If one of his former teammates in Afghanistan had knowledge about his drug smuggling and mentioned it to an FBI investigator, his goose would be cooked."

"He killed all those men and my family to cover his ass?" David asked.

"That's my guess," Gino said.

CHAPTER 8

"*Guten Morgen, Banque Securite Swisse,*" a woman said. "*Kann ich ihnen helfen?*"

"*Kann ich Herr Muther sprechen? Hier ist* David Hood"

"*Ein moment, bitte.*"

"David, where are you?" Willy Muther asked with enthusiasm a moment later. "Are you in Zurich?"

"No, Willy. I'm calling from New York. I need some information."

"David, we've done a lot of business together. Besides, we've been friends for years. What can I do for you?"

"Willy, I've got a list in front of me showing the dates and amounts of large deposits made to an account in your bank back in 2003 and 2004. I need to know the name on the account."

Willy exhaled audibly. "Listen, David. Our banking laws are strict for a reason. We do not give out that kind of information to a private citizen—even if he is a friend. You wouldn't want me to get into trouble by breaking the law?"

"No, Willy, I wouldn't," David said. "But if what I suspect is true, every dollar in that account is drug money. If that's the case, with recent changes in banking laws, your bank could be in real trouble."

Willy again forced the air from his lungs and said, *"Gott in Himmel!"*

David waited.

"Give me the account number, the amounts and dates of the deposits, and a telephone number where I can reach you. I won't promise to give you the name on the account, but I promise I'll call you back."

An hour later, trying to devise their next step if Willy Muther didn't cooperate, David was interrupted by the ringing phone in his room.

"David, is that you? Can you hear me? This is Willy, in Switzerland."

"I can hear you, Willy. Go ahead."

"I checked the deposit dates and amounts you gave me. They exactly matched deposits made to the account number you asked about."

"The name on the account?" David said. "Willy, what's the name on the account?"

Willy paused, and then said, "The first initial is R. The surname Eveque."

David's anticipation dissipated like the air from a punctured balloon. To have come so far for nothing! He would have bet his life the deposits had gone into an account in Rolf Bishop's name. Through his disappointment, he heard Willy's voice.

"Strange name!"

"How so?" David asked. "Why strange?"

"It's just not that common. In French, it translates as Bishop. You know, like a high church official?"

"Bishop, you said?"

"Correct."

CHAPTER 9

The enthusiasm in the hotel room was palpable. David couldn't sit down, while he, Gino, and Shane tried to come up with a plan to get at Bishop.

David suddenly stopped pacing and said, "What's most important to Bishop?"

"Money," Gino offered.

"Reputation," Shane said.

"And power," David added. "He's got all three today. That's what we need to take away from him."

"We kill his ass and that will take care of all three," Gino said.

Shane said, "We can't just kill—" A menacing glare from Gino stopped him.

"I want to make him suffer," David said. "Take away money, power, and reputation, and he's nothing."

"What do you have in mind?" Shane asked.

"Gino, do you have any connections at The Royal Arms Hotel, where the G-8 conference is being held?"

"No, but I have a friend who might."

One of the benefits of the Cataldo Family's relationship with the Hotel and Motel Workers of America Union was the ability to get jobs for the Family's sons and daughters, nephews and nieces. Lois Carbone, one of Joey Cataldo's nieces, had graduated from NYU with a degree in Hotel Management. Cataldo got her a job at The Royal Arms.

She'd worked first as a night clerk, then moved to the Catering Department. After only three years with the hotel, she'd been promoted to Director of Special Events, in which role she was now in charge of making sure of the success of the State Dinner being hosted by the President of the United States. She was on her way to a staff meeting when her cell phone rang.

"Hi Lois, you doin' okay?"

"Sure, Uncle Joey," she replied. *Why is he calling me at work?* she wondered. This was a first. She sighed, thinking about all she had to do.

"Sweetheart, I need to sit down with you today ... as soon as possible. You think you could find time for your favorite uncle this morning?"

Oh shit, Lois thought. *Any day but today.* She wanted to say, I'm awfully busy, Uncle Joey. But, instead, she heard herself agreeing to a meeting. After all, she owed her uncle. "Sure, Uncle Joey. I always have time for you. What time?"

"Let's see. I got ten o'clock now. How about we meet in that little coffee shop down the street from you in about fifteen minutes?"

Lois made a couple quick phone calls, doling out assignments to underlings, postponing the staff meeting, and then hurried from her office. She was waiting at the coffee shop when Joey Cataldo strolled in. She stood when he approached her table and they hugged.

After their coffees were served, Joey looked intently at Lois. "I need to know something," he said. "This is very important or I wouldn't ask. You understand?"

"Sure."

"You workin' on this big dinner tonight with all the hotshots from England, Germany, France ... whatever?"

Lois smiled at the way her uncle glossed over Italy, Canada, Russia, and Japan. "That's right. I'm in charge of the whole thing."

"Tell me what the program is going to be at this *stravaganza*."

Lois hesitated. Joey reached across the table and put his hand on her cheek. He looked into her eyes and said, "Don't you worry about a thing, *mio bambola piccola*. You got nothing to worry about."

"Well, you know, there will be a lot of speeches, and all of the bigwigs will be introduced. A small orchestra is going to play during dinner. And at the end of the dinner there's going to be a presentation."

"That's when the video's gonna be shown?" Joey asked.

"How do you know about the video?" Lois asked.

"Sometimes I hear things, *bambina*. Tell me about this video."

"The President has declared this the Year of the Child. So the White House put together a bunch of clips of the President and some of the senior members of the administration, showing these people today and also back when they were kids."

"What do they got, some guy from the White House to show the video?"

"No, Uncle Joey," Lois responded. "The video's been given to Hal Norris, the head of the hotel's Audiovisual Office. He's the one who will set up all the equipment and play the video. Why?"

"It's better you don't know why. And don't tell anyone we had this meeting. Before I go, I gotta ask you one more question. Where does this Hal keep the video, and when could someone maybe take a peek at it?"

CHAPTER 10

While Lois Carbone met with Hal Norris in her office at five p.m. to go over the schedule for the video presentation that evening, one of Joey Cataldo's men entered Norris's office, searched his desk for a flash drive labeled "G-8 Video," found it, and left the office. He exited the hotel, entered a van parked outside the hotel entrance, and handed the flash drive to another man. That man booted up the G-8 Video flash drive and added content from a disk onto it. He then removed the flash drive from his computer and passed it back to Cataldo's guy, who returned to Norris's office and put the drive back where he'd found it.

At eight-thirty p.m., after dinner, the President rose and said, "We accomplished much the last couple of days. We dealt with key elements of international security, including intelligence, economic, and strategic issues. We are all committed to building a safer, healthier, and more prosperous world for every child on the planet. There is no future without our children, and there is no future unless these children are prepared to provide leadership in their turn. It is for this reason I have declared this year to be the Year of the Child in the United States.

"All of us in this room are privileged. We have the best life can offer. But, if you are like me, you may sometimes forget you too were once a small child, weak and vulnerable, but full of promise. So I thought we all might enjoy a trip back in time to when we were each a long way from our present positions of power."

The President offered his most charismatic smile and waited at the dais as the lights slowly dimmed until the room was almost completely dark. The sound track on the video started while four large screens dropped from ceiling booms. Music started softly, built in volume, and then subsided when an image was projected on the screens and the President's voice filled the ballroom. *Oohs* and *ahs* were heard from every part of the room. On the screens, the President was sitting in the Oval Office, addressing the camera. He spoke of power and privilege. Then the picture suddenly changed to a photograph of the President as a small child, dressed in tattered, dirty overalls, standing in front of a ramshackle house. It was a photo the White House spin-meisters loved. It conjured up an echo of Lincoln. The President spoke of how many children around the planet lived in poverty and lacked any opportunity to escape from it. Other photos showed the President as he grew from a young boy to a teenager to a young adult. "It is opportunity that makes the difference in a young person's life," the President said.

"The next person I want to highlight is a good friend who comes from my home state, and who grew up in conditions of poverty and hunger. He became a military hero and a true American patriot. He has served his nation and the free world at great personal risk and in conditions of hardship, and always without complaint. I am proud to include in tonight's program the image of my lifelong friend, Rolf Bishop."

Rolf Bishop's photo appeared on the screen. He was dressed in a blue pinstriped suit, red tie, white shirt. His white hair contrasted nicely with his tanned face. Then the picture segued to a photo of a small boy dressed in torn clothes, holding a fishing rod in one hand and the hand of a smaller boy in the other. The photo drew a loud murmur of approval from the audience.

The mood in the room was now almost euphoric. So far, the evening had been a tremendous success. Suddenly, the background music ceased, bringing the members of the audience out of their reverie. A new voice and image intruded.

"Good evening, my name is David Hood. Some of you know me. I have provided services to many of you through my company, Security Systems, Ltd. I want to say a few words about the great American hero, Rolf Bishop."

Bishop had an almost uncontrollable, visceral urge to scream. He felt as though he would lose his mind.

He looked around. Although the flow of the video presentation had been broken, most of the people around him had reacted as though Hood's appearance was part of the program.

"Rolf Bishop is known throughout our country as a hero," Hood said. "But that's far from reality. Rolf Bishop is a thief, a traitor, a drug smuggler, and a murderer. He hired the assassin who murdered my wife, Carmela, and my two children, Heather and Kyle."

While these words were spoken, the image on the screens changed. Photographs of the once happy and alive Hood family came up. Then the image changed to a picture of the bombed out Hood home. "The rest of this video includes proof of Rolf Bishop's perfidy and betrayal," David Hood continued. "Deposits totaling fifty-seven million dollars made in 2003 and 2004 into Bishop's Swiss bank account. Deposits that came from smuggling heroin from Afghanistan to the United States in caskets of dead American heroes. I ask you to watch and listen carefully because, as unbelievable as what you will see and hear might seem, it is true in every detail and the proof is incon—"
At this point, someone cut the power to the projectors.

The lights came up. The President called for quiet. People were jostling to get a look at Bishop. The President raised his arms. It took a while for the commotion to subside. When it did, the President said loudly, "It looks as though someone is playing a practical joke. We have had a wonderful evening. I thank you for joining me. I ask you to focus on my message about the world's children and request you go forth and make a difference." Then he wheeled to his right, left the podium, and rushed out of the room. His Secret Service detail had to hustle to catch up with him. When they reached him, the President had buttonholed his Chief of Staff and was squeezing the man's arm so hard that anyone could see he was inflicting pain. The President jerked the man closer.

"I want to know what happened here tonight! I want to know who doctored that video. And I want to know if there's a shred of truth about what that guy said about Bishop! And I want to know now!"

"Yes, Mr. President," the Chief of Staff answered. "I'll get right on it."

"You do that," the President said. "And while you're doing that, get somebody to bring Bishop to my room. After I've talked to him, I want the helicopter to take me back to Washington. I've been in the Big Apple long enough."

The media attendees at the dinner were in near riot mode. They rushed toward the doors that led from the ballroom to the hotel lobby. As they exited the ballroom, rough-looking men in tuxedoes pressed flash drives into their hands.

CHAPTER 11

Rolf Bishop tried with little success to suppress a murderous rage. His hired killer had failed to track down Hood. Instead, Hood had tracked him down and ruined everything. The President had told him he was going to have the FBI look into the allegations Hood had made on the video. Bishop knew the Bureau would dig up more than enough to destroy him. He had to get out of the country. But first he needed to get to his New York bank and empty his safety deposit box. He had two boxes—one in Georgetown and one here in New York City—that he had rented years ago. Each held millions of dollars in bearer bonds, a passport, and identification that he could use to flee under an assumed name. He'd hide out in the condo he owned in the city—also under an assumed name—until the bank opened in the morning.

David was at his wit's end. Bishop had gotten away from The Royal Arms Hotel before he and Shane could grab him. The bastard was now on the loose in a city of eight million people.

Back in his hotel room, he, with Gino and Shane, watched the news, which was covering what had happened at the state dinner. The media had dug up everything they could find about Bishop, as well as about David. It had even made the connection to Gino Bartolucci being David's father-in-law. The media was throwing around conspiracy theories like rice at a wedding.

"What do you think Bishop is doing right now?" Shane asked.

"If I were him," Gino said, "I'd get the hell out of the United States as quickly as possible."

"He'd need a passport to do that," David said. "I wonder if a CIA Deputy Director carries his passport with him."

Shane shrugged. "I doubt it. It's probably back in D.C."

"No way is he going back there," David said. "The press will be sitting on his home and outside Langley hoping to spot him."

"I doubt he could get out of the country even if he had his passport," Gino said. "After that video was shown tonight and the press picked up on it, there's no way the President will want him on the run. If Bishop escapes, the press is going to wonder if the President helped him get away."

"What about false ID?" Shane asked. "Someone as smart as Bishop will surely have 'get-away' money and ID squirreled away somewhere. Maybe in a safety deposit box."

David said, "That's a good thought. It's unlikely that Bishop will be able to access the funds in his Swiss account. Not as long as it's suspected drug money. He wouldn't have all of his cash assets in one account. But maybe he's had money wired to Switzerland from U.S. accounts. If we can identify his U.S. banks, we might be able to locate his safety deposit box."

"Jeez," Gino said. "How many banks are there in New York City? Hundreds? And how many of those banks have multiple branches? It's the proverbial needle in a haystack."

David picked up his cell phone from the coffee table and dialed Willy Muther's number in Zurich. Muther's secretary answered the phone and immediately put David through to the banker.

"Willy, besides the original deposits made to Bishop's account back in 2003 and 2004, were there more recent fund transfers into the account?"

"Yes, David. Dozens of them."

"Can you tell me if there were any American banks those monies were transferred from—starting from the most recent and working backward?"

"The files on Bishop are on my computer. Hold on for just a minute."

David said a silent prayer of thanks for Swiss attention to detail.

Muther came back on the line. "We have the information. Are you prepared to write?"

"You bet, Willy. Go ahead."

Muther dictated the dates of wire transfers into Bishop's account in reverse chronological order, with the amounts of the transfers and the originating banks. The transfers had originated in Atlanta, Dallas, San Francisco, London, Munich, and Bangkok. It wasn't until the seventh transaction back that Muther mentioned a New York bank: Manhattan Merchants Bank.

David asked Muther to go through the remaining records to see if there were transfers through any other New York banks. It took Muther only a few seconds to confirm that Manhattan Merchants Bank was the only one in New York City. And there'd been three earlier transfers through Manhattan Merchants during the past six years.

After thanking Willy, David looked up Manhattan Merchants Bank in the Yellow Pages and found one location in the city.

CHAPTER 12

They had planned to arrive at the bank thirty minutes before it opened at nine a.m., but traffic had been a disaster and they'd arrived a few minutes after nine. David and Shane leaped from the Lincoln Navigator while Carlo and Gino tried to find a place to park. David told Shane to stand outside the bank to keep an eye out for Bishop in case he wasn't inside already.

Inside the bank lobby, a grandiose affair, with brass teller cages, dark mahogany furniture, and marble floor, David spied a "Safety Deposit Vault" sign and arrow pointing at a set of stairs going down from the lobby. He fast-walked to the stairs, descended to a lower level, and looked around. There was no one there. Not even a clerk. Then a woman walked from a vault swinging a ring of keys in her hand.

"Yes, sir, may I help you?"

David shook his head. "No thanks."

The woman frowned but didn't object when David sat in a chair by the entry.

Three minutes passed. No one else entered the area. He pulled his cell phone from his shirt pocket to call Shane, when a tall, white-haired man wearing a blue suit and carrying a leather valise exited the vault. Rolf Bishop.

David stood and blocked Bishop. "Remember me, Colonel? David Hood."

Bishop's jaw dropped. "You!"

Before Bishop could say another word, David smashed his left fist into the man's jaw and followed with a right to his stomach. Bishop staggered backward, hitting the wall behind him. David advanced on him but stopped short when Bishop pulled a pistol from under his jacket. David heard the pistol's report; felt a shock like a massive punch to his chest. A woman screamed. Then darkness.

Carlo had circled the block twice before he said, "Screw it!" and double-parked in front of the bank. He had just turned off the engine when a throng of screaming and yelling men and women ran out of the bank.

"Give me your pistol," Gino said.

"No way, boss. You can't get involved."

"You're going to make someone a great mother someday," Gino said. "Give me that pistol!"

Carlo handed over his .9mm Beretta. Gino disengaged the safety.

"Stay with the car," Gino ordered and slid out of the backseat. He was too short to see what was going on directly in front of the bank and moved through the crowd flowing toward him. He finally got to within ten yards of the bank entrance when he spotted Bishop exiting onto the sidewalk from one of the three doors fronting the building. And then he saw Shane move to intercept Bishop. But before the detective could reach Bishop, another crowd of people burst out of one of the doors and cut him off.

Gino stepped forward and locked eyes with Bishop, who seemed to recognize that he represented a threat. Bishop reached inside his suit coat. Gino rushed at the man, raised Carlo's .9mm pistol, and stuck it into Bishop's stomach. He pulled the trigger and watched the man responsible for his daughter and grandchildren's deaths drop to his knees. Bishop roared in pain. A pistol fell from his hand and clattered to the pavement. Gino crouched over and whispered in Bishop's ear, "That was for Carmela. This is for Heather and Kyle." He fired once into Bishop's chest and then again into the center of Bishop forehead.

The melee outside the bank deteriorated into mass hysteria. People screamed and shouted, pushed and ran in all directions. Gino calmly picked up Bishop's valise, reversed direction, went back to the Lincoln Navigator, and got into the backseat. "Pull around the corner and find an alley or something. I'm going to call David."

CHAPTER 13

It took three hours of surgery to remove Rolf Bishop's bullet from David's chest. The round had just missed his aorta but had collapsed a lung. When he awoke in recovery, still groggy from anesthesia, he saw hazy images in front of him. It took a minute for his vision to clear enough to recognize Gino at the foot of his bed.

"I know I'm not in heaven," he rasped. "You're here."

"Haha," Gino said. "Glad you still have a sense of humor."

"What happened?" David asked.

"Bishop shot you. Someone shot Bishop. Killed him."

"Who?"

"No one knows. Witnesses claim it was either a man or a woman, somewhere between five feet and seven feet tall, weighing between one hundred and three hundred pounds."

David saw nothing but a blank expression on Gino's face. Then, for a beat, he saw a glint in the old man's eyes and knew the person who had killed Bishop was someone with an old world sense of revenge without a new world sense of remorse. David knew only one person like that.

David was in the hospital for eight days before the doctors were satisfied that infection was no longer a big concern. Carlo drove him and Gino to Philadelphia after they drove Shane to LaGuardia to catch a flight. Shane had accepted a job with David's company and was going to Chicago to put in his retirement papers and arrange to have his household goods shipped to Bethesda.

On the way from New York to Philadelphia, Gino asked David what he should do with the twelve million dollars in bearer bonds from Rolf Bishop's valise.

"How about setting up a fund for the families of the men from my team in Afghanistan?"

"Perfect!" Gino said. "By the way," Gino added, "a couple of my men caught a guy hanging around my South Philadelphia house. After an hour of questioning him, he decided to cooperate. He told them what Bishop had paid him to do. Yours was the last name on his target list."

"You should turn him over to that cop in Bethesda," David said.

"Too late for that," Gino said.

David tried to sleep on the trip to Gino's home, but sleep wouldn't come. A few hours later, once he was settled in a room at Gino's place, he sat down on the bed and thought about what he had lost. About the services he would need to attend. He pictured Carmela, Heather, and Kyle and let loose with shuddering sobs and tears that seemed to have no end. With revenge satisfied, his only emotion was overwhelming grief.

Exhausted and spent, he finally drifted off. His sleep was dream-disturbed, full of images of his wife and children, punctuated by voices that made no sense. Not at first, anyway. And then a sweet voice became a trio of voices that sang a refrain that sounded over and over like, "We're okay!"

And then peaceful sleep wrapped him in a soft, comforting cloak.

IMPRESARIO

BY MARIA MASINGTON

The little girl was horrified, at eight years old, to learn that her namesake was murdered. Dr. Cassidy had named his daughter after the opera. His colleagues considered it a pathological choice for an infant, especially since he was a psychiatrist who cared about people's mental health. As she grew up, Carmen wondered if it was punishment for fucking up her father's life.

She liked to pretend she was named after Carmen Miranda in "The Lady with the Tutti-Frutti Hat!" She preferred her version of history, but knew in her heart she was an homage to the infamous gypsy. Some children were planned, some were accidents, but Carmen always knew she was a mistake.

When the obstetrician asked Norma Concordia about her baby's father, she told him, "This kid was conceived up against a filing cabinet at the state hospital, by a shrink old enough to be *my* father." Dr. Cassidy had assumed the young nursing student would agree to abort the product of those four minutes. She knew, however, that this pregnancy would keep him chained to her forever; she would always

323

own a part of him, even though he refused to marry her.

Norma was one of those women who never crossed a bridge she didn't burn. She was an average looking brunette, from an average middle-class background, who deemed herself anything but average. She entered every relationship, expecting to be considered special, and left every relationship resentful and bitter. Norma wanted to be a woman who had it all, but in real life was estranged from everyone but herself.

Dr. Cassidy wasn't a saint, but he did not have the horns and tail that Norma Concordia imagined. After losing a young wife to ovarian cancer, he refused to get close to anyone again. He had a pleasant enough life with a pleasant enough series of girlfriends, hobbies, and work. He enjoyed golf, opera, and his practice. He did not love this nurse, but she had pursued him with a raw desire that flattered his middle-aged ego. It was after the fact that he began to see the borderline traits, the narcissism, the glimmers of paranoia that would soon be his child's mother. Thought and mood disorders could be treated with medication—personality disorders, he knew, were an entirely different beast.

The mistake, conceived among the schizophrenics and psychopaths, was born in 1962, and Kennedy was assassinated before she was eating solid foods. Dr. Cassidy visited twice a month; his child support included a small ranch house, medical insurance, and educational costs for the child. Every other week, he went over for dinner and sat at the Formica-topped kitchen table, where he paid his proverbial dues.

"How is our little Carmen doing?"

"How did she make out at the pediatrician?"

"Look at her smiling!"

Whatever topic he broached, Norma responded with a litany that boiled down to, "My life is so hard and you're an asshole."

Norma loved the baby, or at least the idea of the baby—someone who would always be connected to her and would need her. Unlike everyone else who had let her down, this girl would be forced to love her.

The one thing Norma hated was the crying. It felt like criticism. A little whiskey on the baby's gums did the trick; so did dipping the teething ring in booze, or putting a few drops in the baby bottle. When Dr. Cassidy questioned the practice, she had her retort all prepared. "It won't hurt her. I am a nurse, after all. It's your fault anyway. If we were married I could afford a nanny."

Surprisingly, Dr. Cassidy found that he loved his child. He enjoyed seeing the red-headed baby in the high chair, and listening to her charming stories that changed over the years from ballet and Brownies, to SATs and boys. He never showed up empty-handed—always bringing his daughter a gift, and more important, always armed with his prescription pad. "Norma, I'll write whatever it takes to shut you up." Milltown, Librium, and Valium were her remedies of choice.

Carmen was an average child of the 1970s. She had long red hair and brown eyes, but not a freckle to be found. She was cute, with good manners, and a precocious vocabulary. She loved *The Perils of Penelope Pitstop* cartoon on Saturday mornings, *Curious George* books, and had a crush on Jethro from *Beverly Hillbillies*. She would never be prom queen or most popular, but she fit in—unlike her father, who kept an emotional distance from everyone, and her mother who was always invited because she seemed funny and charming, but was never invited back.

Before and after each of her father's visit, Carmen and her mother sang, "There was a daughter had a dog and Daddy was his name-o! B-I-N-G-O! B-I-N-G-O! B-I-N-G-O! And Daddy was his name-o!" Carmen loved the song because she loved this mysterious, charming man who listened to her and gave her wonderful presents. She had dolls from around the world, hardback books with illustrations, and a tape recorder and a tape of "her" opera. She didn't understand French, but she loved the music and danced to the Habanera.

When she was old enough to see over her mother's bureau, she saw an index card taped to Norma's mirror. *B is for Bastard, I is for Idiot, N is for Narcissist, G is for Garbage, and O is for Old Goat.* One night, when her mother had drunk more than usual, Carmen asked her about it.

"It was my way of sticking it to the good doctor," Norma explained. "I wrote it when I was pregnant and your father refused to marry me and give you a real family. I love that little ditty."

As Carmen's eyes filled with tears, her mother snapped, "Oh grow up, Carmen! When you would sing it, and skip around, and dance, I would think *Fuck him and whatever low-class tramp he is dating this week.*"

Carmen's latent years were set to Vietnam, Watergate, blackmail, hostility, and habitual family conflict. Days were spent in parochial school, while her mother worked at a local psych hospital, and at night they ate TV dinners and talked until bedtime, when Norma would give Carmen Benadryl to sleep through the night and pour herself a glass of wine.

"Who has the best mommy in the world?" Norma would croon.

"I have the best mommy in the world," was Carmen's nightly aria.

"Who loves Carmen?"

"Mommy loves Carmen."

One night, when she was six years old, she said, "Mommy loves Carmen, and Daddy loves me, too."

Without missing a beat, Norma leaned over and whispered into her daughter's tiny ear, in the softest voice possible, "Oh, no, honey, Daddy wanted to kill you before you were born."

Carmen stopped sitting on his lap, was too shy to hug him, and was fearful of his gifts. Was there a knife in the teddy bear? Would he poison her food? How had he wanted to kill her? Carmen didn't know, but one thing she knew for sure, she would never say, 'Daddy loves me' again.

She had nightmares a lot, of both parents trying to kill her, in different ways. Sometimes she was pushed off a cliff, other times she was buried in a dark hole. When the dreams were really scary, she would sneak to the kitchen to see if there were dirty glasses in the sink. She'd scrounge a few sips of wine, some whiskey sour, or a swallow of a Rob Roy if her father had been there. Carmen wished they had parties, or friends that visited, so she could get drinks more often. It made her little body feel warm, as if she were being hugged, and she wondered if other people who were scared knew how much it helped.

The nightmares got worse when Carmen was eight and her father took her to see the opera she was named after. She was so excited to go on their special "date," that she forgot to be afraid of him. Her mother had been mean about it, saying, "He's probably only taking you because he couldn't get a real date." Carmen put on her black velvet Christmas dress, patent leather shoes, and carried a small white muff. She'd asked her mother to curl her hair, but Norma refused, so Carmen braided it herself. She told her mother she was sorry that she was not invited, but in her heart, was happy for an evening alone with her father.

Carmen loved the opera hall with its huge chandeliers, velvet curtains, and ladies in long evening gowns. She didn't understand the words, and fell asleep a few times, but was riveted by the Spanish dancers and the black-haired, big-breasted woman she was named after. At the end of the second act, however, Carmen was horrified when the fickle beauty was stabbed and bled to death on stage. She began to cry. Dr. Cassidy beamed with pride, thinking how perceptive and sensitive his daughter was, but then her crying grew louder.

"Honey, it's ok, it's just pretend," he whispered as he leaned his tuxedoed body next to hers.

"But he killed her!" she sobbed, "Daddy, he killed Carmen!"

She eventually calmed down, but the night was ruined. All she could think about was why her father had given her that name? That night, she dreamt of him stabbing her as she sang the BINGO song, but she also had nightmares that he killed her mother.

"What are you doing in school, Carmen?" Dr. Cassidy asked in the dream.

"A family tree! I need to ask you about your parents," she said excitedly and ran to get her marble notebook and her pencil with the pink eraser.

"Well, my parents are dead—"

Her mother swooped in like a crow over a dead mouse, "Died early to avoid the embarrassment of a bastard grandchild."

The dream ended with Dr. Cassidy grabbing a butter knife, lunging across the meatloaf platter, and jamming it into her mother's neck.

Carmen was too scared to go back to sleep, so she slipped into her mother's bed, where Norma sang, "Who loves Carmen?"

Carmen's mother loved her, but Carmen knew she had to keep earning that love. Her mother's needs always came before her own, so she learned to think of her mother first and herself second. She wished she knew her grandparents, but her mother said they were "losers who don't appreciate me." Carmen wished she had a brother or sister, but her mother never went on dates. When Carmen would ask her mother why she didn't have boyfriend, her mother answered, "They're all dogs!" With no grandparents or siblings, Carmen thought, *I would love a dog!*

Carmen learned how to problem-solve quickly. In first grade, she learned that the lie of a stomachache would lead to a dose of Paregoric, which cured all her woes. It was magic! She felt relaxed, stopped worrying, and was able to sleep in her own bed.

When she was ten, some older girls at school taught her how to smoke cigarettes and marijuana. By sixth grade, she had become the neighborhood's resident problem, turning the other kids onto pot, and by high school, she increased her repertoire to everything from her mother's prescriptions to Angel Dust. She'd taught everyone on the school bus a little song, sung to the tune of *Frere Jacques*, "Marijuana, Marijuana, LSD, LSD. College kids are makin' it; high school kids are takin' it, why can't we? Why can't we?"

She tried to stay under the radar by getting good grades. No one questioned her if she made the honor roll, and the nuns were always impressed by her parents, who stood out among the school's blue collar community. Her father cared, but he wasn't around enough to see what was happening to her.

Her mother was happily getting all her needs met, and when Carmen did get in trouble at school or picked up by the police, her mother had more contact with Carmen's father than ever.

"You use every chance you get to reel me back into your fucked-up emotional netting," Dr. Cassidy whispered gruffly while they waited for the counselor to join them in the school guidance office.

"You have no idea how hard it's been raising this girl on my own," Norma cried.

The guidance counselor, who shared that she too was a single parent, replied, "She is so lucky to have a dedicated mom like you, Miss Concordia, it must be difficult."

Carmen felt sorry for her dad. When they left, he said, "Well, Norma, you look like you were just crowned queen for the day."

Norma was almost happy and calm, and said to Carmen, "You are so lucky to have such an insightful woman at your school."

"Drugs, sex, booze, fun, we're the class of '81!"

Her mother turned a deaf ear on keg parties in her basement, and bong-a-thons in Carmen's bedroom. Through Carmen, she had friends for the first time, at least in her mind. She didn't know they called her Nurse Ratched and whispered, "Carmen, it's medication time" when they saw her. Had her mother known, she'd have turned it from, "They are calling me the horrid Cuckoo's Nest nurse" to "They are comparing me to a movie star."

When Carmen got in trouble at school or with the police, she pulled the "poor child of the shrink" routine. "He understands everyone but me! You know, it's like the cobbler's kid who has no shoes." Dr. Cassidy believed her drug use was his own professional failure. But, in her heart, Carmen knew this wasn't true. In the very deepest part of her soul, she'd made a deal with the devil from the time she stood on a chair to reach the kitchen sink and scavenged sips of wine.

She was madly and deeply in love with anything that made her forget, relax, or feel happy. By high school, she smoked pot every day, sucking the cannabis into her lungs as frequently and as passionately as she could. The first time she tried cocaine, she felt like she found a part of herself she'd never known, a powdery white completeness of her inner void.

She learned by trial and error. Magic mushrooms before school weren't a good idea. She'd thrown up the excess poison before first period, and although she described the effect as "awesome," it was impossible to concentrate and she was sent to the school nurse by two different teachers.

At night, Carmen would light up when she heard her mother yelling on the phone, "You owe me! I raised this kid by myself."

If her mother had been drinking, it changed to "If it had been up to you, I'd have aborted her into a bucket behind the Laundromat!"

Sometimes, when she was high on PCP, Carmen wanted to kill her mother, but she always regretted feeling that way in the morning. Usually, if she had been drinking or smoking pot, she would cry in her room. Her mother gave up everything for her, and she believed what she had been told since she was a baby, that she had the most special mother in the world.

When Carmen announced that she was going to an out-of-state college, Norma fell apart. She yelled, cried, and hyperventilated.

"You're having a narcissistic breakdown, for Christ's sake," Carmen's father yelled. "It's less than an hour away, and you are acting like a martyr."

"A martyr?" Norma screamed. "How dare you call me a martyr?"

"You've done everything but nail yourself to a goddamn cross," Dr. Cassidy growled. "Carmen didn't even consider her first choice schools because they were farther away, and she felt like she'd be abandoning you!"

Norma just kept crying, and mumbling, "She *is* abandoning me!"

Carmen tried to keep up her high school routine once she got to the university. Her grades weren't great—school work interfered with her partying. But she explained to her mother that it was the stress of being a freshman. Without the drain of fulfilling her mother's emotional needs, Carmen enjoyed herself during the day. But, every night after dinner, a drunken Norma called on the phone in the dorm hallway to talk Carmen through the minutia of her day and crescendo with Carmen being an ingrate who only came home two weekends a month. Carmen returned to her room and cried, heartbroken for her mother's sadness and laden with guilt. But, after her first semester, it got better.

In the 1980s, the legal drinking age was eighteen. Jose Cuervo to Boone's Farm Tickled Pink, there was always something to put her to sleep, plus, better marijuana than Carmen had ever found in the suburbs. Even when there was no money, she was decent enough looking that she could always pick up a guy. It was amazing the quality of product they would give her for a night she didn't even remember. In between, there were always ways to get her needs met—speed, or rush, or Quaaludes—but it was in her junior year that, as she told her roommate, "it felt like the skies opened and I saw the landscape of heaven." If cocaine had been her friend in high school, in college it became her lover, and eventually her god.

She did consult her father when the blackouts became more frequent. "Dad, there's something wrong with me. Hours of my day just literally go missing. Maybe I'm like *Sybil.*"

According to her father, the memories could never be regained, and it was disconcerting not to remember what she said or did, let alone what was said or done to her. She learned to take meticulous notes in class.

Her mother was trapped in what Carmen viewed as a world of injustice and loneliness. High or not, Carmen believed to her very core that she did owe her mother, and that Norma loved her. But it felt so good to escape and forget about her mother's pain, at least for a little while.

Even with the self-medicating, Carmen cried a lot and worried about her mother. While the other students got care packages, from home, Carmen became the "parentified" child, sending Norma postcards and long letters, hoping they would help her mother hold herself together.

"Wow, another card to your mom?" the school mail clerk asked, "Is she sick or something? I mean, does she have cancer?"

"No," said Carmen, "she just needs me."

Dr. Cassidy explained to his daughter, many times, "Your mother's not a bad person, Carmen, but she loads you down with guilt! She's turned you into a goddamn puppet! She pulls the strings and you react. If she'd get some psychotherapy, she'd learn coping skills, maybe stop drinking. *You* are suffering because *she* won't address her psychological problems!" Carmen dismissed this as her father trying to ease his own guilt for not marrying her mother and not living with them while she was growing up.

The weekends Carmen stayed on campus, her mother drank and leaked out more hurtful details of Carmen's past—how she'd had colic and Norma never slept, how her father would have sent her to public school if Norma had not advocated for her, how Norma could have gotten married and had other children if she hadn't had Carmen.

"Even with all my hard work you still ended up like your father!" When Carmen would break down on the phone, Norma would sing song, "I know honey, it's just you and me, and we're all each other have in this world. Who loves Carmen?"

Carmen dealt with it by snorting even more cocaine. When she snorted cocaine, she was a star, the wonder around her kicked in, and she was powerful, beautiful, and healed. For a few hours, the world seemed her oyster, her parents loved her, they were normal, and she was enough, until the next morning.

On one visit home, Carmen walked her tipsy mother to bed, and noticed something new taped to the bureau mirror, next to the yellowing Daddy Bingo card. Shocked, she read, *There was a nurse that had a girl and Carmen was her name-o! B-I-N-G-O, B-I-N-G-O, B-I-N-G-O, and Carmen was her name-o! B is for Brat, I is for Ingrate, N is for narcissist (she gets it honestly), G is for greedy, O is for Ordinary!*

"Mom, what is this? *O is for Ordinary?*" she asked.

"The worst insult I could give," Norma slurred, "My plain-Jane daughter with your clown-colored hair and skin that burns too easily.

332

You're too meek to stand up for yourself. You got so few of my good traits, my flare, my wit."

Tearfully Carmen said, "Mom, that's really mean."

To which Norma replied, "I wrote it that night you didn't have time to talk on the phone. I should have mated higher up the food chain," before passing out, like she did more and more often. For the first time, Carmen wondered if her father was right. Maybe her mother was orchestrating all of their lives, and Carmen was playing the role she'd been assigned. Her mother was the star of the show and the producer, her father the Greek chorus, and Carmen the lowly stage hand.

The last semester of her senior year, things started to go wrong for Carmen. She slept through the alarm clock, lost weight, had nosebleeds, a DUI, and two trips to the ER for alcohol poisoning during which she had them call only her father.

"Welcome to your real-life operatic tragedy, Dr. Cassidy," she said during the first emergency room visit. She went days without brushing her teeth or washing her hair, and as the drinking and drug use increased, so did the blackouts.

As her father would say, "All hell finally broke loose" the day before Carmen's college graduation. Her last morning on campus, she woke up knotted into a tangle of Laura Ashley sheets that her mother had chosen, the remnant of a stranger crusted on her thighs. She sat up to do a line through the plastic cover of a BIC pen, the birth canal that would deliver life. The chemical perfume was so tantalizing that every pore of her body screamed for more. Her heart slammed in the brittle cage of her chest like a punch from the inside, so intense that she feared it would burst free and grenade across the room. But mainly, she feared wasting even a molecule of this manna from heaven.

Carmen ran her tongue over every millimeter of the mirror so she wouldn't miss a speck. Lovingly she licked the glass edge, anesthetized, not feeling it slice her mouth until the coppery taste of blood coated her tongue and dripped onto the pillow. She tried to stop the bleeding with the flowered sheet. Then she saw blood running down her leg.

The man next to her panicked and called an ambulance.

She dug a bra and a pair of shorts from a basket of dirty laundry, and for the first time, Carmen wondered how long she could live like this. Smelling the metallic odor of blood, the antiseptic scent inside the ambulance, and the sickening creep of rot between her nostrils, Carmen screamed at the EMT, "I am totally fucked!" to which he responded, "In more ways than one."

Carmen was diagnosed with a sexually transmitted disease, pelvic inflammatory disease, a rotting septum, alcoholism, and drug dependence. Her parents arrived together, fighting as they entered the substance abuse treatment center where she had been transferred.

"Norma, knock it off! This is not the time to put on your psychological tiara! This is about our daughter's life, it's not some soap opera!"

To which her mother smiled and said, "You're upset because you know this is *all your fault!* Your patients will be really impressed with you now!"

IV antibiotics were started, and Carmen was given a pamphlet titled *Chlamydia Is Not a Flower.* All she could think was, *My life has become a fucking Fellini film!*

"Ok, Carmen, tell me about your immediate family." the woman in a denim skirt, with a long braid, and strong Boston accent, asked.

"Well, there are my parents—"

"Who aren't married ..." came the screech from the waiting room.

Through the thick institutional door to the social worker's office, they could hear Norma squawk, "I did the best I could by myself. This is not my fault!"

"How often does that happen?" the therapist asked Carmen

"How often does what happen?" she replied, genuinely unsure of the question.

The therapist stared at her, and said, "Let's continue. Do you have any siblings?"

"I was young and attractive," Norma interrupted. "I could have gotten married. But, no, I told her father to shove his three hundred dollars up his ass. If it had been up to him, she'd have been aborted in a back alley. I gave up everything to end up with a daughter who is a drunk with VD!" Then there was screaming when the staff had a security guard come and manhandle her mother out of the facility.

"We're paying you. You can't kick me out," her mother yelled.

Her father said, "No, Norma, I'm paying, just like I've been paying for the last twenty two years."

The counselor asked Carmen, "You know what we call that?"

"Love and worry?"

"That's not love, that's self-pity. Poor me, poor me, pour me a drink. Is your mother an alcoholic, too?"

Normally, the rehab asked families to make no contact for two weeks, but in Carmen's situation, they recommended longer. Norma called the nurses' station every day, offering to supply anything they needed—old report cards, medical records, 'a laundry list of Carmen's father's failures, just joking,' anything to show that this was not her doing and that she was the one who truly loved this girl.

Her father came to rehab for the family sessions and admitted he had been a crappy parent, but seemed sincere when he explained that it was not because he didn't love Carmen.

"I love her. I just can't stand her mother. Norma's not an evil person, but she's destroying this kid with her refusal to address her own issues."

Carmen raged at him, "You wanted to abort me! My poor mother gave up everything!"

He sat nonplussed, then quietly said, "Carmen, the only things your mother ever gave up had claw marks all over them."

Her mother came down for one session, which she spent talking about her own problems. Afterward, the counselor suggested that the Concordia-Cassidy trio not have any more therapy sessions. The therapists tried to educate Carmen about "malignant narcissists" and how her mother was manipulative. It bothered Carmen, only twenty-two years old, with no siblings and no real friends. Her mother was always there for her. She'd built her whole world around Carmen, and she owed her mother everything. But, at the same time, maybe they were right. Carmen stayed in rehab. She knew if she left, she would die.

After thirty days, she was discharged to a halfway house in another state. Carmen was told that, due to a bed shortage, they would have to send her away. Her mother insisted that her father rent an apartment for her nearby, but for once he refused.

Carmen went to AA and NA meetings every day. It was like an alien world. To Carmen, the people seemed crazy and sick, but seemed to want nothing from her except for her to stay sober. Open with their own flaws and shortcomings, they seemed to care for her, and wanted her to succeed, and they listened. She applied for jobs that allowed her to focus on her recovery and got an entry clerical position at a state-run social service agency.

She did talk to her mother on the phone, but it was limited. There was only one phone located in the group dining room in the house of eight women that had to be shared. It wasn't conducive to long talks. Her mother was allowed to write, and she did—long letters with a litany of complaints and condemnations. She said she looked forward to when Carmen was well enough to move back home with her.

While the letters grew increasingly drunken in nature and more accusatory in tone, Carmen continued to get well. She reached her twelve-month-sober anniversary, and still went to meetings every day. It was difficult, difficult as hell, but she hung in there. Sometimes going to two or three meetings a day, she worked the steps, helped others, used her sponsor, and Carmen felt like she was 100% clean and sober for the first time since she'd been born.

Her father drove into town once a month to meet her for dinner. The conversations were awkward and stilted, focused on politics, weather, pop culture. They never talked about her recovery, or how difficult it was for her, or anything in his private life, but they continued meeting. One weekend, when they went to a performance of *Carmen*, she finally asked him, "Why on earth would you name me after a mean-spirited slut?" He seemed sincere when he told her it was only because he loved the music.

Her sponsor and AA friends recommended that Carmen go to therapy. She tried. Multiple times she made appointments with counselors and psychologists, but they all seemed to obsess about her mother, and want Carmen to blame her, or be angry with her, when all

Carmen could do was feel guilty and heartbroken. She went to her mother's two weekends a month to cook and shop and listen to her mother talk, and talk, and talk. All her mother asked in return for her maternal love and support was Carmen's undivided attention.

At eighteen months sober, her anthem was "My name is Carmen and I'm an alcoholic" or "My name is Carmen and I'm a drug addict," depending on which meeting she attended. Her life consisted of a forty-hour work week with a twelve-step meeting each night, coffee or dinner with AA friends a few nights a week, and weekends with her mother. Her weekends away from her mother were spent with AA friends, and dating a guy named Tom, a roofer, with three years of sobriety.

It was not love, but he was clean and sober, and they enjoyed each other's company. Sober sex was scary, and a completely new experience, but Carmen got over it and had been honest with him about her whole history. She was often tired and had gained weight, but these seemed to be common issues among newly recovered people. She decided to go to a doctor, fearful that, if the exhaustion got worse, she would miss work, and then everyone would assume she'd relapsed.

"It's Murphy's Law," she told Tom, "the soap opera that is my fucked-up life! I slept with the scum of the earth, and never got pregnant! Now here I am in recovery and I'm knocked up! I went off the pill in rehab. I'd been on it since I rode my bike to Planned Parenthood when I was thirteen. With the PID and STDs, I decided no one would want to sleep with me anyway, and I'd give myself a break."

"You don't understand guys," was his response. "Why did you tell me you couldn't get pregnant?"

"Because of the gynecologist the rehab sent me to. He gave me this long lecture about how I'd scarred my fallopian tubes and it would be a miracle if an egg could navigate its way through the wreckage. I can't fucking believe this!"

"Well," said Tom, "you know what we say in NA? Miracles happen."

So do disasters, thought Carmen, *disasters of catastrophic proportion.*

Tom agreed to support any decision she made, but she suspected he wanted her to have an abortion or put the baby up for adoption. Her father took it relatively well. With his detached nature, Carmen found it easy to tell him. He offered financial support, no matter what she decided to do. "Déjà vu, huh Dad? Sorry!"

Her mother didn't notice at first. Carmen had limited her visits home to twice a month, and complained about gaining weight now that she was sober. When she finally told Norma it was, as her father described, "a narcissistic breakdown of gargantuan proportion."

"It's those loser drug addicts you hang around with. I knew they would brainwash you."

"Mom, I'm pregnant, not joining a cult."

"It *is* a cult. Did one of those junkies date rape you? Do any of them even have health insurance? God only knows how far down on the totem pole you've lowered yourself this time, Carmen."

Her mother went days not talking to Carmen, punishing her by not answering the phone, going so far as to change the locks on the front door. Carmen was beside herself with worry and grief, to the point where her mother's emotional pacification became more important than the child inside her.

One day at work, a nurse, who Norma considered one of the least bitchy, said, "Norma, I thought you would *love* being a grandmother."

And it got Norma thinking. She would be the best grandmother.

The more she thought about it, she realized this would be another child she could mold and raise, another being who would need her completely, and Carmen would move back for good.

She had let Carmen's father name her baby, in the hope that it would encourage him to propose, but maybe she'd get to help name this baby. "Norman Cassidy, if it's a boy," she thought, "or Norma Cassidy, if it's a girl. Finally, a Norma Cassidy, which should have been my name all along!"

Norma did a quick flip from hysterical screaming and crying, "Why are you doing this to me?" to "We'll make this work." Every time Carmen brought up adoption, Norma told her, "We can do this! You'll be a great mom because you had a great mom, and we will love the baby so much, and your father will pay for whatever we need." She bought maternity clothes, helped Carmen find the best doctor, and was even nice to "that NA loser" Tom.

Carmen decided not to live out her childhood nightmare and abort her child. An adoption social worker told Carmen that, with her and Tom both in recovery since before she conceived, if she could stay clean and sober for the whole pregnancy, they would be able to place the baby easily.

Tom was all for it, Carmen could keep working, and her father was willing to pay for her to start getting her MBA. But her mother wanted a grandchild so much, and every time she felt the baby move, Carmen loved it more and more. Norma fueled the maternal flame by buying little outfits and stuffed animals, which melted Carmen's heart.

Carmen hoped the baby was a boy.

At eighteen weeks, Carmen had ultrasound. The technician was an older guy, who was nice as he pointed to the screen and ran down a checklist of baby parts.

"See, Mom," he kept calling her 'Mom', "the skull size is normal, the brain appears normal, ten fingers, ten toes. So far so good. All the measurements and weight are appropriate for the gestational age."

Carmen felt relief, but then came the part that she had been dreading,

"So, Mom, do we want to know the sex of the baby? Shall we find out if you are having a boy or a girl?"

A chill ran up Carmen's spine. Fear rose in her throat. *It has to be a boy*, she thought. *Please, please be male!*

Carmen took the next day off work, emptied her bank account, and drove to all her old haunts—remembering her past, seeing how far she had come, and buying as much of the purest cocaine she could find. She considered driving to the State Hospital where her journey began, but decided against it and parked in the lot at the opera house.

Her one year AA coin had a saying on the back. 'To thine own self be true.' She had the child to think of, a child to whom she would be Mommy. A girl. A girl who her mother would help her raise, would sing to at night, and teach about the world.

Carmen's AA sponsor always said, "It's not the lie we tell other people that will kill us, it's the lie we tell ourselves."

Carmen had to stop lying to herself and face her truth. She knew her mother was a bad mother. Norma was an angry, paranoid alcoholic who refused help and spewed her distorted views of the world onto her child. Her only role model for motherhood, had character defects that molded Carmen. Her mother had appointed herself choreographer, maestro, *and* director who cast her only daughter in a tragic role.

"How on earth will I not make the same mistakes?" Carmen wondered. "I've got to protect my baby from my mother, from me."

Carmen turned on her hazard lights and placed the opera cassette into the tape player. She listened to "Habanera" play, mentally translating in her head the one song she had memorized in English:

Love. Love. Love. Love.
Love is a gypsy's child, it has never, ever, known a law;
Love me not, then I love you; if I love you, you'd best beware.

Carmen took the supplies out of her purse and, as if in worship at her dashboard altar, proceeded to snort the purest, most perfect cocaine she had ever experienced, until she seized, her heart stopped and her head cracked onto the steering wheel.

Two days later, her mother and father had filled Carmen's answering machine with increasingly frantic messages. They even spoke civilly to each other in an attempt to find their daughter, both secretly fearing that she had relapsed, but hesitant to report her as a missing person.

Thirty miles away, the police had already found the car, with the "ONE DAY AT A TIME" bumper sticker on the back. The medical examiner was on her way, as the police began processing the evidence, and prepared to call the family.

The police had found Carmen with an ultrasound picture on her lap. A black and white photo of a perfectly healthy fetus. On the back she had written, "I'm sorry. I found out it's a girl. I would have destroyed a girl, if we had lived."

SOMETIMES THE GOOD WITCH SINGS TO ME

BY L.L. SOARES

The entire ride home, after he buried the wicked witch, Jerry Cuttle kept asking himself, *How much longer can I do this?*

Sitting in his driveway, tired and dirty, he felt as if he couldn't move. As if he was completely paralyzed. But that didn't last long. The desire to be clean motivated him to get out of the car.

When he got inside, the phone rang. He stared at it, thinking about how badly he wanted to take a shower. The phone rang again.

He was so afraid it was the witch, calling him from the grave.

He didn't dare answer it.

Jerry stood frozen, staring at the phone. It didn't ring a third time. *I'm safe*, he thought. *Thank you, Glinda.*

Then he went into the bathroom to wash off the dirt and blood.

As he stood under the hot water, Jerry Cuttle thought about the first time Glinda appeared to him. It was after his first suicide attempt. He'd taken a bottle of pills and lain in the dark, waiting to sleep forever. And she appeared before him. All white and shiny. Just like in

The Wizard of Oz. She waved her magic wand over him and spoke to him in that high, childlike, singsong voice:

"Wake up, Jerry. You can't die today."

He opened his eyes and looked at her. He wasn't an idiot. He knew that *The Wizard of Oz* wasn't real. That it was just a movie. And the characters in it were just actors. Glinda was played by a woman named Billie Burke. She was either dead now or very old.

And yet, here she was, young again, in full Good Witch regalia, standing over him, telling him he couldn't die.

"I c-c-can't?" he asked, not believing his eyes. Surely this was a hallucination. And if he just closed his eyes again, he would fall into a deep sleep, and none of this would matter. Perhaps he was dreaming, even now, though he wished the dream didn't seem so real. Here was the same crappy old house, the same sick feeling in his stomach. Why couldn't he feel wonderful in his dream? Wonderful in death?

"No, silly. You can't die yet. You have so much to do."

This struck him as laughable. He'd been a failure his whole life. What on earth, of any importance, could someone like him have to do? His job? It was a dead end, and no one would even notice his absence. His personal life? It was nonexistent at this point. All he did was work and come home. And wish he were dead.

"No," he said. "No point." The discomfort in his stomach was getting worse. He really didn't feel like talking. He just wanted to die in peace.

"Of course there's a point," Glinda persisted, refusing to let go. "I have great need of you."

"Need?" the word was hard to say. But he knew it well. He had needed so much in life. Money, love, respect. Things that always eluded him. Need? He was *made* of need.

"Yes, you must help me. I have a mission for you."

She leaned over him, looking into his eyes. "A wonderful mission. An adventure."

Then she pressed down on his stomach, and the pills all came up in a surge of vomit.

He sat up on the couch, coughing and wiping his mouth. She stood to the side, watching him with a slight smile.

"Now you can live," she said. "And help me get rid of the bad witches."

It hadn't been easy at first. He had never killed anyone before. And even though Glinda had tried to make it clear to him that he wasn't killing a person at all—that he was killing a creature of pure evil—there were certain barriers he had to overcome before he could accept his mission.

He searched the streets for old women who fit the bill. It was much easier than he thought. There was no shortage of vile old women wandering around, glaring at passersby. Most of them were homeless. Glinda spoke to him and told him which ones were witches. *Wicked* witches. So many of them were evil. It was almost unfathomable how they simply walked among us, performing their unholy rites, putting curses on innocent people who didn't stop to acknowledge them or give them a handout.

"That one," Glinda would whisper in his ear. "She needs killing."

After he showered and dressed, Jerry burned the clothes he'd worn when he'd killed the witch, in a metal garbage can in the backyard. Returning to the house, he heard the phone ringing again. It didn't scare him this time.

"Hello?" he asked. A part of him still expected to hear the old woman's voice on the other end, cursing him for his deed.

"Jerry?" a man's voice called out to him. "Is that you, bro?"

It was Henry. His brother. Somebody he hadn't heard from in years.

Jerry hesitated. There were old wounds between them that hadn't healed.

"Jerry? You still there?"

"I'm here."

"You still mad at me for taking off?" Henry asked. "You going to hang up on me?"

Jerry swallowed. "I won't hang up."

343

"I'm sorry. I heard about Mom. I'm sorry you had to handle it alone."

"That was the idea, wasn't it? When you left?"

"I had a lot going on in my life. Bad stuff. I couldn't handle any more. The only recourse I had was to get away."

"Bad stuff?" the anger welled up inside him. "You think you were the only one dealing with bad stuff?"

"Some of us can handle it, Jerry. Others can't. I had to get away to stay sane."

Sane. Jerry thought of what he'd been doing that morning and wondered what the word meant any more. If he didn't have Glinda to guide him through the pain, he wouldn't know what to do.

"My wife and kids leave me," Jerry said. "I move back here. With her. And she's always dying, taking years to die. Always in pain. And you think you had it bad."

"It's over now," Henry said. "She's not in pain anymore."

Henry's words were insensitive, but true. But he hadn't earned the right to say them. He hadn't suffered through the final days. He'd been a safe distance away.

"You don't have the right to talk about her," Jerry said. "You didn't have to deal with it all."

"Listen, I was going through some bad problems. Booze, drugs. You knew that. I had to clean up my act. Get my life in order again. There was no way I was going to do that and watch Mom disintegrate. It just wasn't possible."

What Henry said made sense. He'd been struggling with his addictions all his life, since they were kids. As they got older, Henry seemed to be getting worse. Unable to hold down jobs for any length of time. Incapable of any lasting relationships. Even with his family.

But, Jerry thought, what about *my pain*? What recourse did *I* have? With Henry disappearing all the time, he had always felt the need to be the responsible one. The one who held everything together. He hated Henry for that.

"Are you still there?"

"Yeah, I'm here," Jerry said, trying to keep any traces of anger out of his voice. For all his faults, Henry was still his brother. And he was weak. Jerry couldn't really hate him for that.

Silence. Jerry waited for his brother to continue the conversation, although he already knew what this was about. He refused to make it easy on Henry.

"Jerry?"

"I said I'm here, Henry. It's good to hear from you after all these years. But let's get down to brass tacks. Why are you calling?"

"You're in the house alone now. The house we grew up in."

Jerry didn't answer.

"Things are bad. I need some place to stay. To get my head together."

"And now that Mom's gone, it's safe to come back home?"

"It's not like that, Jerry. I just need somewhere to get my head together."

"You said that already, Henry."

"I want to come home, Jerry. That used to be my house, too. I want to be brothers again. I want to try to make things right between us."

I can't have someone else here now, Jerry thought. *Not with my mission. It's hard enough without someone watching my comings and goings.*

But a part of him wanted to recapture the past. They had been close once. So many years ago. And he didn't want to continue with the mission.

Standing there, the phone receiver to his ear, Jerry thought he saw Glinda in his peripheral vision, darting toward a shadowy corner. Waiting for him to finish the call.

"Jerry," Henry said, his breathing sounded labored. It sounded like he was on the verge of tears. "Please. Give me another chance."

"Fuck off," Jerry said, and hung up the phone.

The first time Jerry killed a wicked witch, it took days to get up the nerve.

The first thing he'd decided was that he wouldn't use a gun. Guns made him nervous. And they were loud! He had a big hunting knife. One of the few things his father had left him. When they were kids, he and Henry used to go hunting with their father. Back before he had a heart attack and died at the age of forty-five. He just went into the office one day, sat at his desk, and never got up again.

Their father was a strict man. Jerry and Henry hated going hunting, but their father would not hear any protests, and they knew better than to even try. One good thing about his death was that they didn't have to go hunting anymore.

Until now. Now, Jerry finally found a use for the old hunting knife.

He'd never been in the military, but he'd seen a lot of movies. Mostly bad B-movies that showed him how to grab people from behind and slit their throats. In the movies, there was lots of blood. So he knew what to expect. He grabbed the witch in a stinking alleyway, the one Glinda had picked out for his first kill, and slit her throat from ear to ear. She made an odd, gurgling noise and struggled at first, but it didn't last long. And suddenly, he had rid the world of some evil. The witch had been disguised as a pathetic homeless woman with hard eyes and no teeth. He'd watched her for days before killing her, wheeling her cart full of overstuffed garbage bags all around the city.

It had been fairly easy to kill her, and leave her body among the piles of trash. It didn't look like anyone had been in the alleyway for years.

It wasn't as easy to forget. He knew she was evil. Glinda reassured him he'd done the right thing. But it didn't make living with it any easier. He'd killed someone. Even if she was a force of evil. He hated the wicked witch for forcing him to do such a horrible thing.

He remembered asking Glinda. Why couldn't he just throw water on them? Like in the movie. Water disintegrated the Wicked Witch in the movie.

This isn't a movie, Glinda told him. *You can't get rid of evil that easily in the real world.*

Sometimes he'd wake from his sleep hearing that gurgling noise. The noise of someone drowning in their own blood.

After he'd killed his seventh witch, Jerry took the hunting knife he'd used and put it up against his own throat, determined to let all the life pour out of him. It was a sharp blade; he made sure to sharpen it every day. But Glinda appeared before him and touched his hand.

"No," she told him. "You cannot do this. Not now. You have so much evil and wickedness to get rid of. Please, Jerry."

He looked into her face. She didn't look like she did in the movie just then. Her face was younger, more attractive. A beautiful face that made him miss Betsy, his estranged wife, all the more. He hadn't even tried to pursue another relationship since she'd left. He loved her so much; he couldn't even think of replacing her. Even now, he couldn't understand why she had just up and left like that.

But here was Glinda, young and beautiful and here with him. She cared about him. She didn't want him to die.

She looked like a golden angel before him. He felt the urge to kiss her.

"Glinda, I can't do this anymore. It is not in me."

"Of course it isn't, sweet Jerry," she told him. "That's because you are *good*. If you enjoyed this, you would be as evil as they are. I am so lucky to have found someone as good as you to help me in this mission. You have been wonderful. The world is such a better place now, because of you."

"I love you, Glinda," he said softly.

"I know," she told him. "Your actions have shown you to be a warm, loving man, Jerry. Don't think I don't appreciate that."

His hand was down at his side. The knife was gone. He saw it on the other side of the room. On the dining table. He didn't have an urge to go get it and draw it across his throat anymore.

He leaned in to kiss her. But she was gone.

Somehow he was able to function at his job. It wasn't something he had to think about too much. And if he was quiet, or distant, it made sense. His mother had died recently. He was separated from his wife. He had reasons to be distant.

Sometimes co-workers tried to seem sympathetic. They'd invite him out for lunch or drinks. But he'd always beg off. Nobody ever pursued it too much.

He kept working at his computer. Kept up appearances. There was no reason not to. Bills had to be paid. And it gave him something to do until the next mission.

"Jerry, please don't hang up."

Henry sounded like he was about to cry again. His breathing was heavy. It was almost like an obscene phone call.

"I know I've been a fuck-up all my life," Henry said. "I know I've always left you holding the bag all our lives. That I've been a disappointment to everyone. Especially you."

"No," Jerry said, trying to reassure his brother. But it didn't sound convincing.

"I really want to make it up to you. I want to show you it's never too late to change. I've been clean for three months now, and it's getting easier. I just need some place I can feel safe. That's all."

"It's not a good time, Henry," Jerry said. "I'm on the verge of getting back together with Betsy. It's touch and go. I don't need the extra stress in my life right now."

"I grew up in that house, too. I know you have room for me. I don't see why I can't come back there. Jerry, I've been sleeping in my car, for Chrissakes."

"Mom left the house to *me*. You were long gone. You don't have any rights to the house. And it's a real bad time, Henry. You've had other places to stay all these years, can't you find somewhere else to get your head together? Can't you give me the space I need right now?"

"Please, Jerry. At least promise me you'll think about it."

"When things are better, I'll call you back. I promise. Give me a number where I can reach you."

"Really, Jerry? You promise?"

"Of course. When things are better here, I'll call you. Hell, if I get back together with Betsy, I'll probably be going back to my own house. You can stay here then."

"You don't realize how important it is to me, to hear you say that."

"But you need to give me time, Henry. You need to make other arrangements for now. Until things are better for me. You owe me that much. After all these years."

"Sure, Jerry. I owe you that much. Thank you so much for reconsidering. Now let me give you my number, okay?"

"Sure thing."

Henry gave him the phone number. Jerry did not write it down. He made no attempt to remember it. He knew he would never, ever call back.

"Got it," Jerry said.

"You don't realize how much this means to me, Jerry."

"I know. I've really got to go now, Henry. I'm expecting a call from Betsy."

"I'll let you go, bro. I really hope you two can work it out. It must be killing you to be apart from your family like this."

Henry actually sounded as if he sympathized with his brother. Like he cared.

After all these years of *nothing*.

"Thanks a lot, Henry," Jerry said, sounding sincere. "Really."

He hung up the phone.

Then he threw the phone across the room.

The ninth time he killed a wicked witch, the vile woman scratched his face. Jerry was convinced that she had injected some kind of poison into him with her nails. He was sure that he would die. He even looked forward to it. For the release.

But he didn't die.

The next morning, he woke up alive and healthy. Like any other morning. He woke to the sound of gurgling, which faded out and was replaced with the buzz of the alarm clock.

When he went to work, he made excuses for the scratch on his face. He said his cat scratched him. He didn't have a cat, but nobody at work knew that. He did not socialize with any of his coworkers outside the office, and none of them had been to his house.

In time, it would heal. And he would try hard to forget about it. But he couldn't. He couldn't forget any of them. They were evil and had to die, but he never got used to it. And it never seemed to get any easier.

He'd read that serial killers find that killing gets easier the longer they do it. But he wasn't a serial killer. He wasn't killing *people*.

He was killing evil monsters that fouled and corrupted the world.

That was why it never got easier. Because he didn't want to keep doing these things. He wanted it to stop. He wanted to go back to his life the way it was.

Jerry hadn't heard from Betsy in months. And he made no attempt to contact her.

Even though he was ridding the world of evil, dirty creatures, Jerry felt dirty too. He took long showers every morning, and at night. To wash the dirt away. But he never felt clean.

He didn't want to get any of that dirt on Betsy, or the kids.

The third time he tried to kill himself, the car was running in the garage and the door was closed. He sat behind the steering wheel, with the windows open, and closed his eyes.

After a while, the engine shut off. Glinda was sitting beside him in the passenger's seat.

"You really have to stop trying to kill yourself," she said, in that childish, singsong voice of hers.

"Glinda, I can't do it anymore. I'm not the right person for your mission. I'm weak. And all this is killing me."

"No," she said. "You are doing a wonderful job. You are much stronger than you think you are. I know you feel sorry for the wicked witches, but you mustn't. It is their bad magic that makes you feel this way. But you must resist it. They know you're on to them, and they're trying to stop you. If you give in to it, they will be safe again. And we're getting so close."

"So close?"

"To ridding the world of them. They are the cause of everything bad in the world, don't you see? All the violence and inhumanity. It comes from them. The bad witches have taken over the earth. And you are my knight, freeing the world from their reign. Don't you realize how important this all is? How much good you're doing?"

"When you say close, do you mean this is almost over?"

"There will be a time when your work will be done," she said. "I promise you that. But don't give up. We can't let them win now. They thought they were invincible, but now you've scared them. Made them realize their days are numbered."

"It's so hard to go on, Glinda."

"I know. I'm sorry this is so hard for you, Jerry."

"So hard," he repeated.

"I love you, Jerry. I love your goodness."

She kissed him softly on the cheek.

"My poor, poor Jerry."

He stared out the windshield. He sat there for about five minutes before he realized she was gone.

He got out and closed the car door. Then he went back inside the house.

"Jerry, is that you?"

"Betsy?"

"Jerry, I was worried. The kids have been asking about you. They want to know why you haven't come to see them in so long. I've been trying to call you. I know we're separated, Jerry, but I never said you couldn't see the kids."

"I can't, Betsy. Not now."

"What is it, Jerry? I know you took it hard when your mother died. Are you okay?"

Hearing her voice created so many conflicts inside him. He wanted to beg her to take him back. He wanted to tell her never to call him again.

"Jerry?"

"I can't talk now, Betsy. Tell the kids I miss them. But ..."

"Jerry, they want to talk to you. I'll put them on the phone."

He heard her go away for a moment. He hung up the phone.

The phone rang soon after, but he didn't pick up. He just stood there, staring at it.

"I'm so tired, Glinda," Jerry said. "I don't want to do this anymore."

He could see her hovering above his bed.

"Glinda, do you hear me? I can't keep doing this. It's killing me."

She stared down into his face. Her face was young and pretty. She looked so sad.

"Glinda?"

She covered her eyes. She seemed to be crying. He could feel himself on the verge of tears, too. He wiped at his eyes.

She was gone.

Someone was ringing the doorbell. It took all his effort to get out of bed and go to the door. All his energy went to the effort it took to go to work every day and appear normal. Once he got home, it all drained out of him and he was exhausted.

"I'm coming," he said. As he moved toward the door, his movements seemed to rejuvenate him somewhat.

He opened the door. It was Henry.

He hadn't seen Henry in years, but it was obviously him. The once young face was harder now. Weathered. His hairline had receded. But in his eyes, Jerry saw the same little boy he used to wrestle with. Who used to cry with him after their father would beat them both with his belt.

"Hello, Jerry."

"Henry," Jerry said. "I didn't realize you were coming here. I thought you were still on the west coast."

"I'm sorry, Jerry. I know I told you I'd wait. Give you time. But I haven't heard from you in so long. I thought maybe it would be better to just come in person, instead of calling you on the phone. Phone calls are a kind of cowardly. I needed to see you face-to-face. To apologize like a man."

Jerry stood in the doorway. "It's been a long time, Henry. It's like seeing a ghost."

"I know. It's been way too long."

Jerry stared at him. Picturing the child's face. Superimposing it over the man's.

"Can I come inside, Jerry?"

Jerry stayed where he was. "No, Henry."

"Why not? I want to talk to you. I need so badly to set things straight between us."

"Now is not a good time, Henry."

"Please," Henry said, and tried to push past him. Jerry struck him in the side of the head with his fist. Hard. He remembered his father hitting him that way once. And the memory was like a flash of fire inside him.

"Jerry!"

His brother looked startled, stumbling backward. His hand went instinctively to where Jerry had struck him, and his eyes were welling up with tears.

"I told you not now, Henry."

"Why?" Henry was trying hard not to cry. He was that same little boy again.

"I told you, it's not a good time. It will *never* be a good time."

"Please. I came all this way to talk to you. To make things right."

"Things can never be right. It's too late, Henry. It's too late and you can't fix things now. You were a fuck-up your whole life and you'll always be a fuck-up. And I don't want to ever see you again."

"Please, Jerry. You don't know what you're saying. You've been under a lot of stress and you don't know what you're doing."

"Get out of here, or I'll hit you again."

Henry hesitated. Then he turned and walked back toward the street. There was an old, beat-up car in front of the house. It looked as used up as Henry did.

Jerry stood in the doorway, watching him go. Thinking that at some point his brother would turn back and say something. One last, parting thing. Something for Jerry to remember this moment by. But he didn't. Henry just got in his car, started it, and drove away.

Jerry stood like that, in the doorway, looking out onto the street, for what seemed like a very long time. Then he went back inside.

He pulled the old homeless woman back into the alleyway and put the knife to her throat. She struggled and grunted and tried to scream, just like all the rest, and dropped her torn, worn valise—something she'd no doubt found in some dumpster and clung to as if she were a tourist and it was her only piece of luggage.

He pressed the knife hard against her flesh. It took only a moment. He was getting to be very efficient. Maybe it was getting easier after all.

She was gurgling as he let her fall to the ground.

Then he pressed the knife to his own throat. He didn't give himself a moment to think about it. He pulled the sharp blade against the flesh of his neck, and felt his blood come pouring out.

It's over now, he thought. *I don't have to do this anymore.*

He stumbled back against the alley wall and slid down to the ground, one of his legs on top of the dying witch, who was still twitching in a puddle of her blood.

He saw Glinda in front of him. Or at least he thought it was Glinda. He couldn't be sure anymore. She looked like Billie Burke in *The Wizard of Oz*. But that was just a movie.

"Poor, poor Jerry," she said, hovering over him.

"I can't do it," he told her. His words sounded like gurgling.

Glinda looked sad. She knelt before him and took his chin in her hand. She looked right into his eyes and started to sing to him. A lullaby. To put him to sleep.

Jerry closed his eyes. Her song was sweet. And even though he knew he was going to die, her song consoled him.

And he knew that, despite his inability to go on, he had made the world a slightly better place.

THE DEVIL INSIDE

BY SHANNON CONNOR WINWARD

"What do you mean by that, Rebecca?" the doctor queried. "What did no one tell you?"

Becca studied the drops of rain on the window, little falling jewels of light.

She felt evil, just saying it, but also relieved. "I read all the books. All the blogs. They warn you about everything that can go wrong. Preeclampsia. Preemies. Feeding problems. But no one tells you what to do when you don't love your baby. Like it's ... unthinkable."

Her words hung for a time, as Dr. Marsh scribbled on his pad. "It's quite common," he said eventually. "Many women experience post-partum depression ..."

"I'm not depressed," Becca countered, tap-tapping her fingers on the armchair. "I just don't love him."

"Why is that, do you think?"

Marsh's office was always an uncomfortable place, hot in winter and frigid in summer. The heat made her choke. She longed for water.

Why? Because he didn't love her back? Because he cried? All the time, always, screeching until his little voice cracked? Because Becca couldn't cry?

"Rebecca?"

Marsh's voice tugged her back, but the baby cried, cried. Becca shuddered. "I just don't feel it," she murmured.

Dr. Marsh smoothed a crease from his pant leg. He let the silence stretch out as if he was making a point. The heater ticked, ticked. The window wept.

"I want to return you to your prenatal dosage of Seroquel," he said, finally, swiveling to face his computer. The pages of her file flicked across the screen—yellow, green and blue.

"You think I'm delusional?" Becca asked the back of his balding head.

"I think we should be proactive." Marsh's hairy hands swept over the keyboard. "The experience of birth can be traumatic. Sleep deprivation, hormonal imbalance. Your body has been through a lot. You might weather it just fine. But, on the other hand, we don't want to precipitate an event."

"Right."

The psychiatrist swiveled back toward her. Colors flickered over his lenses, reflections dancing, chanting. *Precipitate an event.*

"Don't think of it as a setback. This is the hand you've been dealt. It's unfortunate, but we can make the best of it."

Marsh's desktop printer spit out a sheet. "If you're not nursing," he added, holding the paper out for her, "there's no reason not to bring you back up to the levels that were working before you got pregnant."

"Right." Becca took the script and began to fold it into ever-smaller segments.

Observing this, Dr. Marsh reached for his computer again. "Would you like me to prescribe you a sleep aid as well?"

A block from her house, Becca turned down a winding, tree-lined street. Rain pelted the roof of her car and smeared the windows. The constant swoosh of the wipers calmed her. She parked near the little neighborhood playground, leaving the motor running and the wipers on.

On sunnier days, the playground was a Mecca for young mothers and their well-groomed children. In the last months of her pregnancy, after she'd given up her job, Becca used to come here to feed the ducks in the pond. She still had a stash of stale crackers in her purse.

Becca took her purse from the passenger seat, bypassing the crackers and Doctor Marsh's scripts for a pack of cigarettes. She lit one, watching a mated pair of Canada geese navigate the rippling water.

She'd quit smoking the year before, but in the weeks after Micah was born, when she'd failed at nursing and all her other good intentions, she fell into the habit again. Andrew knew, though by silent agreement she never did it in front of him, or in the house. It was a coping mechanism; it was crucial that she avoid being overly stressed.

In college, shortly before she was due to graduate and six months into her relationship with Andrew, Becca had been diagnosed with prodomal schizophrenia; the early stages of the disease that ultimately killed her mother. Because of her family history, Dr. Marsh caught her symptoms early and managed the condition well with medication. She'd been able to finish school, pursue a normal life. Andrew was loving and supportive. They'd been married for six years without any real problems. He wanted children, and so had Becca, before the diagnosis. He'd convinced her to try, in spite of the risks.

She did fine throughout her pregnancy, and Micah was born healthy and beautiful. Andrew was beside himself. But, from the moment she'd held her infant son, Becca could not shake the feeling that something was wrong.

Dr. Marsh thought her problem was psychological.

Becca caught a glimpse of herself in the side mirror and hit a button to make the mirror turn, giving her a view of the manicured street behind her.

"There are bad things in this world, Rebecca," her mother used to say. "There is evil everywhere, hiding in plain sight. You just have to know how to look."

The baby was crying when Becca got home. She could hear him wailing through the door, picking right up with the constant echo of him in her head. Dripping from her dash up the driveway, Becca stood in the foyer, watching the carpet darken under her feet.

"Mrs. Cummings?"

Gigi came around the corner, clutching a blue teddy bear by its ribboned neck. Her mouth was open, ready to give her report for the afternoon, but she took in Becca drooping by the coat rack and paused. "Is everything all right?"

"Did he sleep?" asked Becca, glancing up the stairs.

"Almost the whole time. He just started crying about twenty minutes ago, but he wouldn't take a bottle, so I was going to bring him Blooey."

"Blooey?"

Gigi smiled. The svelte young woman looked more like a rock star than a nanny, with a ring of half-moon tattoos on her wrist and a cobalt streak in her black hair to match the bear, but her expression was sweet and genuine. "He was mine, when I was little. Micah seems to like him."

Becca felt a twist in her stomach. Jealousy, maybe.

It had been Andrew's idea to hire Gigi, an ex-intern from his firm who'd decided to drop law for a degree in early education. Becca had to admit it was a relief to have her. It wasn't Gigi's fault that the baby responded better to her than to his own mother.

The baby's screams had grown more desperate, though Gigi didn't seem to notice. The nanny waited, her dark, mascara-lined eyes expectant—she'd want to finish their business so she could get on with her Friday night. With dull fingers, Becca unbuttoned her coat and hung it on a peg, only to have it slip with a hiss and gather on the floor.

As Gigi made a move toward it, Becca put out a hand to stop her. "What do I owe you?"

"Um. Thirty, I think?"

The baby howled fit to wake the dead. He had slept through her appointment, so he would be awake and inconsolable until Andrew came home. Becca fumbled open her purse and handed a bill to Gigi.

Gigi stared. "This is a fifty."

"For the noise."

"But I wasn't even here two hours."

Becca shouldered past Gigi into the kitchen. She set the teakettle on the stove and turned her back. "Goodbye, Gigi."

"O-okay. I'll just ..."

Becca turned the knob, relishing the *tick-tick-tick* as the gas caught and bloomed into life. Blue flames licked the bottom of the kettle with hungry tongues. Upstairs, Micah wailed as if his heart was breaking.

"Goodnight, Mrs. Cummings," Gigi called from the foyer. There was a pause, and then the front door shut, sealing Becca in with her baby, alone.

She made chamomile tea and drank it piping hot over the kitchen sink. She watched the backyard grow dark. The storm picked up, bending trees and turning the brick pathways into streamlets. The birdfeeders swung as if squabbled over by the ghosts of maddened birds.

The tea burned a little ball of courage in her gut. When she had finished, Becca reheated Micah's bottle, tested it on her hand, and headed for the stairs.

The blue bear was where Gigi had left it, propped on the table in the foyer. Becca picked it up, avoiding her eyes in the hall mirror. She couldn't stand to look at herself; the dark circles, the puffy cheeks. She didn't recognize this person anymore.

The baby's room was decorated with a woodland theme—friendly owls, raccoons, slender deer. The tree in the corner had taken her three weeks to paint; she'd fussed over every leaf and many-fingered branch. It used to fill her with happiness just to stand on the soft green rug and look at what she had done. The dark wood shelves full of books, the tiny clothes hanging in the closet, the empty crib.

The reality had murdered her joy. Now there was only this room of screams, this demanding, restless little thing filling up the world.

Becca leaned over the crib.

Micah was a black-haired baby, solid and long. Becca and Andrew had both been blonde and chubby as children, and blue-eyed. When their baby was born, Andrew had joked that there must have been a mistake at the hospital. If only it were that simple—a switch—and her real baby was out there somewhere, being cared for by someone just as mystified and miserable as she was.

The baby kicked inside the zippered sleeping gown; his fists shook. His skin was flushed red, as if someone had dropped him in a scalding bath. With the bottle pinched in one hand and the blue bear in the other, Becca hefted Micah out of his crib and carried him, still squalling, to the rocking chair.

"All right now," she murmured. "All right."

Micah's lips found the nipple and, thank god in heaven, took it. He sucked with ferocity, his hot little body settling into the crook of Becca's arm. She tucked the bear in beside him and leaned her head back, lulled by the rhythmic tug of the bottle.

Becca closed her eyes, but she didn't rest. Faster than should be possible, the bottle was empty and the baby began to cry all over again. He arched his back as if desperate to escape. She had to wrestle him to get him safely into the crib.

"What do you want from me?" she hissed. Becca clenched the crib's rail until her knuckles turned white. The baby looked back at her, eyes glistening.

"Here," she said, scooping up the bear. It still smelled of Gigi's musky perfume. "How 'bout this? You want this?" She pressed Blooey against Micah's chest. His fingers clutched the blue fur in reflex. His cries abated, and for a moment Becca allowed herself to think perhaps the nanny had stumbled on some magic cure. But he was only catching his breath. Micah kicked the stuffed animal to the foot of his crib and rolled away from it, away from her.

Retrieving the empty bottle, Becca headed back downstairs to fix him another; not that she thought he wanted it but because the trial and error of infant care was all she had to keep despair at bay. Food, diaper, motion, music. Wash, rinse, repeat. She had learned to do this for hours. It was only a stalling tactic, though. Sooner or later the ritual would have to stop. Then she would leave him crying in his crib, close the door to his room, and step off the edge.

The doctors said there was nothing physically wrong with the child. She'd switched him to a hypo-allergenic formula, dosed him with gripe water, and struggled to fix him to a regular schedule. He slept, but in fits and starts, fighting all the way down and rising angry. He just cried. It's just what he was.

At least, it's what he was with her.

At quarter after six, Micah went quiet. It was immediate cessation of sound, as if someone had thrown a switch. Within minutes, Becca heard Andrew's keys in the door.

He found her curled up on the sofa. He knelt beside her and kissed the top of her head.

"How'd your appointment go?"

She'd been clutching the baby's blanket, a crocheted gift from Andrew's great-aunt Sadie in Vermont. While the baby screamed, Becca had worried the blanket until her fingers stuck out like swollen bodies caught in a fishing net.

Andrew untangled them. "What did he say?"

"He wants to increase the Seroquel again."

"To how much?"

"Six hundred milligrams."

"Well, that's what it used to be," Andrew pointed out. He joined her on the sofa, shifting her legs into his lap. "That's not a big deal."

"It is a big deal. I was doing fine on the lower dose. I haven't needed that much in months. I finally convinced him to pare it back since I did so well while I was pregnant, and now all of that is out the window."

"But you've been so unhappy ..."

"*Unhappy*. Not crazy."

"I didn't say—"

"Antipsychotic," said Becca, in staccato syllables. "That's what it means."

Andrew took a breath. His hands circled her calves, massaging, calming.

"Did you say any of this to Marsh?"

"No."

"Maybe you should have. He's a doctor, not a dictator."

Thinking otherwise, Becca let it drop. Andrew rubbed her legs for a few minutes more, then:

"How's Micah?"

He kept his voice casual. It felt like a rope around her heart.

"I'm just saying, it can't be good for him to spend so much time up there on his own."

"I know."

"He needs to see things to ... to ... stimulate development." Andrew was mastering the art of functioning one-handed, with Micah balanced in the crook of his left arm. With his right, he poked at a pot of boiling noodles. He'd rolled up the sleeves of his shirt but forgotten to take off his gold watch, which was getting a steam bath. His light-brown hair stood up from his head in damp spikes. In another life, Becca might have found the sight charming, Andrew softened and flustered with fatherhood. Now it was all she could do to remain upright on the stool at the kitchen island.

"He needs to see your face."

Becca cocked a look at the baby, secure in his father's arm. He was placid, wide-eyed, handsome. Almost a different child.

"You have to talk to him, Beck. Do you talk to him?"

What do you want from me?

To Andrew: "Of course I talk."

Andrew looked as if he were about to say more, but thought better of it. Instead, he shifted Micah in his arms and changed the subject. "What do you think, Champ? Will it be green mush or orange mush?" Leaving the pasta to simmer, father and son went to explore the pantry.

Becca was gone before they returned, seeking solace in her nest of blankets on the sofa. She fell asleep to the bang of Tupperware and tiny spoons, the soft hiss of water boiling on the stove, and the absence of infant screams.

"What are you waiting for?" urged Dr. Marsh, who was not really Dr. Marsh. He wore an apron and scowled at her with mist fogging up his glasses. "Cook the bastard."

The roasting pan was heavy in her hands, the baby greased and naked as a Thanksgiving turkey. The weight of him pulled her down, down into the baking heat of the oven.

"I'm not ready," she murmured, feeling panic, the sense of things slipping away from her like steam rising. "I don't—"

"He's ripe," said not-Dr. Marsh. "He will only start to spoil if you wait any longer. Look." With a roasting fork tongue he jabbed the baby in the thigh. The skin gave way with a *pop*, spraying stinking liquid over her face. Becca closed her mouth to keep from swallowing. The carcass in the pan began to fall apart, already tender and rotting—here an arm, there a meaty slab of belly.

"It's not human," the Marsh-thing told her, in a voice almost consoling. "It's only meat."

She knew then that doctor was really her mother, dressed in a costume to teach her a lesson. She could see her mother's sandy curls trying to burst from his scalp, and the ragged red necklace-scar on his-her neck.

"But it's my baby," Becca insisted, though she was already sliding the pan onto the center rack. A part of her curled away from the blaze, the grief of it, but only a small part. Up came the oven door. Down came the not-doctor's hand on her shoulder. There-there.

"Come now, Rebecca. Come now. You know that isn't true."

Andrew woke her with a gentle shake.

"Come on, Becca. Wake up."

"I'm up. What?" she protested, rubbing her eyes.

"It's time for your meds."

Dr. Marsh swam before her in a blood-red haze.

Becca blinked. Her husband sat on the edge of the sofa in the dark room, his hand out. She had an urge to knock it away—a feeling so strong she had to clamp her teeth down on her tongue until it passed.

"Beck."

Becca took the pills. Andrew offered a glass of water.

"You slept through dinner."

"What time is it?"

"Ten."

"God." Sluggish, Becca fought to disentangle herself from the blankets.

"Do you want me to heat up something?" Andrew got up, took the glass, and helped her to her feet.

"I just want sleep."

She let Andrew lead her upstairs. They passed the baby's room, the door cracked, soft light pooling in the hall. From within, silence.

In bed, Andrew curled his arm around her waist and fell asleep. Becca tried to follow, leaning into his deep, rhythmic breathing, but that road was blocked to her now. She lay wide-eyed in the dark, waiting, until the screaming began again.

"Good morning, Sunshine!"

Andrew breezed into the kitchen, smiling and well-rested, smelling of aftershave. He kissed the baby in his bouncy chair, then Becca.

"Looks like it's going to be a beautiful day." He stood at the French doors, taking in the view of the backyard while he adjusted his tie. The forsythias were in full bloom after the night's rain, riotous against a bright blue sky. A flock of starlings had settled around the feeders, fluttering and readjusting themselves in a dance of greed.

"You should go to the park," Andrew suggested. "Get some fresh air."

Becca murmured, noncommittal. Micah's eyes followed his father, ignoring the bite of mashed bananas Becca waved under his nose.

"Andrew, take this, please." She'd been trying for half an hour to get the baby to eat, knowing that once Andrew left there'd be little hope of getting food into him.

"Come on, Champ," Andrew said, taking the spoon and Becca's chair. A sputter of airplane noises followed her across the kitchen. While she poured coffee into a travel mug for Andrew's commute, and packed his lunch, Micah took a spoonful, then another, as agreeable a baby any parent could hope for.

Becca stood back, out of view. When the bowl was empty, she traded Andrew's mug and lunch for the dishes and moved to the sink.

"Try to get out," Andrew repeated, nuzzling her disheveled hair. "It'll do you both some good."

Becca nodded. She stayed where she was to watch him leave, did her best to smile. The front door closed. Becca turned back to the sink as Micah began to wail.

"Right," she said.

She filled the dishpan until the water ran hot, washed her hands, splashed some over her face. She began to hum, something tuneless and desperate, and poured a cup of black coffee for her own breakfast.

She turned on the television and watched a morning talk show at full volume for a while, hearing nothing but the baby's cries. She bounced the chair with one hand, mechanically, up and down, up and down, letting the coffee mug grow cold in the other, until something thumped behind her.

Becca jumped at the noise. Seeing nothing, she was about to turn back, when a smudge of darkness caught her eye just outside the French doors.

A starling lay sprawled on the flagstones, dead or stunned. Becca stared at it, the beautiful blue-black sheen of its little body iridescent in the morning sunlight.

It took a moment to realize that Micah had grown quiet.

He, too, was looking at the bird. His face, still tear-laced, was soft with interest. Becca muted the television and watched him, unused to seeing him like this, alone with her, calm and quiet. He seemed to be studying the starling, which still hadn't moved. His eyes were wide and dark, completely unfathomable to her.

She jumped again at the second thud—another bird, falling down the glass. It came to rest on top of the first, a mass of feathers.

The third time, she saw the impact—a speckled black body, seemingly out of nowhere, flew into the French door like a kamikaze pilot. This one dropped to the ground, staggered, and tried to fly again. Becca watched in growing horror as it rolled across the flagstones, found its ground, and flew off, only to circle once and dive right back into the glass. She could almost swear she heard its neck crack. The doomed bird dropped to the stones beside its brothers and lay still.

Micah laughed.

When the fourth bird hit, Becca picked the baby up, seat and all, and moved him to the family room. With shaking hands, she fumbled a disc into the DVD player and set the baby in front of the TV. He fussed, but settled himself to watch, sucking his thumb with a look of sleepy interest.

As classical music chimed happily in the next room, Becca fetched a trash bag to collect the feathered harvest.

"Damn it, where are you?"

Becca knelt on the hard cement floor where, in the farthest corner of the basement, she had stashed the remnants of her mother's life. A trio of cardboard boxes lay open, their contents disgorged and strewn around her. Photo albums, old-fashioned scarves, felt bags of jewelry— things she never looked at but could not bring herself to give away. Somehow, in spite of age and the damp of the basement, they still carried a ghost of her mother's scent. It brought tears to her eyes, but she tore through them, searching for what she knew was there, had to be there.

When at last she found it, Becca let out a cry of relief. Strange, that it should give her comfort, this instrument of madness, but as she lifted the small wooden box from its nest of yellowed tea towels, Becca felt a warm thrum of power under her fingers. Almost reluctantly, she set the box aside and put everything else back, safely tucked away in the dark, as if she had never been here.

Back in the kitchen, Becca cleared the aftermath of breakfast. She lit a scented jar candle, set it on the island, and ran her hand over the marble surface in a clockwise circle once, twice, three times. She still knew the ritual; she'd seen her mother do this a hundred times.

In the family room, Micah's cries began again in earnest. Becca placed the box before her.

It was a lovely thing, made of walnut and smoothed to a shiny finish, except on the lid, where her father had carved a rose motif. An anniversary gift from years ago, when her parents had still been in love, before he left her mother with an infant daughter and a mortgage she couldn't afford. Becca traced the carving, remembering the way her mother had handled it with such sweet reverence.

"He was a good man, Rebecca, don't you ever think otherwise." She never blamed him, despite the long nights, the part-time jobs, dinners of Spaghetti O's and Wonder Bread. "It was the Devil that got to him, that yellow-haired bitch. Once you let the Devil in, you can't tell up from down anymore. That's why we have to be so careful. That's why you've got to learn to see people for what they are *inside*."

She'd shown her how, when they started to take in boarders; each one carefully, ritually screened. With the kitchen table scrubbed, the candle burning, her mother would open the box and take out her cards. One by one, she'd set them aside, face down by the candle, whispering the Lord's Prayer. "Deliver us from evil …" When the candle sputtered, that was the card; she'd turn it over.

"What do you see, Rebecca?"

"It says 'The Hanged Man'," Rebecca had answered once, while a migrant worker waited on their front porch, hoping for a room. "Does it mean he's a bad man?"

"Don't read the cards, baby. The words don't matter. Look at the picture." So Rebecca had taken the card and turned it, studying the picture upside down; a man strung to a cross by one foot, his arms lashed behind him. Though it looked like torture, the man in the picture was luminous, serene. A golden orb surrounded his inverted head.

"How does he make you feel?" her mother had asked.

"Hopeful?"

Her mother had nodded. They'd kept the boarder, a man named Jorge. He'd stayed with them for three years, until he'd saved enough money to send for his family and buy a house of his own.

Others, they'd turned away. The Seven of Wands, a man with bad eyes and a sneer on his lips. The Star, a woman gazing openmouthed at the sky while life slipped through her fingers.

"This one," her mother said once, after the screening was done. She pulled a card from the deck and flung it on the table. "This is the one who lured your father away."

Becca had stared at it, the Empress, with long blonde hair and ample bosom. Mama told her the young clerk from her father's office was only pretty on the outside; within, she was a demon. She had consumed him, destroyed him, and their family with him.

"Do you see it?" her mother had asked. "Do you feel it?" Becca had nodded, though she was never quite sure what her mother had wanted her to see, the sickness in her belly when she thought of them was real enough.

She'd believed in her mother, when the cards were the start and end of it. They never did take in a boarder who did them wrong. It got to a point, though, when her mother would not speak to a stranger until she had consulted the tarot. A new doctor, a cashier at the grocery store. Becca's friends. Once, she'd demanded that the school assign Becca to a new fifth-grade class because the cards said her teacher was evil.

Later, her mother claimed she no longer needed the cards. She could see the demons with her own eyes, and they were everywhere. She'd tried to make Becca use the cards for herself, but Becca had put them in a box and lied about it. People laughed at her mother. They said she was crazy. Becca hadn't wanted to live her life that way.

When she went away to college, her mother stopped leaving the house altogether. Then one Thanksgiving, while Becca was on her way to Virginia to spend the holiday with friends, Mama cut her own throat with an electric bread knife. It was one of the boarders that found her, slumped over the kitchen table.

Micah's cries had reached a frantic pitch. Becca took the cards from the box and removed the first one. "Our Father, who art in heaven," she began, but the words failed her. *Let me not be crazy.* Tears slid down her cheeks as she set each card aside, trying to focus on the candle while her baby screamed, sounding less like an infant than a demon raging.

The flame sputtered, bent, straining to go out, though there was no wind in her warm kitchen. Becca turned the card in her hand face-up.

How does it make you feel? her mother asked, as Becca wept.

Grinning up at her, triumphant, was The Devil.

She thought about killing him. She left him, screaming, while she paced the house, struggling to decide what was real. The face of the Devil laughed at her behind her eyes, her head pounded like black birds slamming against her skull. But when she went to the family room to look at him, she saw only an infant, red-faced and helpless. He looked like her father, she thought all at once, and the realization knocked the breath from her. For an instant, a feeling like love guttered in her chest. She wanted to go to him, hold him, protect him from what was rising inside her.

But then she remembered, *"Once you let the Devil in, you won't know up from down."* And so she backed away, hands pressed against her belly to smother the ache.

"He's soaking wet," said Gigi. The reproach was clear in her voice, though the nanny avoided meeting Becca's eyes as she removed Micah from the bouncy chair. The DVD was on instant repeat; she had to raise her voice to be heard over the music. "How long has he been like this?"

"I changed him an hour ago," Becca lied. She stood in the archway, hugging herself.

The nanny glanced at Becca, still in her robe and nightgown. "Do you want me to give him a bath?"

"Fine."

Gigi carried the baby upstairs. Becca returned to the kitchen, where she had spent the morning, and laid her head down. She heard the sound of the tub running. Once, she'd dreamt of bathing her child, slippery and laughing. Now another woman tended him, scrubbing at a taint that could not be washed away.

"Am I crazy?" she asked herself. On impulse, she pulled the next card from the deck.

"Who are you?"

Gigi had just emerged from the hall with Micah, wet and pink under his hooded towel. The nanny jerked at the sound of Becca's voice.

"He never cries when you're here."

Becca waited by the crib, the blue teddy bear crushed between her hands. Casting her a nervous glance, Gigi brought the baby to the changing table and set to swaddling him. "I guess it works, huh?"she said, her back to Becca.

"What works?"

"Blooey. My mother said he always calmed me down, when I was little. I guess it works for Micah, too."

"Right," said Becca. "Like a charm."

Gigi turned at that. She gave Becca a dark look, then hefted Micah, zippered into a sleeper, onto her slender hip. "Are you all right, Mrs. Cummings? You look ... really tired."

Becca's legs began to tremble, as if she had been standing in one place for hours. She stumbled to the rocking chair and sat down, hard.

Gigi crossed the room to put Micah in his crib. She cooed to him and churned the handle of his mobile, sending the bright jays, owls, and blackbirds in a flight of circles above him. Obediently, the baby turned his head to the wall. His little chest rose and fell to the tinny, tinkling music.

Becca tried to rise, but found that she could no longer move, as if invisible bonds tied her hands and feet. She could only flinch as Gigi came nearer.

"We had a feeling you were catching on," the nanny said.

The starlings crashed in Becca's brain. *Maybe this is just a dream*, she thought, but the young woman standing over her seemed solid and real, right down to the scent of her perfume.

"Who are you?" Becca demanded again.

For a moment, Gigi just looked at her. Then, she sighed. "Oh, honey."

The nanny lowered herself to the floor in front of Becca. "Your mother wouldn't have needed these," she said, reaching for the tarot in the pocket of Becca's robe. Helpless to stop her, Becca stared as the nanny pulled the top card from the deck and showed it to her.

The High Priestess wore a moon, like the tattoo on Gigi's wrist. The eyes were the same, dark and full of secrets.

"You know, we wanted you first, Rebecca. All that raw power. We tried for years to get close to you, but the damn witch saw through every avatar we sent. By the time you got out from under her, you were no use to us. Too influenced by what she taught you, too old. But not too far gone to give us another shot, hmm?

"He is so beautiful. And so ripe. All he needs is the right teacher." With a look of great tenderness, Gigi reached between the crib slats to stroke the sleeping child's head.

"Whatever you think you're going to do with him," Becca managed, "I won't let it happen."

"Oh, it's too late. We already own him. I think you see that." The nanny clucked her tongue. "But, now, what to do with you?" Gigi drew the next card—the Eight of Swords, a woman blindfolded and bound, trapped by her own indecision. "We kind of hoped you would just take care of it for us, like your mother did. She knew, you know. When we started working on you, made you think the sight wasn't real, just ... madness. She had nothing left to live for, so one day she just ..." Gigi made a slicing motion against her own throat, and let out a cruel laugh. "What a mess."

Becca felt something shift, then—the invisible bonds that held her began to loosen. With a cry she hurled herself from the rocker, but the nanny sidestepped, and Becca's legs gave out beneath her. She fell to her knees.

Becca grabbed the slats of the crib and tried to rise. Grief and rage lodged in her throat; she gasped, struggling to make her body obey, but she felt as if she were a hundred years old. Too weak. Too tired.

Gigi watched Becca for a moment, calculating, then circled around her to the head of the crib.

"Get away from him." Becca pulled herself to her feet, but the other woman was faster. Gigi grabbed the baby from the crib and slipped away from Becca's reaching hands.

"Everything's okay, Mrs. Cummings," Gigi assured her, backing toward the door. The girl's face had changed, suddenly void of all mocking and malice. She looked terrified. "It's all going to be okay."

Becca lurched, too late. The nursery door swung shut. She heard Gigi's padded footfalls down the stairs, and the front door slam.

Becca staggered to the bedroom window, looking down in time to see Gigi climb into her yellow Volkswagen with Micah in her arms. Becca banged on the windowpane.

She felt a cold spike of fear, expecting the bug to drive off, but it remained in the driveway. Gigi put a cell phone to her ear and looked up, her face a pale oval through the glass. Becca could swear she saw the nanny grin.

"Beck?"

Andrew's voice, from the bottom of the stairs. Becca lifted her head from the floor, where she'd been curled in a fetal ball. The stairs creaked under Andrew's cautious steps. A moment later, he opened the door to the nursery, saw her, and let out his breath.

"You're all right. Thank God."

He took Becca in his arms. She tried to cling to him, but he held her away from him, searching her face.

"Gigi called me, hysterical. She said you attacked her. What happened?"

"What time is it?"

Andrew paused, taken aback. "It's ten-thirty."

"Did you see me this morning?"

"Beck ..."

"Did we talk? Have breakfast? Did I see you off to work?"

"Of course, Beck. Don't you remember?"

Becca looked at her husband, feeling the heavy weight of resignation sinking in her bones. She saw the look in his eyes. If she told him what Gigi had said, what she was, he wouldn't believe her.

They'd already gotten to him. Just like her father. But like her father, Andrew was still a good man.

Becca took a shaky breath, and laid her head on his shoulder. "I'm sorry. I'm so tired. I don't think I slept at all last night. I don't know up from down anymore."

"She could have called the cops, Beck. Thank God she called me first."

Becca swallowed bile. "I didn't mean to scare her."

After a moment, she felt her husband's hands, warm and comforting on her back. "I know. It's all right."

"I think ... I need to lie down."

Becca allowed her husband to take her to their room. He tucked her into bed, kissed her, and moved to leave.

"Andrew?"

He turned in the doorway.

"Tomorrow, let's call Dr. Marsh."

"Okay, Beck. I think that's a good idea." Andrew gave her a smile she could see right through and went out, leaving the door ajar.

When he was gone, Becca crept out of bed and went to the window. She saw Andrew walk down the drive to meet Gigi by her car. They exchanged words that Becca couldn't hear. Gigi's face was drawn, looking for all the world like a scared young girl. She seemed reluctant to give the child back, but with Andrew's reassurance, Micah was transferred into his father's arms. When he fussed, Gigi kissed the top of his dark head. Then she kissed Andrew, full on the lips. At first he resisted, and Becca's heart skipped a beat. Maybe he was strong enough, after all. Maybe ...

Then Andrew's shoulders relaxed, leaning into the kiss.

Becca turned from the window.

"I know what you are," she heard herself say.

Andrew slept in the next room, oblivious as ever to the night screaming that had kept her awake since Micah had been born. She'd said nothing all evening, watching her husband croon to the baby, feed him, tuck him in. She'd pocketed the pills that Andrew gave her and went to bed, pleading exhaustion, which was true enough. She washed them down the bathroom sink and then hid under blankets until he crawled in beside her hours later. When he fell asleep, and the crying started, she took her pillow and crept to the nursery.

The caterwauling had stopped at the sound of her voice. Swathed with moonlight in his crib, Micah turned his round head toward the nursery door.

"I loved you, when you were inside me." It came out as a whisper, her chest so tight she could hardly breathe. She clutched her pillow against her belly. His eyes were like dark stones, watching through the crib slats.

"I loved more than just the idea of you. I felt you, growing, moving. You were a part of me, and a part of Andrew. You were everything we ever wanted. Now all of that is gone."

The silence filled her head. Becca took a faltering step into the room, then another, her bare feet soundless on the carpet.

Above the crib, the mobile began to sway. Round and round the birds flew, without music, without wind. Becca halted, shaking so badly she feared she might fall. She lurched the rest of the way, grabbing the crib rail for support. The crib rocked, and the infant's hands jerked in reflex.

Becca raised the pillow.

"That's how you fooled me, isn't it?" she whispered. "All those years, Mama kept us safe from the Devil outside. And now I've let you in."

Micah stared up at her, his eyes twin black moons.

"But I know how to see now," Becca told him. "And I know what to do. We can start over. We can be a family, just like we dreamed."

Becca leaned over the crib rail, and kissed the baby gently on his dark brow. "Don't worry. Mama loves you," she said.

Then, moving softly, so as not to disturb the blessed silence, Becca returned to her room and put the pillow to her husband's sleeping face.

THE WRITERS

JOSEPH BADAL

Joe worked for thirty-seven years in the financial services industry, retiring in 2007 after six years as a director and senior executive of a New York stock exchange-listed company. Before beginning his finance career, Joe was a decorated military officer, having served in the U.S. Army for six years, including tours of duty in Vietnam and Greece. He also served in the New Mexico House of Representatives. He has had six suspense novels published: *The Pythagorean Solution*, *Evil Deeds*, *Terror Cell*, *The Nostradamus Secret*, *Shell Game*, and *The Lone Wolf Agenda*. His short story, "Fire & Ice," was included in the Smart Rhino anthology, *Uncommon Assassins*. He is a member of International Thriller Writers and was recently named one of the Fifty Best Authors you should be reading. Joe has written dozens of published articles about various business topics and is a frequent speaker at conferences and civic organization meetings. He has extensive experience as an interviewee on radio and television.

DOUG BLAKESLEE

Doug Blakeslee lives in the Pacific Northwest and spends his time writing, cooking, gaming, and following the local WHL hockey team. His interest in books and reading started early thanks to his parents, though his serious attempts at writing only started a few years ago. He often blogs about writing and other related topics at The Simms Project at http://thesimmsproject.blogspot.com/. Published works can be found in the anthologies *Uncommon Assassins* and *Zippered Flesh 2* from Smart Rhino and the upcoming anthologies: *ATTACK! of the B-Movie Monsters*, *Astrologica: Stories of the Zodiac*, and *A Chimerical World:*

375

Tales of the Unseelie Court. His current project is an urban fantasy novella featuring a group of changelings in the modern world. He can be reached on Facebook or simms.doug@gmail.com.

CARSON BUCKINGHAM

Carson Buckingham knew from childhood that she wanted to be a writer, and began, at age six, by writing books of her own, hand-drawing covers, and selling them to any family member who would pay (usually a gumball) for what she referred to as "classic literature." When she ran out of relatives, she came to the conclusion that there was no real money to be made in self-publishing, so she studied writing and read voraciously for the next eighteen years, while simultaneously collecting enough rejection slips to re-paper her living room ... twice. When her landlord chucked her out for, in his words, "making the apartment into one hell of a downer," she redoubled her efforts, and collected four times the rejection slips in half the time, single-handedly causing the first paper shortage in U.S. history. But she persevered, improved greatly over the years, and here we are.

Carson Buckingham has been a professional proofreader, editor, newspaper reporter, copywriter, technical writer, and comedy writer. Besides writing, she loves to read, garden, and collect autographed photographs of comedians and authors she loves, as well as life masks of horror movie icons. She lives in Arizona, with her wonderful husband, in a house full of books, orchid plants, and pets. Check out her blog at carsonbuckingham.blogspot.com. Carson is a member of the Written Remains Writers Guild.

WELDON BURGE

Weldon Burge, a native of Delaware, is a full-time editor, freelance writer, publisher, and creator of Web content. His fiction has appeared in *Suspense Magazine*, *Futures Mysterious Anthology Magazine*, *Grim Graffiti*, *The Edge: Tales of Suspense*, *Alienskin*, *Glassfire Magazine*, and *Out & About* (a Delaware magazine). His stories have also been adapted for podcast presentation by *Drabblecast*, and have appeared in the anthologies

Pellucid Lunacy: An Anthology of Psychological Horror, Don't Tread on Me: Tales of Revenge and Retribution, Ghosts and Demons, and *Something Dark in the Doorway: A Haunted Anthology.* He has a number of projects under way, including a police procedural novel. He also frequently writes book reviews and interviews for *Suspense Magazine.* He is a member of the Horror Writers Association, the Authors Guild, the International Thriller Writers Association, and the Written Remains Writers Guild. Check out his Web site at www.weldonburge.com.

ERNESTUS JIMINY CHALD

Ernestus Jiminy Chald was born in Salt Lake City, Utah, but has spent the bulk of his existence in Chicago, Illinois. His published works include *The Rubbish Bin* (a polymorphic novel in the form of an actual trash can filled with crumpled pages of narrative prose, handwritten correspondences, and various forms of "garbage") and *Black Carnations* (a collection of elegiac poetry). He is also the author of *The Philosophy of Disenchantment; or The Ephemeral (mis)Adventures of Arthur Snowpenhauer* (a comic book). Chald is the founder of Peisithanatos Press, an underground publishing enterprise.

LIZ DEJESUS

Liz DeJesus was born on the tiny island of Puerto Rico. She is a novelist and a poet. She has been writing for as long as she was capable of holding a pen. She is the author of the novel *Nina* (Blu Phi'er Publishing, October 2007), *The Jackets* (Arte Publico Press, March 2011) *First Frost* (Musa Publishing, June 2012), *Glass Frost* (Musa Publishing, July 2013) and *Morgan* (Indie Gypsy, Summer 2014). Her work has also appeared in *Night Gypsy: Journey Into Darkness* (Indie Gypsy, October 2012). She is currently working on a new novel. Liz is a member of The Written Remains Writers Guild.

PATRICK DERRICKSON

Patrick Derrickson has been a fan of speculative fiction from the age of nine, when he first read *The Stand* by Stephen King. Since then, he has been the majestic hero of kingdoms, galaxies, and unspoken horrors. A member of the Written Remains Writers Guild and the Written Remains Mixed Genre Critique Group, he has finally found the outlet for the bizarre thoughts that chase each other inside his head. Patrick is a soccer referee, follows technology obsessively, and listens to too many podcasts. He lives in Delaware.

MIKE DUNNE

Michael Dunne is a freelance technical writer, author, and blogger. Drawn from more than ten years living and working in the Middle East, "The Fire of Iblis" is the first in a series of Arabian-themed dark fantasy stories. Current projects also include *Night's Edge* and *Dawn's Light*, the first two novels in his New Kingdoms trilogy. A member of the Written Remains Writers Guild, Michael currently lives in North Alabama with his wife Nance and white German Shepherd Abby.

GAIL HUSCH

Gail Husch lives in Wilmington, DE, teaches art history at Goucher College, and has published articles and a book about aspects of nineteenth-century American art. In recent years, she has turned to fiction, completing *The Button Field*, a novel set in the late nineteenth century based on the real-life disappearance of a student from Mount Holyoke College, as well as several short stories set in the present. She is currently working on another historical novel, this time dealing with the consequences of a mysterious appearance. Gail is a member of the Written Remains Writers Guild.

RAMONA DEFELICE LONG

Ramona DeFelice Long's writing has appeared in literary, regional, and juvenile publications, including *The Arkansas Review*, *TOSKA*, *Literary Mama*, *CRICKET*, *10kToBI*, *Handspun*, *Delaware Beach Life*, *Blue Lit*, and *FamilyFun*. She has been awarded artist fellowships and scholarships from the Mid-Atlantic Arts Foundation, the Virginia Center for the Creative Arts, the Delaware Division of the Arts, the Pennsylvania State Arts Council, Philadelphia Stories, the Society of Children's Book Writers and Illustrators, and the Rehoboth Beach Writers Guild. Ramona is a member of the Written Remains Writers Guild. She is a native of Louisiana and now lives in Delaware, where her day job is as an independent editor and online writing instructor. She maintains a literary blog at ramonadef.wordpress.com.

MARIA MASINGTON

Maria Masington is a writer from Wilmington, Delaware. Her poetry has been published in *The News Journal*, *The Red River Review*, and *Damozel Literary Journal*. Maria is a member of the Written Remains Writers Guild, the Wright Touch Writer's Group, and was selected to participate in the 2012 Delaware Division of the Arts Poets and Writers Retreat. The first Tuesday of every month, you can find her at the Newark Arts Alliance where she emcees their open mic night, for writers of all genres to share their work. Masington's day job is serving as president and executive manager of Lutz Engineering, Inc., which she co-owns with her husband. Their life consists of two sons, two dogs, and too many interests to count.

SHAUN MEEKS

Shaun Meeks lives in Toronto with his partner—model, Burlesque performer, and corsetiere, Mina LaFleur—where they own and operate their own corset company L'Atelier de LaFleur. Shaun is a member of the Horror Writers Association and his most recent work has appeared in *Zombies Gone Wild*, *Zippered Flesh 2*, *The Best of Dark Eclipse*, *Dark Light 3*, *Fresh Fear*, *Fifty Shades of Decay*, *A Feast of Frights* from the Horror Zine, *Shadow Masters* an anthology from the Horror Zine, and *Miseria's Chorale*, as well as his own two collections, *At the Gates of Madness* and *Brother's Ilk* (with James Meeks). He has work coming up in numerous magazines and anthologies and will be releasing his new novel, *Shutdown* and latest collection, *Dark Reaches*, in late 2013. To find out more or to contact Shaun, visit www.shaunmeeks.com.

CHRISTINE MORGAN

Christine Morgan divides her writing time among many genres, from horror to historical, from superheroes to smut, anything in between and combinations thereof. She's a wife, a mom, a future crazy cat lady and a longtime gamer who enjoys British television, cheesy action/disaster movies, cooking, and crafts. Her stories have appeared in many publications, including *The Book of All Flesh*, *The Book of Final Flesh*, *The Best of All Flesh*, *History is Dead*, *The World is Dead*, *Strange Stories of Sand and Sea*, *Fear of the Unknown*, *Hell Hath No Fury*, *Dreaded Pall*, *Path of the Bold*, *Cthulhu Sex Magazine* and its best-of volume *Horror Between the Sheets*, *Closet Desire IV*, and *Leather, Lace and Lust*. She's also a contributor to *The Horror Fiction Review*, a former member of the Horror Writers Association, a regular at local conventions, and an ambitious self-publisher (six fantasy novels, four horror novels, six children's fantasy books, and two role-playing supplements). Her work has appeared in *Pyramid Magazine*, *GURPS Villains*, been nominated for Origins Awards, and given Honorable Mention in two volumes of Year's Best Fantasy and Horror. Her romantic suspense novel *The Widows Walk* was recently released from Lachesis Publishing; her horror novel *The Horned Ones* is due out from Belfire; and her thriller *Murder Girls* was just accepted by Skullvines. She's delving into steampunk, making progress on an urban paranormal series, and greatly enjoying her bloodthirsty Viking stories.

BILLIE SUE MOSIMAN

Billie Sue Mosiman's *Night Cruise* was nominated for the Edgar Award and her novel, *Widow*, was nominated for the Bram Stoker Award for Superior Novel. She's the author of fourteen novels and has published more than 160 short stories in various magazines and anthologies. A suspense thriller novelist, she often writes horror short stories. Her latest works include *Frankenstein: Return From the Wastelands*, continuing the saga of Robert Morton from Mary Shelley's classic, and *Prison Planet*, a near-future dystopian novella. She's been a columnist, reviewer, and writing instructor. She lives in Texas where the sun is too hot for humankind. All of her available works are at Amazon.com. Check out her blog, "The Life of a Peculiar Writer," at www.peculiarwriter.blogspot.com.

CHANTAL NOORDELOOS

Chantal Noordeloos (born in the Hague, and not found in a cabbage patch as some people may suggest) lives in the Netherlands, where she spends her time with her wacky, supportive husband and outrageously cunning daughter, who is growing up to be a supervillain. When she is not busy exploring interesting new realities or arguing with characters (aka writing), Chantal likes to dabble in drawing. In 1999, she graduated from the Norwich School of Art and Design, where she focused mostly on creative writing. There are many genres that Chantal likes to explore in her writing. Currently Sci-fi Steampunk is one of her favorites, but her "go-to" genre will always be horror. "It helps being scared of everything; that gives me plenty of inspiration," she says. Chantal likes to write for all ages, and storytelling is the element of writing that she enjoys most. "Writing should be an escape from everyday life, and I like to provide people with new places to escape to, and new people to meet."

RUSSELL REECE

Russell Reece is a Delaware native whose stories and essays have been published in numerous print and online journals including

Memoir(and), *Crimespree Magazine*, *Delaware Beach Life*, *Sliver of Stone*, and *Vine Leaves Literary Journal*. His work has appeared in several anthologies, most recently in *Proud to Be: Writing by American Warriors* released in 2012 by Southeast Missouri State University. Russ has received two "Best of the Net" nominations and was named a finalist in the 2012 Pirate's Alley William Faulkner Creative Writing Competition. Russ is a co-host of 2nd Saturday Poets in Wilmington, Delaware and a board member of The Delaware Literary Connection, a nonprofit championing the literary arts. He is a University of Delaware alumnus and lives in Bethel, DE in rural Sussex County along the beautiful Broad Creek. You can learn more at his web site, russellreece.com.

JM REINBOLD

JM Reinbold is the Director of the Written Remains Writers Guild in Wilmington, Delaware. She is the author of the novella "Transfusions," published in the anthology *Stories from the Inkslingers* (Gryphonwood Press, 2008). "Transfusions" was nominated for a Washington Science Fiction Association Small Press Award. Her poetry has appeared in *Red Fez Magazine*, *Strange Love* (2010), and *A Beat Style Haiku* (2012). In 2011, she received an honorable mention from the Delaware Division of the Arts Individual Artist Fellowships for her work-in-progress *Prince of the Piedmont*. She has been selected twice (2008, 2012) by the Delaware Division of the Arts as a fiction fellow for the Cape Henlopen Poets & Writers Retreat. In 2009, her novel-in-progress, *Summer's End*, was a finalist in the Magic Carpet Ride Magical Realism Mentorship competition. She is currently working on a mystery/crime novel, a number of short stories, and haiku. You can visit her online at www.jmreinbold.com.

BARBARA ROSS

Barbara Ross is the author of *Clammed Up*, the first in a series of Maine Clambake Mysteries, published by Kensington in September 2013. She is the 2013 co-chair of The New England Crime Bake and a co-editor/co-publisher at Level Best Books, which produces an award-winning anthology of crime and mystery stories by New England authors every November. Barbara also blogs with a wonderful group of Maine mystery authors at Maine Crime Writers and with a group of writers of New England-based cozy mysteries at Wicked Cozy Authors. Barbara's first mystery novel, *The Death of an Ambitious Woman*, was published by Five Star/Gale/Cengage in August, 2010. In her former life, Barbara was a cofounder and Chief Operating Officer of two successful start-ups in educational technology.

L.L. SOARES

L.L. Soares is the Bram Stoker Award-winning author of the novel *Life Rage*, which was published by Nightscape Books in the fall of 2012. His other books include the short story collection *In Sickness* (with Laura Cooney), published by Skullvines Press in 2010, and the novels *Rock 'N' Roll* (from Gallows Press, early 2013) and the upcoming novel *Hard*, coming from Novello-Blue in the fall of 2013. His fiction appeared in such magazines as *Cemetery Dance, Horror Garage, Bare Bone, Shroud,* and *Gothic.Net,* as well as the anthologies *The Best of Horrorfind 2, Right House on the Left, Traps,* and the one you're holding in your hands. He also co-writes the Bram Stoker-nominated horror movie review column *Cinema Knife Fight,* which now has a whole site built around it at cinemaknifefight.com. No matter how many times he forces radioactive arachnids to bite him, he just can't seem to get the amazing abilities of a spider. To keep up on his endeavors, go to www.llsoares.com.

JUSTYNN TYME

Justynn Tyme is a Buddhist, Dadaist, and multi-talented experimental artist. He is currently the Director of Radioactive Mango Recordings' ALL-OUT MONSTER REVOLT PROJECT, a member of the Written Remains Writers Guild, and steward of the Dada Network. Justynn has been a long-time fellow in many experimental arts organizations, most notably: The New Absurdist, 391, The Dada Network, and Taped Rugs Productions. Justynn's work has appeared in both national and international publications, most notably KBOO's

101 Hours of Innumerable Small Events, The Written Remains Writers Guild's *Stories from the Inkslingers* anthology, Full Of Crow's *Corporeal Flux 2*, Mill Stream Book's *Bust Down The Door and Eat All The Chickens* and Three Room Press's premier Dada magazine "Maintenant." Justynn is the founder and director of America's most obscure Absurdist comedy group, The Whimsical Icebox; the curator of the Omphalos Dada Yow's Digital Dada Museum; and the founder of the annual, international event, Dalikrab Day. Justynn currently lives in Dada, Delaware—where he believes himself to be a ten-foot-tall eggplant from outer space—in a house of antiquity with six cats and a liquor cabinet.

SHANNON CONNOR WINWARD

Shannon Connor Winward is an author of literary and speculative fiction and poetry. Her work has appeared or is forthcoming in such venues as *Pedestal Magazine*, *Flash Fiction Online*, *Strange Horizons*, *Illumen*, *Ideomancer*, *Jabberwocky*, *This Modern Writer* [*Pank Magazine*], *Inkscrawl*, *Vine Leaves Literary Journal* and *Enchanted Conversation: A Fairy Tale Magazine*, as well as in genre anthologies on both sides of the pond. In between bouts of parenthood and other madness, she is at work on her second novel and her first collection of poems. Shannon is a member of Science Fiction and Fantasy Writers of America and the Science Fiction Poetry Association, and a Rhysling Award nominee. She lives and writes in Newark, Delaware, and is a member of the Written Remains Writers Guild.

THE ILLUSTRATOR

JAMIE MAHON

Jamie Mahon is a photographer and graphic designer based in Leeds, England. He's also the director and lead designer of *Soundsphere Magazine*, and often provides freelance work to various venues.

Much of his work reflects his interest in the gothic subculture, which he finds "visually stimulating."

You can see more of Jamie's work at jamiemahon.wordpress.com.

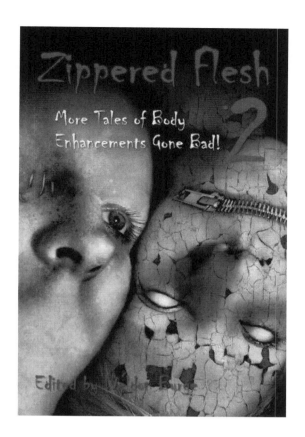

ZIPPERED FLESH 2:
More Tales of Body Enhancements Gone Bad!

So, you loved the first **ZIPPERED FLESH** anthology? Well, here are yet more tales of body enhancements that have gone horribly wrong! Chilling tales by some of the best horror writers today, determined to keep you fearful all night (and maybe even a little skittish during the day).

Bryan Hall * Shaun Meeks * Lisa Mannetti * Carson Buckingham * Christine Morgan * Kate Monroe * Daniel I. Russell * M.L. Roos * Rick Hudson * JM Reinbold * E.A. Black * L.L. Soares * Doug Blakeslee * Kealan Patrick Burke * A.P. Sessler * David Benton & W.D. Gagliani * Jonathan Templar * Christian A. Larsen * Shaun Jeffrey * Jezzy Wolfe * Charles Colyott * Michael Bailey

Available in paperback and Kindle eBook from Amazon.com.

Also visit smartrhino.com for the latest from Smart Rhino Publications.

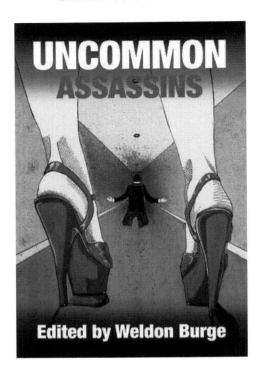

Made in the USA
San Bernardino, CA
27 November 2013